I0613019

PSYCHIC STORM

THE OVERLORD

A Science Fiction Novel

J J ECKHARDT

This is a work of fiction. All characters, organizations, and events portrayed in this novel are either products of the author's imagination or are used fictitiously.

Copyright © 2022 by J J Eckhardt

All rights reserved. No part of this publication may be reproduced in whole or in part, or stored in a retrieval system, or transmitted in any form or by any means, electronic, mechanical, photocopying, recording, or otherwise, without written permission of the author, except for the inclusion of brief quotations in a review.

For information regarding permission, please write to:
info@barringerpublishing.com
Barringer Publishing, Naples, Florida
www.barringerpublishing.com

Design and Layout: Linda S. Duider, Cape Coral, Florida

Photographer: Amanda Walker, Wild Spice Photography

ISBN: 978-1-954396-22-7
Library of Congress Cataloging-in-Publication Data
Psychic Storm: The Overlord / Eckhardt

Printed in U.S.A.

This book is dedicated to my family and to all the generations to follow. Remember, it is never too late in life to start something new and explore something you never thought possible.

J J Eckhardt   April, 2022
Joseph John Eckhardt

"The best dreams to achieve, are those you never knew existed."

~ J J Eckhardt

ORIGINS

The Triberions

The planet Triberon once existed in a solar system over three hundred thousand light-years from the Sol system. A more massive planet than most other rocky worlds in the universe capable of supporting life, its strong gravity well caused the planet's intelligent life-form to be squat and heavily muscled. Although they were short in stature due to the high gravity, the Triberions built a large and peaceful civilization that lasted for centuries.

Early in the development of their civilization, vast distances of ground and oceans separated the three major races on the planet; still, it didn't stop them from knowing of each other's existence early on in their emergence. The universe had granted the inhabitants of this world not only the ability to communicate verbally as in most other galactic species but had also given them the power to communicate mentally.

When they were a young species consisting of one race, before the great migrations, it only worked in direct genetic groups and in close proximity. As their societies grew, the ability grew as well and became stronger, enabling the Triberions to sense and communicate over greater distances and to those outside of their genetic family. Over many centuries, the ability grew until they started hearing voices in their heads that were different while using a distinctive but familiar language.

At first, when this new ability started, many feared they were going insane or it was communications from gods or evil spirits. Many Triberions did go insane from the noise in their heads, and others were put to death for possession by malevolent spirits. Eventually, the Triberions learned how to block out these other voices as they had learned how to block voices of their own race with whom they didn't want to have communication.

Over time, the elders and educated class realized the voices were other tribes of Triberions, which had broken off from the original race and left in search of food and fertile land. The migration happened so long ago, it became lost to history and legend, and the one race had become three distinct races, genetically altered by their surroundings. Years later, the civilizations learned how to understand the language of the other two races. A century later, they communicated with only one common language, verbally and mentally across the entire planet.

When the Triberions first learned more than one race existed on the planet, all descended from the original; they desired more than basic communication. The aspiration caused a major scientific expansion worldwide to develop travel methods across the vast distances between the races. They eventually built what Earthlings would recognize as railroads and large ocean-going vessels. These advancements enabled the Triberions to become one race of people but did not unite them as one race with one set of priorities, moralities, or gods. For almost a century, the races fought over land, morality, religion, and freedom. When a widespread famine ran wild across the planet, they knew the time had come to end the fighting and work together.

Centuries later, they had built an impressive society free of war, prejudice, and hatred. Their abilities almost made them of one mind and one being, but they still highly regarded and encouraged individual freedom of thought.

Because of the high gravity, the Triberions never made it into space or even invented air travel. In its place, they created a vast underground network of computerized travel tubes, which enabled them to travel from one city, one country, and one continent to another with extreme efficiency.

After many more years of development and practice, some of the Triberions could use their minds to move small objects and influence lesser non-intelligent species. The additional abilities were leading to even more discoveries than had ever been found on other planets with intelligent life. Everything was good.

The Destruction of Triberon

What the universe gives, the universe can take away.

Unknown to the Triberions, out across the vastness of space, a menace headed for them at a tremendous speed. A microscopic black hole, too tiny to be detected by even the most advanced space-faring races, approached their solar system, unseen and without warning.

It started as a beautiful sunny day over the Tribat continent as the inhabitants of the cities were going about their various chores and business ventures. On the far side of the planet, facing away from the sun, the inhabitants of the Tevil continent slept; sleep would not last for long.

When the tiny black hole interacted with their sun, it exploded outward with such a boundless force, it ripped apart the planet's surface that faced the sun and eventually destroyed the entire world, followed soon by the destruction of the entire system. The shock wave it created moved out across the galaxy at an incredible speed until it became a barely detectable wave of charged particles. But the waves, which moved from the direction of the backside of Triberon, contained more than charged particles.

When the sun exploded, there was enough warning to cause great fear among those Triberions awake on the daylight side of the planet. The fear and anguish spread around the world and eventually to those asleep on the dark side. When they awoke from the agony they experienced—a millisecond before the end—their feelings were strengthened and released as a vast psychic wave. The wave spread outward from the planet's dark side, being pushed, carried, and intensified by the shock wave of charged particles.

The black hole quickly sucked into itself, all the matter in the system. Unfortunately for other inhabitants of the galaxy, thought and psychic abilities are not matter, so the psychic wave of fear, anguish, and extraordinary capabilities continued spreading outward.

The Wave of Triberon

The wave traveled on and on for hundreds of thousands of years. As it moved through the universe, the storm it created passed through many other star systems. Some had intelligent life beginning to form a civilization, and some were almost as advanced as the Triberions.

Although the wave had traveled for a long time, its impact on many civilizations remained devastating. On one minor planet where humanoid intelligent life had recently begun to form tribes and a sense of self and religion, the storm wave caused devastation. The inhabitants experienced not only an intense feeling of anguish and despair from the wave, but it also filled their minds with images of the Triberion civilization, which they considered to be images of the Gods. They became so paralyzed by the lasting effects of the wave they didn't realize they could now control the world around them. They thought the strange occurrences must be the anger of the Gods, who were punishing them. They fled and hid in caves and huts, afraid to leave for fear of the Gods, but even hidden away, things still moved by themselves, and many unintentionally killed themselves and their neighbors. In less than a planetary year, the entire civilization perished.

And still, the wave sustained.

Three hundred thousand years after the death of Triberon, the wave passed through a highly advanced civilization with colonies on a few of the system's planets. The first planet to be hit became so filled with fear of death and the images flooding their minds, they quickly went insane.

Shortly thereafter, they accidentally destroyed the planet by allowing the energy plants to go critical and explode.

On one of the other smaller colonies, the fear, anguish, and despair caused all the inhabitants to commit suicide by opening the airlocks and allowing poisonous gas to enter their biosphere.

The principal planet in the system, from which all life had originated, mainly inhabited one giant continent. When the invisible storm hit, the continent was on the far side of the world, so it didn't impact the inhabitants at full force. However, the wave remained strong enough to instantly give them the psychic abilities it had ripped away from the Triberions. Immediately, everyone could hear the thoughts of all those near, and everyone gained the ability to move objects and control the space around them.

The mentally stronger inhabitants used their abilities to control others for amusement and perversion. Soon, small groups had mental wars with each other, while in other parts of the continent, citizens murdered with only the thoughts in their minds.

Many committed suicide, and thousands of others attacked and killed their friends and neighbors simply because of their thoughts. Eventually, society crumbled, and few individuals remained alive, while those enduring spread far apart, trying to get away from each other's thoughts. The separation worked well, until in the night when their thoughts invaded the dreams of others. Eventually, nothing remained of the once-great civilization except a few enclaves of inhabitants who spent their lives eating a plant that prevented their minds from hearing others' thoughts. The plant, an addictive drug, also caused people not to have any ambition or desires. Eventually, the entire population became extinct.

And still, the storm wave continued expanding for many thousands of years until the only thing remaining was the ability to impart its gift or curse onto other sentient creatures. A few thousand years later, the wave approached a small blue and white planet orbiting around a yellow sun.

ARRIVAL

The Day the World Changed – The Event

Jonathan Bartram was of slender build and the kind of guy no one ever would pick to be on their team; he would never catch the eye of the pretty girl in the office, and never be the go-to guy for anyone. He would always be the guy most suspected of being a womanizer or worse. His dirty blond, uncombed hair hung limp around his somewhat odd facial features.

His childhood had been filled with misery as most of the other children in school avoided him, sensing something wrong about his demeanor. The other parents would often complain to the school principal about Jonathan's behavior around their children. Some parents, including his own, feared him, though no one could explain why.

He was twenty-four years old and a graduate of the Drexel University School of Engineering. Even at school, where he excelled in all his classes, Jonathan had no friends to include him in the more enjoyable aspects of college life. Even among the nerds, he became an outcast.

Being unattractive and shunned by most, no one would be surprised he remained a virgin until his twenty-third birthday when he paid a prostitute to service him in his apartment. Even she hurried to leave after they finished their transaction, sleazy even to her standards. It may have been because Jonathan wanted more than he desired to pay for and expected her to perform things she felt uncomfortable undertaking, even for more money. Jonathan was sick by most standards, too sick for even the lowest of hookers.

Jonathan hated most people and appreciated the opportunity he had to work from home on most days. At the office, no colleague ever missed him when home, and when he appeared in the office, he didn't fit the corporate mold. He always arrived disheveled whenever he had to come in for a meeting or presentation, and he never stayed long. He liked no one in the office except for one person. Her name was Patricia Stevenson. She was beautiful, with medium-length, blond hair and piercing blue eyes, causing him to desire her more than anything in life.

Patricia, like most others, didn't like Jonathan, but neither did she dislike him. A compassionate person, she recognized his talent and felt sorry for him, sort of the way she felt sorry for the shelter dogs she visited at least once a month. She always said hello to him, even though he sometimes made her uncomfortable by the way he would leer at her when he didn't think she would notice.

Jonathan could tell it bothered her, but he didn't care. He liked her; he wanted her but knew their coupling would never happen. She dated and Jonathan felt sure she fucked Mark Givens, an accountant who worked across the hall from Patricia. Mark had the looks and body type the girls desired, and he used it well. Jonathan ran into Mark a few times and instantly knew, like many others, Mark hated him.

Jonathan could always tell when people disliked him, feared him, or outright hated him—like Mark. It was one of Jonathan's talents, as he liked to call it. He also always knew exactly what his bosses and the clients wanted from him even before they were sure themselves. His ability to consistently provide what they wanted unerringly was the only reason they tolerated him and kept him as an employee.

Jonathan always felt he had some unique power, and he proved it during his sophomore year at Drexel. He needed money, so he signed up for a study on E.S.P. conducted at the Pennsylvania University a few blocks down from Drexel. He achieved a forty percent correct rate during all the studies they performed. The researchers told him they had never met anyone like him, and they weren't happy when he informed them, he had enough and no longer wanted to participate. He knew they didn't like him; like everyone else, they only wanted to use him. He wished his ability could be strong enough to show them what it genuinely felt like to be used.

The universe heard his wish.

Because of the way the Earth faced at the time, the undetectable storm wave of Triberon first hit France and the British Isles, followed by Spain, Portugal, and the western African continent. The wave quickly moved across the ocean to South America, North, and Central America before moving on to touch Australia, eastern Russia, and parts of the Asian continent. The only places partially spared when the energy storm pushed past the Earth were western Russia, parts of Europe, and most of the African continent. Eventually, those not immediately touched areas would also experience a severe impact as the world fell into disarray, and those with newfound powers would arrive to conquer.

It was late evening, on a day that had earlier been bright and sunny when the storm hit the city of Philadelphia. The wave of psychic energy hit as if someone threw a switch, and all hell broke loose. Across all areas of the world struck by the wave, as in Philadelphia, tens of thousands of people collapsed and died on the spot—the experience being more than their brains could handle. In cities and towns where night had fallen, many died in their sleep, as those who were not so lucky became immersed in nightmares commonly shared by their neighbors. So much horror filled their minds, that many thousands perished in minutes from heart attacks brought on by intense, unrelenting fear.

Many who did not succumb during the evening—unaware of the event—awoke as drooling idiots, incapable of taking care of themselves, and died after starving to death or worse. Others awoke the next day to voices in their heads, some loud, some soft, angry, and perverse. People felt as if their bodies were not their own as they moved in ways they didn't want to move and did things they didn't ever want to do. The nightmare had begun for many, a dream from which they would never awake until the day they died. If they were lucky, the day came quick.

Human minds were different from the Triberions, so the wave gave humans different abilities and powers than the Triberions, such as the ability to control another's actions, cause pain, or influence their dreams. Other newfound skills and capabilities from the wave would not manifest themselves till years later for most. Still, some like Jonathan had immense powers immediately after the wave hit, and they didn't hesitate to use them.

There were also powers the Triberions had, which humans did not. Although one human mind could control another, most humans could not sense another's thoughts or use the ability to communicate wordlessly as the Triberions had for centuries.

Roberta Welkson waited tables at the local twenty-four-hour diner on Market Street, near the city's historic district. She finished her shift, and while walking home, experienced extreme pain in her head, causing her to stumble as if drunk. Her knees hit and scraped the pavement when she fell, and her body curled into a fetal position. She didn't care about the blood pooling under her as the pain continued along with images of creatures she had never seen before, as they chased people through a landscape only visible in her mind.

A few minutes later, the pain started to ease. She continued walking until new agony ravaged her body as the assault on her mind continued—images of men and women fighting with knives and shooting each other with guns flashed in her mind. As one person shot or stabbed another, she could feel the pain as if she were the one cut by the knives and pierced by the bullets.

The pain grew to such an extreme, she stumbled into a small, dank, and dirty alley where she repeatedly smashed her head against the wall to stop the images and agony. She was unsuccessful and eventually knocked herself unconscious.

Later, when Roberta woke, things were not as bad, and she thought whatever happened was over until she felt an extreme fear as if something was coming to get her. She didn't see anything, but she knew the end was near, the unseen menace approached. Roberta started to run, so afraid of the menacing evil, she didn't pay attention to where she ran and ended up running down the middle of the street. She stumbled over the median curbs several times until an out-of-control minivan driven by a tourist hit her and ended her torment.

Randolph VanPelt worked for the Southeastern Pennsylvania Transportation Authority for many years. He loved working the night shift as there weren't many passengers at night, and he felt it relaxing to drive along the mostly empty streets. On the day of the event, however, he worked the early evening shift, having switched with a friend. A decision he would soon regret.

His vehicle sat waiting at a red light on South Broad Street when the event started. Randolph experienced severe vertigo—everything around him began to spin along with images he couldn't identify. His face flushed, and he had the look of someone about to lose their lunch as his eyes glazed. He sat in the middle of the street, he thought for only a few minutes, but when he looked at his watch, an hour had passed—screams, laughter, fire, and blood filled the once quiet street.

He watched the disarray in horror until startled when someone banged on the bus door, and he looked over to see two young men waiting to board. He opened the door; they entered the bus and moved to the seats behind him without paying the fare. He turned to tell them to pay when one man said, "Just shut your damn mouth and drive."

Randolph didn't want to move the bus without the fare, but he had no choice. Something now forced him to drive the bus as if a puppeteer controlled his every move. Behind him, the young men laughed as one said, "hit that row of cars along the street. Hit them all." When he tried to resist, his arms and legs twitched and moved on their own while he felt a growing pain behind his eyes. After a minute of fighting, he drove his bus along the sides of all the cars he could find—his pain eased.

A block ahead of him, a woman ran out of a house and started running down the street. The two behind him saw her as well and said, "run the bitch down." He fought to resist for a short time, muscles trembling. The bus lurched under him and started speeding down the street even though his foot wasn't on the gas pedal—someone else controlled the bus. He tried to move his foot to the brake or turn the bus, but no matter how he tried, he couldn't move, and he watched, helpless, in pain and horror as the bus struck the woman, and she disappeared underneath him at the intersection of Tasker and Broad.

Soon after, still in a daze and alone on the vehicle, he realized the two men were standing on the corner laughing. He started to rise from his seat when the bus suddenly lurched. It traveled down the road, turned, and crashed at full speed into a brick wall, crushing the people who were standing there trying to deal with their individual demons and sending Randolph through the window.

Twenty-five-year-old William Paterson woke from one nightmare to fall into another as he found himself in an unfamiliar room. He tried to look around, but his eyes remained, forced to stare into the full-length mirror standing in front of him. In the mirror, he viewed his image clad only in the underwear he remembered wearing to bed that evening, his brown hair tousled as if he had just risen from bed.

While he stood there, his hands moved to his underpants, pulled them down, and he started fondling himself. William didn't understand why he stood there masturbating; it wasn't something he usually did and thought he must be asleep and dreaming. He tried to stop, and he wanted to wake up, but instead, he continued to uncontrollably stroke himself. His body started to glisten with sweat as his heart rate increased.

Behind him, laughter erupted as he fully dropped his underpants to the floor and continued, unable to stop, even as the stroking began to hurt. He tried to turn around; he wanted to see who laughed at his expense. However, all he could do was stare into the mirror. After what felt like an eternity, he unloaded onto his sweaty hands and, against his will, stuck them into his mouth.

He spun around, pulled by some handless force, to face those laughing behind him. What he saw made him cringe. Two men he recognized as his new neighbors in the Rittenhouse Square apartment building were visibly drunk and in bed together, naked with beers in their hands and many empty bottles lying in the bed and on the nightstand. While the men continued laughing and mocking him, he felt his body pulled over to the bed, and he finally came to understand he wasn't having a dream. William shouted as he realized he was powerless to stop the assault.

Many people across the world who didn't die soon after the wave hit, realized they could control other people, control things in their environment, and move tiny objects around with their thoughts. It didn't take long for one person to try and manipulate another. Many battles of the mind resulted, and countless more died when used as toys to fight like gladiators of old. The strongest fell into two categories; those who wanted to help others and those who desired to dominate, abuse, and play with humanity.

The helpful individuals soon learned the abusers outnumbered them. They disappeared from the major cities and fled to the countryside, where they banded together and worked on using their collective powers to hide and help as many people as possible. They knew those who would abuse the power, or abilities as they soon became known, would continue to fight until few were left strong enough to resist.

Those in society who wanted control over their world and the people around them were far more numerous than most would have realized before the storm crashed into their lives. They were quickly becoming the masters, and the weaker becoming the slaves.

The masters started using the slaves for their amusement and enjoyment, forcing them to commit violent murders and fantastical suicides, performing sex acts of all kinds and varieties that would make Sodom and Gomorra look like paradise. The masters were cruel, and they quickly went through many bodies until they had nothing else to do but turn on each other. They consolidated their power and used the slaves, not providing other enjoyments, to fight their battles for them and become human shields and weapons.

Many people died in horror as the masters forced them to fight with no control over their bodies. Those who died quickly were the lucky ones since those only wounded were left where they fell to suffer a slow death.

Hell on Earth had begun.

For Jonathan Bartram, his life became Heaven on Earth. He had gotten himself blind drunk and had partaken in some extremely potent, almost deadly, cocaine the evening the wave hit. The combination of the two, shielded him from the immediate fear and confusion others felt and allowed the wave to give him more abilities than any other human in the vicinity or maybe the world.

When Jonathan awoke, he could hear a multitude of voices in his head. It took him only two hours to gain control, and in that time, he learned to quiet the voices and zoom in on only those he wanted to hear. The next hour, Jonathan found he could communicate with others, and he laughed as he used the ability to torment people and fill their minds with vile thoughts, images, and fear of an unknown enemy.

He tormented one person so severely they committed suicide by cutting their wrist. As his victim slowly died, Jonathan found their death caused him a wonderful sense of euphoria and sexual excitement. He became excited without touching himself physically; he ejaculated in his pants as his entire body quivered. He could only imagine the thrill of having this drama occur in person instead of through the victim's mind.

Later, Jonathan stood at his window, looking out on the world with his eyes and mind, seeing and feeling the fear and carnage. As the days passed, his power grew, and he fought off others, trying to take away his supremacy and increasing domain. But all of this wasn't enough; he wanted more. He thought for a while, and he realized he knew who he wanted to find. He only hoped they remained alive.

The next few weeks were a combination of sick pleasure, fear, and torment. Far worse than could be imagined in the lowest depths of hell, agony and pain waited for many who survived the first few days after the storm wave washed across the world. Not only were many people physically violated, but they also endured mental violations, rape, and enslavement.

Those who escaped the cities hid in small enclaves. They tried not to use their newfound abilities, but over time they couldn't avoid feeling the fear and utter degradation of so many victims. Even in the countryside, numerous people died from the fear they couldn't keep out of their minds, while other entire groups succumbed to the anguish and despair—eventually, they committed suicide.

The more powerful enclaves managed to keep the feelings away, keep themselves hidden, and help those less powerful. Over the years, they grew to become towns that protected the citizens from all the torments experienced by others not so lucky to escape. The new reality of life set in, and they fought as needed to defend their existence. They could only hold out for so long, for the emerging Overlord of Bartram Fortress knew of their existence and wasn't pleased.

PERVERSIONS

The Fortress

The Overlord of Bartram Fortress gazed out from the top of the tower, once the base of the almost forty-foot-tall William Penn sculpture. The beloved icon had stood atop the Philadelphia City Hall tower, overlooking the city that William had helped design and build centuries ago. The statue was now a memory to some and a symbol of despair and oppression to others.

Workers completed the grand building, now known as Bartram Fortress, at the beginning of the twentieth century. The architects designed it to be the tallest building in the world at that time, but the Washington Monument and Eiffel Tower surpassed it before completion. When first constructed, the building had over seven hundred rooms, most of which the Overlord converted to his own perverse and military needs.

The Overlord had the lower ground floors ripped apart and replaced with dormitories and storage for his growing army. The upper levels were his, and he had them remade into living space and bedrooms for his many servants, slaves, guests, and sexual partners. The below-ground levels and the subways beneath the building were converted into his prison and torture chambers for his extra special guests. They became his favorite places to visit.

The Overlord, once known as Jonathan Bartram, thought back to the time, almost three years ago, when he first learned how to steal others' power and abilities. Jonathan realized he could link minds to his own and boost his abilities to give him incredible power to do almost anything he wanted. There wasn't a mind in what remained of the city of Philadelphia, Jonathan couldn't control; however, moving objects, especially the size of old Willie, took more power than any single mind could wield. It turned out to be easy for him to manipulate people since moving electrical impulses in the brain was a simple task, but moving matter required great mental strength he could only get by stealing from others.

The effect for the man soon to be known as the Overlord became better than the finest orgasm he could ever experience. However, for the people whose minds he stole, only the end of life awaited. When he finished with them, nothing remained but an empty, brain-dead shell he would feed to his dogs.

Jonathan stood that day in the middle of North Broad Street across from the now ransacked Academy of Fine Arts. He reached out and grabbed the minds of those he had picked to be his helpers. Their master had promised them the reward of pleasures of the flesh and full stomachs to get them to cooperate. As he grabbed their minds, they realized the mistake they had made. His strength grew, and he used the power to push against the statue, and slowly it began to rip from its base. A few minutes later, the icon fell, tumbled, and crashed into the middle of the City Hall courtyard.

To Jonathan's surprise, the bronze statue only bent but didn't break. What to do with the fucking thing now, he thought, before inspiration struck him. The next day after the empty shells that once were people had been gathered and disposed of, he enticed another group of fools and used their abilities like the first. Connecting his mind to his victims' minds, he lifted the statue above the ground and moved it through the west portal of the fortress, all the way out past the old Philadelphia Electric Company building.

He stood at the foot of the Market Street bridge and concentrated, stealing his victims' last bit of power. The metal bulk moved silently over his head and high into the air before it began to turn, its head facing the street below. Jonathan closed his eyes and used the last drop of stolen power to ram the statue upside down through the middle of the bridge and into the Schuylkill River. He positioned it there to remind anyone coming at him from the west of his immense power. It was at that moment he became the Overlord, and only one accomplishment remained.

The memory of that great day made him smile as he released his load into the mouth of the old hag he forced to give him his moment of pleasure while he gazed out across his empire. When he finished forcing the old bitch to clean him up and zip his pants, he casually kicked her off the side of the tower base and walked away, not bothering to watch her fall to the courtyard below.

"Thank you, hag," he said as he walked away. He couldn't stand to have anyone around who would perform such an act of perversion at such an advanced age, whether forced or not. He both loathed and desired his minions for all his pleasure and material needs. He required bodies to do his work, and he needed the flesh to satisfy his perverted sexual desires. Once used, they were foul and disgusting to him—nothing but trash. There remained plenty of flesh to go around for numerous years of enjoyment, and he knew he could always make more. He had already sired over thirty children.

He could please himself with the abilities he possessed by merely thinking about it, but he considered that as bad as giving himself a handjob. Why keep slaves around if you were not going to abuse them for your pleasure. He thought himself a good ruler. He would allow them to pleasure themselves, sometimes voluntarily, before he molested them for his gratification. What more could they expect? That is what happens to the weak-minded.

Only one person existed that he used for his pleasure—on rare occasions—and still kept around, but theirs was a special relationship. She had months ago given herself freely with a small amount of coercion and control, simply to protect the love of her life. He used her when needed but treated her with gentle respect, which even surprised him. She would become the mother of his true heirs, and he wanted her to be both physically and mentally sound.

Twenty-two-year-old Patricia Stevenson, a co-worker before the day of deliverance—as he often called it—had to Jonathan the look of a beautiful goddess. Her blond hair and piercing blue eyes caused him to desire her more than anyone or anything he knew, but she didn't feel the same. She pitied him, which he found revolting, and as payment, he enjoyed staring at her when at work to make her nervous.

When Jonathan started taking over the city in earnest a few years ago and declared himself the Overlord, he still missed the one thing he desired. The Overlord needed a woman at his side to provide him companionship—one to lift above the scum he kept as his slaves.

Jonathan knew who he wanted; he had searched for both since the day of deliverance. He could only hope she lived. He had to find her, and hopefully, the bastard, as well, as it became a constant obsession. Using his abilities, he put her image into the minds of everyone he could with the instruction to report back to their Overlord and be greatly rewarded.

It took almost three years before a rewarded dead fool located her living in a house in Pennsauken, NJ, across the river from his growing empire. And even better, she lived with that bastard Mark Givens, the man she truly loved.

Three and a half years after the day of deliverance, toward the end of a long, hot, Philadelphia summer, he gathered ten of the strongest, best-trained men he had under his control. Riding in one of the old SEPTA buses he had in his possession, they crossed the Ben Franklin Bridge to retrieve Patricia and her lover. It was always a risk to leave the city since his control only extended through the center city area, the northeast and south, but these were his best fighters, and he could always use his power to hold off any attacks.

Most survivors were afraid to attack the Overlord, as his reputation and control spread quickly, but there would always be those few idiots. The fools still living in the area knew his reputation and knew it best to get out of his way, even though he didn't control the area—yet.

The mission across the river and up to Pennsauken was uneventful. They had to work around many cars and skeletal remains still littering the streets. The houses along the way showed signs of decay and were overrun by animals and vegetation no longer meticulously maintained by the former residents.

When they arrived, the Overlord could sense his quest inside the house and feel they were having sex in one of the upstairs bedrooms. By lightly touching their minds, he could feel the sweat running along their bodies, caused by the hot summer and the passion of their activity. As Jonathan stood outside, he trembled as he could feel the sensations they were experiencing as the climax quickly approached—but he wanted more.

The situation is too wonderful, he thought, *let's have some fun.*

The Overlord stood outside, reached with his abilities, and forced his mind into the bastard's. He learned a few months prior, he could, if he desired, feel everything his subjects experienced, and he wanted that now, in full glory. It felt good as he took complete control of the bastard's mind. He looked into Patricia's eyes as he made her lover thrust harder and deeper, faster, and faster even after she started to complain and asked him to stop.

Patricia started to resist and panic just as Mark's body climaxed, and the Overlord quivered in the delightful pleasure. He abruptly pulled his mind away, leaving Patricia and the bastard free to deal with what had happened, and while they argued, the Overlord enjoyed the last thrill of his orgasm.

He had his fun, time to move in. He used his power to keep the two lovers from hearing their entry into the house. Jonathan and his men went upstairs and kicked the door open, finding the lovers still naked, and in the middle of the argument about the violent lovemaking, Mark couldn't even recall.

"Hello, Patricia, remember me? More importantly, did you enjoy that last fuck? I know I did. It may have been your bastard's dick inside your twat, but I controlled his every thrust."

Patricia sat on the bed, confused; it took a while for her to react and grab a pillow to cover her body. At first, she didn't recognize him, but when she did, she became sick to her stomach, knowing now what had happened to Mark. She heard Jonathan controlled Philadelphia, and she had heard about his many abilities, atrocities, and murders. It was because of Jonathan, they left Philly as soon as possible. They intended to relocate further north away from the city but never had the chance.

"Yes, Jonathan, I remember. What are you doing here, and how did you find me?"

Before he could answer, Mark yelled and lunged for him, but the slaves were on Mark and took him down with little effort. Jonathan told Mark to stand. When he didn't, the Overlord used his mind to force him to stand, and Mark jumped up from the floor like a marionette on strings.

"I very much enjoyed using you, bastard, to pleasure Patricia, even though your dick is quite a bit smaller than mine. From now on, it will be me and my body only; she will enjoy. You won't need that pathetic thing any longer."

Jonathan walked over to one of the slaves now holding Patricia on the bed as she sobbed and told him she would never willingly have sex with him. He took the knife from the slave's holster and walked back to stand in front of Mark and held out the magnificently polished and sharp blade.

"Take this knife, bastard, and cut off your little dick. You won't miss it."

Mark had a powerful will and possessed some minor abilities he used to try and resist, but his event-granted abilities were no match for the Overlord. Slowly he reached for the knife and held it in his right hand.

The Overlord could see the fear in the bastard's face, and a tear appeared in his eye as his hand trembled.

"Do it, bastard, cut off that miserable excuse of a dick."

Mark reached down with his left hand, grabbed the head of his manhood, and pulled it away from his body as another tear fell from his eye.

"Please, Jonathan, stop. Don't make him do this," Patricia cried from the bed.

"Sorry, my love, but I must do what I must do, and my name is Overlord—you would be wise to remember."

He paused a moment to reflect on his conquest. He now had the one last thing he needed to banish away forever—the person known previously as Jonathan. The Overlord of Bartram Fortress would let nothing stand in his way.

His reflecting done, the Overlord reached out again with his abilities, overcoming Mark's will. He forced the quivering man to bring the knife down and cut off his shaft a small fraction of an inch before the sack.

When Mark completed the deed, the Overlord released his hold, and Mark screamed out in agony as he fell to the floor, holding his hands over the fresh wound—blood leaking between his fingers.

"Be glad, bastard, I don't force you to eat it.

"Take him out and attend to his wounded stub. I want him alive. If he dies, you will all suffer the same fate, and I will make you eat yours."

The slaves left with Mark, still crying, while blood dripped across the floor as they prodded him down the stairs.

"Now, my lovely Patricia, let's talk about you and your Overlord."

The Overlord stood atop his fortress as the day darkened, still looking over his kingdom. He smiled and thought about all the changes since the

Day of Deliverance. He became, in all manner, the Overlord of everything he could see before him. He found his true love, and soon, one way or another, she would be his wife, his lady by his side. As he headed back to his throne room, he thought about the first time he took her for real, and the last time it was by force.

The Throne Room

The Overlord's throne room had been the Philadelphia City Council chambers. He instructed his slaves to remove all the chairs and desks, except for in the upper gallery, and the space made open to allow his subjects room to prostrate themselves before him. His slaves also created a large hole in one corner with a shaft leading down into the old sewers. When the Overlord tired of one of his toys, he would have them throw themselves down the shaft to their deaths—if they were lucky.

A large platform sat at the front of the room, raised ten feet above the main floor and surrounded by steps. In the middle of it sat a large throne the Overlord took from an exhibit showing at the Philadelphia Museum of Art when the deliverance had come upon the world. The throne, massive and covered with fine cloth trimmed in gold and silver, served him well, but someday he decided it would be more extensive and made from his enemies' bones.

When they arrived back at the fortress from the mission to retrieve his future wife, he had her brought to him in his throne room. She stood in front of him, still naked and shaking from the earlier activities.

"Bring the bastard," he yelled to one of his slaves, "and the three remaining men we captured from the North Philly Resistance. Strip them naked before you bring them to worship me."

The North Philly Resistance was a group that had developed some unique mental abilities from the event. They had used their power to hide from the Overlord for a short while, but when they started to raid the northernmost portions of his kingdom, they became known to him and could no longer hide. He had captured a group of five men the day before—two were already dead, and the three remaining he had saved for further entertainment. *This should be fun,* he thought.

"Come, Patricia, my love, sit to my right on the step so you can see and fully enjoy the entertainment."

When she refused to move, he used his mind to force her to sit where he had instructed.

"You will learn you cannot refuse me. It can be a painful lesson if you want, but I sincerely do not want to hurt you—more than is necessary."

His slaves brought Mark and forced him to kneel on the bottom step facing the throne. He kept his face down, too ashamed to even look up at Patricia. Some of the others in attendance gasped when they witnessed the fresh bloodstain on the small diaper Mark now wore.

"Enough!" The Overlord yelled to quiet his guests.

"The one thing I remember I liked about you was your hatred for gays. I don't much like them either; they were always judging me and getting special privileges. You, bastard, I sense to have more than hatred; you fear them, and maybe fear deep down you might like it. Let's see!"

The Overlord forced Mark to turn to the right and guided one of the resistance prisoners prostrating before him, to stand facing Mark. The prisoner, a large black man, in every sense and body part, stood directly in front of Mark with his crotch in Mark's face. The Overlord knew the bastard had a dislike for blacks and gays, being a homophobe and a staunch racist—the latter being something the Overlord could not tolerate.

"Now, bastard, take him into your mouth and give him the last enjoyment of his life."

After a bit of hesitation while Mark tried to resist, he did as the Overlord demanded. The Overlord then freed their minds enough to be repulsed and sickened by what he had forced them to do in front of all his worshipers.

He turned to Patricia, still trembling, crying, and begging him to stop. She tried to look away, but he forced her to watch.

"Does your bastard give better head than you, Patricia? Later I will find out."

After minutes of agony for Patricia and the two men, the big man unloaded into Mark's mouth, and the Overlord forced the bastard to swallow.

"Next!" The Overlord yelled to his slaves.

As he forced the first man to walk over to the hole and throw himself down to the sewer, he also forced a young white man, the second of the NPR, to stand in front of the bastard and get his enjoyment. This one liked the experience and enjoyed the pleasure. That was most unacceptable.

"Bite it off!" The Overlord yelled at Mark.

The young man screamed in pain as Mark, unable to resist, bit off the man's penis, and spit it out onto the man's feet.

"No one gets to enjoy pleasure in this thrown room except me!"

As the young man now walked dripping blood to follow the first down the hole, the Overlord pulled the third man up behind Mark and had him face the throne.

"Face us bastard and watch as I take your lover for my own. You will never have her again."

The Overlord forced the man standing behind to grab Mark by the hair of his head and pull it back so he couldn't look away as the Overlord compelled the man to remove the bastard's diaper and enter him from behind.

As Mark endured the torture, he had to watch while Jonathan forced Patricia in front of him, and he began to cry as he witnessed Jonathan take his pleasure with her, this time for real with his own body.

As the Overlord enjoyed Patricia, he forced her to look down and watch Mark's abuse. The moment alone could almost make him explode in delight. He waited years, and now this time belonged to him—the Overlord.

The room filled with laughter from those in attendance as he continued to take his pleasure and enjoy his moment of conquest. The sound of her cries made the experience even better than he could have imagined, and he exploded in her way too soon.

The Overlord laughed again to himself as he sat on his throne and remembered that day. He wasn't totally without shame for what he had done and what he made his love endure, but months had passed, and things were now different.

Patricia and the Proposal

Patricia awoke from a dream of a happy time, a time before hell broke loose in the world, and her life changed forever. She didn't know what happened four years ago; she only knew her life and the lives of everyone, drastically changed that day and the act of survival became harder thereafter.

Patricia had what she considered a perfect life before the day of hell. Mark and she had moved in together two years after they first met. She had moved from Wilmington, Delaware, for the job she had started two days before she first met Mark in the office. They both felt it to be love at first sight.

Jonathan assigned her a spacious and well-appointed room. Heavy ornate curtains lined the windows; furniture and art adorned the room with what would have been considered eighteenth-century antiques back in the days when anyone would have cared. The bedroom had once been the Philadelphia City Council President's office. Jonathan, her captor, and tormenter, designed and converted it into a bedroom for his bride-to-be.

The room looked beautiful; they fed and cared for her well. However, the bedroom existed in a prison run by a madman who wanted to be her husband. He would come to her some nights, lie beside her, and occasionally have sex with her. She had stopped fighting his advances after he threatened to torture her former fiancé, Mark.

His advances were not harsh or cruel, as he saved that for his slaves but it remained a violation, unwanted but repeatedly tolerated. He would tell her how much he loved her and how he would surround her with luxury, but she cared for none of it and told him so repeatedly.

She had learned from the servants of unspeakable things Jonathan did to her and Mark the first day in the throne room. However, she remembered none of it, which she considered a blessing. They told her he had wiped her mind of all the events so she wouldn't hate him and would want to be with him. They would not or could not speak of what exactly happened, but it didn't stop them from talking.

Patricia knew Jonathan abused Mark repeatedly that day, but the last thing she could remember before waking for the first time in her room was Jonathan forcing Mark to cut off his penis at the house in Pennsauken. She didn't understand why he let her remember that horror, but he did for some sick reason. She also knew from what little conversations she had been able to have with Mark; he could remember everything Jonathan did to them, but Jonathan had made it impossible for Mark to discuss. Jonathan forced him to suffer alone in silence.

Mark loved Patricia, and she loved him. They shared a secret Jonathan could not pull from their minds and an answer to a question he didn't think to compel them to answer. Patricia doubted Jonathan would care, but it might be an excuse he could use to justify killing Mark. She couldn't take the chance, so the secret remained. She had no one to tell or anyone in whom to confide.

Jonathan had not come to the bedroom last night, and for that, she was grateful. She knew he probably spent the night having drunken sex with his slaves.

Better for me if he spends time with them instead of here in my bed.

When washed and dressed, the handmaid told her the Overlord would be having breakfast with her this morning in his private chambers. He expected her to be ready by eight, which gave her only a half-hour to prepare mentally.

"Hello, my lovely Patricia, you are looking splendid today. Did you sleep well?"

"Yes, I sleep very well when I'm alone."

"Oh, don't be so snarky; you know you enjoy our times together, more than you want to admit. Now, please sit down with me and enjoy some wonderful breakfast."

Patricia looked at the table set with fancy dishes, most likely stolen from the department store once known as John Wanamaker's, many years ago, back when she was a child. She couldn't remember who owned it more recently, but it didn't matter now since true civilization had disappeared, and Jonathan had used his power to take control of everything in the city.

Breakfast consisted of eggs benedict, sausage and bacon, and some croissants with various jams. Jonathan fed her well and tried his best to make her happy, but she would never be happy as long as he held her prisoner in his fortress.

Patricia spent most of the breakfast listening to Jonathan talk endlessly about lucratively raiding most of Bensalem to the north and Eddystone to the south. He loved to talk about his conquest of resources, territory, and people. The way he abused and killed off his slaves, he always needed more.

"The lands to the west I leave to the pigs. As long as they don't bother me, I won't bother them. They are lower than my lowest slave, not a talent or valuable trait among them.

"You are silent today, my love. What is your problem? Are you not happy?

"It is hard to be happy while kept a prisoner."

"My dear, you are not my prisoner. You are free to go anytime you wish, but the bastard is mine and will stay mine. He is my favorite court jester and throne room servant, but that can change. If you were not here, he would become of less value to me."

As the Overlord waited for her response, he thought about what the bastard did when he wasn't performing or serving. He often could be found tied up high on the rafters, and the Overlord's army slaves would use the bastard for target practice. His vital organs were protected, but there were still many places where a forceful blow would cause him much pain. The bastard could never tell Patricia, and the Overlord always made sure to have the many wounds covered if he and Patricia were going to have an opportunity to meet.

The Overlord would use Mark as a servant when it suited him and when he wanted to assure Patricia that her former lover remained healthy and unharmed. The breaks from being a live target often included being forced to watch the Overlord have sex with his slaves. Since the bastard no longer had a dick, the Overlord knew this drove him mad with desire he could no longer fulfill. The Overlord smiled at the thought.

Patricia spoke up, which drew him out of his happy thoughts.

"What did you say, my dear?"

"I said, I would like to see him and talk to him. It has been a while, and I want to make sure he is really okay."

"My dear, do you not trust me?"

She sat there a moment, afraid to answer. She knew Jonathan had strong feelings for her, but she also knew he was quick to anger.

"I just need to see him, to let him know he hasn't been forgotten."

"I can assure you I will not forget your former lover, but I guess I could arrange a visit or two, on one condition. When you see him, it would be nice to show him this and let him know you have consented to be my wife."

To Patricia's shock and disgust, Jonathan pulled out a diamond ring from his pocket. It had one huge diamond with two smaller diamonds to the sides. Before the fall of civilization, the ring would have been worth well over twenty thousand dollars.

"You know I could force you to do whatever I want, but that is not what I want to do. I want you to be with me willingly. I love you and hope you will grow to at least like me one day for what and who I am."

"I don't want to marry you; how could I, after what you have done to Mark and me? I know you wiped my mind, so I don't remember, but I have heard talk of—"

"From whom? Who would dare to tell you of things I have deliberately made you forget?"

"So, you admit it's true?"

"I admit I have done some terrible things to you and the b—Mark, and I am sorry. I admit I have done these things in the past out of anger and jealousy. They were wrong, and I regret them. It is why I wiped your memory. I want to be with you, and I want you to be happy.

"You have a week to make up your mind. I will not force you to marry me, but if you don't, I will take out my anger on the one you do love. As a show of good faith, I will not torture or kill those dirty perverts who watched and told you of my past sins.

"I must go now. Please consider my proposal carefully."

The Overlord's Prison

The Overlord's prison existed underneath Bartram Fortress—built for the Overlord by his many slaves. You could quickly get a project complete when you could control a worker and force them to work until they dropped dead. The Overlord had many slaves, so there were always more workers available to perform for the great cause. He didn't have to control each person all the time; the fear of him and his abilities kept them all in line. As long as they stayed in the city and worked, he kept them fed. As bad as it may be in the fortress and the city, it could be far worse outside the area under his control.

The Overlord had the prison constructed into the former Broad Street and Market-Frankford subway platforms and tunnels under his fortress. The many alcoves along the tunnels were a great place to hold a prisoner, and he could use the tracks for many hours of torture. He even had a subway car at his disposal. They maintained no electricity in the subway to power it, but the Overlord had other abilities to move the car along the track and over a prisoner.

The tunnels were also home to many hungry rats, and he didn't mind if they played and ate in his prison. They were always happy when a new meal arrived, prepared for them, tied to the rails.

Today, the Overlord had come down to check on a special new prisoner. A young man, barely an adult, and only a few years younger than himself, the year the powers were bestowed upon him. His guards caught the suspected spy in the city a few weeks ago, and the Overlord needed to know who he worked with and to what end. The Overlord had the prisoner tied upside down and stripped of his clothes to make the cold and dampness as unpleasant as possible, while he had his army throwing railroad spikes at him as a game. Unknown to the Overlord, the young man had his own abilities, and he could deflect some of the material thrown at him, with no one being the wiser.

The latest torture had been ongoing for over a week, and the Overlord wondered if the boy felt ready to talk. He could not allow anyone to spy on him regardless of apparent age. He had to know what the boy's accomplices were planning. If only his powers had allowed him to read minds in addition to controlling them, no one would ever be able to stop him. Not being able to read minds was one of his weaknesses and one that kept him up at night. He had many enemies out beyond the city, so he always had to be on guard.

The Overlord discovered another vulnerability the hard way, a couple of years ago when he had an accident during some rough sex. He realized when unconscious, he lost all control of his subjects, and for some reason, sleep was not the same. When he slept, he still had control and could sense when someone approached him. His sexual partner that evening would have maimed him, or worse had his guards not been attentive.

His people were attending to the young traitor's wounds when he arrived, so the Overlord instead headed over to the training area to visit the bastard. He built the training area a city block away in an old concourse section below South Broad Street. He enjoyed the walk back and forth between the lower levels of the fortress and the training facilities, thanks to the many connecting corridors built for changing from one train line to another. The walk gave him time to think and plan without distraction.

He would come back to question the young man after he visited the bastard. He looked forward to telling the bastard about his proposal. Anything he could do to drive Patricia's former lover crazy with grief and despair made him unimaginably happy.

On his way to the training area, as he walked through the tunnels, he thought about the first time he had walked through here as a boy. His father took him on little trips to ride the subways and other train lines around the city. It had been their special time together before he became abusive and ended up in jail.

Later in his life, he would walk through the tunnels to get out of the cold or to find someone to follow and make them nervous. It was fun, but not as much fun as he now had controlling those around him. A lot had changed since the first time he walked these tunnels, and it delighted him.

Before the day of deliverance, the city had built offices down in the tunnel to service the needs of the homeless who used to sleep there to get out of the cold. The Overlord disposed of the homeless scum years ago as they became the first group forced off the Market Street Bridge and into the river as soon as he took control of the city. Those higher up in command of his armies used the offices for some relaxation with the women they conquered. It kept them happy, and a happy soldier is less likely to turn on his commander. He only allowed men in his army. The women he kept for enjoyment.

His men were taking the bastard down from the rafters when Jonathan arrived in the training area. This latest session had left him with severe injuries, and he would need some time to heal, for the Overlord wanted him able to serve dinner at the engagement party he had planned for Patricia when she agreed to his proposal.

When his tormenters unhooked him from the ropes, he dropped on the floor, and the medics started treating his wounds. The bastard wasn't conscious, and that wouldn't do for the Overlord's enjoyment.

"Throw some water on the animal," he yelled to one of the medics. "I want him awake."

The medic grabbed a bucket of wastewater from a nearby pit—the only water available and poured it over the bastard's face.

Mark regained consciousness and moaned from his pain as he lay there in agony. When he saw who stood above him, he spit, but he remained so weak the spit merely fell back upon his face, where the embarrassment and understandable old rage was apparent to the Overlord.

"Ha, ha, ha, you're a pathetic piece of animal shit; you can't even manage to spit. I'm glad you are awake, for I have news. I have decided to take the hand of your former lover, as well as her pussy, to be mine. I have waited too long—too many months for her to come around to my charms, time to push the issue. Push, push, push in the bush, right bastard?

"I have officially asked her to marry me, and I wait only for her answer."

"She will never willingly marry you!"

"That is where you are wrong. For some strange reason, even after using my abilities to manipulate her mind, Patricia still has feelings for you, and I will use that to my advantage. Yes, I could force her, but it will be more fun for me and more torment for you if she lies in my bed for the rest of her life, willingly.

"Enough of this conversation," the Overlord yelled. "Sit him up against the wall."

The Overlord looked over and saw one of the sex slaves pleasuring the winner of the last target practice challenge.

"You, whore, come over here.

"Now watch closely, bastard, as I take this slave in the same manner, I will soon take Patricia."

Stephen Estrada

He had been hanging, upside-down, in one of the small alcoves that lined the walls of what had at one time been the Broad Street Subway for close to twenty-four hours—the longest of the many sessions he had endured the past week. They tied the young spy there so Jonathan's army could torture him by throwing railroad spikes at various parts of his body as a game. They were not allowed to aim for his head, but the game consisted of getting points for every shot that hit his privates. To make their aim better and cause his pain from the cold and dampness more severe, they stripped him naked and threw cold water on him whenever he fell asleep.

Before this torture began, they held him in a perpetually wet, smaller alcove for over two weeks. They fed him scraps and didn't let him out to relieve himself, no matter how much he complained.

Thankfully, his training and hidden abilities prevented him from feeling the cold coming from the cement wall they tied him against, as well as the pain from all the brutality an average person wouldn't be able to endure. Unknown to Jonathan, the abilities the event had given the human race went beyond controlling others. It enabled some people to control their minds and allow them to suppress pain and fatigue, at least for a little while.

Stephen's latest torture had been off and on for well over a week, and still, they asked no questions of their captive. They told him they were waiting for the Overlord. Even though he could control his suffering, his body was getting damaged, and the constant faking of his pain became hard to keep up. The mental strain became torture in its own way, though it helped to allow some of the actual discomforts through when it suited his purposes.

In between the torture sessions, Stephen would relax as much as possible and try to make contact with Patrick. They had practiced for weeks the ability to communicate while separated. The talent worked somewhat to around three city blocks distance—short messages, not a real conversation—but Stephen feared his location down in the subway tunnels, prevented Patrick from hearing him. He hadn't heard from Patrick since being captured.

One thing he couldn't control—his hunger and thirst. He could handle the feelings of being hungry and thirsty, but he couldn't control the effect it had on his body; he couldn't manage the everyday needs of his body beyond a day or two. The more he became dehydrated or starved, the harder it would be to protect himself. They were not starving him completely since Jonathan wanted him alive, but what they did give him remained barely sufficient. He could endure the pain and dampness, but he still needed to have his strength if he hoped ever to have an opportunity to escape if necessary. However, escape wasn't the plan.

They were about to begin another round of the game when Stephen heard a loud voice. "Stop! Take him down, give him a chair and a robe so he can get warm and rest.

"Hello, young man, sorry to keep you hanging around waiting for me for so long."

Stephen Estrada—a baby-faced, average fifteen-year-old, going on sixteen when the wave struck the Earth. A boy of standard height for his age, with sandy-brown hair and green eyes he inherited from his mother.

His good looks and natural charm made him popular with the girls in his class, but he usually didn't notice since he focused mainly on his studies and sports. Stephen had many friends who knew they could count on him to help anyone in need, but he never would volunteer to be a leader. Two of his teachers had encouraged him to run for student council. He told them he didn't feel he had the right temperament to lead. He liked to follow, wanted to help, but he never craved the spotlight.

Since his birth, he lived in Aston, Pennsylvania, with his parents, followed by his sister, Cynthia, a few years later. They celebrated her eleventh birthday a week before the event—the last happy memory he would have for a long time.

The town of Aston, located close to Chester, was a short train ride from Philadelphia, where his grandfather would often take him to ride the trains and spend quality time together. Those times ended a year before the event when his grandfather suddenly passed away from a heart attack.

The town, part urban, part suburban, had the best and worst of both. Stephen's family lived in a two-story, colonial-style house, complete with a porch and a small backyard. They were close to their neighbors, and they all watched each other's homes whenever they were away. He attended the regional public high school since his parents couldn't afford to send him to the local Catholic high school. For the most part, he had a good happy life.

Stephen had finished baseball practice, ate, and completed his homework, so he decided to go to bed early for some extra rest. He had a big math test the next day, and unlike most of the sophomore jocks in school, he wanted to go to college on his own intellect and other merits. He went to bed as an innocent, young teenager and woke up to a world that sent him feelings and experiences of a man. Stephen was about to be thrust into adulthood.

After having vivid dreams, he could hardly remember, Stephen, awoke the next day and found a different and terrifying world. In his head, he could hear voices, and he experienced a wide range of emotions—fear, part of which, his own—to sexual excitement, revulsion, and deep sorrow. He could see images in his mind as if he walked in another body, sharing their experiences. In one image, he lay on top of his young neighbor across the street, and she cried, begging him to stop. In his groin, he could feel a familiar sensation, and when he realized what was happening, he cried out and managed to push the image out of his mind.

The following image started with someone he didn't know punching and kicking him as he fell to the ground. He could feel the pain of each blow almost as much as if it were happening to him. The unknown victim looked up to see a gun pointing at his face, he heard a gunshot and the image quickly changed to that of being on his back with a large middle-aged man lying on top of him. When he understood the situation, he again cried out and successfully pushed the image from his mind. As the minutes wore on, he discovered he could keep the obscene experiences from his mind but found the task challenging.

He spent the rest of the morning curled up on the floor of his bedroom closet, crying out weakly for mom and dad as if again a small child, while trying to get the voices and painful emotions to stop. Eventually, Stephen found he could block out almost all of the noise and feelings, but it remained difficult, and they were always there pressing on his mind.

He still experienced his personal fear, but eventually, he knew he had to get up and see what had happened to his family. He worried about them because he knew things were not right, and from outside, he could hear screaming, alarms, sirens, and an occasional explosion. It sounded like a war zone to Stephen, as if he now lived in the middle of a new world war.

When Stephen became able to deal with his fear and felt he could no longer hold his piss, he went to the bathroom and took care of business. He realized he had soiled the front of his pants, and as much as Stephen wanted to find his family, he first had to get washed and dressed quickly. When he left his bedroom, he called for his parents and sister. When he heard nothing other than the continuing commotion from outside, he went to his parent's room and found them in bed—dead. It didn't look like anyone hurt them, but on their faces were expressions of horror and pain.

After standing there shaking and again crying for a few minutes, he pulled himself together, moved closer to the bed and after kissing his parents on the cheeks, covered their faces and went to find his sister.

Cynthia's bedroom stood across the hall from Stephen's parent's room and when he approached her door, he could hear her sobbing inside. He entered the room and found her with the covers pulled over her head, curled up in her bed, in the same manner, he had curled up in his closet.

He sat with her for over an hour, holding her tight and softly telling her to fight the images in her head and concentrate on his voice. When alone in his room, he would often sing along with the radio, practicing his vocal talents for the band he wanted to start with his friends. Cynthia would hear him and sit by his door, listening. He knew of one particular song she loved, so he sang it to help distract from the images in her head. When Stephen started singing, he found it helped him as well. He knew he needed to call the police, even though they wouldn't be able to help, but right now, he needed to be with his sister and needed to make her feel better so he could feel better.

A few minutes passed with Stephen softly singing before she asked him about their parents, and he had to tell her they were dead, which caused her to start crying again. After a few minutes, she asked him what had happened, and Stephen told her he didn't know. All he knew was that his mind remained flooded with horrible images of bad things, and he told her any images she saw were not real even though he suspected they were genuine and somehow projected into their minds.

When she calmed down, he told her they had to leave the house and find somewhere safe. He had no idea where to go since their grandparents were dead, and their only aunt and uncle lived hundreds of miles away. He had hoped to find a government shelter where they would be protected and safe. He didn't know what exactly was happening, but he knew to be alone on their own would be dangerous.

He felt sure it would be a waste of time, but he took his sister downstairs, grabbed the phone, and dialed 911. As he expected, the call didn't go through. He tried a couple more times but had no success. Before giving up entirely, he tried calling the non-emergency number but connected only to a busy signal.

Stephen took his sister back upstairs, and they spent the next hour packing some clothes and as much water and food as they could manage. Before they left the house, he cooked breakfast so they wouldn't have to worry about eating for a little while. When finished, he quickly went back upstairs by himself to say a final goodbye to his parents.

The day, sunny and warm, barely displayed the horror and chaos he knew lurking nearby, even though the neighborhood became quiet and still. He could feel the images and compulsions pushing on his mind, and at one point, Cynthia started to walk away from him as if in a trance. He reached out and held her while she continued to try and pull away. After a few minutes, he managed to wake her from the apparent trance, and he decided they should try the police station first to see if anyone remained there and if they knew what happened.

They only encountered a few living people as they walked to the police station but witnessed many dead bodies in the street. One older woman they found drooling as she stumbled down the street while talking to herself in a trance. The next block, they encountered a naked man who had cut off his privates. The man had jumped out in front of them, with no way for Stephen to protect Cynthia from seeing the man still dripping blood from between his legs.

The man yelled for them to help him find his Johnson.

"They took it from me, right out of my hands after I cut it off. Why did they do that? Why did they make me cut it off? Help me, please, help me find my Johnson!"

Cynthia began to cry again, and he could feel her fear penetrating his mind as he pushed the man to the pavement and pulled his sister along behind him to get away before the man could get up from the ground and start following. Stephen felt awful about pushing him down so forcefully, but he feared the man was dangerous.

When they arrived across from the police station, he stopped and quickly pulled Cynthia aside and hid behind the corner of the building. Something was wrong; he could somehow feel it. It wasn't safe. As they stood there, he heard a gunshot from inside the station. Shortly after, two men came out, and he heard them talking about how easy they could make the pig kill himself. Stephen knew they had to move on, but he had no idea where to go.

After walking around for a while, Stephen decided to try the high school. He thought the school would be a place where the Red Cross or some other government organization would be likely to set up a shelter and offer some help. On their way, they had to stop a few times to avoid people walking around in a trance, and gangs of men, boys, and even women he could tell were looking for people to terrorize.

Along the way, they continued to encounter people lying dead on the sidewalks and in the middle of the streets. They saw a mix of individuals lying in the middle of the road, apparently run down by cars and trucks based on the condition of their bodies, as well as other people dead in vehicles mangled against walls and light posts. Some had been mutilated and still had knives and even large forks sticking out of their bodies.

Eventually, they reached the high school to more disappointment as only emptiness and silence greeted them in the building. Stephen expected someone to be there, even if only people looking for safety in numbers, but they found no one. They entered through one of the side doors they found unlocked, and he decided to head for the cafeteria. They had walked around for a few hours, and he thought it would be a good idea to have some more to eat and drink without having to use the supplies they were carrying in their backpacks.

Stephen made some sandwiches with the lunch meats and cheese he found in the refrigerators since he didn't know how to work any cooking appliances. In the kitchen, he also found juice boxes and water to drink. After they both took some time in the bathroom, they continued on their way. He didn't know where to go, but it would be best, he thought to go somewhere out of the area, maybe to the countryside where they would be less likely to run into any trouble.

They walked down a side street with houses on both sides, taking a shortcut to the highway where he thought it would be safer. He would be able to see farther ahead to determine if it remained safe to continue. They didn't get far before four older teenagers jumped out in front of them from behind a truck.

"Well, well, boys, look at what we have here. Are you out for a little stroll with your girlfriend?"

Stephen recognized the boy talking as a senior from his school. He knew the boy only by his reputation. He knew they were in trouble.

"We're trying to find some help. We can go back the way we came."

"No, you won't!"

As Stephen turned around, two other boys grabbed him from behind and were holding him tight.

"Run, Cynthia, get away," he yelled to his sister.

"Stop Cynthia," yelled the boy, obviously in charge. "Come over here and stand next to me."

As Stephen watched in disbelief, unable to do anything, his sister walked over to the boy and stood beside him as he took her hand.

"She is such a beautiful little girl with a beautiful mouth. I can't wait to take her back to my bedroom and show her what it is like to be a woman."

Stephen screamed at him in rage as the other boys all laughed.

"You mother fucker, if you so much as lay a hand on her, I will—"

Stephen stopped suddenly, unable to speak, and he started to comprehend what was happening. This boy had the means to control others. Now he understood some of what he had seen on the road.

"Such language from a little boy. My name is Ralph, King Ralph," said the boy. "What's yours?"

He tried to resist, but he couldn't. He felt like a puppet—mouth forced to move, controlled by someone else.

"My name is—Stephen."

"Let Stephen go, boys; he won't be any trouble. He is going to stand there and do whatever I tell him."

"How old are you, Stephen?"

"I'm—" he tried to fight the urge to answer, "fifteen."

"A fifteen-year-old giving orders like a man, but are you indeed a man? Pull your pants down, grab your dick, and stroke it like a real man."

All the other boys laughed and taunted one another about joining Stephen.

Stephen's hands reached for his belt as he tried to control his movements. He started to unbuckle his belt when he realized he had a slight ability to resist. He didn't want to let on; he maintained some control of his body, so he continued to unbuckle his belt. When he felt sure he could move freely, he quickly jumped at Ralph and grabbed him.

It didn't take long for Ralph's friends to grab Stephen; pull him off and hold him tight. Looking at Ralph's eyes, Stephen could tell the boy now feared him, but even more, he was angry.

"You little fucker. You and your sister will pay for that stunt."

Ralph walked to Stephen and punched him hard in the stomach, causing Stephen to fall to the round as pain shot through his stomach and into his chest and groin. He labored for each breath, panting like a dog, rolling on the cement.

"Stand him up," Ralph yelled to his friends, "So he can watch his sister."

They got him back on his feet, holding him tight by supporting him under his arms and around his neck.

"Cynthia, my dear Cynthia. Take off all your clothes."

"No, please don't do this to her."

"You should have thought about that before you attacked me, Stephen. Now you will stand there and watch your sister do as I say."

Unable to resist the order Ralph had given, she now stood in front of the boys, naked and shivering.

"Cynthia, move your hands and rub them down there between your legs. Tell me, you little sweet thing, how does it feel?"

She resisted, fought hard, and screamed, "No, I don't want to do that!"

"Too bad, now follow me, Cynthia; we are going to go have some fun, and to make it more interesting, I'm going to allow you back control of your mind and body when the time is right."

He turned and spoke to Stephen, who had tears running down his face while trying hard to fight back as he became able to suppress the pain while rage grew in him. The intense rage strengthened Stephen, and he started to feel something he had never felt before.

"I would invite you inside to watch, but I don't perform well in front of an audience."

As Ralph walked away with his sister, Stephen's captors laughed and began to tell him all the fun things they would do to his sweet sister when Ralph finished. The more they taunted him, the more he could feel the odd strength continuing to build in him—not the strength of body, but a strength of the mind.

Minutes later, as they still held him pulling on his hair, and rummaging through his things, he heard a scream coming from the house in which Ralph had taken his sister.

"Stephen, help me—please help me—make him stop! Stop! Stop—it hurts."

The screaming continued until all of a sudden, it stopped as if choked out. Somehow knowing what had happened, Stephen screamed a sound like he never had before, and his captors all went limp and fell to the ground, with blood flowing from noses and ears. He started to move but he couldn't. Whatever happened, whatever he had done, it drained him so completely he collapsed next to his captors. As consciousness faded away, he could feel blood flowing from his nose as it pooled on the sidewalk.

When he woke up later, Stephen knew many hours had passed. The older boys lay on the ground where they fell. He could tell they were dead, and he didn't care. The sun went behind the building as he stood there—he had to find Cynthia before dark.

He ran into the house where Ralph had taken Cynthia and bolted upstairs to look for her in one of the bedrooms. What he found made him sick. She still bled from where Ralph raped her, and there were red hand marks around her neck. Ralph had strangled her to death, and Stephen again collapsed, but this time from sorrow and pain. As he lay there crying, he wondered why Ralph hadn't come back and killed him while unconscious. Maybe, being a sadistic bastard, Ralph thought letting Stephen live would be a more severe punishment for killing his friends. The demented devil on Earth may have been right. As Stephen sat on the floor next to his dead sister, he wished more than anything else that he also was dead.

Stephen and the Overlord

Stephen's captors had him hanging in the subway alcove, off and on for over a week. Even when they gave him food and water or laughingly tended to his wounds, he still hung against the alcove wall. First, they dangled him by his wrists and arms, then when bored, they attached him by his feet, leaving him upside down. When they really became bored, they would tie ropes to his wrist while he hung upside down, and his tormentors would pull him away from the wall, release the ropes, and let him slam back against the rough cement, hitting his head, while they laughed and spat on him. They were about to go back to the spike throwing game when the Overlord had him taken down.

The robe the Overlord ordered given to him felt soft and warm. It felt refreshing not to have to use his abilities to keep warm for at least a short time; however, he still made his body shiver so the Overlord, who now sat immediately in front of him, would not be suspicious.

"Give the boy some fresh water and a non-moldy piece of bread. I am sorry if they have not been treating you well, but we do not take kindly to spies."

Stephen knew he had to make this look good, so he released as much control as he dared, which caused his body to have muscle spasms and minor convulsions as he took a much-needed sip of water.

"I am not a boy and not a spy," he said in a low voice, faking fatigue, and defeat.

"Speak up, boy; I don't believe I heard you properly! Did you say you are not a boy? Certainly, you are not a girl, and no self-respecting man would get caught so easily."

The surrounding guards and prior tormentors laughed at the Overlord's joke. Partially because they enjoyed abusing Stephen, but also because they wouldn't dare not laugh.

When the laughter faded, Stephen again responded, "I'm not a spy."

Stephen decided not to pursue the boy issue. He didn't want to push Jonathan too far.

"Really, and you expect me to believe that? What's your name?"

"Stephen," he responded as he took a bite of the bread and then pretended to choke on it a little before taking another drink.

"Stephen, you were caught trying to enter my fortress in the middle of the night; why?"

"A gang was chasing me, they had partial control of my body, but I managed to get away when . . . ," he winced in almost fake pain, "they stopped me again and started fighting over who would get to play with me first."

"You look like a powerful b—young man, well-built and strong; why couldn't you fight them off with your physical and mental abilities?"

"I have none or very little mental ability. The gang . . . they were going to make me do things to . . . to a young girl."

"What a lovely story, Stephen; don't you all think it's a lovely story?" the Overlord asked all the men standing around, waiting to continue their games. "I never met anyone who had no ability. I think you tell a good tale, for we had no reports of any gangs when my guards captured you, and my subjects wouldn't dare have that kind of enjoyment without my permission."

After a brief pause, while the Overlord stared intently at Stephen, trying to decide if any of the boy's story was true, he mockingly continued.

"I hear you like to sing while you are hanging around. You can't be too uncomfortable if you are singing."

"It keeps my mind off the pain," he said as he took more water and bread while he still could. "I sing . . . and think back on better times before the event unleashed its evil."

"How dare you, young prick," the Overlord said as he quickly got up from the chair and knocked the bread and water out of Stephen's hands. Stephen stood—not of his own volition—so fast real pain shot through his body as the robe fell to his feet, and for the first time, his nakedness made him feel vulnerable.

"Evil? The power is not evil; I am not evil; my servants and soldiers are not evil. Look at you, standing there well-endowed with your muscular young body, thinking you are better than me. Did it help you survive these past years? Did you use it to get what you wanted, your enjoyment, your perversions?

"No, you young prick! You came here to mock me, steal from me, and spy on me. You will tell me what I want to know, or you will slowly die by your own hands!"

The Overlord released his hold, and Stephen let his body fall to the ground as if he had no control or strength left at all. *At least I had some food and water,* he thought, but he remained worried about what would happen next.

"Take this little boy prick, piece of self-righteous filth and lock him in one of the isolation chambers," he instructed one of the soldiers. "Pick one close to the steam pipes so he can keep extra warm."

Anger flowed through the Overlord as he physically grabbed the worthless young man by the back of his hair, pulled his head off the floor, and gleefully spat in the little prick's face.

I could easily destroy this prick with my mind, but no, keep control, keep control.

The Overlord had to admit he enjoyed using his own body to inflict pain instead of his mind. A refreshing change he should engage in more often.

"If the pain doesn't make you talk, maybe the isolation and heat will."

The Overlord dropped Stephen's head to the floor and gave him a hard kick to his balls. Stephen lay there, using his abilities as best he could to fight off the pain as the Overlord of Bartram Fortress stormed away.

Well, at least I got to meet Jonathan—

Three of the Overlord's soldiers immediately pulled Stephen to his feet, interrupting his thoughts. They tied a rope around his neck and another binding his hands behind his back. They pulled him down a long hallway like a dog till they arrived at a metal door guarded by another soldier.

"Unlock the door; we have an additional pig for roasting."

When the door opened, the first thing Stephen noticed after the heat was the stench of human sweat mixed with urination, defecation, and rotting flesh. He could use his abilities to suppress his urge to vomit, but one of the younger soldiers who looked about the same age as he, wasn't so lucky.

The young soldier quickly walked away and threw up in a corner. The older soldier, apparently his superior, kicked him in the face while he knelt on his knees.

"Your disgusting weakness cannot and will not be tolerated. If the Overlord knew of your softness, he would have us both killed. Maybe you need some time in isolation alongside this pig to build your strength?"

He grabbed the young soldier and pulled him into the room filled with what looked like storage lockers, old and rusted, each one barely large enough to hold a full-grown normal-sized man. He pulled the young guard over to one of the lockers, unlashed it, tossed the dead body residing inside, onto the floor, and forced the young soldier inside. Although he didn't resist, Stephen could hear the young soldier whimpering and asking for forgiveness, but his superior offered no sympathy.

"Your turn now, little piggy. You can be braver than that pussy and walk into the isolation chamber yourself, or I can beat the shit out of you and then toss you in. Your choice!"

Stephen obediently walked into the opened locker. The guard cut loose the ropes around his hands and neck and slammed the door, leaving Stephen in almost complete darkness. While he tried to adjust his body as best he could in the tight space; he could hear the young soldier still whimpering nearby, and pitied him.

Stephen's Journey Begins

Stephen appreciated the fact he could shut down his normal bodily functions to stay cool and conserve energy while at the same time, his body would absorb the steam escaping from the supply pipe to keep hydrated. In a few minutes, he had his physical body prepared, and as he fell into a meditative state, his mind wandered back to the events and days after he awoke to find his sister dead.

An hour later, after shedding all the tears he had, Stephen knew he needed to get up and get moving if he wanted to have any success finding Ralph and making him pay for what he had done. Blinded by grief, he couldn't realize how impossible it might be to do anything to Ralph when the boy had abilities, and he didn't. Or did he, Stephen wondered? He didn't think so until remembering what he had done to Ralph's gang.

Stephen started thinking about what had happened outside when he somehow took down the other boys who were part of Ralph's gang. He knew he had to get up and go outside to take a look at the bodies, to see if he could figure out what he had done.

When Stephen made his way back out to the street, darkness had fallen, but a still working streetlight illuminated where the bodies lay. He slowly walked over, making sure as best he could no one else remained in the area. All five boys were lying on the ground with dried blood around their ears, noses, and eyes. He bent down next to one of the boys and could find nothing else visibly wrong with him. He saw movement out of the corner of his eye and turned to see a dog and some rats feasting on one of the other bodies, and he almost vomited.

He stood up not, sure what to do, and started thinking about what had happened. When Ralph had taken control of him, he was partially able to resist, and then when angry and enraged, he somehow caused this bloody carnage. Stephen also realized he no longer experienced vile images in his mind of sex and murder and gathered he could somehow unconsciously block the imageries.

As Stephen stood there, he tried to open his mind, and the vile images returned, so he quickly closed his mind again. He now knew how to control the block his mind had automatically developed, and he wondered what else he could manage. As if a light turned on in his brain, Stephen suddenly comprehended; he had seen Ralph as part of the images and now knew where to find the sick bastard.

Before leaving to find Ralph, he located the backpack he had been carrying, lying a few yards from the bodies, where an animal dragged it. He ensured the pack remained intact and went back to the bodies to rummage through their pockets, looking for and taking anything useful. He found three pocketknives, two small, powerful flashlights, and even a Swiss Army knife.

He put everything in the backpack except for one of the knives he held open in his hand as he headed to find Ralph back at the high school. He understood now Ralph and his gang had probably followed them from the school and then surrounded them on the street. He needed to make sure it could never happen to him or anyone else again.

A short time later, he stood outside the school, looking for any indication of where Ralph would be hiding. He sensed Ralph inside, another new ability, but he didn't know how to find him without walking into a trap. He decided to go around to the school's back entrance and enter through the cafeteria door he used earlier.

When Stephen had approached the school, he noticed light coming from the first-floor teacher's lounge window. He hurried into the school and started walking down the hallway, which would take him to the lounge. When he crept close, he heard voices, and when close enough, listened to what sounded like a woman crying and begging for her life.

He quickly entered the room with the knife held out in front of him, shocked and revolted to see Ralph standing with his pants down around his ankles while a naked woman lay, face down over a chair, begging him to stop. He couldn't directly see Ralph's actions, but he knew how Ralph abused the woman.

"Haven't you gotten your fill, yet today, Ralphie?"

Stephen caught Ralph by surprise, but the thug sprang quickly to action as Stephen immediately could no longer move toward Ralph, no matter how hard he tried. Ralph hastily pulled up his pants and came over to Stephen, took the knife out of his hands, and threw it across the room.

"Hello again, Stephen; I'm not surprised you found me, for I knew you were an idiot. I could have taken that knife, slit your throat, or gutted you like a little piggy, but what fun would that have been for me? I can make you kill yourself later, in some enjoyable and bloody way, but first, how would you like a lollypop?"

Stephen felt his body being pushed down to his knees and knew what Ralph had in mind, but no matter how hard he tried, he couldn't stop until Ralph made a big mistake by not keeping his boasting mouth shut.

"Let's see if you can give better head than your sweet little sister. She didn't like it, so I did her like I was doing that bitch over there when you walked in and so rudely interrupted my pleasure."

The thought of his sister and what Ralph had done to her gave him a strength of mind he didn't realize he possessed, as he broke free of Ralph's control, reached up, and punched Ralph in the balls. Without hesitation, Stephen, using abilities that shocked him, flung Ralph across the room and halfway through one of the windows. Blood flowed from the cut on Ralph's throat, and he slowly bled to death while Stephen stood and watched.

After Ralph died, Stephen could hold on no longer, and he collapsed to the floor while expelling the contents of his stomach. Before today he had never thought of killing another person, and now he had killed six people, barely older than himself. Even though he knew they were deserving, it made him sick, and he vowed never to kill again unless in self-defense—a vow that wouldn't last long.

When he felt better, Stephen decided the best thing to do would be to spend the night in the school. The woman who Ralph had been raping fled quickly without even taking her clothes. He hoped she would be alright, but he doubted she would survive for long unless she developed some abilities to defend herself.

Stephen couldn't stay in the lounge, not with Ralph's dead body lying halfway through the window, and he didn't want to be upstairs where he knew another teacher's lounge existed. He decided to go to the principal's office since he knew she had a sofa in her office, but first, he needed to eat—he felt starved. He went back to the cafeteria, pulled some chicken strips out of the thankfully still working freezer, and cooked them on the stove after figuring out to make it work.

The school had a gas stove, which still worked but, it had an electric pilot light, and the electricity to the school appeared to be off. Thankfully he thought to grab matches from his home before they left. The thought of home, made him break down and weep, more than he had since he woke up to this new terrible reality.

After eating, he went to the principal's office, which he found locked. He banged against the door to no avail and finally smashed the glass with his bare hand to reach the lock. He walked over to the sofa and collapsed, almost sliding off in the process; too tired to care, he remained vulnerable. He didn't wake up until he heard someone smashing windows in another room.

Stephen grabbed his backpack and one of the other knives before slowly leaving the office and heading out to the hallway. The smashing came from down the hall; he quickly went through the main entrance and into light rain. He didn't see anyone around, and he hastily left the school parking lot and stopped between two parked trucks to think.

Now all alone, he had nowhere to go and didn't know what to do. He couldn't go home, and he had no relatives in the area. After some thought, he decided to make his way out to state RT 1 and follow it until he had a better idea.

He didn't walk on the road unless necessary. He sensed it better to follow along the route via backyards and behind buildings as much as possible. He saw a few people along the way, as well as many dead bodies. He encountered some in a world of their own, walking dazed, almost like in a zombie movie, except these people were alive, though not mentally there.

When he did see others alive, he stayed away, so there would be no trouble. He trusted no one and thought he might never again. A couple of days after the event, Stephen entered the town of Kennett Square and saw a small mini-mart with doors wide open. He figured it might be a good idea to pick up more food, so he wouldn't starve for a while. He entered the store and headed toward the lunch meat counter. The power was off, but the food remained cool, so he cut a few pieces of meat and cheese. He quickly ate them before grabbing protein and granola bars.

He looked out the front and saw a group of older men, and he decided to try the back door instead. He walked into the storage area when out of nowhere, a man stepped in front of him, holding a shotgun. The middle-aged man began to yell, but before Stephen could even think, his mind reacted and sent the man flying through the back door, cutting a deep wound on one of his legs as blood shot out of his artery, and the gun went off. Stephen wasn't hit, but he knew the men in the front would hear the gunfire and come to check it out, so he ran away from the store as fast as he could into the woods behind.

Ten minutes later, he lay on the ground, exhausted, repeating over and over again, like a mantra to cleanse his soul, "I'm sorry, I'm sorry, I'm so, so sorry!" He had killed again, and it not only made him weak, it also made him sick. Stephen didn't want to be spending his life killing people; he couldn't and vowed again he wouldn't.

Stephen lay there in the grass and dirt for almost an hour before he got up and began walking again, still staying off but following RT 1 south. After what felt like many hours, it started getting dark, and up ahead along the RT 1 and the 896 interchanges, he saw a group of buildings that looked like small warehouses. When he moved closer, he found all but one had smashed open doors, so he decided to find a way into the one that looked and felt safer.

In the back, behind a couple of dumpsters, Stephen saw a window only about eight feet from the ground, so he moved one of the empty dumpsters right below the window and stacked some pallets in order to climb and reach his goal. He smashed the glass, hoping no one remained around to hear, and looked inside. He could see with the minimal amount of sunlight remaining to the day that he was in luck. There were boxes below the window looking strong enough to hold him, so he dropped his backpack first and then climbed through the window, careful not to cut himself on the broken glass. He hung by his hands from the ledge about a foot above the boxes, and he let go.

Unfortunately, the boxes were not as strong as he hoped, and they caved in under him, sending him flying. Stephen thought he would smash headfirst into the floor when he somehow almost instinctively brought his feet around, and when they hit the floor, he curled up and rolled across the floor before coming to a stop, unhurt against a bunch of other boxes.

He quickly grabbed his backpack and hid in case anyone heard him. After a few minutes, it looked and felt clear, so he grabbed the flashlight and found an employee's lounge with a sofa bed. With the incident among the boxes behind him, he stretched out on the bed, and soon without worry, fell asleep.

The next morning, he took a walk around the warehouse and checked out a few boxes to see if there were anything useful inside—all he found were a bunch of party supplies. Stephen had managed to break into one of the most useless warehouses possible, a warehouse for one of the big party stores in the area. He did find a couple of utility knives he took as well as some heavy-duty packing tape. He wasn't sure what he would do with the tape, but he sensed taking some would be a good idea.

He then went back to the break room and smashed the glass on one of the vending machines to have some protein bars for breakfast. "No sense using up the supplies I'm carrying when I have better ones here," he said out loud merely to fill the silence with something.

As Stephen ate, he thought about what happened when he broke in the day before. Although he played football and baseball, he never learned any gymnastics moves, so he had no idea how he knew to land like that without getting hurt. He wondered what other abilities he might have gained from whatever had happened. The thought made him think about putting on the television in the break room to see if there were any news reports. He found only disappointment and fuzzy snow images on all channels.

The clock in the break room—probably battery-powered—showed almost 10:00 in the morning. Outside, a storm poured heavy rain across the grayed-out landscape as it had done since Stephen woke up. He had nowhere to go, so he decided to spend the day in the party warehouse. He went to the main office and found some money while rummaging in the desks, which he used to buy some water since he couldn't break into that vending machine.

The rain continued all day, and he heard no noises from outside other than the rain and thunder. When darkness arrived, he went back to the breakroom and slept, where he dreamt all those people he killed were chasing him through a graveyard.

The following day the sun glared off the cars and broken glass littering the parking lot and streets, and the day began with the sound of silence. The thought made Stephen cry as he remembered the name of his mom's favorite song and phrase she used often. He ate another couple of protein bars and bought more water from the vending machine before cautiously venturing out the warehouse's front door to continue his journey south, following along RT 1 through muddy farms and woods. After about an hour, he decided to try walking on the highway.

Stephen stood listening at the interchange for RT 10 and RT 1. When satisfied, no one hid near; he walked up the ramp to find vehicles sprawled along the road's visible length. Most of the cars had crashed, and dead decaying bodies inhabited some still, especially the vehicles that experienced horrific crashes. It looked like some people had stopped in the middle of the road and walked away with their cars still running. He tried starting a couple of the abandoned ones, but they all had run out of gas since apparently not one person shut off the cars when abandoned.

He didn't know how to drive but thought driving slowly on the road would have been better than walking. After relieving himself against one of the cars and feeling guilty about it, Stephen continued walking. He walked for another couple of hours before stopping to sit in one of the cars to have lunch, which consisted of more protein bars and a now warm iced tea he had brought from the warehouse. Other than the sounds of birds and insects, it was eerily quiet, and he wondered what happened to everyone. He could see smoke in all directions and some still smoldering accidents as he had walked, but no people. He felt lonely but realized after what had happened so far, it might be a good thing there were no other people around.

After eating lunch, he walked on the highway for another three hours, stopping only once to hide in a car. He sensed something wrong, and after a few minutes crouched behind the front seat, he heard screaming and yelling, slowly becoming louder. When it felt safe to raise his head to look out the window, he saw two young-looking women, maybe still teens, chased by a group of boys who appeared barely older than himself.

It appeared none of the boys had acquired strong enough abilities to work over a distance, but as they got closer to the women, they both stopped, and he knew the boys had them under their control. He didn't want the boys to see him, so he put his head down again and continued to hide, even though the stench from the dead body in the front seat began to make him nauseous. The smell became almost unbearable, but he remained terrified of being caught, so he had no choice other than to stay hidden.

He couldn't hear much of what the boys were saying to the women, but it was enough to know what the boys were doing to them, and he felt like a coward hiding there, not helping. Maybe his ability would prove to be stronger than theirs, or perhaps not, but he was too terrified to find out. After a few minutes, he realized the fear and terror to be unlike him. As he lay in the car shaking, he began to believe the terror he experienced came from the women.

After about an hour, it sounded quiet again, and he slowly crept out of the car to look around, but all he could see were the young women gathering up their clothes. He thought he could see blood on their faces, and at least one remained crying. Eventually, they walked away, back in the direction from which they had come while being chased.

Stephen felt ashamed but had to keep going, and he told himself, at least the boys hadn't killed the women; maybe they wished the boys had. He didn't know where he headed, where it would be safe, but he knew standing there exposed on the highway wasn't the place to remain. After almost another hour of walking, he saw a sign for Nottingham County Park and felt that was where he should go.

He followed the signs off the highway and through the park entrance. The map showed it to be large enough that maybe he could find a place there to hide for a while. He knew it would be dark in a couple of hours, and he needed somewhere to spend the night.

Stephen walked about fifteen minutes into the park when he heard what sounded like children playing, but when he came closer to the sound, he found two boys, younger than the two who raped the women. They set up a tent in the park, probably trying to hide, but what they were doing sickened him almost as much as what happened to his sister and the two women. The boys were torturing a dog whimpering in pain. They were throwing stones at the dog, and it just stood there as he assumed the two boys or at least one of the boys used his newfound ability to keep the dog from running away.

Stephen couldn't take it anymore. He knew he had to stop hiding and being afraid—this would be where he became a man instead of a child. He ran toward the boys yelling—

Stephen emerged out of his meditation to the sensation of icy cold water thrown on his hot body. Bucket after bucket for almost a minute. It felt magnificent, which he knew wasn't his captor's intent, and as before, he acted innocent, weak, and in pain.

"Are you ready to talk now and admit to the Overlord you are a filthy spy?"

Weakly he responded, "I am not . . . a spy."

"So, help me, I will beat you to death with my own hands if you do not admit you are a spy, because if you don't submit, he will kill me, or worse. Please admit you are a spy; I will make your death as quick and painful as possible."

"I am . . . not a spy," he repeated.

"So be it," the guard said as he slammed the door, and Stephen once again found himself happily in darkness and ready to go back into his meditative state to conserve energy and protect his body.

Before entirely beginning the meditation, Stephen wondered if the guard remained next to him and if he lived. He heard nothing and hoped the guard was no longer subject to punishment.

Proposal Accepted

Patricia stood at one of the windows in her room, which she considered her cell, looking out over the city. She had finished the lunch provided when one of Jonathan's minions came to escort her to the throne room. He politely knocked on the door and patiently waited as she ignored him until he knocked a second time.

"What is it?" She yelled through the door.

"The Overlord requests your presence in the throne room immediately, and I'm to escort you."

"I doubt very much if it is a request. What would happen if I said no?"

"Please, Lady Patricia, don't get me in trouble with the Overlord."

"What's the matter? You don't want him to compel you to cut off your dick and eat it before he forces you down his garbage hole?"

"Please, just open the door and come with me; he will be agitated if you don't. I will force you if I must."

"I need to get dressed. I will be ready in a few minutes."

She wanted to delay as much as possible, but she relented and reminded herself this guard was as much a prisoner as she, and it wasn't his fault. They were all in a living hell of the universe's making, and nothing they could do would change the situation.

During her time at the fortress, Patricia realized she had developed some abilities, which she occasionally used on the servants to get what she wanted. It made her feel filthy and as immoral as Jonathan. She made sure she hid her ability well, for she knew Jonathan wouldn't like it, and God only knew what he would do to her if he found out.

She decided it best not to delay any longer, so she opened the door and greeted her escort, a tall, handsome young man, much younger than her. Patricia recognized him from conversations she had with him previously. Before the scourge that gave Jonathan his powers, he grew up and had still lived in Bensalem, Pennsylvania. He attended Rowan University in New Jersey and had been getting drunk at a party in Philly when all hell broke loose.

"Let's go, Paul; take me to him so I can soon get back to my cell and some peace when he finishes tormenting me."

"Thank you for not causing any trouble, and sorry I'm a part of this," Paul said as they started walking. "I have tried many times to fight his commands, but I cannot. Whenever I try, I get images in my head of my limbs cut off, lying on the ground in a pool of blood, and the pain is as real as possible without actually happening."

Paul's torment was something new she had not heard of before. She always wondered how Jonathan managed to keep his guards, soldiers, and slaves in line, and now she knew. Thankfully he had never used that ability on her; for whatever reason, he wanted her to be as free as possible, which wasn't saying much.

They made their way through the hallway, at one time lined with the council members' offices, now used as guest rooms and sex chambers for Jonathan's actual guests. Many came to the fortress, willing to serve, and in return, Jonathan provided them with whatever deviant pleasures they desired.

Eventually, they reached the elevator and silently descended to what had been, years before, the council chambers level—the chamber which now served as Jonathan's throne room. They exited the elevator, and Paul asked her to remain by the door with the other guards in attendance, so he could introduce her.

Paul opened the double wooden doors—which Jonathan had reinforced with steel—entered and introduced Patricia as if she were a queen. The thought made her sick to the stomach.

"My pardon, Overlord, Lady Patricia, has arrived."

"Well, don't stand there, you fool, bring her in, and then go fetch her some tea."

"Yes, my Lord."

Paul went back and held the door for Patricia to enter the spacious ornate room, which she found filled with visitors, soldiers, and poor souls to be judged and probably punished by Jonathan. If he kills them, at least their torment will be over, while mine is just beginning, she thought as she walked through the door.

"Patricia, my dear, please join me up here by my throne."

She walked up to the platform where he sat on his showy chair, and next to it now sat a smaller yet still ornate chair in which she sat down, feeling all eyes upon her. She could sense anger, lust, and even pity coming from those in attendance.

"I have some business to attend to, my dear, and then we shall talk."

Before Jonathan, an older man and a woman stood, both with heads lowered and eyes looking to the floor.

"Look at me," the Overlord said to them, as instantly their heads raised. "You have both been found guilty of stealing and need to be punished. Luckily for you, I'm in a good mood today and feeling merciful, so I will not throw you into the garbage; however, you must receive your punishment."

"Step forward, woman. In honor of Lady Patricia's presence here today, I shall be merciful to you this time. Your punishment shall be to watch your husband suffer."

The woman started to speak, and the Overlord bellowed, "Silence," and her mouth instantly shut by the force of his will. "Try to speak again, and I may need to change my mind and toss you both in the garbage."

The Overlord motioned to one of the guards, who moved to stand before the man, holding out a knife in his hands. Patricia looked over at Jonathan and softly asked him not to harm the man, but he ignored her.

He looked at the man intently and smiled as the frail individual, shakenly reached out, took the knife in his right hand, and walked over to the stone pedestal in front of the Overlord. The man placed his left hand on top of the cold grey stone, put the knife on his wrist, and started to cut through the tissue, muscle, and bone while the Overlord laughed.

The excruciating pain showed on the man's face as tears started to run down his cringing expression. He couldn't scream, and his wife trembled before him from the pain she endured by being forced to watch. When the man finished, as blood continued to flow down the pedestal's sides, the Overlord released them both, and the room instantly filled with their screams as he rose from his throne and bellowed once more.

"This and worse is what will happen to anyone who dares to break my laws. Take them away, tend to his wound, and then toss them both back out into the street, where they belong."

Two of the Overlord's servants and a guard pulled the couple out of the throne room as another servant began cleaning up the mess and disposing of the severed hand. The Overlord looked over to Patricia to see tears still on her face as he reached out to take her hand. She wanted to pull her hand away but knew better than to fight.

"Clear the room except for my personal guards, who are to wait outside the door. I will pass judgment on the rest of these animals later. Take them back to their holding pens, and then escort my guest to their quarters where you are to provide them with whatever pleasures they desire."

The guards cleared the room and escorted the guest away as Patricia sat there, still upset and repulsed by what she witnessed.

"How can you do that to people, have you no shame, no regard at all for others?"

"I assure you, my dear, I hold you in the highest regard, but I am growing impatient. It is time for you to give me your answer. If what you witnessed upsets you, consent to be by my side as my conscience and wife."

"Where is Mark? You told me I could see him?"

"I did, and I will uphold my end of the bargain. Bring in the bastard," the Overlord loudly commanded.

The guards re-entered, went to the side door, and escorted Mark into the throne room wearing a jester's costume that would have been commonplace in eighteenth-century Europe. He had a slight limp as he walked, and Patricia couldn't wait for him to approach the dais. She jumped out of her chair and ran to him as Jonathan sat there, trying to hold his temper and contempt for their relationship. When she reached Mark, she threw her arms around his wasted body and gave him a long kiss, which transferred some of his makeup onto her face.

"How are you? What has he done to you?"

"Patricia, I have missed you so much. I'm well. How are you? Please tell me you have not consented to marry this evil, twisted man."

"I heard that," Jonathan yelled as he stood up from his chair and forced Mark to his knees. "Now, bastard, crawl here before me and beg for my forgiveness."

As Patricia watched, Mark crawled the rest of the way. She wasn't sure if Jonathan forced him or if Mark, so broken, crawled on his own accord. When he reached the dais, he spoke.

"I'm sorry for my outburst, and for Patricia's sake and Patricia's sake only, I ask for mercy."

"That's better. Now, Patricia, I have upheld my end of the bargain. If you give me the answer I desire, I promise the bas—Mark, will be well treated and will not see another day in my prison as long as you both cooperate and play nice."

With tears running down his face, Mark spoke again. "Patricia, please do not do this for my sake; I don't care if he kills me or tortures me; please do not marry him."

Jonathan held his temper as he looked over to Patricia, awaiting an answer from her luscious red lips. He wanted her more than anything else in the world, but he didn't want to force himself on her. He wanted her to be with him willingly, even if coerced.

"I have one other condition—"

"I am tired of these games," Jonathan interrupted, his voice filled with anger. He paused to control his temper and asked, "What is your new condition."

"All I ask is that you treat him with dignity and allow him to serve you without this ridiculous, demeaning outfit."

"If you will marry me, I agree."

Patricia sat down in the chair, looked over at Mark, and quietly agreed. "Yes, I will marry you."

On the floor, Mark collapsed in sorrow and despair, while on his throne, the Overlord of Bartram Fortress smiled, as his plan worked, and she would soon be his for life.

The Overlord sat on his throne, relishing his victory, and finishing his lunch in the silent, empty room. He looked forward to his marriage to Patricia with a smile on his face. He awakened from his wedding night thoughts when he heard a tentative knock at the main door to the room. He used his ability to partially open the door revealing the guard assigned to the little prick spy, and he motioned for him to enter and report.

"Excuse the interruption, my Lord, but I do have an update on our spy."

"I certainly hope it's good news!"

The guard stood there a moment to calm his nerves before responding.

"I checked on the prisoner this morning to make sure he remained alive and questioned him further; however, the young man still insists he is not a spy. He remains strong enough to withstand another day or two, so I left him roasting in the chamber."

The guard stood there, trying to control his breathing and calm his pounding heart, not sure what to expect as the Overlord sat unmoving with no decipherable expression on his face. Eventually, he stood up and paced around the top of his dais for a minute before speaking.

"Leave the little prick there another two days and see what he has to say. If he still doesn't admit to being a spy, we will try something else. There is more to this prick than meets the eye. I think we will add him to the jester troop to keep me amused and keep him handy in the throne room close to the guards. I will have the little prick be roomies with the bastard, where he will hopefully loosen his tongue, and I can then pry the information out of the bastard.

"It could be fun. If I get bored, I can make the boys pleasure each other, as long as neither one likes it, and if Patricia does not behave, I will make her watch her old lover boy get it in ways she could probably never imagine."

The thought made the Overlord laugh hysterically, and the guard knew this to be his cue to leave while he wasn't the subject of the Overlord's attention. His life would be over if his master knew of his desires and activities with some of the other guards in the fortress.

Stephen's Journey Continues

The guard slammed the door and left the room to make his report. Stephen hoped the Overlord would be merciful to the guard when he brought him the news.

Stephen prepared to re-enter his meditative state when he realized someone occupied the locker on the other side. He could hear what sounded like a woman softly crying and asking for mercy. He couldn't do anything to help other than use his powers to put her to sleep—ease her torment. He recently discovered the ability and never expected to find it useful.

When he finished doing all he could for the woman, he prepared his own body and mind.

Stephen sprinted toward the boys yelling for them to stop when, unexpectedly, he felt as if he ran against a heavy wind. He wasn't sure which boy, if not both, held him back, but he wasn't going to let them get the better of him, so he closed his eyes and pushed back as hard as he could.

Stephen escaped their power, lunged forward, and lost his balance. He fell face down on the ground, scraping across the cool, wet grass, while he heard screaming coming from the boys. He shot up on his feet to see the boys sluggishly getting up from the ground, almost fifty feet away from where they were before. Stephen now understood, his ability became stronger when he was angry, and he made a mental note to be careful not to hurt anyone out of anger.

Stephen looked around and saw the dog had managed to get away and hide somewhere as he started walking toward the boys to make sure they were okay, but they weren't staying around to talk, and they hurried away, both limping. He didn't know if they were returning, but he decided to make the best of the situation.

The boys had set up a sizeable, rugged tent with essential supplies and a few pieces of cooking gear. He quickly took their shelter down but didn't wrap it up. He looked around their campsite and then put all of the supplies he wanted onto the tent, grabbed a couple of the tent ropes, and started pulling everything into the woods. Stephen didn't care if the tent ripped since he had duct tape he could use to make repairs, and he didn't care what the boys would do without their supplies; they were now his.

Stephen remembered from the map a clearing deeper in the woods that looked like an excellent spot to hide and prepare for whatever lay ahead. He was exhausted but knew he needed to keep moving. An hour later, the sun below the horizon, he found the clearing. Mentally and physically exhausted, he stopped, pushed the supplies out of the way, and collapsed on top of the tent, where he slept for hours.

He awoke sometime in the dark early morning, feeling a light mist on his face. His clothes were damp, and when he sat up, pain shot through his entire body. Whatever he had done yesterday, it drained his body, and he probably made it to his new home on adrenaline only. He wasn't in bad shape since he did lift weights at school, but he wasn't muscle-bound. He grasped if he were to survive, he would need to build his body, become tougher, and work on using the abilities to suppress and control pain. He managed to find the flashlight, and he set it on a nearby rock to give him some light to set up the tent before the mist became heavy rain.

He didn't want to lay in the tent with wet clothes, so he hesitantly stripped and hung them across the tree branches. He felt nervous and vulnerable, standing out in the open, naked. He didn't like changing in the locker room when at school; he looked young for his age, and he always thought the older boys were judging and talking about him behind his back. He remained a virgin and had never been with a girl in anything less than a bathing suit, but as Stephen stood there in the dark naked, with no sound other than the insects and night creatures, he found the experience to be freeing and exhilarating. Realization set in, and he knew his life would change in many ways. Like it or not, he had to grow up.

It was too cold to sleep without wearing something, so he pulled his dry clothes out of his bag and got dressed before going into the tent to go back to sleep. His sleep became restless as he dreamed about his sister screaming and Ralph's gang laughing at him before he used his abilities to silence them. As he watched, their skin melted off as their skeletons fell to the ground, still moving as if they remained alive and in great pain. He started to walk away when he heard shrieks from behind him and turned to see the smoldering skeletons of the boys moving toward him, hands outstretched. He awoke, screaming, sweaty, and heart pounding. Stephen eventually fell back to sleep, this time without dreams or nightmares.

When Stephen awakened later in the morning, the sun shimmered through the outstretched tree branches above, and the air was warmer. He hung and laid out all the wet clothes and supplies, which had gotten soaked during the night, and noted what he had. He estimated he had enough for about five days between the food he seized from the boys and what he had with him. He wanted to stay longer and avoid others as much as possible, but he knew he would have to go looking for food.

Stephen had been a boy scout a few years back from age eight to twelve, so he did have some knowledge about what berries and nuts were available to eat out in the woods, and he wasn't above killing and eating a rabbit if he could manage to catch one. He had the small propane stove he also removed from the boys, so cooking wouldn't be a problem for a little while if he found something edible to cook.

He pulled an energy bar from his supplies for breakfast. After eating, Stephen decided to walk about his camp to make sure no one else lurked nearby. He went around a mile away and did a circle around his campsite as best he could. He took note of water sources and open areas to exercise as he walked around in the woods, thankfully hearing, and seeing no one.

When he arrived back at his campsite, everything other than his clothes had dried, so he organized what little he had and put the items into the tent to protect them from animals and any rain coming along later. His work done; he turned his attention to himself.

To survive in this new world, he needed to be stronger, faster, and more agile. He started by doing three sets of twenty sit-ups, followed by three sets of push-ups. He then used a thick tree branch to attempt some pull-ups but could barely complete three. Arm strengthening would need a lot of work, he thought, as he looked down at his now sore red hands, making a mental note to try and find some gloves.

Next, it was time to run. Stephen followed the same path he had used to scout the area and ran around the camp three times, stopping only twice to do a few vertical push-ups using a perfectly-positioned set of rocks. Stephen had flashes of memories as he ran—the man he killed in the store, Ralph bleeding out while his body lay over the windowsill. At one point, the images were so bad he had to stop to throw up.

When he finished running and arrived back at his campsite, he decided to try something he hadn't done since the scouting days: mediation and yoga. Being young boys, they didn't get much training, but he did learn a good yoga position and a few mediation techniques, so he decided to try it.

He found the position uncomfortable at first, but then after some practice, it became more comfortable to hold, and he decided he needed to add more stretching to his daily activities. As he relaxed, Stephen let his mind drift, but no matter how hard he tried, he couldn't dispel the images of the people he killed. After about an hour, he gave up and went running again.

For the next week, all Stephen did was stretch, exercise, run, and meditate repeatedly. All the activity made him tired, and as the week progressed, he slept well at night without the bad dreams he had been experiencing. While running along a new path, he found a little waterfall he used to bathe and wash out his clothes, getting ripe from all the exercising. His clothes were not meant for exercising, so he eventually spent most of the day wearing only underpants. He figured if he met anyone in the woods, embarrassment would be the least of his problems.

The yoga position became more comfortable to hold each day, and his meditation periods were getting longer. The images of those he killed were falling from his mind, but now as Stephen meditated, he had visions of others being abused, tortured, raped, and murdered. Occasionally he saw through the victim's yes, most times through the eyes of those inflicting the torment. He hated what the world had become, and he wished he had the power to end it all for good.

By week's end, his supplies were running out, and he knew he would have to leave the park and look for food. He could only supplement his supplies with so many nuts and berries. He also hoped to find a place to get shaving cream and a razor. He needed a haircut before the world went to hell, and now his hair annoyed him, falling into his eyes as he ran. He had his head shaved in the past as part of his high school sports initiation, but he had never done it himself.

Stephen grabbed what he thought he would need for his expedition, including a knife and a large stick he could use for defense if needed. He didn't have protection for the mental abilities he could encounter, and he hoped not to need his abilities again; he didn't want to kill.

Sunset started as Stephen emerged from the park's edge, and he spent a few minutes looking around from behind a large bush before venturing out into the open. A slight breeze carrying the stench of death blew down the empty road. He knew many bodies were up on the highway, and he believed there were many more lying nearby, slowly decaying.

He had no idea which way to go, so he decided to head away from the park and go to the left. He had only gone a short distance when startled by a dog that ran out in front of him. Thankfully, the dog had no interest in Stephen, but he wondered if maybe the dog ran away from something or someone. He picked up his pace to get farther down the road in case roaming nearby, someone or something did startle what probably had been someone's pet.

A half an hour later, he noticed farther down the road, a small drugstore that didn't look too severely damaged. He hoped things looked as good when he got closer. He didn't feel it a good idea to approach from the front since there were large windows, and someone could be watching, so he slipped behind a furniture depot and made his way to the back entrance.

The sun had fully set by the time Stephen tried the back entrance, and surprisingly, the door silently opened for him. Now inside, he felt it safe to use his flashlight, and he started looking around for supplies. The store shelves were mostly empty, but a fair amount of prepackaged food items were lying around to gather. As he walked, his feet crushed packages of snack foods missed by those who visited the store before him. The crunching sound made him nervous—afraid someone would hear.

After Stephen filled most of his backpack with sausage snacks, protein bars, and sports drinks, he went looking for medical supplies like band-aids, gauze, antiseptic, socks, and the shaving supplies he wanted. To his surprise, he even managed to find gloves he could use to protect his hands when he exercised. He uncovered everything he wanted in under ten minutes, including a good pair of scissors made for cutting hair, but as he started to move to the back door to leave, Stephen froze as he sensed danger.

Stephen couldn't explain the feeling. The hair on his arms wasn't standing on edge, the back of his head wasn't tingling, but he knew. He waited five minutes, but although he saw no one, he still sensed danger, but he had to get moving. He slowly opened the door and slipped out, heading for a parked truck to hide out of sight. He made it halfway to the vehicle when a shot rang out and luckily missed him and hit the truck. He quickly, instinctively dove under it, rolled out to the other side, and jumped a fence into a back yard of one of the homes backing up to the store.

He crouched behind a plastic storage bench that wouldn't offer much protection but would provide cover. He could somehow still sense he was in danger, and a minute later, a husky male voice called out.

"I know where you are, come out and give me everything in your backpack."

Stephen didn't respond; he just stayed put, unmoving, while figuring out what to do. He didn't want to kill the man and didn't even know if he could when not angry. He could try to use his newfound abilities to knock the man down, but he wasn't even sure how to make that happen. When he sent the boys flying, he responded to a direct threat. His life was not right now directly in danger; he didn't think the man truthfully knew where he was hiding.

"This is your last warning, come out here and give me the backpack, or I start shooting."

Stephen reached out with his mind, but as expected, nothing happened. He thought he probably needed to see the man to be able to defend himself in any way. He paused a moment, took a deep breath, and ran for the fence on the other side of the enclosure. He only went about ten yards when another shot rang out, and the bullet struck a few feet ahead of him.

He had no choice now; Stephen stopped, put his hands up, and turned around as the man came out of hiding and stood on the other side of the fence he initially jumped.

"That's a much better boy; now walk over here."

Stephen slowly walked towards the man, visibly overweight and panting now as he spoke. Stephen's heart raced as he felt trapped with no way out, and he felt more afraid now than he had been since that first day. When Stephen stopped walking, he stood about ten feet away from the man.

"Please, sir, I need these supplies, my mom is sick, and she needs the medicine and food. There is plenty more still in the store you could take."

"You're a young one, aren't you? I wish I had more light to see your face and body. No matter, fun is fun, maybe we can make a deal? Come closer so I can see you better; yes, all the way to the fence."

Stephen reluctantly walked closer to the fence with his hands still in the air. The man held the gun in his right hand, and when Stephen came close enough, the man reached out with his left hand and ran it down the side of Stephen's face. He worked hard to keep his composure as he continued to hold up his hands, knowing full well the pervert's intent.

"Yes, you are a pretty one. Now give me the backpack, and then we can talk about what you must do to earn it back. If you are outstanding and cooperative, I might even let you keep all the contents."

"No, I can't," Stephen said, starting to cry to get some pity from the man. "My mom is waiting; she needs the supplies."

"Okay young man, how about this deal instead. You can keep everything in your backpack as well as your life by taking me to your mom. When I finish with you, I can fuck her as well while you watch."

The man's words were the last mistake of his life and all Stephen needed to hear. The man's vile ideas made him think about his parents lying dead back in his old home. This time the tears came for real as he reached out in disgust and anger, sending the man flying backward, many feet in the air, smashing through some low hanging branches, before falling to the ground, landing head-first.

Stephen ran back towards the other side of the yard, hopped the fence, and kept going. He didn't look back to see if the man or anyone else followed, and he didn't care if he only knocked the man down or killed him; as far as Stephen was concerned, the man deserved to die; Stephen's innocence vanished for good.

He ran blindly back to his campsite, seeing no one. He tossed the backpack into the tent, ran a few yards into the woods, and heaved against a tree. When finished, Stephen wiped his mouth, sat down against another tree, and cried while thinking about his parents and sister. He felt utterly alone.

Early the following day, Stephen immediately ran in the woods for two hours, thinking of nothing but the task at hand. The new socks he found the night before felt good on his feet, and he ignored the blisters his old socks had started. He ran through the woods without looking where he was going, running through bushes, being hit by tree branches, but not stumbling once. When finished, he went to the little waterfall, and without hesitation, stripped off his clothes and let the water run over his body as he worked hard to keep the events from the day before out of his mind. His reluctance to be out in open naked, and the sense of vulnerability it formerly gave him, had disappeared with his innocence. The icy water brought out goosebumps on his skin, inter-mixed with trails of blood from the many cuts on his body.

Finally, he felt clean, grabbed his clothes off the ground, rinsed them out before putting them on, and walked back to his campsite. He finished unpacking the supplies he grabbed the night before and then went running again. The rest of the day and the rest of the week were back to the routine of running, meditation, and exercise, day after day. His meditation skills improved each session, he ran longer every day, and his body began to show the new strength he built.

Another week later, Stephen felt better equipped and prepared for what lay ahead—time to move on. He started organizing what he would be able to take, but before he continued his journey, one thing remained to accomplish. He had put it off long enough. Stephen took the scissors and began to cut off as much hair as possible. When done with the scissors, he took the shaving supplies to the waterfall, and using the razor, shaved the rest of the hair from his head. He couldn't see what he was doing, but it felt like he had done a decent job. An hour later, a few minutes before noon on a cloudy day, he continued his journey.

Stephen wanted to keep heading southwest on the highway, but the smell from the dead bodies in some of the cars became too intense, so he decided to walk along the highway as best he could. In some places, a minor road paralleled, and in others, he had to cut across parking lots, go around warehouses and jump fences to cut through properties he sensed were empty.

He saw no one, but occasionally, he would hear a scream or feel a bit of pain as he experienced the torment inflicted on others. Stephen knew he could push the pain and the emotions away if he stopped to do some meditation, but he needed to find somewhere safe, and he didn't want to stop.

Something compelled him to move on. He wasn't sure what it was, but he somehow comprehended he had to keep moving. To delay would mean trouble, or he might miss something important. The farther along he went that day, the more he became convinced.

I will miss something or someone, if I don't continue moving alongside the highway.

He continued to walk till well after eight that evening before finding an office building with an open door. The building contained three floors, so he decided to go up to the second floor in case anyone else came in via the ground level. After checking his exit options in case of trouble, he found an office, locked the door, and had something to eat before doing two hours of meditation.

When Stephen completed meditating, he felt much better. He wasn't feeling pain or anyone else's distress, but still, he felt compelled to journey on, and he lay down to sleep, wondering what or who waited for him when he continued his journey.

The next morning began bright and warm, the sun burning his now bald head. He stopped to pull a baseball cap from his pack, thinking sunscreen might be another needed supply. With his hair a memory, the cap required adjustment. If Stephen didn't know any better, he would have thought it the beginning of a day too pleasant to have a care in the world.

Stephen's morning started with a small bite of food from his supplies. He found some juice and water in a storage cabinet in the office's break room an hour later, which he finished before leaving. He had hoped to find more supplies, but his search ended in vain.

He continued his journey minutes later to who knew where, but at least today, Stephen experienced no pain or mental anguish from others who might be nearby. An hour after he started his journey, Stephen realized he had crossed into Maryland when he noticed a Maryland motor vehicle office.

Stephen had never been in Maryland before that he could recall, even though it wasn't far from his home. His parents had talked about taking him and his sister to the Baltimore Aquarium, but the trip never happened, and he fought down the urge to cry as he continued, making his way toward something he still knew beckoned.

A couple of hours later, he had to drop behind a trailer parked by a grocery store when he heard voices coming from ahead. He crouched there a few minutes, listening to the sounds coming closer, and realized he heard laughter among the voices.

Stephen moved closer to the front of the trailer and was shocked when he saw a gang of five young women, probably in their early twenties, walking down the street with two guys of about the same age. Both guys were naked and wearing what looked like dog collars around their necks, with leashes two of the women were holding.

The guys appeared to be in a trance, probably controlled by at least one of the women. While Stephen watched, a woman with bright pink hair kicked the taller captive in the backside and told him to eat something she saw lying on the ground. He immediately got down on his hands and knees and put the item into his mouth as the women stood there laughing.

The sight made him sick to his stomach, so he backed farther behind the trailer and waited for a half-hour to make sure they were nowhere nearby when he continued his journey heading southwest following along highway 1. Stephen spent the rest of the day walking and hiding as needed when he sensed trouble up ahead. If asked, he wouldn't know how to explain his new ability, but he somehow knew when to hide, when to move faster and when to find shelter.

He stopped briefly under a large tree in the backyard of an abandoned house to have lunch and rest. He wanted to stay under the tree and forget the world, but knew he couldn't. He traveled a few more hours, avoiding trouble while occasionally hearing gunfire or screaming coming from not too far away. Part of him wanted to help if he could, but Stephen knew he shouldn't get involved; he couldn't help everyone and still help himself. He wasn't usually so self-centered, but he felt like the future had something more important for him to do with what remained of his life.

A couple of hours before sunset, he reached the Susquehanna River and could see the highway 1 bridge less than a mile away. He thought about heading up to the bridge to cross the river, but his newfound senses made him feel it was a bad idea, so he decided to walk the other direction towards some riverfront homes. He couldn't sense any trouble as he approached the first house and was happy to discover the answer to crossing the river.

There were several small canoes up against a storage shed in the backyard of the first house. He looked out over the river and didn't see any apparent currents in the water to cause concern, so he grabbed one of the canoes and a paddle and prepared to put it in the water when again something told him to wait. After a brief moment of indecision, he decided to sit under the house's deck and have what passed for dinner nowadays as he waited for the cover of darkness to cross.

Three hours later, he stood on the other side of the river, having made a smooth, uneventful crossing, and began to set up for a night sleeping in some woods he found on the far side of the river. Tomorrow was another day, and he had a feeling it would be eventful.

Light rain greeted Stephen in the morning. He wondered if his ability could now predict the weather since he had thought to pull out and set up the small tarp he had taken from the boys. It kept him and most of the supplies dry, at least until he had to take it down and continue his journey. The rain didn't last much longer, and a couple of hours later, after walking through backyards parking lots and woods, he came upon State RT 440 and decided to walk along the road for a while, heading west.

The road mostly passed between farms not yet planted, long stretches of forest, and a few seemingly empty houses along the way. When he came near a gas station, he went off the road and approached the back of the building as a precaution. He saw and sensed no one, so he picked up more water and nonperishable food.

An hour later, it remained cloudy with a light, cool breeze. Stephen reached the end of 440 and had to decide which way to go: left, right, or directly ahead into a forest. He chose to go with the forest and crossed the road into the woods. He didn't know why he wanted to go in that direction, but he knew it was the correct thing to do. Unfortunately, the going wasn't easy, for a clear path didn't exist, and he ended up getting scratched by numerous thorn bushes and low-hanging tree branches.

Stephen bled from more than a few scratches but not bad enough to cause him any worry as he pushed through the brush, continually wiping the water from his eyes to clear his vision in the now heavy rainfall. The trees protected Stephen for a while, but the cold rain now made its way past the sparse canopy, soaking him. He thought about putting on the light jacket he carried but decided it made no point since his t-shirt and jeans were already soaking wet, and at least the rain washed the blood off his body.

As if rain wasn't bad enough, he came to a creek and had to walk through water a foot deep. He almost slipped and fell along the muddy bank on the other side before finding a tree branch he could use for support.

An hour later, the rain became a fine mist clinging to the forest underbrush as he emerged out of the woods onto a road called Rocks Road, county RT 24. When he looked to his right, Stephen saw a sign for the entrance to the Rocks National Park. He had arrived at the destination—how or why remained a mystery.

A minute later, Stephen reached the sign. He started walking up the access road but stopped when he sensed someone watching him. He didn't detect any danger and prepared to yell out 'who's there,' when he felt an imminent threat from farther up the park road. He looked, saw a parking lot and small building, but no people.

He stood in the middle of the road a moment, deciding what to do when his legs turned, and Stephen started walking towards the woods. He tried to fight it at first, but he sensed no danger from within the forest, so he decided to let go and see what happened. A few moments later, after being pulled through the trees and getting more cuts, he came face to face with the person who controlled him.

He stood there, staring at a tall, dark-haired woman in a green raincoat. Stephen was at a loss for words when she spoke up with a soothing and commanding voice.

"Come with me, get attention for those cuts, or stay here and get caught by the thugs in the Welcome Center building, be tortured, and die. Your choice!"

"I knew this day would be eventf—"

Roommates

Stephen again awoke from his meditation to the feeling of icy cold water flowing over his hot body, making him more than anything else, annoyed. He wasn't bothered by the cold water, but they kept interrupting his meditations. He allowed goosebumps to show for the sake of his captors.

"Thanks for cooling me . . . off, but this is . . . becoming annoying," he said, just barely making it sound and look like he was exhausted from the torture.

"I will save you the trouble . . . of asking, and I will say it slowly. I . . . Am . . . Not . . . A . . . Spy!"

Stephen could see the anger on the guard's face as he slowly spoke, and the guard answered by a hard smack across Stephen's face.

"You have your orders, don't fuck this up. I have to report to the Overlord."

The head guard turned from his companions and stomped out of the room, his contempt for Stephen evident by his demeanor. Stephen recognized one of the remaining men as the young guard they locked in the cabinet next to him.

The older guard pulled Stephen from the so-called isolation chamber and led him, still naked, down the hall with a spear against his back until they came to and entered an unmarked room. More lockers filled the place very similar to the other, except this one wasn't for torture and had bathroom facilities and showers.

"You smell! Go clean the stink off of your body, so we don't have to put up with it any longer," the older guard said, with a look of disgust.

"And then what," Stephen asked?

"Do what the hell I say! You will find out your fate soon enough."

The guards left the room, locking the door behind them as Stephen headed to one of the shower stalls. He found the water ice-cold as expected, but it didn't bother him as he had grown used to extreme conditions. He used plenty of soap, glad himself to wash away the smell, and a few minutes later, he air-dried and stood to wait for the guards to come back as there were no towels and nowhere to sit. With nothing else to do, he stood in front of the single dirty mirror and looked at his body.

Well, at least they helped me lose some unwanted pounds.

He looked at his face wishing they would have provided him something to shave. He hated having a beard, and he now had many weeks of growth.

He closed his eyes and reached out with his mind wishing he could sense his wife in the same way she could sense him. Stephen wasn't sure if his ability had strength enough to broadcast his presence to her, but he hoped she would be able to know he remained alive.

Stephen tried again to send a message to Patrick. A short few words—I'm okay, nothing to report. He had no way of knowing if Patrick had received the message. He heard no response.

Stephen knew he hadn't much time left, so he took a deep breath, forced his body to relax, and his heart to slow as he stood there, flexing various parts of his body to strengthen his muscles in the way his wife had taught. It wasn't as good as a real workout, but it kept the muscles from deteriorating.

He completed his routine when he heard the key put into the lock, and he stepped back a few feet to not piss off the guards. If he appeared cooperative, it would win him favor and possibly allow him to manipulate the men in the future, especially the younger one who had spent time in the isolation chamber.

"You smell better; now put this on," the guard tossed a robe-like piece of clothing to Stephen. The robe appeared to be of cheap linen fabric like a potatoes sack. It would itch most people who wore it, but it wouldn't bother him. He pulled it over his head, surprised it fit as well as it did.

"I'm all washed and dressed. Where are you taking me tonight?"

"Shut up and get moving out the door to the right," was all the guard said as he grabbed Stephen by the shoulder and pushed him to the hallway, where the second, younger guard waited.

As they walked down the corridor, Stephen took in the scenery. He had never been in Philadelphia's City Hall before, and this was the first time Jonathan's guards had taken him to this section of the building. Most of the original decoration had been destroyed or removed. However, the halls were still reminiscent of a much different world.

After a few minutes, they stopped at one of the many doors, and the guard told Stephen to get in and make himself comfortable. "Your roommate is busy performing for the Overlord in the throne room and will be back soon. I'm sure the two of you will be best buds."

Both guards laughed as they slammed the door behind him. He knew the door was locked and could sense one of the guards, he believed the younger, standing on the other side of the door.

Stephen looked around and realized the small room had no windows and only one other door off to the far side of the room. When he opened the door, he found a closet with some odd clothing inside plus some garments that resembled the piece of cloth he now wore.

The space had no bathroom, but he did see a bucket of water in the corner he guessed his mysterious roommate used when the guards wouldn't let him out to use the proper facilities. Old and dirty, ornate paper, which probably dated back thirty or more years, covered the walls. It had ripped and peeled away in places, and in other areas, he could see where pictures had once hung. He gathered the room had been a low-level flunky's office, back before the event.

Two cots sat against the walls, one on each side of the room. One had a pile of dirty clothes and costumes thrown on top. The additional, only slightly cleaner cot, Stephen assumed to be his. Stephen wasn't sure exactly why they stuck him here, but he knew whatever the plan; Jonathan directed the action and called the shots, no doubt hoping to discover the truth about his guest.

Stephen moved to sit on his future bed when he heard the door unlock. He expected the guard or his roommate to enter as the door opened; what he wasn't expecting to see standing in front of him was a man dressed in a ballerina's tutu.

Aspen and the Overlord

The senior guard gave his underlings their orders and hesitantly walked away to give his Overlord an update as his men pulled the young spy from the isolation chamber. The younger of the two guards, he considered an untrustworthy sissy. He hoped the time in the heat locker taught him a lesson. The older guard, Scott, would make the sissy more of a man worthy of serving the Overlord, or they both would die after he enjoyed them first.

The guard laughed to himself as he walked down the ornate corridor of the fortress's upper level. He would love to be a fly in the room, hearing conversations that would ensue between the bastard and the spy. He doubted the Overlord's plan would work, and he looked forward to seeing them both eviscerated and tossed down the garbage hole.

Aspen, the guard's given name, wished he had powers like his Overlord. He hated the name his parents cursed him with, which was one reason he killed them a year before the event occurred. If he had the powers the Overlord possessed, he could have bloodlessly tortured the two before killing them for inflicting him with that always-hated name and for trying to have him arrested when he wouldn't leave their house.

Growing up, the other kids teased him without mercy, making fun of his name and his onetime hippie parents. They would make jokes about him being a terrible specimen of a tree; skinny, weak, and easily broken. One time, they even tied him to a tree in the forest to be with his kind. He remained there for many hours before a friend found him and cut him loose. If he had powers then like the Overlord, he would have enjoyed watching his tormentors suffer.

No one in the fortress knew his real name. The name he gave when he volunteered to work for Jonathan before he became the Overlord was Ander. A strong name, it made him feel like the man he knew himself to be.

Aspen admired the Overlord and hoped to one day be his most trusted guard and advisor. He would kill Nathan, his Overlord's current advisor, if he thought he could get away without being caught. Aspen knew the Overlord liked him about as much as he liked anyone, but the Overlord also knew Ander didn't need to be controlled or watched. He enjoyed enforcing the Overlord's orders, especially when they were to inflict misery on someone.

He told the fool spy he feared for his life, simply a bullshit story trying to get the punk to talk. Aspen didn't trust the young man and would like nothing better than to torture the truth out of him, but that was a decision and task for the Overlord.

Aspen had gone to the throne room, and the guard on duty told him the Overlord had departed for his special pleasure chamber. The space, more for torture than pleasure, received its nickname from the guards. The Overlord would take certain people for a personal demonstration of his vast powers, giving the Overlord the only real pleasure.

He arrived at the pleasure chamber to find Nathan keeping watch at the door. The hatred Aspen felt for the man immediately surfaced and reminded him how much he wanted nothing more in life than to replace Nathan and be by the Overlord's side, day and night. In this, Aspen was obsessed.

"Hello, Nathan, is the Overlord almost finished with his pleasure? I have an update for him concerning the spy and Mark."

"Don't let the Overlord here you use that name. He will skin you alive for sure. Is the bastard enjoying his new roommate?"

"Sorry for the slip. I didn't stay around long enough to find out. I wanted to update the Overlord as soon as possible."

"Well, Ander, you will have to wait a little longer," Nathan said, as a loud and long scream came from behind the door.

On the other side of the door, in a chair, sat a naked woman, fondling herself while being forced to watch the Overlord torture her husband. He never touched the man; the man tortured himself, fully aware of what he did but unable to stop.

The man's body was full of bleeding wounds he had inflicted upon himself with a large knife the Overlord supplied for the task. The long scream the guards had heard came from the man when he forced the man to dig out both of his eyes with his own bare hands.

The man stood in front of the Overlord with his bloodied hands held out, and each hand held one of the eyeballs. The Overlord laughed at the sight.

"Be thankful I do not force you to cut off the balls hanging between your legs," he said to the man as he took the eyes from him.

The Overlord walked over to the woman and told her to take the eyeballs from his hands. When she hesitated, he advised her to do it willingly, or he would force her to eat them. The woman slowly reached out her moist hands and took the eyeballs from the Overlord.

"Now, my lovely, shove them up that wet cunt of yours and spread those legs for your master to fill will his glory.

The guards standing outside the door couldn't hear anything beyond the man's screams, now silent and merely whimpers. While waiting, Aspen had a bulge in his pants, thinking about the fun going on inside the room.

Ten minutes later, the Overlord came out and instructed Nathan to dispose of the two pieces of filth by whatever means he desired. Nathan was more than happy to oblige as he entered the room and closed the door with a smile on his face. He never minded having the Overlord's sloppy seconds.

"Follow me to the throne room and report," the Overlord instructed Aspen as he started walking away.

"Yes, Overlord, your plan is progressing as you ordered. I placed the spy in the room, and the bastard, if not already there, will be soon."

"You have done well, Ander, but let's be fair and not prejudge our friend Stephen. Make him feel like another trusted slave and instruct everyone to follow and observe them at all times. Anyone who brings me solid evidence Stephen is a spy will receive a handsome reward."

"Yes, Overlord, I will see to it personally."

"I have promised Patricia not to make the bastard perform as my court jester any longer. Make sure he has appropriate attire to be a throne room servant and find some appropriate jester costumes for our friend Stephen. I can hardly wait to see him perform."

They arrived at the throne room, and Aspen assured his Overlord he would do as instructed. The Overlord and Aspen were smiling as they parted.

Stephen and Mark

Stephen stood there for a moment, not sure what he looked at, many thoughts racing through his mind before he spoke.

"What the hell are you dressed for?"

"Who the fuck are you? Is Jonathan going to torture me even more by forcing me to have a roomy—a kid? Is he going to get his jollies by making us screw each other? Well, maybe he forgot he cut off my dick, so not much is going to happen unless I'm to serve as your girlfriend."

Mark paused as it occurred to him what Jonathan could do using this new person as a surrogate. He shuddered at the thought. If this newcomer touched him in any way, he would find the means to strike back, no matter his fate.

"I can't speak to Jonathan's intentions. His guards captured me a few weeks ago and accused me of being a spy. They tortured me in the old subway for a couple of weeks and then held me locked in a sweltering locker to try and break me, but as I told them many times, I'm not a spy.

"By the way, my name is Stephen," he said as he held his hand out to the person standing in front of him dressed as a ballerina. Stephen could hardly keep from laughing.

"My name is Mark, a pleasure to meet you, I guess. It will be good to have someone to talk to instead of the bugs. By the way, feel free to laugh at me. I know you want to. I see it on your face."

He took Stephen's hand and shook it like a man afraid to trust anyone.

"I'm sorry, I don't want to be rude and laugh, but have you seen yourself?"

"Unfortunately, I have. You told me your story, at least part of it, so I guess I should tell you mine.

"I had the misfortune of being in love with the same woman he wanted for his own. The fucking pig has been submitting me to various forms of torture just for the hell of it, and this is the latest. I get to be one of his court jesters, so he can repeatedly belittle and abuse me in front of his perverted kiss-ass guests.

"Until recently, they held me in the subway rooms, while not being used for target practice, until they moved me here a few days ago. Welcome to what constitutes paradise around this God-forsaken place. If you don't mind, I would like to get out of this thing."

Mark undressed in front of Stephen, having long since lost any sense of embarrassment or modesty. Stephen winced when he saw what Jonathan had done to Mark and started to think about how he could recruit Mark and maybe get him out of the fortress; however, he knew he had to be careful. Stephen had no doubt he roomed with Mark in the hopes he would admit to Mark he was indeed a spy. Jonathan would undoubtedly torture Mark to get whatever information he learned. At that moment, Stephen came to realize Mark could be in trouble whether he confided in him or not, and it would be his fault.

"Why do you think he moved you here, Mark?"

"Patricia, my . . . former fiancée, and the desire of Jonathan's affections has agreed to marry him; in exchange, he agreed to no longer torture or abuse me. I assume this is his way of no longer abusing me, at least not in public. As you could see by the outlandish costume I wore, he is not living up to the full agreement."

"Does she genuinely expect him to keep his word in the future?"

"I doubt it, Stephen, but he has prevented me from telling her about anything he does to me. If I try, the words don't come out, and my head starts to hurt. He grants her permission to see me occasionally, and she told me she overheard her attendants talking about what was happening to me before their agreement."

"I'm sorry, Mark. This entire world has gone to hell since the event. It has brought out the worst in almost everyone. Hopefully, someone will find a way to stop Jonathan."

After a pause where Stephen considered his next words carefully, he moved closer to Mark and spoke in a low voice.

"I might be able to remove whatever block he put into your mind. I'm sure he used his ability the same way a hypnotist puts ideas into a person's subconscious. We can talk more about it later."

Mark had a look of surprise on his face and was about to ask for more information, but Stephen shook his head no.

"Thank you, Stephen; it's good to have some friendly company, but it is late, and I would like to get some sleep while I can. I never know when they are going to come to drag me out of here to satisfy some desire of the Overlord of Hell."

"That's fine; I need some sleep as well; we can talk more tomorrow if they let us. I also am happy to have someone else to talk to other than the guards; they are no fun at all."

Stephen went to his cot and lay down, putting himself back into a restful and recuperative sleep. His breathing and heart rate slowed to what a doctor would consider dangerous, and his face lost all expression. He dreamt about Nicole and recalled their time together at the cabin, following the strange meeting in the woods.

Nicole and Stephen—His New Life

"Just shut up, kid. Are you going with me, or are you going to take your chances with them?"

Stephen shut his mouth and thought to himself how beautiful she appeared. He could sense no danger from the woman, but he could sense danger behind and up the road.

"I'll go with you."

"Good. Keep your mouth shut and follow me until I tell you it's okay to talk."

The stranger turned and pushed her way through the brush and tree branches behind her as she quickly started moving through the dense forest. A person out of shape would have had trouble keeping up with her. She was fast, determined, and appeared to know exactly where to go to get through the dense brush and had no hesitation as she moved forward.

On the other hand, though easily able to keep up, Stephen continued to get pummeled and cut by branches and thorn bushes. He didn't notice the woman getting hit, but he had to keep his head down a bit to avoid cuts across his face or getting more in his eyes than just the water whipping off the soaked branches.

They walked for at least a few miles before they came out of the woods and into a clearing. He stopped a moment, surprised by what he found in front of him, a log cabin in the middle of a clearing with a small unplanted garden space off to the side. He saw a large boulder on the left with a United States Forest Service flag painted on its surface. When he looked beyond the other side of the building, he saw a crushed rock road running off to the right, heading back into the forest. The road looked large enough to accommodate two vehicles passing at once, and he believed it led back to the park's entrance and the trouble of which she spoke.

A sign on the cabin read, 'Rocks National Park – Ranger Station and Nature Center'. An American flag flew above from a pole attached to the pointed roof, which again made him sad to think about everything changed since the event. The Stars and Stripes were clean and looked new. He was about to ask if she had put it up when the strange woman interrupted his thoughts.

"Yo, kid, stop gawking and move your ass."

Stephen started moving again and followed the woman into the building. The first thing he noticed was the musty smell as it assaulted his nose, almost causing him to sneeze. He didn't see much in the cabin except for some old wooden chairs and a desk. The main room also contained a small kitchen area with a micro-fridge, sounding like it still worked but ready to die. Across from the kitchen area, he saw a fireplace with ash and partially burned wood from a recent fire.

Stephen put his backpack down in a corner and whispered, "Am I allowed to talk now?"

"Yes, you can," The woman answered while grabbing a bottle of water from the refrigerator and tossing it at him."

"Why did I need to be silent while making our way through the forest? Is there genuinely anyone around here who could hear us?"

"No, I only wanted to make sure you could listen and do what I told you without question."

"As suspected. I guess I passed!"

While they talked, the woman removed her rain gear, and he realized she wasn't as old as he thought, and he began to think of her more as a girl rather than a woman. He understood it to be a minor difference, but it did make him feel more comfortable with his new situation.

"I'm surprised there is still electricity in this cabin; it looks like they abandoned the place. My name is Stephen, by the way."

"I'm Nicole," she answered between gulps of water. "The Forest Service abandoned the cabin a few seasons ago. The rangers used it when they were on extended duty, and for various educational purposes, at least one ranger lived here at all times.

"Enough talk, for now, Stephen. There is still running water here, so I suggest you shower while you can and properly clean those scratches. There's a bottle of antiseptic on the shelf you should use as well."

There were two doors on the far side wall of the cabin. "Which door is the bathroom?"

"The one on the right, the other is my bedroom. You'll be sleeping out here, assuming you are staying."

"I guess so," Stephen said, grabbing his bag and pulling out dry clothes. When he turned back, Nicole headed into her bedroom without saying another word, so he went in the other door to get cleaned off and tend to his cuts.

He found a standard but small bathroom with a tight shower stall, a sink, and a toilet. Stephen turned on the shower and stood waiting for hot water before realizing there wasn't any. She hadn't mentioned it would be a cold shower, but it wouldn't be a problem after cleaning off with cold water from under waterfalls the last few weeks.

He looked in the little mirror above the sink and realized he looked like shit. His head, face, neck, and arms were full of bleeding cuts, and his shirt had holes in multiple places, exposing more bleeding cuts along his chest. Luckily, he did manage to pick up a few more shirts during his travels.

Stephen moved to take his clothes off then decided they needed cleaning anyway, so why not wear them in the shower. He took off and discarded the ruined shirt, followed by his soaked sneakers, which he put to the side, before getting in the stall to find a bar of soap and shampoo.

He instinctively shivered a second or two as the cold water hit his head. As frigid as it was, the water felt great, and he one by one stripped off his remaining clothes, rinsed them out, and tossed them on the stall floor. Stephen's hair hadn't yet grown back, so he grabbed the bar of soap and cleaned himself while paying particular attention to the multiple cuts.

When finished, Stephen realized he hadn't seen a towel, but one waited for him on the toilet seat when he stepped out of the stall. He dried off, wrung out his clothes, and hung them on the shower stall curtain rod. He found the antiseptic, took care of his scrapes and cuts, and got dressed. When he returned to the main room, he found a cot set up by a wall with his pack sitting next to it on the floor.

"You may want to put something on your feet, kid. This floor is old and full of splinters."

He rummaged through his bag and grabbed the soccer slides he had with him and wore them as he thanked her for setting up the cot.

"How did you know this place was here, Nicole?"

Since she called him kid, Stephen thought about calling her girl but decided not to cause trouble. The cabin would be far better than being back out in the rain.

"I spent a couple of summers living at my aunt's house in Pylesville, only a few miles from the park. My cousin and I were junior scouts, and we participated in many nature lessons at this cabin. I . . . wanted to get out of my house in West Chester, where I lived, and remembered this place."

"Are we safe here? I saw the road leading to this cabin from I suspect the Welcome Center, and if you know about this place—"

She cut him off before he could finish.

"Trees block the road. They probably fell during the last two harsh winters, and the entrance to the road is also overgrown with brush. If others show up, we will have to deal with it then, but the thugs I saved you from appear to be content staying upfront for now. The Welcome Center is larger and far more comfortable."

"For now!" he repeated, not hiding his skepticism from his voice.

"It's getting late, kid," she said as she walked towards the bedroom. "Do what you want, but I'm going to sleep."

"No lights," she shouted as the door closed behind her. Stephen had nothing else to do, so he grabbed a snack bar from his pack, and when he finished, he went to sleep on the cot as darkness fell through the room.

The next few weeks became the basic routine of getting up, eating, and starting his exercise regimen. Nicole wasn't pleased about him running around the forest, and she made her feelings known with piercing looks and a cold shoulder. She worried someone would see him, but she got used to it and stopped complaining after a few days; however, the silence continued, and she only spoke to him when necessary.

More weeks passed, and she informed him they needed to make a supply run, so they planned an excursion for the next day. She led him through the forest the opposite way from the entrance he used the first day. They came out onto a small road that led down to a warehouse still filled with plenty of canned goods and some other non-perishable foods, including dried beef and jerky. He never liked the stuff, but food was food nowadays.

The next day after the excursion, she told Stephen he needed to earn his keep by preparing the garden for planting. He thought it mid to late May, having lost track of the days, so he figured it to be about the right time. There were some seeds left at the cabin the rangers used as part of the education programs they offered, and Nicole also picked up some on an earlier supply run.

Stephen worked the dirt to make it suitable for planting. The day became hot, and his body sweaty, so he took his shirt off to enjoy the cool breeze, and a couple of times, he caught her staring at him, which made him uncomfortable.

A few days later, the silent treatment began to fade, and they spent time talking about their past lives and what they thought had happened the day they both, at the same time, called the event. Neither one divulged too much detail about the time before they came together; however, he could tell she deliberately withheld something from him, as he from her.

Life continued, such as it was. Talking, and at times, ignoring and avoiding each other as the days passed, and they began to feel something they didn't want to allow coming to the surface. One day, to distract himself from the growing feelings, while they were pulling weeds from the garden, he finally asked the question, nagging at him since his arrival.

"How were you able to control me and force me to come to you in the woods?"

Nicole gave no immediate answer, so he asked again, making sure he had her attention.

"Nicole, how were you able to control me and force me to come to you in the woods?"

She appeared hesitant to answer the question, but after a moment of silence, she admitted she didn't know.

"Truthfully, I had never done anything comparable before. I worried you were going to get yourself killed, and I wanted you to move my way, and it just happened."

"You were worried about me? A young stranger, walking down the road."

"Yes, get over it. No different than protecting a lost puppy," Nicole said as she hurried into the cabin.

Comparing him to a puppy hurt in a way he had trouble trying to understand. He wanted to talk more about her abilities and his but decided it could wait since she evidently hated talking about her new skills or the event. He wondered if he brought up memories she didn't want to remember, and he felt again, she wasn't telling him everything.

A few days later, while walking in the woods, Nicole found Stephen meditating—something she didn't realize he did as part of his workouts. She informed him she used to teach meditation and yoga as an instructor and could teach him some new positions and techniques. Her only condition, they would have lessons in the cabin, not outside on the ground. Over the next couple of weeks of instructions, she complimented him on being a fast learner, and they spent many hours together each day doing yoga and meditation.

Stephen found he needed both to help him cope with his new life, concentrate on keeping the new feelings he experienced at bay and control his body from doing things he wouldn't want Nicole to see. He never had an actual girlfriend, and even though he thought her too old for him, he felt something starting to happen.

Weeks went by, Stephen figured it was now late June, and as the temperatures became warmer, he would stop to get refreshed under a waterfall in the park before heading back to the cabin. On one particular day, it had begun to downpour with severe lightning on his way back, so he ran into the cabin dripping with water and getting mud all over the floor. He started stripping off his wet clothes and dropping them on the floor as Nicole came out of her room and saw the mess.

"You had better be planning on cleaning up that mess yourself, kid. I'm not your mommy, and I'm not going to clean up after you."

Stephen stopped as the comment registered in his mind. After a brief moment, his pain returned. He fell to the floor, eyes tearing, as the memories of his parents and sister all came crashing back in his thoughts. He fought so hard to keep the pain at bay. Not caring about Nicole,

Stephen put his hands over his eyes and cried harder than any other time since the day of the event. He thought about his parents, dead in their bed, but mostly he thought about his sister and the hell she went through before she died.

Nicole immediately came over, saying she was sorry; she didn't mean it. She sat on the floor and put her arms around his body, trying to give him comfort.

"I'm so sorry, Stephen. I didn't think first about what I said; the last thing I want to do is hurt you."

The touch of her arms across his bare chest and her hair lying across his neck, again stirred up other feelings he continued trying to ignore even though his body couldn't. Stephen composed himself and asked Nicole to please leave him alone for a while. It wasn't only his emotions and memories he needed to control, and he hoped to God she hadn't noticed.

She reluctantly agreed and went back into her room, where he thought he could hear her softly crying while he sat there for a few moments, alone on the floor. When his body finally relaxed, Stephen stood and cleaned the floor before going into the bathroom to wash out his clothes and hang them up to dry. He needed the distraction to get the thoughts of what he lost and Nicole out of his head.

A couple of weeks later, Stephen's hair and the small amount of beard were getting to be more than he could endure. He put his hair in a tail, but it still annoyed him when he ran. He had spent a lot of time out running in the forest; he didn't need all the hair on his head, collecting insects and sweat, and decided he would need to shave again soon.

Later in the day, while looking for a snack, Stephen happened upon a calendar in one of the room's cabinets. He discovered Nicole had been keeping track of the days. It mattered not to him what damn day it happened to be at this point; he found it meaningless. Then Stephen noticed his sixteenth birthday coming up in two days, on the nineteenth of July, and decided to shave on that day. Probably the last time in his life that he would even know it was his birthday.

His emotions started pushing to the surface, but he immediately put them down as fast as possible by looking at the pictures in the calendar—places and images that had no memories for him. As he looked through the months, he was surprised to find out Nicole had marked the day they met. He didn't know what to make of the notation of his arrival; did she consider it a good thing or bad?

He put the calendar back where he found it and decided not to let her know he saw it or tell her about his meaningless birthday. As he ran and completed his other exercises, he couldn't help but wonder if Nicole's marking the day they met meant anything, and he started to think about what he wanted it to mean.

The water had stopped working a few days ago, so they could only get washed in the creek or at the waterfall, which had begun to slow as spring turned into summer. On the morning of his birthday, he went out to get washed with a bucket in hand. After washing up, he filled the container with water and went back to the cabin to shave.

Stephen didn't care that the water was cold; it would work just as well, so he grabbed his razor and shaving cream, which he took outside to sit on the large rock in front of the cabin. Why not enjoy the warm sun while shaving? He started with his little beard and face stubble and then tried to cut his hair shorter with the scissors.

Nicole had been picking some early vegetables from the garden when she saw him sitting on the rock, trying to cut his hair, and she laughed out loud at the sight. She offered to help, to which he reluctantly agreed, and she took the scissors. When his hair appeared short enough to shave, she took the shaving cream, gently spread it across his head, and shaved him with the razor.

As he sat there, enjoying her gentle touch, his body again started to react, and he could only hope Nicole wouldn't notice. When she finished the shave, she took a wet rag and gently wiped his now bald head. Before Stephen could thank her for the help, she put her arms on his shoulders and began giving him a massage.

Her touch felt tremendous on him, and he felt ready to explode as her hands now worked their way down his chest and eventually to his pants. She stopped, came around to stand in front of him, and grabbing his hands, she pulled him up into her arms, where she gave him a long, deep kiss. Without saying a word, she led him into the cabin and into her bedroom, where she stripped off her clothes and his and laid him down upon the bed.

Stephen had been through much over the last few months. He had done things, experienced things, and seen things no boy should, but after all of that, it was on his sixteenth birthday, he indeed became a man.

The following morning after Stephen's birthday, their relationship began to change. He no longer felt awkward being around Nicole, and the next evening they began to sleep together every night. It wasn't merely sex with the only person available; it was love, at least for him. She said she felt the same, even though their ages were different, and the relationship would have been taboo before the event.

Stephen eventually told her everything that happened to him and everything he had done on his journey. Nicole did the same, but he felt she still held something back. He didn't care; whatever secrets she kept, it wouldn't change their relationship. However, he noticed one change; she never again called him kid unless she wanted to be deliberately cute.

Three weeks later, after a session of meditating together, he pulled a little ring out of his pocket he had made from string, got down on one knee in front of her, and proposed.

"It probably doesn't matter now, but my parents raised me as a Roman Catholic, and one day when things are better, I want to marry you in the sight of God."

Nicole took the ring, put it on her finger, and cried as she said yes.

As the months passed, they spent most of the day working on their bodies and developing their abilities to be as strong as possible in case of future trouble. They would run, exercise and, meditate together, and refine their skills by attempting to use them on each other and the environment.

They would have power duels where Nicole would try to control his body while he used his power to resist. They would set up cans, balls, stones, or even large branches and try to move them with thought alone. Nicole could use her mind to move some things but not enough to make the ability useful. Stephen couldn't move them at all, but they did notice a slight breeze would shake the leaves behind what he tried to move. They both laughed at the sight.

One day after a meditation session, Nicole suggested they go out to the Welcome Center and see if anyone still lived in the building. She felt it better to be well-prepared and check the gang out rather than be surprised if the group decided to explore the area and found the cabin.

When the pair arrived at the Welcome Center, they could sense the building was empty, and when they went inside, they found several decayed bodies lying on the floor. Nicole turned over a few corpses and recognized one of them as the man who had been their leader. His throat appeared to have been slashed by his own hand using the knife still held in his decayed appendage.

"It looks like someone came here and killed him and a few of the others."

"No, Stephen, this one at least killed himself and maybe the others. Someone came here and used abilities on them. There were about fifteen guys here at one time, plus a couple of girls they had as prisoners. I wonder what happened to the girls?"

Nothing more could be done other than gathering up some still usable supplies and heading back to their cabin. Stephen left feeling disturbed by what he saw, and he believed something was going on he or they would have to deal with another time.

The end of September arrived, and the sun still shed warmth but winter would be coming too soon, and they had to prepare. The electricity had stopped two months ago, and the propane tank, which fed the heating system and stove in the kitchen, approached empty, so they were going to have to rely on the fireplace for heat and cooking. They had both been able to use their abilities to capture wild turkeys and deer, so meat wasn't a problem. Nicole knew which plants and berries were safe to eat, and they had vegetables from the garden.

Before winter set in, they made a few trips to gather supplies. They both needed winter coats and new clothes; Stephen especially needed new clothes since he had grown taller and more muscular since he had left his home. In addition to clothes, they also used their trips to get matches, canned goods, dried foods, a couple of axes for firewood, and other tools they thought might come in handy. They were as stocked and prepared as possible.

When they arrived back at the cabin and finished putting away the supplies, Stephen took Nicole's hand and then hugged her as tears fell from his eyes.

"It was so empty out there. Nothing but bodies and dead quiet. Are we alone? Is no one else out there?"

Nicole hugged him tightly, holding back her own emotions.

"I'm sure we are not alone; I feel it. I also feel we may find it's better to be alone, just the two of us."

The next few months together they spent building their bodies, minds, and talent. They would spend hours in meditation, and they both learned how to put their bodies into a deep meditative state that would allow them not to be affected by the cold and preserve their bodies and strength even after days of not eating. By March, they could spend days in the meditative state without any severe effects on their bodies.

One day late in March, they could both sense an approaching storm, another ability they developed. They stripped off their clothes and lay outside in the middle of the garden awaiting the storm. They knew they would be safe from animals, as sensing danger even when mediating was an ability they both had developed. Stephen often wondered if their physical intimacy could be responsible for the talents they had developed on almost the same timeline.

The snow piled up to nine inches before it stopped, and Nicole and Stephen were both buried in snow several inches above their faces. After being immersed in the drifts for almost two days, they awoke when the sun came out and quickly melted the snow.

By the time summer came around, they required little to survive. If they weren't building their bodies with daily exercise, they wouldn't have bothered to hunt, but their bodies needed the protein to grow and become stronger.

With each day, their abilities grew, and they were able to sense each other and occasionally communicate wordlessly, especially if their bodies were touching. They could detect animals for miles and the occasional but rare human passing close. They found they could also take control of other's minds to allow them to be unnoticed, as if not in existence.

One day in June, they awoke from their meditation and looked at each other, wondering what had happened.

"Did you feel that Nicole, or was it just me?"

"I felt something; I'm, however, not sure what. It felt as if someone called to me, but not by name."

"Yes, I experienced the same, as if I was being . . . beckoned. That is the only way I can describe the feeling."

They felt uneasy, but they needed to go hunting to replenish the meat supply. The mystery could wait to be solved another day, and the day didn't take long in coming.

They had celebrated his seventeenth birthday with a stale old Tastykake, followed by an hour of sweet slow lovemaking where Nicole pleasured him in new ways they had never done before. Their ability to control their bodies gave a whole new dimension to sex. Of all the hell the event had brought, at least it brought them together.

His birthday gift complete; they lay down on the floor and entered into deep meditation. They had been meditating for two days, only this time they were practicing controlling the environment around them while they lay on the floor. Stephen could create a slight breeze and move around dirt and dust, but Nicole discovered how to reach out with her mind and kill insects as large as a cockroach.

Stephen was the first to sit up; Nicole soon followed.

"I felt it again, the same as a few weeks ago, this time stronger. Someone is calling me—calling us."

"Yes, Stephen, I felt it too. They want us to come to be safe."

"Sanctuary!"

They said the word simultaneously, and they knew that soon the day would come to leave.

Stephen and Mark—Jesters

Aspen waited until the two jester bastards were in their room, and he slammed the door behind them. He and Mikal, a new guard originally from the commie country of Russia, had escorted the fools back to their room. Aspen would love to beat them, shove a knife up their asses and watch them bleed to death, but the Overlord wanted them treated well, for he still had plans for the fools. Aspen hoped he could be present when the Overlord disposed of them. He hoped it would be bloody, and he became aroused thinking about the scene.

Nathan told him to observe the two bastards and listen to them as much as possible, but he had heard nothing of importance so far. If the younger one was a spy, he wasn't talking about it, and he had no way to get out and report to anyone. If the young one tried, Aspen would enjoy being the one to put him down—hard.

Aspen considered his assignment a waste of time, so he decided to delegate to the new guard. He appeared to be a hard ass like all former commies, so he should work out well. Aspen gave the guard the same instruction Nathan and the Overlord had given to him. Confident all would be well, he left to relieve his tensions before it caused him to do something the Overlord would not appreciate.

As Aspen walked away, inside the room, Stephen and Mark were taking off the jesters' costumes they wore to the throne room to entertain Jonathan. The humiliation of having to wear them was almost more than Mark could endure as he tossed it aside. At least, he no longer endured the humiliation alone and knew from experience that things could be worse. Patricia believed this torment to be over, for the Overlord hid it well, and he prevented Mark from telling Patricia the truth during the short times they were allowed to be together.

Stephen spoke first, as this was the first opportunity to talk without being overheard. He knew Ander left, and the remaining guard he sensed had stepped away. He knew the time had come to start confiding in Mark.

"That had to be the most disgusting thing he has done in the last few days, while we had to be his fucking entertainment."

"Be careful what you say, Stephen, the guard, will overhear, and we will literally be fucking jesters for all to watch—just like today."

"The remaining guard has stepped away from the door; we can talk freely without being disturbed. I need to talk; I need to let it out."

It wasn't true, but he needed to feel Mark out.

"I'm no prude, but Jonathan taking her like that from behind while he forced her to give the old man a blowjob while everyone watched and gawked was horrible. You could see tears falling from her eyes, especially when he forced her to walk into the pit. The Overlord of Hell is a sick murderer, and someone needs to stop him for good."

"Damn it, kid, you need to shut your mouth, or we will be next in that pit. For someone so young, you have a lot to say, much of which could get you killed."

"I told you, the guard left. No one is listening to us."

"You can't know that!"

"Yes, Mark, I can. I have abilities of my own. I have kept them hidden, but it's time to confide in you. I am, what the Overlord suspects, I am—a spy. They sent me here from a place called Sanctuary to see first-hand what was going on here, and it is worse than what we heard. One way or another, someone needs to step up and bring it and him to an end."

"A spy? You're just a damn kid—sixteen, seventeen, maybe. Why are you telling me? What if he tortures me to find out what I know?"

"First of all, I'm nineteen, not that it matters. Second, because I like you, and although I have only seen her in the throne room, I like Patricia and don't want to see her married to that monster."

"Third, I need help. I need people in here I can trust."

"I don't know what powers you have, but there is no way you can take on Jonathan."

"Not alone, no, that is where you come in. I can tell you have powers you either don't know you have or you refuse to use. Either way, I'm going to help you develop those powers, and you are going to help me."

"The two of us against him, are you serious? The best we could ever hope would be to get out of here ourselves. We wouldn't even be able to help Patricia, let alone get rid of Jonathan."

"Escape is not my plan. I told you Jonathan needs to die, and we will have help from outside. I only need to be able to contact them. I don't know if I'm strong enough. That is one place you may be able to help me."

"The guard is coming back; we will talk more when we can and start your development. I suspect we don't have a lot of time. Let's get to sleep."

Stephen lay down on his cot, but sleep wasn't his aim. First, he sent another short message to Patrick, and after a few minutes, he received a brief confirmation of message received. Finally, a response. Stephen feared his friend might be captured or dead. He was relieved it wasn't the case.

The evening's events did disturb Stephen; even though he was a man—twenty years old—he at times still felt like the young teen who woke up one day to an abrupt end of his childhood. Mark was correct; in one sense, he remained too young for so much big bravado and responsibility. He felt alone and wanted to think and dream about his wife, Nicole. As he went into his meditation, he recalled their journey to Sanctuary.

Nicole and Stephen—On to Sanctuary

Two weeks had passed since they felt the call to Sanctuary, and they barely discussed or acknowledged what had happened. They were reluctant to trust the feelings, telling them it was the right thing to do. They knew they couldn't stay in the cabin forever, as tempting as it might have been. Stephen would have loved to stay and ignore the world, but deep inside, he knew that wasn't who they had become over the last year and a half.

"Stephen, it's been two weeks since we shared the vision, or calling maybe would be a better word, and we haven't directly talked about it at all. We can't ignore what we both felt."

"I know we can't. I'm just worried about what we will find when we get there. It could be a trap; it could be a way of enslaving people or God knows what. The world has descended into chaos and anarchy—I want no part of it."

"Do you want to hide here and ignore the world?"

"Yes, I—no, I don't really. Something inside of me wants me to leave, but I worry, is it to help or seek revenge? I don't want to fall into the trap of my life becoming nothing but revenge for what happened to my sister."

Nicole took his hands in hers and looked into his eyes.

"You are not that person, Stephen; I know it, and deep inside, you know it too. We need to go."

On that day, she convinced him it was time, no matter what the future held. A week later, they were ready. They packed as much as they could carry on a journey they knew would take weeks. They didn't need much, just shelter and some tools. If required, they could find food and water or go without it for days. Their ability to control their bodies and their needs had grown in the past year.

Stephen stood outside the cabin staring at everything and nothing. He fought many emotions as Nicole came out to join him. She stood next to him facing the cabin, put her backpack on the ground, and grabbed his hand, as they both just stood there a few minutes before speaking.

"What are you thinking, Stephen?"

"I'm thinking about how much I am going to miss this place. It became my home—our home for over a year. I'm going to miss it—after all, I became a man here and met my future wife."

"No, Stephen, you did not become a man here. You became a man on the day of the event. Only a man could have gone through what you did and survived to be a better person. You were a man the day I met you, and while here, you became a better, stronger man—the man I love. You still have, after all that has happened, an innocence about you, which makes me love you even more."

Stephen turned to her, gave her a big boyish smile, followed by a kiss. He picked up his backpack and started walking away.

"Well, come on, girl, don't just stand there. Pick up your backpack, and let's get moving; our futures are waiting."

They made their way out the back end of the park along Rockridge Road over farms and across property once owned by wealthy individuals who could afford the acres of rolling hills and lush landscapes. They made their way to RT 165 and on to RT 23 west. Somehow, they knew the way to go, and after a few days of traveling, they decided to camp for a couple of nights at the White Pony Golf Center.

Neither one had ever played golf, but they enjoyed laying naked on the eighteenth green with their bodies enjoying the now overgrown grass as they practiced their meditation and listened for further callings from Sanctuary.

Stephen hadn't much opportunity to work on keeping his body strong, so he took advantage of the health center there to work out on genuine weightlifting equipment instead of using rocks and trees. To their surprise, the showers still worked, and they enjoyed the first real shower together in many months. The water came out ice-cold, but to Stephen and Nicole, it was a piece of normalcy they had missed more than they realized.

After a few days, the time had come to move on along Troyer Road, passing over Highway 83, which they found littered with abandoned and burnt-out trucks and cars. The sight caused them to pause as it reminded them how many had died since the event. After a few moments, they continued along RT 137, which took them near the town of Brandy Spring.

They were deciding where they wanted to spend the evening when a feeling of impending danger struck Nicole. She grabbed Stephen's hand and led him into a house on the side of the road, by going around to the back and breaking in the kitchen door.

"What going on? Why did you bring me in here?"

"Something is wrong, Stephen; I feel it. We are in danger, or we would have been in danger if we had stayed on the road. Something or someone is coming, and we need to stay hidden."

While they waited for something or someone to pass, like the ancient Jews waiting for the angel of death to pass them by, they pulled out their last remaining energy bars. They didn't have long to wait. Less than fifteen minutes had passed when they heard an old yet familiar noise from outside, which started low but was getting louder—a helicopter.

They both realized what the sound was at the same time, and when Stephen went to the window to look, she pulled him back.

"No, Stephen, it's not safe; in fact, we need to move down to the basement—now!"

They found the door to the basement and ran down the stairs, closing the door behind them as they found a spot on the cramped dirt floor to wait for the danger to pass.

The helicopter had passed, and all remained quiet for a few minutes, but Stephen could tell by Nicole's face, they were not safe yet. A few minutes later, they heard voices from outside and heard someone say they would check it out. While they sat on the floor, they heard a crashing as the person who spoke kicked in the front door and entered the house, causing the floorboards above to squeak in the process as the person looked around the rooms.

They heard another person come in, and they listened to the conversation.

"Find anything in here, Butch?"

"No, it looks abandoned, but I felt sure I sensed something from in this house."

"Well, we have to go. The copter is getting low on fuel, so we are going to camp up north a bit in Parkton, and tomorrow we will continue to Pennsylvania without our air support unless we can find some fuel."

"Did you leave the bitches all alone with Frank, or is Scott back? You can't leave Frank alone with them too long, or he'll fuck them without us."

"Scott is back, but you are right; we need to go. I don't trust that little prick either."

A few minutes later, all was quiet, and Stephen felt like it was okay to talk.

"We have to follow them and help those girls they have as prisoners."

"No, Stephen, we can't fight four men plus whoever is in the helicopter. They may have guns, and even if they don't, they outmatch us by all but maybe abilities. We can't take the chance."

"But you know what they are going to do to those girls; I can't just sit here and do nothing."

"Stephen, for now, you must. Your time—our time to help will come; I feel it now more than before. We have to get out of here and get quickly into the park down the road. We can camp deep in the woods, and we will be safe."

Stephen reluctantly agreed, and they made their way along Masemore Road and into Gunpowder Falls State Park, where they set up camp for the night. Stephen didn't sleep well as he dreamt all night about his sister and how he took his revenge on Ralph.

The next morning, they woke to high winds and light rain. Again, Nicole had tapped into something which Stephen couldn't, and she told them they had to find some good sturdy shelter, such as a warehouse or factory building. They had passed a few buildings before reaching the park, so they headed back out of the park as the wind quickly became severe.

An hour later, they were breaking into the Furniture Plus warehouse on RT 83. It looked like no one had recently been in the building, but they did find a few rotted bodies upstairs in the employee break room. Stephen had seen an office down by the loading dock, so they went there and decided it would be an excellent place to wait out the storm.

A day later, they still waited. Although rare but not unheard of, unquestionably, inland Maryland experienced its first severe hurricane in years, and they were stuck in the middle of the storm. The wind had ripped away part of the roof, thankfully on the other side of the building, and the parking lot and roads they could see from the dock had become covered with at least a foot of water.

Nicole told Stephen she hadn't known what was coming, but she knew it would be dangerous, and they would need shelter. Stephen knew if they had remained in the park, there was a good chance they would be dead from flash flooding or falling trees.

The following day, the rain had ended, and the clouds started to break and show a blue sky of wispy clouds, causing shadows to move across the flooded roads. They couldn't leave, and they didn't expect anyone would be able to get in the factory, so they laid on the floor and worked on putting their bodies into a protective sleep. Stephen was still learning but proficient enough not to require clean drinking water or food at the moment.

A few days later, the water outside had finally receded enough to allow them to leave the building, and they walked into what looked like a war zone. The event had caused the destruction of society, but most of the earth and structures had not changed and showed little sign of society's collapse. Now, however, the world was in ruin; trees were down across the roads, along with the useless power line poles and road signs. Many buildings had roofs blown off, and the roadside stores, there a couple of days ago, were in ruin or gone.

Stephen and Nicole proceeded back along RT 137, winding through the debris on the road until they had to stop again when the road and surrounding landscape was impossible to pass from a combination of water and wreckage. They entered a small, old colonial house, which appeared not to have suffered much storm damage, and they made themselves comfortable. There were some canned goods in the kitchen and enough propane still in the tank to allow them to have a stove-cooked meal. The first one they had since the propane ran out at the cabin.

They slept in comfortable beds, made love a few times over the next couple of days, and enjoyed warm showers until they knew the time had come to stop playing house and continue the journey. Stephen enjoyed staying in the house and acting like everything remained normal in the world. He hoped Nicole and he could someday have a traditional life together, living in a house with a kid or two playing in the yard, and a dog barking at the postman. He knew he remained a bit immature to be talking about having kids and possessing a home; after all, he was only seventeen years old but felt much older, as life had aged him more than he liked.

When they continued their journey, the roads were dry; however, some of the surrounding lands were full of downed trees and still soggy.

The travelers stayed on RT 137 for the next couple of days, spending the nights in non-damaged houses and picking up valuable supplies, including a gun and bullets they found hidden in a closet of a home office they explored. Stephen hoped never to have to use it but having the gun in his backpack made him feel safer knowing it existed within reach.

Perfect, dry, and bright weather had been their constant companion over the last few days, but the weather remained cool for August, and the breeze helped to dry the land, so they started cutting through fields when it looked and felt like a good short cut. On their third day on the road, when they saw a sign for Hampstead, Nicole told him she felt danger ahead and told him they needed to cut across the fields below the town. In some places where the farms had grown soybeans, the going was easy, but cutting through tall corn, wildly growing on unkept land, became a bit more demanding, but even Stephen felt their lack of visibility to others to be a good thing. They continued cutting through fields until they stopped for the night at a house a mile below the town.

The next day, they continued walking through fields, deep woods, and streams. The couple walked across the land in soaking wet boots from hiking through the water, and Stephen started to feel blisters developing on his feet. When they came out onto RT 30, they saw a sports shoe store down the road and were ecstatic to find it remained undamaged and full of boots. They found new boots and dry socks, a few extra of which they grabbed for future needs before continuing their journey.

They continued through overgrown farms and pastures until they came out onto Gorsuch Road, which they followed to RT 140, then RT 27 into Westminster. Stephen wasn't happy about walking directly into the center of town; he felt exposed. Nicole assured him she could sense no danger—she thought they needed to be at that place at that time. The buildings appeared to have only minor damage from the storm but did show signs of looting.

"The streets are empty, except for the usual carnage; I hear nothing, and you sense no danger; what would we need to do other than look for some supplies?"

"Someone needs our help, Stephen; I can feel it. This way, quickly."

Stephen followed her down a side street, littered with decaying bodies and into a brick building where a door had been propped open. When they ducked behind a wall, Nicole motioned for him to be quiet, and after a moment, Stephen heard the faint noise of a person crying.

They silently moved closer to the sounds and ended up outside a room with a door partially open enough to see the scene inside. A middle-aged, scruffy, unkempt, half-naked man stood at the bottom of an army cot. The man had a young woman, probably in her late twenties, strapped down on the bed. The young woman cried and repeated over again, "No, no, no."

They could also see the body of another man, half-dressed, lying in a fresh puddle of blood on the floor. He looked to have been about the same age as the girl, and Stephen figured him to have been her boyfriend or husband, which the man soon confirmed.

"I warned him to cooperate," the man said, "All he had to do was fuck you while I watched, but no, your boyfriend had to be stubborn and play the hero. I'm glad I sliced his throat before he could use his mind tricks on me."

"The girl responded between her cries of misery, "He couldn't do that. We simply wanted to be left alone."

"Liar!" The man yelled as he bent down to the body on the floor, used his knife to cut the underpants off the body, and then used it again to cut off the dead man's penis.

"If he had no ability, why couldn't I control him like the others, and why can't I control you? No matter, bitch, you will open those pretty legs of yours for me to take my pleasure, or I will shove your boyfriend's cock down your throat. I'm sure it wouldn't be the first time."

As they stood behind the door looking through the small opening as best they could, Stephen took out the gun with shaking hands and released the safety. Nicole reached out and pushed his hands down to indicate not to use the weapon. As he stood there with the gun in his trembling hands pointing towards the floor, Nicole pushed the door open, walked into the room, and confronted the man.

"You're a weak, poor excuse of a man, and you don't deserve to live," she shouted, louder than Stephen had ever heard her yell in the past.

As the words left her lips, the man flew across the room, smashing into the wall with enough force to cause his body to dent the plaster before it lifelessly fell to the ground. Nicole walked over to the motionless man, picking up his knife on the way, and plunging it deep into his heart to make sure he would cause no more trouble.

Stephen stood watching in amazement as he realized he needed to put the safety back on the gun and put it away before he accidentally shot himself. He knew Nicole had better ability than he to move small objects, but he had never seen her do anything similar before. He knew from his own experience it was probably her tremendous anger, which allowed her to throw the man with her mind.

He silently watched as Nicole untied the victim from the cot, sat next to her, and held the shaking woman until she could calm down. It felt like an eternity for her to become composed, but eventually, she did, and Nicole asked her to get dressed and come with them to safety.

A short while later, they were sitting in a former real-estate office on West Main Street. The building looked completely undamaged by any looting, and the office in the back had a couple of comfortable sofas to sit on as they ate, and the girl told them her story.

"Thank you for saving me from that madman. I thought I would die a horrible death—part of me wishes I did. I don't know how to go on without Damon; he was the only thing getting me through this, whatever it is—this hell brought down on our lives."

"Where are you from, ah—"

"Susan, my name is Susan. I didn't even realize I never gave you my name."

"I'm Stephen, and this is Nicole. We were passing around the town when Nicole sensed someone in trouble, needing our help. We heard you crying, and the rest, you know."

Susan took a drink of water to compose herself before speaking.

"Damon and I are—were, from up north, from a town in Pennsylvania called Carlisle, about ten miles west of Harrisburg. We barely made it through last winter, so we were heading south before the cold weather to hopefully find somewhere warm and safe to try and build a new life. Now I don't know where to go."

"You can and should come with us," Nicole said from over in the corner where she had been sitting. Stephen suspected Nicole experienced remorse and may need time to deal with what happened. He knew first-hand what it was like when you took a life, even if the person deserved death. Stephen continued, giving Nicole time to deal with her emotions.

"We are traveling to a place we believe to be safe. We think it's called Sanctuary; we have felt a calling to the place, so it's where we are heading. I feel like we are getting close."

"Is that another one of your things you can do since the end day, besides throwing people across the room?"

Susan said the words with a small smile, finally coming to her face.

Nicole stood, a bit shaky at first, and came over to Susan.

"End day? I like to think things are not that bad, but we have been in seclusion, or you could say, hiding for the last year. We have started calling it the event," Nicole said as she sat down next to Susan.

"To answer your question, yes, I feel something calling to us, we both do. I can also, at times, sense danger, and apparently, when someone needs help. What about you, do you have any abilities?"

"Damon had no abilities at all, but I have the ability or immunity maybe from whatever happened. The abilities some people have, don't work on me, and I can somehow extend the protection to people around me."

"Really," Stephen said. "We should see if it works on us; what's the range?"

"No, Stephen. Not now," Nicole answered. "We need to get moving. We are getting close, and this town will not be safe for long."

"I have learned not to doubt you. Susan, are you coming with us?"

"Why not? I have nowhere else to go."

The balance of the journey remained uneventful. The weather continued to be fair, the group encountered no one else in their travels, and Nicole felt no warnings of danger. Nicole and Stephen didn't practice their meditating since they now had a traveling partner. Stephen wanted to try some experiments with Susan's ability, but Nicole insisted they keep moving. The new friends spent the nights in various farmhouses and took as many helpful supplies as possible.

A week after the encounter at Westminster, they came out of a cornfield onto RT 31 and followed it into Liberty Town. The town appeared deserted, but Nicole and Stephen felt the presence of someone watching. Nicole sensed no danger, so they spent the night in an office that used to belong to a lawyer and had a comfortable set of sofas the girls used to get a good night's sleep.

The next day they followed RT 550 out of Liberty Town for a few hours before seeing a sign showing the town of Woodsboro two miles ahead. On the left-hand bottom corner, they noticed a small letter 's' with an arrow indicating to go straight ahead.

Half an hour later, they crested a small hill and stopped to look down into the town of Woodsboro in the valley below. It was a small town with no distinguishing features other than a tall church steeple near the center of the town.

Stephen and Nicole stood there, Susan close behind, looking down at the town for a moment until at the same time they both spoke.

"Sanctuary."

The Day is Set

"Wake up, lazy filthy bastards," Aspen said, while Mikal stood outside the door and cringed as Aspen brought his stick down hard on Mark's back. "The Overlord wants the two of you in the throne room; get dressed now."

Stephen pretended to be groggy and tired, but he had sensed the approach of the guard Ander. He felt him and oddly saw the guard in his dream as he recalled when he and Nicole first arrived at Sanctuary. Mark, however, genuinely remained tired, as he suffered more from emotional than physical exhaustion. Stephen watched Ander reward Mark's slow movements with a punch to the kidneys to accompany the strike to his back. Stephen hated the guard and vowed he would one day make him pay.

A few minutes later, in full regalia and after being pushed along so hard, Mark fell multiple times; the guards escorted the haggard men into the throne room where Jonathan called an audience with a bunch of scoundrels hoping to win the Overlord's favor.

"Oh look, here come my prized jackasses now."

The Overlord no sooner spoke the words when Mark fell to the floor, where, on all fours, he made sounds like a donkey. Stephen felt the compulsion and could easily resist, but he needed to play along or risk exposure. He threw himself down to the floor and began making the same gestures as Mark. Stephen felt the force pushing him to Mark, and although he didn't want to, he mounted Mark like he was his lover.

Finally, Stephen felt the compulsion cease, and they rose slowly off the floor and staggered over to their spot against the wall.

The Overlord stood and applauded his jackasses, loudly slapping his hands together and whistling like a lusting, construction worker. His guests quickly got up on their feet and mimicked his actions, as Mark and Stephen experienced the compulsion to bow to the audience.

"Where is that bitch who is to be my wife? She should know better than to keep me waiting. No matter, I will take my pleasure as I wait."

A young woman, standing against a far wall, started walking toward the dais and stood in front of her Overlord, fear showing in her expression. She trembled as she dropped her thin, tattered robe to the ground while slowly being forced down on her knees in front of the Overlord's throne. The guests watched as he moaned in pleasure from the movement of her mouth along his—

"You are a vile and disgusting pig," a voice yelled from the doors that were again standing open where Patricia, flanked by two guards, now stood with anger visible on her face.

"Well, finally, my future wife has arrived."

"You expect and want me to marry you willingly, but then you continue these obscene behaviors in front of a bunch of practically drooling, mindless rogues, who would barely pass as human."

"No need to insult my guests," he responded in anger! "Hold your tongue, or I will force you to cut it out as my wedding present to you."

The Overlord paused as a smile came across his face.

"However, you are right, my dear Patricia; I should not behave in this way."

The woman in front of him immediately stood up, with extreme fear on her face, as she unwillingly walked towards the pit. The guests watched, some in silence, some egging her on as she walked to the edge of the hole. She looked back at the Overlord, and without hesitation, stepped into the pit and disappeared as a scream came from her lips as she fell to her death.

Patricia yelled in horror and stormed further into the chamber approaching the Overlord, but before she could direct her enhanced anger at Jonathan, he spoke.

"You have only yourself to blame. You didn't want the woman to continue, so I disposed of her."

Patricia was about to respond but found she couldn't.

"You may speak when I finish. I have decided, my dear, to make our engagement official by setting a date. You shall willingly become my wife exactly one month from today at noon. Please try to be on time.

"As a sign of my love for you, I promise not to engage in sexual activity with any of my whore subjects from this day forward. I will keep myself pure from this day until the day I take you as my wife. I'm sure your loins are getting wet, just thinking about me entering you. Isn't that right, bas—Mark?"

She noticed Mark standing against the wall when she entered, before she had gazed upon the disgusting scene on display atop the dais. Now her eyes moved to Mark's companion. The man, who had the face of a boy, was dressed the same as Mark. He looked as haggard and defeated as Mark looked since the day they were captured and taken to the fortress so long ago, but this man was more than he appeared. She felt something from him, and it gave her the slightest glimmer of hope that she quickly hid for fear Jonathan would notice.

"You also promised to leave Mark alone, yet here I find him still being forced to wear that silly costume and perform for you at your command, probably also by force."

"I'm sorry, my dear; I can assure you I have not harmed Mark in any way since I promised you; however, I am reluctant to lose my favorite jester. As you can see, the situation has changed, and I now have a new jester to abuse for my enjoyment, so I do promise you will never see Mark in that costume again. He will be elevated in status to be one of my proper servants and throne room attendants.

"That is now two wedding gifts I have given you, and it's not even our wedding day yet. Do not ask for more, or you may see my anger no matter how much I love you."

As he spoke the last sentence, he looked over at the bastard, just to see the look of disgust on his face, and the Overlord wasn't disappointed.

SANCTUARY

Professor James Oswald

Professor James Oswald tried to relax, but his mind wouldn't cooperate. He sat in his study at the old parish house he had moved into a few months following the terrible day that forever changed the world. The house sat next to St. John's Church; a non-denominational Christian house of worship built back in the mid-nineteenth century.

The professor completed reading the report he received moments before from his people in Philadelphia. The report detailed the activities of Jonathan Bartram, the so-called Overlord of Bartram Fortress, the former Philadelphia City Hall building. The professor found it difficult to read. There were so many violations of life and liberty, with cruelties he had only seen in the most horrid movies, which he could never watch in their entirety.

Professor Oswald remained after the event, a man who believed in science, and he knew no matter what caused this change to humanity, it was up to humanity to decide if it would be a blessing or a curse. He believed the abilities could be used for enlightenment, to improve the world by bringing science together with the new skills many now possessed.

He envisioned schools where children would learn how to use their abilities to expand their knowledge and marry their skills with science to create a better world with freedom and respect for all people. However, he knew first there needed to be a place where people could feel and be truly free from persecution, harassment, and torture. A place where people of all ability levels could feel safe—for this reason, he and a few followers came here and created Sanctuary.

The professor had earned his degrees in Teaching, Life Science, and School Management at the University of Pennsylvania in Philadelphia. He loved the time he had spent in the city last visited more than twenty years ago and hated what it had become. He had always wanted to return, but his multiple jobs in Columbus, Ohio, kept him busy. He had little free time and had never married, though he always had a woman by his side. The professor had been quite a playboy until the day of the event made him realize how trivial his life had been.

The town of Woodsboro, which he called Sanctuary, was only one of the many across the country, and he hoped, across the world. He communicated with many of the other groups in what had been the United States, and they all wished to slowly build their towns and influence until people like Jonathan and also the abolition front could be eliminated or converted.

The Abolitionists were a new group, which had come to Sanctuary's attention. The faction, almost a religion now, believed the abilities were nothing but a curse, and they were something to be exorcised from the world. The professor didn't think such a thing would be possible. He understood their concerns and motivation, but this enhancement to humanity needed to be embraced and used wisely for the betterment of all. The new abilities were not something to be suppressed or eliminated.

When his newly formed group first arrived in Woodsboro, Maryland, almost a year after the event, they encountered little resistance. The few remaining inhabitants embraced the idea of learning how to use their abilities for good. They helped set up housing and an official government to take care of the town while the professor and his people helped everyone cope with and use their abilities.

A few years before the event, the Woodsboro area had been part of a pilot project to equip the town with as many renewable energy sources as possible. The project area generated seventy-five percent of its electricity from renewable energy. All the houses, the church buildings he now used, and most municipal buildings had solar power panels mounted to the roofs. In addition, an experimental hydro-generation system continued to provide power from the nearby waterfalls and creek, and farther up the main road, three giant windmills continued to generate power.

With the town secured, they began to send out emissaries around the area to bring others to Woodsboro. Now, almost three years later, they controlled and protected an area nearly one hundred miles around with Sanctuary at the center.

A few months after they had started sending out emissaries, they also used their collective abilities to send out a message of safety and hope. Waiting for anyone who was interested, it was a place called Sanctuary. They knew many people roamed the countryside, trying to survive—who they hoped would follow the signal to safety.

As he sat behind his modest church desk, he recalled three of the first people to respond to the call. They included a young couple, both of whom had extraordinary abilities and control.

Professor Oswald wasn't having a good day. One of his latest recruits had been ambushed and killed the day before while on a patrol and rescue mission. She was only twenty-five years old, with an ability that would, with the proper training, allow her to impart learned information to large groups of people by projecting the knowledge from her mind. Her death would be a significant loss to the community.

As with life in general, every terrible thing becomes balanced by something good if we are lucky. To prove the point, he had received word the two people, whom they believed had answered their call to come to Sanctuary, had made it to the outskirts of town, and they had picked up a third person they had rescued along the way. His team had been watching them since before they entered Westminster, and from the reports, he felt confident they would be an asset to the community.

They appeared to be brother and sister; the younger, looking to be a minor boy, and the older, a young adult woman. He anxiously waited for his team to escort them to his office. He didn't have long to wait.

"Hello, and welcome to Sanctuary. My name is Jim." He said as the three entered his office. "Please sit and relax. Is there anything I can get you to drink or eat if you are hungry?"

The younger woman they thought to be the boy's sister responded first.

"No, thank you, I think what we all need now are answers. My name is Nicole Newbert, and I'm sorry, I shouldn't be speaking for my companions."

The other two responded in turn, again saying thank you, and they were fine. The boy introduced himself first as Stephen Estrada. He was seventeen, and he appeared nervous, sitting in front of the middle-aged stranger. The woman whom he knew the other two had rescued introduced herself as Susan Karley.

"I just realized; this is the first time I have used my last name since being rescued by my two friends."

"I hope that means you feel comfortable here. What about you, Stephen, Nicole?"

"I sense no danger," Stephen responded and admitted it wasn't one of his more developed abilities.

"You do appear nervous, Stephen, is there a reason?"

"I've been through a lot and have matured since the event, but sitting here, I feel like the seventeen-year-old boy I actually am. I feel . . . not in control, but in a way, relieved."

Nicole reached out to Stephen and squeezed his hand in a show of support and affection.

"I too sense no danger here," Nicole replied. "I sense only friendship, and I also feel relieved but curious."

Jim folded his hands in front of him on his desk, knowing it was a gesture many interpreted as signifying a trusted authority.

"My full name is Professor James Oswald, but everyone calls me 'Professor' even though I continuously ask to be called just Jim. Again, welcome to what we call Sanctuary. I and some companions started this place to be a refuge from the world. We wanted to create a place where people could be free to use and develop their abilities without fear and ridicule, as long as they respected the rights and privacy of their fellow citizens.

"We also in the future want this to be a place where people can learn to accept and control their abilities and use them if they choose, in the best possible ways. We hope one day we can use our newfound talents to educate and help rebuild the world with a combination of various abilities and science.

"I believe you may have experienced one of our combined aptitudes?"

"Yes, we both—Nicole and I, heard or felt is maybe a better word, the calling while we were meditating. The feeling was of nothing specific, merely the sentiment of safety and the word sanctuary. How did you manage to make that happen?"

Jim sat back with a smile on his face, proud their technique worked.

"One thing we have done already is to succeed in linking our minds to a sort of radio broadcasting device. We take turns at various times, two or three together, sitting at the machine and sending out our thoughts. I'm glad you heard the calling. You are the first to answer.

"I must admit my people have been watching you since you entered Westminster, and the reports are fascinating. Susan, we regret we didn't know what was happening to you, or we would have come to your rescue."

Jim looked over to Nicole and Stephen and asked how they knew Susan needed help and where to find her.

"I could sense it," Nicole answered.

When she neglected to elaborate more, he decided it best to wait until later to explore their abilities, assuming they stayed and joined the community.

"I'm sure you are all tired and would enjoy a comfortable, clean bed for a change. I hope you will choose to stay with us permanently, but that is not a decision you need to ponder and make immediately."

Jim stood to escort the group out to meet his assistant.

"I can have Debra show you to the rooms we have available for you, Nicole and Susan, so you can freshen up if you like before the evening meal."

Stephen was about to interrupt, but Jim continued with hardly a pause.

"Stephen, I'm sure you would like to stay with your sister, but we have dorms set up for the teenage boys over at the old community college building."

Nicole laughed, about to speak up, but Stephen answered much faster, and Jim thought the boy had been expecting separation from his sister. What Stephen said next, Jim would never have expected and it caused him to sit back in his chair.

"Nicole is not my sister; she is my fiancée, so I suggest you find a place where we can both stay together, or we leave right now."

Jim was taken aback for a moment and felt sure he had a look of disbelief on his face.

"I'm sorry, Stephen, but I believe you did say you were seventeen."

"That is correct, and Nicole is twenty, turning twenty-one. In less than two weeks."

"I'm so sorry, I just assumed—"

Stephen abruptly cut him off.

"I can assure you; our ages are as we have said, but Nicole and I have been together for more than a year, and we intend to be properly married someday. If it's a problem for you due to your beliefs, I understand, but it is what it is. I can assure you we are in love and have been for some time."

"I know Jim," Nicole added, "back before the event, whatever it was—our relationship would have been considered improper and, to some, illegal. Now, there are no more laws and what's happening out there is far worse than a twenty-year-old being in love with and having a sexual relationship with a seventeen-year-old."

Jim knew his face had flushed.

"I'm sorry, I meant no offense; I was merely surprised. I can assure you there will be no judgment made by me or anyone else here. There is room for you at a house we have set up for couples, any type of couples. So please go and relax and be my guests at dinner tonight. Debra will tell you all you need to know."

The professor chuckled to himself as he remembered their conversation. Things had changed since that day, and the four of them were now close friends. Nicole and Stephen loved to tease him and remind him of the conversation.

They had grown to be valuable assets over the next few years, and they were part of his advisory board. They led many training sessions with other town members to teach them how to improve and control their abilities and use them for the good of all. Stephen was a big proponent of strengthening your body and your mind. He developed strength training regimens for anyone who wanted to improve their physical abilities, which were popular in the town and a must for security. He would always argue you could not rely entirely on your mind talents alone to help you survive in this new world in which they now lived.

Another valuable training Stephen and Nicole brought to the community were the exercises. They both were capable of amazing things with their bodies while meditating. Their skills allowed them to go without food or water for much longer than would usually be possible while still using some of their abilities to manipulate the environment around them.

When it came time for an extra, unique spy to investigate the happenings in Philadelphia, Stephen became his first choice, and even Nicole believed their best option, but Jim had received word things may have taken a turn for the worse.

News from Philadelphia

Professor Oswald received word the Overlord's troops had captured Stephen—holding him prisoner in the fortress. It took time for the news to travel from Philadelphia, and the information he just received happened three weeks ago. Jim hoped Stephen wasn't already dead. His thoughts were interrupted when Debra excused herself and entered his office.

"Good evening, Professor, I heard about Stephen. Please try not to worry; he has been well-trained, young, and strong. He will be okay; I just know it."

"Thank you, Debra; I hope you are correct. You always are the optimist, and your bubbly charm always makes everything better. Do you have any good news for me this evening?"

"Yes, I do. Here is the detailed report concerning the new recruits and the expansion of the territory being helped and protected by Sanctuary. I have read the report, and it is excellent news throughout."

A smile crossed Jim's face. Debra shouldn't be reading the reports, and they both knew it, but neither cared. They were family, no matter what their titles suggested. However, the event hadn't changed the need for structure, and titles were a necessity, even if meaningless.

"Thank you, Debra. Could you ask Nicole to come to see me after she completes the evening classes?

"I will, Professor, and I will also have dinner sent in for you since it appears you are not planning to leave the office any time soon."

"You know me too well. Thank you."

After Debra left the room and quietly closed the door, he thought about Stephen and the last meeting they had together before he and Patrick began the mission.

They had talked at length about the dangers of the mission. Although Stephen did have extraordinary powers and a healthy, resilient body to protect himself against physical and mental torture, it remained a dangerous mission. The professor didn't like guns, but life made him a realist, and they did have access to many types of firearms. Stephen declined to take any weapons with him, as expected.

"You know I'm going to worry about you while you're gone, Stephen."

"I know, Jim, but please don't; you have enough here to worry about, like Nicole. Who is going to keep her in line while I'm gone?"

Jim smiled; he welcomed the humor and appreciated Stephen trying to improve his friend's mood. For one so young, he knew exactly what to say to lighten a mood. Nicole, who also attended the meeting, sat unexpectedly silent.

"This is my choice; I know what I'm doing, and it's not like I will be alone in Philly. The Philadelphia team will now consist of seven operatives, including Patrick, who will accompany me there. He and I have been working on a connection that, if successful, will allow us to partially communicate with each other over a distance equal to about three city blocks. Success has been spotty, but it's something. He is already working with the contacts in Philly, setting up a secure base."

"I know we have other operatives around the city Stephen," Jim replied, "but they are trying to stay hidden. Your idea of trying to flush out the situation by working your way into the fortress is a different situation entirely.

"How do you feel about this, Nicole? Are you on board with your husband putting himself in this much danger?"

"I will not lie and say I won't worry, but I know Stephen, and I know his abilities; he is the best person to try and work their way into the fortress. We need to know what's happening there and if there is any way for us to stop the Overlord before he becomes stronger and expands his territory even farther."

Nicole wondered if she was trying to convince Jim or herself. Her heart raced as she sat listening. It was something she could usually control.

"Jim, I know the risks, and you know my abilities and training. I agree with Nicole, and I know you do as well. Someone needs to get inside the fortress. We need to know the full scope of his abilities, and most importantly, we need to know his weaknesses. Everybody has them, regardless of any special ability bestowed upon them."

After a brief pause where Jim tried his best not to let his friendships and emotions get the better of him, he wished Stephen good luck on his mission.

A knock at the door awoke him from his thoughts. He knew Nicole had arrived.

"Please come in."

Nicole came into his office. He rose, and he greeted her with a hug. She sat in front of his desk with the usual smile of calmness on her face.

"How do you do it, Nicole? How do you remain so calm and outwardly worry-free while I sit here feeling knots in my stomach wondering what has been happening to Stephen?"

"If you would attend a couple of my meditation sessions, you might be able to relax more. The empathy you feel can be a curse or a blessing, and my meditation techniques can help you better channel all your abilities."

Jim never spoke much about his particular abilities, even with his friends, but Nicole knew one of them was a profound sense of empathy.

"I know, I counsel new people who come here all the time about learning how to cope with and use their abilities, but I don't heed my own advice. I maybe would have been a good politician if the event hadn't happened. Do as I say, not as I do!"

Nicole laughed as she reached out to grasp Jim's hands to comfort him.

"Stop worrying; he is fine. I can feel it. I would know if he were . . . well, you know, not fine. We need to give him time; eventually, he will have an opportunity to contact the other team members. You know he won't risk their exposure no matter what he has to endure to protect them, and you know he can endure a lot. It's one of the reasons you choose him for this mission."

"I know Nicole, and I know everything you say is true, but I can't help but be worried."

Nicole stood, ending the conversation before she lost emotional control.

"Now, your dinner is waiting, and Debra will kill me if I stay here too long, so if you feel better, it's time for me to go."

"Yes, I do feel better. I just wanted to make sure you were okay."

Nicole again assured him she was fine and advised him not to worry. She wished Debra a pleasant evening and went outside, stopped, and looked up at the bright night sky filled with stars. She wondered if Stephen could see the stars as well, or did they confine him in some dark prison. She wasn't completely truthful with Jim; Nicole knew Stephen was alive as fact, but she only felt he might be okay; she couldn't be certain.

Nicole began walking back to their house as she started thinking about her life after the event. It hadn't started well, and she continued to be more disturbed by what she had done before meeting Stephen than she ever admitted to him.

Nicole's Terror and Escape

Nicole had awakened the first morning after the event to find her head filled with voices, a jumble of words, and screams, which gave her a tremendous headache.

She lived in her parents' house in West Chester, Pennsylvania, a small town about ten miles southwest of Philadelphia, and attended West Chester University, studying marketing and business. She didn't have many friends outside of school, and her neighbors were all older couples and widows, except for the mid-thirties couple who moved in next door a few months ago.

Her parent's named her Nicole Elizabeth, and as usual for all Catholics, she added another name when she received Confirmation. Nicole then became Nicole Elizabeth Angelica—a mouthful that she heard often when in trouble while attending Saint Agnes Elementary School. Young Nicole had many friends through high school, but they all moved out of the area or attended far away colleges.

Nicole's parents were killed in a car crash by a drugged-out drunk almost nine months ago to the day. Their life insurance was more than adequate to cover her school costs and provide for a good portion of her future. Her aunt, the only other living relative other than her cousins, wanted Nicole to live with them in a town outside of Chicago. She respectfully declined and told her aunt she wanted to stay in her childhood house at least while she attended school, and then she would maybe go out to Chicago to look for a job.

Her neighbors tried to comfort her as best they could and help her out, but there wasn't much they could do, and the new neighbors were a little bit on the peculiar side. At various times, she had caught both of them looking at her in a way, which made her uncomfortable. One day while outside cleaning the front garden, getting it ready for spring planting, the woman named Gloria came over and started talking about how beautiful Nicole looked and what a waste it was she had no one special in her life.

Gloria had started talking about her sex life with her husband in graphic detail and even mentioned how they liked to invite others to join them when they became bored. Before Gloria went back into her house, she had patted Nicole on her ass and then stood at the door with her husband watching Nicole work. The disturbing encounter had occurred one week before the event. One week and two days before the nightmare would begin.

Nicole had spent the first day after the event in her bed, wishing for the voices to stop. She didn't put on the television or radio, and she barely heard the sounds of sirens starting to fill the air outside around the town.

The following morning, she realized the voices were still there but quieter. She could understand the voices more clearly, and what she heard made her sick. Such depravity wasn't something she experienced in her life, and she started to realize these voices were coming from somewhere outside her home. Shortly after she came to that realization, she found she could silence the voices by pushing them out of her mind. She didn't understand how she managed to do it, but how didn't matter. With the voices silenced, she felt ready to go outside and see what was happening.

When Nicole walked out of her house to stand on the porch, she first noticed the screaming and gunshots coming from all around the area. She stood there a few moments, unsure what to do, when Gloria called to her and told Nicole to come inside with them. It was no longer safe out on the streets for a young woman.

Nicole didn't want to go in their house. She had been invited many times and had always made up some sort of excuse or another. She said no, thank you, and moved to go back in her own house, but her body had another idea as she started walking over to Gloria. Before Nicole knew what had happened, she found herself inside their home, standing before Hamlin, Gloria's husband.

"Hello, Nicole, how nice of you to finally join us in our home."

Hamlin sat in front of her in a reclined lounge chair in nothing but a pair of skimpy yellowed underpants, smoking a cigarette. He put the cigarette out in the ashtray, raised the chair to the normal position, and slowly stood while staring intently into Nicol's eyes. He moved closer and began to play with her hair before running his hands down her shoulders. He smiled as he ran his now sweaty hands across her breasts before reaching down between her legs.

"Hey Casanova, how about you cool it for now. Time to play later."

Nicole wanted to run, wanted to cry, wanted to scream, but she could do nothing but stand there as Hamlin put his hands around her waist, pulled her close, and gave her a long kiss on her lips.

"Go upstairs . . . Yvette, yes, that will be your new name. Go upstairs to the backroom," he said to her after he sat back down. "Take off all your clothes and lay on the bed. Gloria will bring your new clothes up to you shortly."

Nicole didn't want to go upstairs, she didn't want to stay in their house, but she had no choice. To her horror, no matter how much she tried to stop herself, she began to walk up the stairs, and a few minutes later, she was lying naked on a dirty, stain-filled bed in a room with mirrors on the ceiling.

As she lay on the bed looking up at her naked body, she felt ashamed. She didn't understand how they could control her, and she became frightened, thinking of what was to follow. She needed to get out of the house, but she couldn't move off the bed, no matter how hard she tried.

A few minutes later, Gloria came into the room with an old box, which she put down on the dresser by the wall. Gloria came over to the bed and started running her hands up and down Nicole's body as tears began to fall down Nicol's cheeks and onto the yellowed pillow. Gloria leaned over and licked the tears from Nicol's face as she continued to move her hands up and down Nicol's now quivering body.

"We are going to have so much fun together, Yvette, but we don't want to rush these things. I think we will play with you first for a few days, a few weeks, or maybe a few months before we let you fully partake of the ecstasy of our bodies. Now put on your uniform and come downstairs, so you can make us our dinner."

The following month became the worst of her life—crueler than being stood up for her high school Junior prom, more terrible than even the death of her parents. The clothes in the box were a French Maid costume she had to wear every day as they forced Nicole to cook and clean for them, do their wash, and take care of their pets, one of which was a giant snake they would use in their sex games.

Day after day, they compelled her to watch them play their sick games and forced her to watch as they made men, women, boys, and girls do things to them that repulsed her. All she could do was observe and pray they didn't force her to participate in their dirty games, although Hamlin threatened it many times. He would touch her and lick her face as he whispered in her ear what he wanted to do to her and force her to do with him. He would tell Nicole, one day it will be your turn—one day, I will fill you with my joy, and you will scream in ecstasy.

As the weeks passed, one good thing began to happen. Nicole found she was starting to develop abilities, like the ones Gloria and Hamlin were using against her and their victims. She found she could move dust with her mind, and more importantly, Nicole found she could occasionally resist. She was careful not to let it show, but there were times she could not have done what they asked, times she maybe could have left, but she remained afraid. She knew if she weren't strong enough to get away successfully, they would punish her, and it would not be pleasant.

One day, during one of their sex games with a teenage boy they had forced into the house, she reached out with her mind and managed to take partial control of the boy. She could make him stop doing what they were telling him to do. Gloria thought the boy had the power to resist, and the more Gloria tried to force him to her will, the more Nicole forced him to resist, but they pushed too far.

The boy raised his hands to his head and screamed as blood started flowing from his ears before he collapsed on top of Hamlin. The young boy died, and it was her fault. The power play between her and Gloria became too much for his mind. Nicole stood there in shock, horrified at what she had caused, and trying not to let on it was her fault. At that moment, she vowed never to use another person to fight Gloria and Hamlin, but at least she had learned her abilities had grown greater, and her time to escape would eventually come.

A few days later, the time would come but not as she had expected. Gloria had gone out to try and find additional food. Their supplies were running low, and she started to worry. Hamlin figured it would be an excellent time to have the thing he had desired for weeks, while Gloria was out of the house.

Nicole stood before the sink in the kitchen, cleaning dishes, when Hamlin came in and grabbed her from behind. He ran his hands up and down her arms and legs as he started to pull the maid costume off her quivering body. She tried to resist, but he remained too strong for her. She desperately wished her abilities were strong enough to make him stop. Eventually, he removed all her clothes, turned her around, and stood in front of her, naked himself.

He compelled her to lie on the kitchen table, and he began to climb on top. She felt him rub her between her legs, preparing to force himself upon her with pure lust in his eyes. She couldn't let this happen, and she screamed in panic, which he returned with a slap across her face. Now terrified, in pain, and angry, she screamed again, but this time something happened.

Across the room, lying by the sink, lay a carving knife she had been cleaning. It started to shake on the counter as if shaking from an earthquake, and then it quickly shot across the room and plunged into Hamlin's neck. He screamed as he jumped off Nicole and pulled the knife out of his neck, which became the last mistake he would ever make. While his blood shot out of his punctured artery, she could feel him trying to hurt her with his mind, but she pushed back and held him at bay. She watched as he became weaker and died; finally, his grip on her ended for good.

Nicole stood there paralyzed, not knowing what to do, when she heard the front door open as Gloria came back from searching for supplies. Nicole yelled out to her; they were in the kitchen as she pulled the knife out of Hamlin's body and stood behind the door, waiting for the last of her tormentors to enter the room.

Gloria opened the door about to give an order when Nicole screamed from behind her target and plunged the knife deep into her back. Gloria spun around, eyes wide open, and reached out with her mind. Nicole instantly felt dizzy and experienced pain in her head like nothing she had experienced before. Gloria tried to speak but couldn't, and as her captor sank to the kitchen floor, the pain gradually left Nicole, and she knew, finally, she was free from the horror.

Nicole could think of nothing except to get out of the house. She ran out the front door, not even thinking about the fact she remained naked, and she thanked God that no one else was around. She knew she had to leave and go away from there quickly and find somewhere safe. She ran to her house, took a quick shower to get the filth and blood off her body, and got dressed. She found a backpack she hadn't used in years, filled it with some clothes, food, and other items she might need, and left what had been her home for the final time.

Nicole was about to run away as fast as she could when she felt a familiar touch in her mind—Gloria. Her tormenter remained alive and still tried to control her. Nicole wasn't going to leave without finishing the job she started, so she went back into the house and found Gloria sitting on the floor, trying to reach the knife protruding from her back.

"No, you don't bitch, you are going to die like your fucking bastard of a husband."

Nicole went upstairs, grabbed some rope from the playroom, took it downstairs, and tied Gloria to the kitchen table. All the while, she could feel Gloria trying to take control, but Nicole was now too strong to let that happen. When she finished tying Gloria to the table, she grabbed the lamp oil from under the kitchen sink they used in fancy lanterns around the house for light. Nicole poured the oil on Gloria's head and then poured a trail of oil out to the living room while Gloria pleaded for her life in a gurgling blood-filled voice.

Nicole took the matches out of her pocket she had grabbed from the kitchen, lit one, and stared at it, hesitating only an instant as she thought about the fact, she was going to take another life. It wasn't for self-defense; it was pure, straightforward revenge, and she liked it. She let the match drop from her hand, watched it fall into the oil, and continued to watch as the flame followed the path into the kitchen. Gloria screamed as the fire hit her; Nicole smiled as she turned and left the house forever.

Like her days in school, when they had fire drills, she stood in the street facing the house. Eventually, smoke came out of the windows, followed by fire. Nicole watched the fire spread from her neighbor's house to her parents' house, the home in which she had been born and raised. As she watched the fire consume her once happy home and spread down the row, tears fell from her eyes before she turned and walked away.

Nicole's Journey

A week later, Nicole stood outside the town of Quarryville, on RT 372, staring at the sign welcoming her to town as she tried to decide what to do next. The last week had been uneventful as she traveled roughly westward, passing smoldering fires, dead bodies, and abandoned cars. She thought about going east to the ocean but felt there wouldn't be many resources there or along the way. A girl had to eat, even if it was canned goods and granola bars.

She stayed away from major roads and population centers as she traveled. She didn't want any confrontations, and she didn't want to end up being someone's slave again, maybe this time forever. She occasionally felt pain and anguish from others, but she suppressed those feelings as much as possible, although she would wake up at night, sensing her name, called from a distance.

She realized she couldn't stand out in the open forever, so she decided to go into town. She was low on water and granola bars, so she felt she had no other choice. She decided to stay on the road but be vigilant as she started walking. There might be someplace along the way to get supplies, which would mean she wouldn't have to go all the way into town, which would make her happy, but no such luck. The only things on the way into town were houses, a few more dead bodies, and an occasional dog.

RT 372 became E. State Street as she entered the town proper, and ahead of her stood what she was looking for, a convenience store, and it looked like it may still have some needed supplies. When Nicole entered the store, she found a huge mess, and she doubted she would find anything there safe to eat or drink until she decided to look in the back storeroom.

She found boxes of granola bars, energy bars, fruit juices, and water. It looked like someone had already taken some of the bars and maybe left in a hurry, leaving a few scattered along the floor. Nicole quickly grabbed what she needed, had a bite to eat and some water before leaving, and then headed out the back door into the beginning of a horrifying afternoon.

Nicole had only walked a few yards into the woods behind the store when she heard voices from farther ahead. She hesitated a moment, then started to move away. As she walked, she heard a scream from the same direction and felt pain in her right arm as the cry intensified. The pain wasn't great, but it did hurt as if her arm was exposed to heat and burned far worse than in the past when using sports creams on her lousy bicep and elbow.

Nicole heard another scream as the pain in her arm worsened, and she knew she couldn't leave, so she headed deeper into the forest. She went about forty yards when she came to the edge of a clearing and stumbled. She had intended to stay behind the bushes and evaluate the situation; however, she inadvertently tripped on a tree root and fell into a clearing dropping her backpack in the process.

"Well, well, what do we have here," a man's voice spoke as she stood back onto her feet.

What she saw made her sick to her stomach. A young man, probably mid-teens, stood next to a fire. He wore a long-sleeved shirt, which was on fire. Most of the scorched right sleeve smoked, and she could see flames down by the boy's wrist. From his eyes, tears were falling as he started to mouth the words, help me!

"What the fucking hell are you doing, don't just stand there, help him!"

Nicole started to move toward the boy but found she couldn't move. It only took a split second for her to understand. The man, or the woman behind him, had abilities they were using to stop her, and worse, to torture the boy.

The man spoke again.

"You are not going to do anything bitch, but watch, and when we finish with him, it will be your turn."

Nicole pushed again to move, but this time toward the man, not the boy, and she was successful as she lunged toward him. The man raised the club he held in his hand over his head to use against Nicole. As he brought the club down, Nicole quickly rolled onto the ground, which caused the man to miss her head by only a few inches.

Down on the ground and unable to get up in time, Nicole watched the man bring the club over his head. Before he could strike, she felt something inside her, like the feeling at the house before she escaped. As the man brought the club down, she reached out and was able to stop him from completing the movement.

The man screamed in anger, which caused the woman to grab another club from the ground and come after Nicole. As the woman advanced behind the man, Nicole was able to take control of him and caused the man to swing the club behind and into the woman's stomach. She collapsed to the ground in pain, holding her hands on her stomach. When the enraged woman started to get up, Nicole caused the man to bring the club down hard on the woman's skull, killing her.

"No, Betty, Betty, wake up; I didn't mean it; she made me.

"You fucking whore bitch, you will pay—"

Nicole took control of him again and stopped the man from talking as she forced him to pick the club off the ground and bring it down hard on his left foot, and then his right. The man fell to the ground writhing in pain, but Nicole hadn't finished with him yet. She made him bring the club up again and bring it down repeatedly on his knees until she could see blood coming through his jeans.

She stopped the man from beating himself and looked for the boy to help him, but he had run away during her fight with the two insane people. She hoped he would be okay, but she could smell the lingering stench of burning flesh, and she realized he would probably die from an infection. She hoped he would not linger too long in pain.

Nicole turned back to the man as a couple of dogs came into the clearing, probably drawn by the smell of burning flesh.

"I could kill you right now, walk away and never think of you again, but instead, I think I'll leave you to my hungry friends over there. Goodbye."

Nicole picked up the backpack she had dropped when she tripped over the tree root and began to walk away as the man crawled behind her. She had only walked a short distance before she heard the man scream, and she kept walking with a big smile on her face.

A day later, Nicole woke from a dream in which she relived the events with the boy. In her dream, the boy was standing with her as they together were forcing the boy's former tormentors to light themselves on fire, She stood there laughing while the couple cried out in pain.

The experience slightly sickened her because, in her dream, Nicole enjoyed the pain she inflicted on the couple. She knew it was wrong, but she also knew they were terrible people and deserved their punishment. She decided then and there she would use her powers to defend those who couldn't protect themselves, and she would burn and kill anyone who tried to inflict suffering on others, including anyone who would try to stop her.

A week later, she had crossed from Pennsylvania into Maryland, following along RT 222. She was a couple of miles outside the town of Oakwood when she heard two men talking from a short distance away. She decided to move away in a different direction when she heard one of the men say the word, 'rape.' She worried they might have had a prisoner there; they were going to abuse, so she slowly walked closer to hear what they were saying.

"She was a beauty, and oh, the things I wanted to do to her. I could have used my powers to force her to give me the time of my life."

The other man started to laugh and then said, "Maybe next time you can fill her with your overwhelming charm, but for now, let's go take care of business so we can eat."

The two men, one many years older than the other, got up as Nicole moved out of the bushes to stand in front of them, blocking their way.

"You two pigs are going to do nothing but pay for your crimes. Where is the girl?"

When the men didn't immediately answer, she pushed them to the ground with her mind. It was the first time she used her powers in that way, and it wasn't easy.

"I'll ask one more time. Where is the girl?"

"What, girl?" The older man asked as he tried without success to stand.

"The girl your friend talked about raping."

The other, younger man who Nicole now noticed was cut and bandaged in many places, stood ready to defend himself.

"There is no girl, honey," the older one said. "That was a dream, but if you want to make my dream a reality, I'm game."

The older man now slowly stood up all the way while the second man grabbed his friend's arm to get him to stop. He realized they might have been in trouble, and he wasn't wrong.

"You are both pigs, and I'm not stupid. I'm sure it wasn't a dream that cut you like that, and I heard you say you were going to take care of business."

The older man raised his hand to point behind another grouping of bushes, but before he could say anything, Nicole had run out of patience. She screamed; both men raised their hands to their heads and collapsed dead on the ground a few seconds later.

Nicole immediately went through the bushes expecting to find a girl tied up, but what she saw made her regret what she had done for only a short moment. Lying on the ground was a deer barely alive, with a tree branch stuck in its side. She didn't know if they had hurt the deer or were only taking advantage of the situation and finishing the job to use the deer for food.

It doesn't matter what they were doing with the deer; they were disgusting men who needed to die for thinking about raping a girl. Only an appalling pig would dream such a thing.

In another time, another place, Nicole would have understood how wrong her thinking had become, and she maybe would have realized she suffered from a form of post-traumatic stress syndrome, but not now. In her mind, what she had done was justified. She would protect those who couldn't defend themselves.

Nicole continued her journey, still not knowing where it would take her, yet feeling compelled to go in a specific direction. She went south along RT 222 until RT 1, which she found littered with cars containing dead bodies. The only way to cross the Susquehanna River was on the highway bridge, so she waited till nightfall, and when she felt it safe, she crossed.

She continued for a couple more days and had stopped one night outside the town of Dublin Mill, along RT 440. A storm was approaching, so she wanted to be somewhere inside and had found an empty farmhouse that looked and felt safe.

The following day, after having a couple of energy bars and some water from bottles she had found in the house, she started again on her way west along RT 440. She hadn't gone too far when she heard a dog barking and whining in pain. She followed the sound and became horrified to find two young girls, not even teenagers, using their abilities to torture a small brown dog.

They were laughing as they were seemingly forcing the dog to put its head into a deep puddle of water from the night's thunderstorm, and Nicole could tell the dog was having trouble breathing from the water in its lungs.

Nicole didn't even confront the girls before screaming and reaching out with her mind like she had done to the men before, but this time she concentrated on pushing the girls as hard as possible. The two girls flew through the air, and both smashed hard against a stand of trees, with one girl ending up impaled on a branch; both were dead.

Nicole awakened from her rage-induced ability trance to see the dog walk over to one of the dead girls and start to lick the young girl's hand hanging down within his reach.

Immediately Nicole broke down, her guilt unbearable, as she fell to the muddy ground and began to cry. She wondered what kind of life these girls had before the event, as she now called it. This dog might have been their pet, and though what they were doing was wrong, the dog couldn't have realized, and he now missed his companions.

What have I done, what have I become? I murdered two young girls, for what? I deemed myself judge, jury, and executioner. I'm as bad as Hamlin and Gloria, only in a different way. I want to die; I can't go on.

She lay there on the muddy ground crying off and on for hours as she stared at the dog now lying at the feet of his dead companions. Eventually, she fell into a haunted sleep in the mud.

Nicole didn't sleep well that evening, but not because of the cold mud, which made her bed. She remained for hours, haunted by visions of the two girls running through a clearing of tall grass in pink and green fancy dresses, chased by their dog. In her dream, she watched as red stains appeared on the dresses, and the girl's skin began to melt from their faces.

Nicole ran the other way, right into the two men she had killed days before. They pushed her to the ground and picked up an impossibly large rock they were going to drop on her head. She began to scream and woke up still screaming as the sun started to hurt her now wide-open eyes.

The first thing Nicole noticed when she could see clearly was a sign along the road giving directions to Rocks National Park. She knew these roads had looked familiar, and now she understood. She had visited the nature center many times in the Rocks National Park—the two summers she had spent with her aunt and cousin when they lived in Pylesville, a town only a few miles up the road.

The cabin.

The thought came to her, and she began to understand why she had come this way. The Nature Center cabin was also a fully-equipped, long-term ranger station. She decided it would be the perfect place to go and hide from what remained of the world. She wanted to hide, not to protect herself, but to protect the world, or at least the local area, from her misguided judgments and damned abilities.

Nicole slowly got up out of the now mostly dry mud, brushed herself off as well as possible, and headed along RT 543 north, until she came to Cherry Hill Road, RT 646 west. She followed the road for the entire day, and by nightfall, she stood at the entrance to the park.

She knew there had been a visitor's center up the road, but she had a feeling or sensed it would be a bad idea, so she headed into the woods, hoping to find her way before total darkness. She continued for another two hours in light only from an almost full moon until she collapsed exhausted in front of the cabin door, where she spent the night.

She awoke the next morning, not remembering having any dreams or how she eventually found her way to the cabin. While she lay on the ground in front of the cabin door, fully coming awake, she felt lucky no one else was around.

No, it wasn't luck. I knew this would be safe, just as I knew how to find my way here.

Nicole found her backpack lying a few feet away. An animal of some sort found it during the night and helped itself to a couple of her energy bars. She cleaned the mess out of the pack and then went to open the door, but of course, she found it locked.

Not a problem, I hope!

The ranger stationed there when she visited those many summers ago had lost his key in the woods a few times, so he had gotten one of those fake rocks people use to hide house keys in their garden. He had told her he knew it wasn't a brilliant thing to do for a house, but he felt sure it wouldn't be a problem with so many rocks lying around the cabin. It was, after all, merely an old rundown cottage in the woods.

Her memory was now a bit rusty. She vaguely remembered in what area to look, and after ten minutes of kicking rocks, she found the right one, and happily, the key remained. She opened the door, not surprised to find little had changed, other than the fact the cabin had been abandoned before the event. The main room still looked the same, with several wooden chairs and an empty desk with a lamp. She tried the light and was surprised to find electricity still coming into the cabin—and the bulb even worked.

The cabin had a kitchen with a small refrigerator and a stove powered by propane. Nicole plugged in the fridge and smiled as the sound of the little compressor filled the cabin. After a minute of looking around, she found a few matchbooks, and she used a match to confirm the stove worked. The room did contain a fireplace but having a regular cooktop for meals was something she figured would come in handy, especially after she discovered a couple of pots and pans in the cabinet.

For as long as the propane lasts, anyway.

Next, she went to the bathroom and rejoiced to find the water working in the sink and shower. Her skin had an oily sheen mixed with dried mud, and the idea of a shower was like heaven. She used the matches to re-light the water heater's pilot and, when ready, spent the next ten minutes enjoying the warm water. She knew she couldn't afford to waste whatever gas remained on a wasteful luxury, but she needed this and decided to endure cold showers in the future.

After being cleaned and dried, she felt free of Hamlin and Gloria. They would never haunt her future dreams.

There is just one more thing I need to check before looking around the exterior of the cabin.

She knew there was a bed in a separate room since the rangers were stationed there for weeks at a time. Nicole opened the door to the room and yelled with delight as she saw the bed. As she sat on the thin mattress, raising a cloud of dust, she realized it was the first she heard her voice since she screamed at the girls. Her voice sounded unfamiliar, harsher, harder, nasty, making her think she was no longer innocent—she had become a murderous woman.

The thought of the girls made her again cry as she became enveloped with guilt. She didn't deserve a bed; she didn't deserve a warm shower or hot food to eat. She deserved to rot in hell if such a place existed.

"Nicole . . . Nicole, hello?"

Nicole had stopped for a moment to sit on a bench and enjoy the evening as she thought more about her journey. She had become so lost in her thoughts she didn't notice Susan sit beside her on the bench and call her name.

"Hi Susan, I'm so sorry, I was thinking about . . . things. I didn't even realize you were there. You would think my abilities would prevent that from happening. How are you doing? I haven't seen you for a couple of weeks."

"I'm doing well. I returned yesterday from out west, where I helped our forward scouts and security learn how to resist others' abilities."

"Is that going well? Are they able to learn?"

Susan hesitated a moment. Nicole felt she was unsure of how to answer.

"Some are better and quicker than others, but I believe it is a latent ability in everyone."

"If that's true, Susan, it could dramatically change the world, almost as dramatically as the event itself. If everyone could resist the commands and urgings of others, we could start to use the other new abilities we have to repair society and build a great new world where the abilities are used only for the good of all."

"It's a wonderful vision, Nicole, and one that may be possible someday."

Susan sat for a moment, lost in her thoughts, while she also enjoyed the night air. She wanted to ask Nicole about Stephen, but she didn't want to be reminding Nicole of what she was probably trying not to have running through her mind. Off in the distance, she could hear an owl and a few other night birds, and she wondered not for the first time if the event had caused any changes in the animal kingdom. A slight breeze flowed from the south as they watched the full moon emerge from the clouds to brighten the rolling landscape.

"He's been captured by the Overlord. That was the last bit of intel we received."

Susan wasn't surprised; Nicole knew what she wanted to ask.

Nicole continued, "But I know he is okay, at least for now. Our bond is strong, and I can feel he is alive, and I believe . . . well. Only time will tell if he is indeed okay, and being here, with no way to help, is driving me crazy. Which is probably why I didn't hear you talking to me," she laughed.

"It's nice to hear you laughing, and good to know your bond is still strong with Stephen.

"It's getting a little cold, and I do have mission reports to write by morning. Don't sit here too long; go home and try to relax."

"I will. Thank you, Susan, for caring; you are a good friend."

"I will always love and care for the two people who saved my life."

Susan walked away to her home, but Nicole wasn't yet ready to be alone in her house without Stephen. She sat there, thinking now about the day they first met.

A couple of weeks later, Nicole completed cleaning the cabin as best she could. She found an American flag in a cabinet and decided to hang it above her new home. In addition, she completed a few successful supply missions and now had ample provisions.

She had picked up some new clothes, food, of course, matches, another ax, and a calendar. The store where she found the calendar had a battery-operated clock that still displayed the date and time. Knowing the date the clock displayed made her feel better. She couldn't part with the idea of time, even though she knew it now meant nothing, but she told herself the calendar would help her keep track of the seasons. It would be essential to know when winter approached.

Nicole also had spent the last few weeks working on her meditation skills to help her cope with what she had done in her travels. She had become able to control some things around her as she meditated, and she became able to slow her body down and spend almost ten hours in meditation without any need for food, water, or even a bathroom break.

Another thing she accomplished with her abilities, for convenience's sake and cleanliness, was to stop her menstrual cycle altogether. Not worrying about or tracking her period was a small victory, but even small victories mattered now.

The morning and night before had been rainy, and she enjoyed the sound of the wind blowing through the pine trees surrounding the cabin.

After having a small breakfast, Nicole lay down on the hard floor and began a new meditation session. She was determined to break the ten hours record she had set the previous week.

A few hours later, while deep in her meditation, she suddenly woke and sat up as if ready to attack an intruder, but as usual, the cabin remained otherwise empty. The structure was out of the way, and the trouble up front never seemed to care about heading her way, but something wasn't right; something approached.

No, she realized not something, someone!

The hour grew late, and Nicole started to have a chill. She was tired of sitting on her ass, accomplishing nothing, so she got up and headed home to get ready early for bed. She had a busy day in the morning, helping train the newest community members, and she wanted to be at peak performance.

A few minutes later, Nicole entered her empty home. Walking into the house reminded her how much she missed Stephen. She knew his mission was critical, but she constantly worried about him even though she could feel his presence.

She went to the kitchen and poured herself a glass of wine, which she drank in one long sip before heading to the bedroom. The bed felt warm and inviting, but even with the wine, Nicole found she couldn't yet drift off to sleep, so she lay there thinking about how she met Stephen, how he saved her from herself and how their relationship evolved and led them here to Sanctuary.

Meeting Stephen

An hour later, after realizing someone approached who needed help, Nicole stood watching and waiting in the woods. Water poured down her hooded raincoat while she continued looking for—the person. All she could sense was someone, which caused her to experience a frustration she hadn't felt in some time. The person could be male, female, older, or younger; she could do nothing but wait and hope she wasn't sensed or spotted by the group up the road at the visitor's center.

Another half an hour had passed before, finally, the person came into view. It looked like a young boy in his teens, dripping wet from the downpour with bleeding cuts on his upper body, some showing through his torn shirt. Nicole watched and began to panic as he started walking toward the visitor center. The people there were trouble, and she knew they would do unspeakable things to this young boy, just for fun. She had to stop him, but she didn't want to expose herself if anyone else watched.

The next thing Nicole knew, she felt a connection to him, and she somehow, without trying, made him stop. She closed her eyes and pictured him walking toward her in the woods. When Nicole again opened her eyes, he walked in her direction.

She was as shocked as he appeared to be, but she didn't let it show. She told him to follow her or get caught by the thugs in the welcome center—his choice. After a few words back and forth, she walked away deeper into the dripping wet forest and toward the cabin as he followed.

When they arrived at the cabin, Nicole told the boy where to put his things and encouraged him to use the shower to clean his wounds. As he walked away, she realized he had a well-built body for a boy of his age, and she started feeling things she quickly suppressed. She realized there wasn't a towel in the bathroom, so she quietly put one in there and set up a cot for him in the main room.

When he came out of the bathroom, she warned him about the splinters on the floor while trying not to stare at him. She repeatedly called him kid, even though he had told her his name. Calling Stephen, kid, reminded her he was a young man—no, a boy.

They spent a few more minutes in conversation. Nicole warned him about the group at the visitor's center, told her she was going to bed, and ordered no lights. Alone in the bedroom, she couldn't get him out of her thoughts. She felt glad to have some company, but she had concerns about the feelings she had experienced.

He's barely fifteen years old, if that. You need to stop these feelings before it becomes a problem.

She went to bed in hopes of putting him out of her mind, but her dreams had other ideas.

In the next few weeks, Nicole tried to suppress her surprising feelings about him as much as possible. She continued to mostly call him kid, thinking using his name would bring them closer together in a way her mind didn't want even though her body wanted otherwise. He spent a lot of time exercising and running through the forest, which worried her. They didn't need anyone seeing him and coming to investigate. The trouble down the road had been content to stay at the center, but that could change.

After a couple more weeks passed, she took him on a supply run, including getting him some new clothes. He was quickly growing out of what he had brought. She then explained to him about the garden she expected him to work and maintain to earn his keep.

The weather turned warmer, and when he worked in the garden, he often took off his shirt, which only made her feelings toward him stronger, and she became certain she could feel something from him as well.

He practiced meditation as she did, although he wasn't as experienced, so she started helping him with his meditation and yoga, which he used to learn how to control his body. They started spending more time together, meditating, which Nicole didn't mind.

Unfortunately, Nicole tried too hard to hide her feelings, which led her to say something to Stephen; she still regretted all this time later. He had come in from running during a heavy rainstorm, trailing mud, and water over the cabin's floor.

"You had better be planning on cleaning up that mess yourself, I'm not your mommy, and I'm not going to clean up after you."

Oh my God, I can't believe I said that to him. I can feel the pain I caused him as if it was my own. Stephen, I'm so sorry!

He fell to the floor with his hands over his face and cried. Nicole felt like the worst bitch she had ever known, but she couldn't let it show. However, she went over to him, hugged him, and apologized, but he asked her to leave him alone, which she also thought best. She went into her room, threw herself onto the bed, and began to cry, hoping he couldn't hear her in the next room.

Things were a little strained between them for the next couple of weeks. They still did meditation exercises together, but other than that, Stephen was spending a lot of time alone, running, and building his body in the woods. She would try not to stare at him when he returned, but he looked so good to her, and she realized when he wasn't there, she missed him tremendously.

One day she saw him trying to cut his hair, and she offered to help as nothing more than a gesture of friendship. After cutting his hair, at his request, she applied shaving cream to his head and shaved him gently. Her feeling and sex drive rose in her again; she knew at another time what she wanted would have been taboo and even illegal, but she began not to care.

He may be a boy, but he had the body and the mind of a man.

Nicole wiped the remaining cream from his head, and then without thinking what she was doing, she put her hands on his shoulders and began to give him a massage. She could tell by looking down, Stephen enjoyed her hands on him, so she continued. She moved her hands down his chest and into his shorts. He said nothing, but he also didn't resist or pull away.

Nicole moved in front of him, pulled him up into her arms, and proceeded to kiss him like she had kissed no other man in her life. After the kiss, neither spoke; she led him into the cabin to her room, where they made love for the first of many times.

Afterward, he told her that day was his birthday; he had turned sixteen and no longer remained a virgin. In another time, another place, now worlds away, she would have been concerned, but not in this new world in which they now lived.

Their relationship changed, and they confided in each other the things they had done to survive. Stephen remained upset at what he had done even though she would have done the same if not worse from what he told Nicole. She told him of her journey but couldn't bring herself to say to him about the little girls she killed.

A few weeks later, Stephen had made a little ring out of string, which he placed on her finger as he bent down on one knee and asked her to marry him. Nicole had cried as she said yes, and as she began to cry again, thinking about that day, Nicole absent-mindedly played with the piece of string she still wore on her finger as she lay there recalling the memory.

Months passed as summer changed to fall and winter set in, but it mattered little to them. They had continued to grow their abilities together, and they could spend much time out in the cold without any ill effects on their bodies.

Winter changed to spring, and their abilities continued to grow. They both felt the calling to Sanctuary and knew it was time to move on. After a couple of weeks of preparation, they began the journey that eventually led them to the next chapter of their lives. They had made a new friend along the way, and as Nicole lay there, she realized how much she had enjoyed her short conversation with Susan. It had been a while since they talked, and Nicole realized she needed the companionship.

She recalled how the people of Sanctuary had accepted them into the community and how quickly they became close friends and allies with Jim. They were assigned a house and started teaching their meditation techniques to others in the town.

They had been officially married a short time later and celebrated their second anniversary before Stephen began his mission in Philly. She loved and missed him so much, and as she drifted off to sleep, she reached out and could feel his mind also falling to a night of restless sleep.

Welcome to the Resistance

The following week was uneventful as Nicole continued her training classes helping the new members of the community learn how to manage their various abilities. Working with them helped keep her mind off Stephen and enabled her not to feel so lonely.

She had finished the morning class when she received a note inviting her to have lunch with Jim in his office. She knew such an invite meant he had a new project for her, he received further information about Stephen, or some other situation for which he needed her assistance. The information shared with her at the meeting surprised and intrigued Nicole—so much for uneventful.

Jim wasn't in his office when Nicole arrived, and she felt too concerned to sit down. She paced back and forth in the small office, wondering what could be wrong. She couldn't sense anything wrong with Stephen, but their connection wasn't perfect. Jim may have learned something new about to happen; Stephen may not even be aware of the development.

Finally, five minutes later, Jim came into his office, sat at his desk, and motioned Nicole to sit in the chair in front of his desk.

"I'm sorry about the delay getting here; I had another matter needing attention.

"Just spit it out; what's wrong? What happened to Stephen?"

A concerned look spread across his face.

"Nothing I know of; I'm so sorry it didn't occur to me you might think I had news about Stephen. Again, I'm sorry, but this does concern Stephen, in a way. The time will be coming soon when we will need to go to Philadelphia and take care of Jonathan, and Stephen is a significant part of the operation."

Nicole was intrigued and a bit annoyed since she knew nothing of this plan.

"Stephen and I, as well as others, have planned this operation, and Stephen getting caught was part of the plan. He is our inside man, and we have many operatives outside the fortress monitoring the situation. Susan has trained them all to be immune to others' powers."

"What, Susan never mentioned this to me, only that she trained some forward scouts."

"She has been sworn to secrecy. It wasn't necessary before to bring you into this plan. I had decided more than a year ago to keep most of what I'm telling you limited to a few people. Many here would not approve, but we cannot put our heads in the sands and do nothing. Let me start with a little history.

"I knew we couldn't build a safe community without also having the ability to defend what we were building. I was never a military man; I spent most of my life earning my degree to become a professor—I prefer to teach. I do know; however, the best offense is a good defense, so I created a secret group called the Resistance, separate from Sanctuary. They are in Creagerstown just up the road."

"I thought that was only a base of operation for our scouting teams and security."

"That is, Nicole, part of what they do, but since being set up, they have also been, shall we say, the military arm of our town. They not only scout and patrol, but they also seek out and engage troops loyal to

Jonathan."

"We have defeated many of his scouting and abduction squads, but we think he may be getting wise to our presence. We have tried to throw him off by sending teams out to other areas north and south of the city, but we think he knows his enemies are out to the southwest of Philadelphia. Thankfully we are sure he doesn't know exactly where."

Our people are primarily well-trained former military. We recruited many individuals over the last year and added them to the ranks of our soldiers; some have never even been to Sanctuary. Jonathan's troops are mostly untrained and weak-minded. He can't afford to surround himself with too many who could seek to overthrow him. We aren't even sure how he keeps the people and troops he has in line and obedient. We have come up with some theories, all of which are horrible to contemplate.

Jim got up from his chair, grabbed two cups from the cabinet, and poured them some coffee. The pause would allow Nicole to digest all he explained. He could tell Nicole was a bit surprised by all he had told her so far. When he sat back down, he continued.

"Susan has worked with all the troops to give them the capability not to be influenced or controlled by others' abilities; however, it isn't perfect and probably useless against Jonathan."

"Give them the capability? Don't you mean trained them how to resist?"

"No. Please don't be mad toward Susan, or me for that matter, for not explaining this to you before. The defense is not something, in most cases, a person can learn, as originally thought. It is something a brain has to be altered to achieve."

Nicole sat there stunned, a little angry, and a bit concerned, as Jim continued.

"She had learned how to alter a person's mind to have this power when she was traveling with Damon and her brother."

"Brother! She never mentioned a brother."

"Yes, I know. Susan kept it a secret. I think it is too painful to share. He died when they were trying to get away from one of Jonathan's abduction squads. She had learned how to make him able to resist before he perished. She thinks it may have been because they were siblings; she could extend her ability to him, but what she learned before he died enabled her to bring out the capability in others. Susan was trying to foster the skill in Damon when the man you killed captured them.

"To get to the point of our meeting. Susan has completed doing her part; now, I need you to do yours. I would like you to go to the base and teach as many of our soldiers in the Resistance as possible to control their bodies. We need them to be ready to go without food, without sleep, and to be able to endure the elements the way you and Stephen taught yourselves.

"Things are coming to a head. We need to move soon. Jonathan has announced he will be taking a bride, and we think the wedding would be a perfect time to strike. When we strike, we want you to be part of the strike force, assigned the mission to rescue Stephen, which means while you are training them, they will be training you how to fight."

Nicole sat there, not sure what to say. She was upset they lied to her; and that Susan couldn't confide in her. She also had strong concerns about their community becoming militaristic. However, she did realize Jonathan's rule over helpless individuals needed to end before worrying about building a proper future.

"I'm in. I will do whatever I can and whatever I need to do to help."

If I can. I may have created a little problem that would prevent me from fighting.

Jim interrupted her thoughts.

"Great!"

He went to the door and asked Susan to come in and join them. She immediately went to Nicole, who had stood up, and she gave Nicole a huge hug, which Nicole returned.

"I'm sorry, Nicole, I hadn't confided in you earlier, but you have enough to deal with, and we didn't want to burden you more, but now we need you."

"Please sit, ladies; there is another development."

"We have been contacted by a woman named Mary Croy. She says she is from the group called the Abolitionist, and she wants to talk. I don't know what this is about, but she is waiting for us at Creagerstown. Can you be ready to go in an hour?"

Both responded, yes. Jim stood behind his desk and had one last thing to say.

"Nicole, welcome to the Resistance."

The Ride to Creagerstown

Nicole gazed out the window of the military-grade Jeep as she thought about the last four years of her life. It read like a sci-fi novel with twists and turns she could never have foreseen. She felt lucky to be alive, and for that, she was grateful, but if she could re-set time and somehow prevent this all from happening, she knew she would, even though she would probably never have met and certainly never married Stephen.

Nicole loved him more than she could ever have imagined, and she feared he would be hurt or killed during the events coming to a head. Could she go on now without him if he didn't survive? Far better maybe to never know his love than to bear the pain of loss. She had already lost too much in her life.

She was momentarily distracted by a family of deer frolicking in the woods as the caravan passed. The deer were oblivious to all the turmoil, and she envied them their ignorance. They didn't have to worry about near-impossible tasks. Could Sanctuary and the Resistance successfully take down the Overlord of Bartram Fortress? He was extremely powerful, and they were, in comparison, weak. Yes, they had a variety of individuals with a diverse set of abilities, and they had, according to Jim, a well-trained army at their disposal, but would it be enough?

If they did succeed, what then? Would everyone who served Jonathan be happy to be set free, or would they be disappointed they could no longer carry on with their sadistic ways? Her journey to Sanctuary showed the worst of humanity, including the worst of herself. Destroying the

Overlord would not instantly make the world perfect, but it would be a start.

And what of the new life she may be carrying? A small part of Nicole regretted having allowed her menstrual cycle to restart, but if something happened to Stephen, she had wanted a piece of him still in her life. They had only been together one time after she allowed her cycle to resume, but she knew, one time is all it takes.

I may not even be pregnant. I should stop worrying about what may be, at least for now.

Nicole pushed the memories of her relationship with Stephen out of her mind and thought about this person they would soon meet.

Abolitionist group? How exactly do they plan to abolish the abilities? They could end up being worse than Jonathan.

'Nicole, Nicole . . . hello."

"Oh, what? Oh, I'm sorry, I was daydreaming and didn't realize you were talking to me. What did I miss, Jim?"

"I was talking about the Abolitionist group. We did know of their existence and had been watching them as best we could. I don't know of Mary firsthand, but she does match the description of a woman they call the Priestess."

"It sounds like a religious cult."

"Yes, Susan, it is. The leader is a former reverend who has turned the idea of living without using abilities into a religion that appears to have quickly become a cult."

Nicole began to worry more about Mary's motives.

"So, what do they want with us?"

"That is an important question. I hope we can get some straight answers from this woman. Should be fun, I have never met a Priestess before, and I hear she is pretty."

"Jim, we need to get you a girlfriend," Nicole laughed as she once more turned her gaze to the woods.

She didn't see Jim look into his rearview mirror and give Susan a wink and a little smile.

Jim drove the Jeep into Creagerstown, and Nicole thought it looked like any other, mostly abandoned, small town in the area. They drove past a city hall, and a hospital Nicole could see remained open and active. A few blocks down, they entered the parking lot of what had been the high school before the event. She could see out on the football field a few groups of soldiers training in what looked like hand-to-hand combat. The sight made her uneasy.

A young man greeted them, probably about Stephen's age, who led them to a waiting room, which had been a small schoolroom. Chalkboards on the walls contained notes for planning. She could see on one of the blackboards, mostly smudged, the words city hall fortress. She knew it referred to Bartram Fortress.

"How many soldiers are here, Jim?"

"Here, there are currently only one hundred."

"Only?"

"Yes, Nicole. Most are recent recruits in training. We have modified the schools to serve as barracks and training facilities. We can house almost three hundred fighters here at any one time."

"Do you not like the term soldier, Jim?"

Before he could answer, Nicole continued.

"What do you think about all of this, Susan?"

Nicole didn't know why this all bothered her so much. Was she so naive about the world before and after the event? She worked to remove the scowl from her face before she met Brian. Jim had never mentioned the man before the ride to town, all part of the secret.

"I think we need to be prepared to defend ourselves, and we need to be ready to do what's right, and what's right is getting rid of anyone like Jonathan. I hate myself for not being repulsed by the need to fight, but his cruelty and evilness must stop. I believe we can build a great society around the abilities we have discovered in ourselves, but we need to finish cleaning house."

"Cleaning house, Susan? Billions have probably died, or soon will!"

"I know, Nicole. But I wonder why. I don't want to sound like a cultist myself, but I do believe in God, and I believe this happened for a reason."

The room became quiet as they waited for Brian Crawston. According to Jim, Brian was a friend of his before the event. They had worked together since the event to create a safe place to rebuild society. Before the event, Brian had served as a Marine Captain and had been home on leave after a recent tour in the Middle East when the Hell on Earth started.

Nicole started to break the silence when the door opened, and Brian came into the room. He was a tall man, and you could tell by his build, short hair, and overall demeanor, he had been a Marine. She knew enough about the Marines to know he would say to her, he still was a Marine and always would be a Marine, even if the corps no longer existed, nor the country they served.

"I'm sorry to be late; I had an emergency situation to defuse."

"Anything I need to know about?"

"No, Jim, only the usual problem with guys and girls needing to blow off some steam. Training can get intense; people get hurt; they forget and use their abilities to even the score. No damage done, and I think both participants have learned their lesson, for now anyway.

"Down to business. Mary, the Priestess of the Abolitionist, is waiting for us next door."

Brian couldn't help but snicker as the words left his lips.

"The Priestess says one of her abilities is to see certain aspects of the future, and she doesn't like what she sees. That is all she will tell me since I apparently am not important enough."

"Maybe she just doesn't like jarheads," Jim said with a massive grin on his face.

"Let's go meet this Priestess."

Brian led them down the hall to the next door, into another smaller classroom. As they entered, Mary stood with her hands on her hips.

"Well, it's about time!"

ABOLITIONIST

The Purple Weed

The weed had grown wild across most of the eastern seaboard for more years than anyone could remember. It flourished as far north as Vermont and New Hampshire, as far south as the northern counties of Georgia and Alabama, and as far west as Ohio, Kentucky, and Tennessee. It became known as the purple weed by many backwoods' inhabitants and nature lovers. The flowers, which bloomed briefly in early spring, were purple, but the plant itself was dark reddish and green, sort of like red beet and chard stalks. The weed was the bane of serious gardeners. They had trouble keeping it out of flower beds and vegetable gardens since it took a potent herbicide attainable only by farmers to kill it off and keep it away.

Back in the early twentieth century, someone decided to dry out some of the small leaves, and then for some reason known only to them, smoke it like tobacco. It had a bitter taste when smoked, but it became, in other ways, enjoyable. It wasn't addictive like tobacco and didn't smell as bad as some cigars. Although it was sometimes mistaken for the other weed, it wouldn't make you high like cannabis, but it did relax you like a mild sedative, and it eventually became known to some as the poor man's high.

When cannabis became more acceptable and used for medicines by extracting its oils, someone decided to try the technique with the purple weed. They were disappointed to find nothing happened when used as oil rubbed into the skin. The oil tasted much too bitter to drink, but when watered down and taken as a tea, with some sugar or honey, it was far better than chamomile or peppermint tea for various mild ailments.

Almost three years after the world changed, someone in the Larson Colony of Limerick, Pennsylvania, found some old purple weed oil. They decided to drink it straight, on a dare, not knowing of its history as a tea.

It left a horrid taste in the mouth worse than smoking the bitter weed. It was hard to keep the substance down, but unlike smoking the weed or rubbing its oil on your body, drinking the oil had an unexpected effect on the brain. The discovery could have happened anywhere, but it occurred in the Larson Colony by chance or universal design. As the months passed, the Colony became known as the Abolitionists, devoted to the suppression of all the abilities the universe had bestowed. They now had the tool to change the world again, this time to their liking.

Revered Thomas Larson

Thomas Christian Larson started life in an exceptionally religious family. He grew up and went to school in Emmaus, Pennsylvania. Thomas became a good student, especially in Sunday School, where he always had high marks in his classes. Thomas believed in and loved God tremendously, and he knew when it was time, he would go to seminary school.

When he came of age, Thomas attended the Kutztown College of Bible. He spent two years learning more about the Bible and how to be a good reverend. The more he learned, the more he began to doubt. Thomas developed his own beliefs, and they eventually threw him out of the school less than a month into his third year.

Thomas didn't care. He knew all he needed to know to start his particular church and lead his own flock. All his religious upbringing never removed from Thomas the sins of pride and self-importance. He felt he knew best how to lead a congregation, and he was sick and tired of the puritanism the school had been pushing. Thomas believed God created the human body to be used and enjoyed, something frowned upon and difficult to practice in a seminary school.

He broke off all contact with his family and started a small congregation in Perkiomenville, a town not far from his hometown but far enough. He loved Pennsylvania, and if it weren't so secluded, he would have set up his new church in the Pocono mountains.

Reverend Larson was charismatic and good-looking, with blond hair and blue eyes. He had no problem attracting women of all ages to his flock and less trouble attracting men who agreed with his philosophy of using their interpretation of God's gifts.

He didn't care much about the money except when it could help him grow his congregation and build a proper church for his audience. After years of work and patience, 'Reverend Thomas Larson's Church of Joy' opened on his thirtieth birthday. It was a small church, capable of holding less than two hundred congregants but large enough for a great beginning.

The opening occurred nine months before Hell on Earth began. At first, Thomas thought the event would be a good thing, a gift from God to help him enlarge his flock. The reality became far different. Instead, his congregation turned upon itself, and Thomas's philosophy of Joy turned into a philosophy of violent self-indulgence and infliction of pain.

The reverend had no abilities immediately apparent, a fact he managed to conceal, as he lost control of what he built. Thomas could do nothing as members of his church began to use the building for forcible copulations of all kinds. Men forced women into unspeakable acts, while some men even turned on the congregation's younger, weaker male members. The women of the church were no better, ganging up to abuse the women who the devil decided would have no abilities.

It disgusted Thomas, but he did nothing but watch and hide. Reverend Larson was a coward who, more than anything else, wanted to protect himself. When the first murder happened in his church, he knew he had to leave before he became a victim. Thomas could do nothing to fight the curse, and he vowed never to use any abilities he might still acquire for evil or personal gain—a promise he wouldn't keep. Thomas also vowed to God, he would one day abolish this scourge from the world, now believing it wasn't a gift from God but a curse put upon the world by the devil himself.

Larson fled the church he created and almost became a victim himself when he was captured and tortured by a group of young girls who wanted to make him pay for all men's sins in a unique manner. When they found his collar and realized he was a religious man, they decided it would be fun to reenact the crucifixion with Larson taking Christ's place. They had him stripped down to his underpants and used their powers to force him to lie down on a crudely constructed cross of pressure treated two by fours.

The young women had nails and a hammer they were about to use when all hell broke loose. A group of men had heard what the girls were doing, and they came to exact their revenge for the men and boys they had murdered. When the girls had to defend themselves, their control of Larson ended, and he hurried away before becoming involved.

He hid in one of the nearby buildings the girls were using. He knew he had to get out, but he remained afraid. He found clothes and sneakers that had belonged to the men they had killed and entered a closet to get dressed and hide. Later, as he snuck out to get some food, he listened to the men rape and slowly kill the girls one by one. He hid for another day before making his way out of the house and continuing his journey.

He fled to Limerick, where after hiding for a few weeks, he started looking for others like himself who believed the abilities were a curse. He surrounded himself with those who had talents he could use to defend the community, and Thomas also made sure to recruit beautiful women because he still believed in the joys of the body.

Mary Croy

Mary gazed out and above the field of purple weed, standing atop one of the watchtowers scattered around the town. As she watched, the cool breeze which moved through her long black hair also had its way with the tall weed now in bloom. The purple flowers bent slightly back and forth in the breeze, causing a wave of color to move through the fields.

The sight was beautiful to watch, but she hated the weed. She hated what it did to the mind. Mary didn't hate the abilities the universe bestowed on her; what she despised was how the various abilities were being abused and used to hurt and enslave what remained of humanity.

After the day of the gift, as some called it before she developed her particular abilities, Mary suffered abuse by other women who had enslaved her and used her in their sex games. The women abused and violated her many times before she developed her ability to see glimpses of the short-term future.

For as long as Mary could remember, she had some minor ability to see the future. She couldn't communicate with the dead, see spirits, or read a person, but she would know when she would have a visitor or know when not to go down a particular street. She could occasionally see trouble or disasters, but only if they involved her. She didn't foresee the end of civilization.

When her captors learned of her ability, it elevated Mary in their eyes, and she became their early warning system. Her elevated status meant they would no longer abuse her or force Mary into sex games, but she wasn't free either, and she longed to get out. Her abilities had enabled the women to capture and enslave others, including young boys whom the women would force to fight one another, some to their death.

Their enclave outside Conshohocken, Pennsylvania, became a place of violence made worse by free-flowing alcohol and drugs. Boys and young men they captured never made it out alive. If lucky, the women would pick them to be studs, but even then, the sex became sadistic.

Mary had enough; she wanted out; she wanted away from these sick women; she wanted to be free. After many months of meditation and practice, Mary learned she also could control others, but not physically. Mary acquired the ability to make others see what she wanted them to see. After practicing for a few weeks, Mary felt ready to leave by making her captors see her in her room when she had already walked away. She wished she had a way to stop the women and put an end to their sick cult, but in the end, all she could do was get away and save herself.

After her escape, Mary wandered around to the west and temporarily used a house in Lionville. Eventually, she headed north to the Pottstown area and moved from place to place to avoid trouble until she dreamed about a man of the cloth she needed to find. After a few months from mid-summer to late fall, Mary found her way to what later would become the Abolitionist Cult. She found the man she dreamt of but sensed something terrible from him. However, it was almost winter; she needed to stay somewhere safe and warm. The other people there appeared friendly, and she liked their philosophy of not using abilities.

After a few months, she realized she had escaped one cult to become part of another, but this group was different at first. Yes, they used their powers occasionally but only to help others and to defend their community. Their laws forbid the use of abilities in any way to harm or take advantage of others.

Mary loved being there at first. She didn't tell them of her ability to influence what a person could see; she informed them only of her ability to see the short-term future. As she did with the women, she used her talent to warn of danger soon to come.

After almost two years, things began to go wrong. Thomas Larson, their leader, struck a secret deal with the Overlord of Bartram Fortress in Philadelphia, to supply power from the nuclear generation station near the town. The Overlord promised to leave them alone to practice their silly ban—as he called it—on using the abilities, as long as the power flowed, and they stayed obedient.

A few months after the deal with Jonathan, Thomas Larson officially turned their community into an Abolitionist Cult. He created a religion around the complete abolishment of what he now called the curse. He declared himself a reverend of this religion, and eventually, Mary became known as the seer and Priestess of the cult. She didn't like it, but she felt it harmless until some fool discovered the weed's power.

Mary didn't believe the abilities humanity acquired were terrible. Some survivors used the new talents well, while others used them for what Mary considered evil. Her original skills had become sharper after the event, as had also happened to other unsuspecting people. Larson called it the curse, brought to the world by the devil, and it became simply hell day to many of its victims, including the reverend.

Mary wanted no parts of Larson's plan to rid the world of abilities by using the weed. She knew total suppression was impossible, and if only some people lost their powers, they would soon become slaves to the likes of the Overlord. She could not allow that to happen, but she needed help.

Someone needed to prevent Larson from implementing his plan, and the Overlord required elimination. She could see a future where this would be possible, but she needed to form an alliance between the Abolitionists and those at a place called Sanctuary.

Mary felt the call to Sanctuary for many months. Her powers allowed her to see a future which would also include another place called the

Resistance. She thought they were in some way connected. She had to leave, and she had to find the Resistance. The Overlord had to be stopped, one way or another.

William Paterson

William stood on the top of a broad hill, overlooking the fields of the purple weeds. They had cultivated almost thirty acres of the reddish-green-stemmed weed, but more had to be grown and plans made. They needed a much larger supply of the plant if they were ever going to remove the scourge brought down upon the Earth.

Work progressed on alternate ways of disseminating the weed. Eating the ground stems and flowers worked well, as did drinking it like a strong tea, but the process worked too slowly. They needed a way to dose a large population at one time, secretly. Unless you drank a large amount of the oil, the effects of merely eating the weed took time to work, and depending on the person, the effect only lasted for a month at most without repeated exposure.

This scourge had to end, and this was the only way to do it. They had to stop the perversions and abuses perpetrated by those who gained mental power to control others. No one should have to suffer the injustices he endured, and the tyrant Jonathan who dared to declare himself Overlord, had to be stopped.

Reverend Larson allied with Jonathan only because it became necessary at the time. They needed to gain his trust to get closer to him in his fortress. The reverend didn't believe Jonathan was aware of the weed. William hoped it to be true.

William thought back to the day almost three years ago when he arrived at what later became the center of the Abolitionist movement.

The center of the new religion was constructed around the suppression of the abilities and destruction of those who would not willingly give up the power.

He had been traveling for a few months before he had made his way to the reverend. He left his Rittenhouse Square apartment before Jonathan took total control of Philly and most of its surrounding area. He heard of Jonathan from his captors, who threatened to sell him to the maniac.

He had only the clothes he took from his captors and some food when he started his journey. He was weak from the torment they put him through, but he had gotten his revenge. William had become their captive sex slave from the day hell started. One of his two captors was always on guard when they didn't have him locked up or restrained, so it became impossible to escape. He couldn't fight their mental powers. He knew because he had tried, and they made him pay the price by violating him with objects other than their bodies, which always remained their first choice.

Eventually, the opportunity came after many weeks of torment. They had gotten themselves drunk, and William realized too much alcohol weakened their powers. He wanted to try to run away that day, but he had no food and no clothes. They loved to keep him naked as part of his torment. Having no clothes would not have stopped him, but he needed to have at least something to protect his feet.

One day when they were drinking heavily after a long session of getting their pleasures with him, he could tell their powers were extremely weak. Robert, the older one, left the room to shower, and Philip said he would keep an eye on the toy while he forced him to make their lunch. They were separated and drunk. He knew this to be his chance.

When Philip threatened him with punishment if he wouldn't willingly make lunch, he agreed and went out to the kitchen, as Philip sat in a chair to relax and eventually fall asleep. William grabbed a long, sharp knife from the drawer and quickly came behind Philip, raised the

THE OVERLORD

blade high, and thrust it into Philip's chest as the man sat there snoring. They never thought to get rid of the knives because they assumed they could always control him, but Philip learned his mistake.

As William pulled the knife out of Phillip's chest, he heard the shower water stop. He knew he couldn't wait; he couldn't take the chance Robert would sense his intentions or Philip's death. William knew Robert would dry off in the shower before opening the curtain, so he quickly went into the bathroom, pulled back the shower curtain, and cut deep into Robert's throat. He could feel Robert reach out with his mind, and he was almost able to make William cut himself, but Robert bled out quickly and died before he could do anything more to fight back.

William stood there and watched the blood mix with the water droplets still in the shower as it slowly flowed into the drain. His tormentors were dead, but that wasn't good enough for William. He reached down, grabbed Robert's dick, sliced it off, picked it up, and took it with him back to the living room, where he did the same to Philip's lifeless body. He then went to the window, opened it, and threw both dicks out the window for the birds and dogs to fight over and devour.

He felt ecstatic and was about to take the knife to mutilate more of their bodies when he finally came to his senses. He needed to leave, but there was no big rush since they were both dead. He went back to the bathroom, pulled Robert out of the shower, and took a badly needed shower of his own as he thought about what he needed and where to go. When he finished getting their filth off him, he grabbed some of their clothes, made himself lunch, finished packing some supplies, and then left on the journey that brought him eventually to his savior, Reverend Thomas Larson.

Weed Bombs are Born

"Excuse me, William. I have great news."

William's reminiscing of how he gained his freedom ended as he heard his name called. The person who disturbed him was Russell Boom Gulla, a self-proclaimed anarchist who joined their group a few months ago. His middle initial stood for Barry, but his friends changed it to Boom to recognize his bomb-making abilities.

Russell was a pervert, and William had no desire to be near him more than needed. He reminded William of Philip, the way he sometimes caught Russ looking at him. He sensed Russ considered him a friend—nothing could be further from the truth.

Russell had a pale complexion and skinny body, almost sickly looking, and since he shaved his head, the jerk looked even more like Philip. William would love to see Russ dead, but the reverend wouldn't be pleased.

"Yes, Russ, what's up?"

"I did it, well, we did it. I guess I must give Sandra some credit. We succeeded in turning the purple weed into a bomb we can use to disperse over a wide area."

"How the fucking hell does that work, and to what purpose? You need long-term exposure—"

"Not when it's super powderized!"

"What are you talking about Russ, you make no sense?"

"Well, buddy, try not to miss the update meetings."

William had been away for almost three weeks, looking for that bitch Mary. Larson wanted her back one way or another, and William had volunteered to find her, but to no avail. It was as if she had disappeared from the face of the Earth. He had heard stories about a settlement down south in Maryland, but he figured she would go more towards Philly. He had been wrong, he assumed.

"I was busy doing the reverend's work. Do you have a problem with that, Russ?"

William moved closer in front of Russ as if to start trouble. William just wanted to put him in his place, but he felt a distinct impression, Russ enjoyed the close contact. He moved away and turned his back to Russ as if to dismiss the bald asshole.

"Okay, William, I'll fill you in. Sandra developed a way to concentrate the weed into a super robust powder that works by being inhaled. She found it worked within a matter of seconds. All abilities are rendered mute. It doesn't last long, but then again, how long does it take to slit a throat?"

"We don't want to kill everyone, just free them."

"Yea, yea, yea, I know. But first, we have to incapacitate them, then force them to drink the long-term mixture, and keep them on it forever, apparently."

Russell stopped as if thinking about a plan. A devilish look appeared in his sunken eyes.

"What we must have, William, is a way to make the effects permanent, but this will do for now. I developed an explosive delivery system which quickly disperses the super-powder. We just finished testing it on the women out west of Pottsgrove."

The women, William knew, were a small group of middle-aged hags who used their powers to enslave a group of younger men. They used the men for all the manual work around their camp and their never-ending pleasure. They forced the captives to perform every sex act ever conceived. William thought it sick. Even though he supposed some of the men probably enjoyed the experience, it reminded him too much of his captivity. He asked Reverend Larson for permission to have them destroyed, but Larson had other plans. Now he understood.

William also knew Russell took much pleasure out of watching the torment the woman inflicted on their captives. Russ would sneak close enough to use his powers to experience what he considered pleasure by feeling what the men felt. More proof indicating Russ was a sick pervert.

Russell again brought William out of his thoughts as he continued his explanation.

"We hit the compound with twenty bombs. The women were powerless, so we walked into their camp, and they could do nothing to stop our advance. We beat some and raped others, but the best part happened when we told the former captives they could do with the women whatever they wanted. Such great entertainment to watch the men take their revenge. You should've been there, friend, to share it with me. It was glorious watching those boys fu—"

"Thank you for the report; now go and inform Thomas so he can plan."

William watched as Russ went on his way to inform the reverend of the successful test. Russ was disappointed he couldn't tell the whole story, but William felt relief to see him leave. Russ represented the worst society had to offer before and after the event. Russell B Gulla reminded him of some he met on his way to being saved by Reverend Larson. William had been a different person then, and he thought about how much he had grown and healed since he began his journey.

William no longer felt guilt; he was no longer afraid; he would never again be the instrument of another's pleasure unless by choice. He stood taking in the breeze while he thought of his journey, and the day, months later, when he first met the Reverend Thomas.

William's Journey

William began his journey to Reverend Larson a little over two months from the day of the event. His time in captivity left him with physical and emotional scars; he feared anyone he might meet in his travels.

He left the apartment and headed for the river drive. He walked along the drive, hidden in the bushes until he climbed his way up to State RT 1 and headed south. William continued walking along the side of the road and hiding anytime he heard a noise that could be another person. He walked with his head down, looking to anyone who would have seen him as a broken man, depressed and barely able to carry his weight, all of which were true.

His head became hot, and he sweated even though he wore his Phillies hat taken from his former apartment when he packed. He walked overdressed for the day's warmth, afraid to expose his body after many weeks of being always forced to be naked. Even with head down, looking at nothing but the pavement, the brightness of the day bothered his eyes because he hadn't been outside since before the event.

William walked for over six hours before he heard voices up ahead. They sounded like they were coming closer, so he hid behind tall bushes in front of one of the big, old, presumed- empty houses, which lined the historic road. He wanted to hide with his head down between his knees, but curiosity got the better of him. He wished he hadn't looked.

Passing about fifteen yards in front of him was a pack of six men all about his age holding ropes, and on the other end of each line, a naked woman danced down the street, and he could tell by looking at them it was against their will. Each woman had tears running down their cheeks, and a few had bruises on various parts of their bodies. Still, the worst part was when he looked down at their feet and saw most of the women's feet were bloodied and leaving a trail of bloody footprints behind.

An hour after they had passed, William still sat behind the bushes trying to forget the horror he witnessed. The sun began to set, so he pulled a bit of bread and a bottle of water from his backpack. When finished eating, he grabbed a blanket, wrapped it around his now cold body, and slept on the porch of a house across the road. It was the best night's sleep he had since the event.

The next three days passed in about the same manner. William slept hiding behind a bush or a wall and found more food and water from ransacked stores along the road. His mental state improved, and he no longer walked with head down, eyes looking at the ground. However, he remained afraid and walked farther away from the road when possible. While traveling, William witnessed many atrocities he spent the next few months erasing from his memories, but one he could never forget, even though it, unfortunately, wasn't the worst.

William walked for a few hours before he stumbled upon a man and a woman a few years older than himself. They were torturing a young boy, barely a teenager, by making the boy repeatedly stab himself in his hand with a sharpened stick.

The boy's hand looked mangled beyond recognition, blood flowed down the post his hand laid upon, and William knew, if the kid didn't get help soon, he would probably bleed to death.

"What are you doing to him? Stop, nothing he did to you could deserve such a punishment."

The man spoke as the woman appeared in deep concentration.

"The little bastard tried to steal our food. No one steals from us and gets away with it, not ever again."

William looked over at the boy, who had tears streaming down his face. He didn't make a sound, and William felt sure it was the woman preventing the boy from screaming. As William watched, the boy managed to mouth to him, help me, but there wasn't anything he could do, nothing he was brave enough to do. He tried one more time to reason with the man.

"Please stop; he is going to bleed to death if he doesn't get help. Do you want to be a murderer?"

The man approached William, which caused him to stumble back and trip over a rock, landing on his ass.

"You pathetic piece of shit, you can't even take care of yourself. I suggest you get the fuck up and walk away before we make this thief use that stick on your eyes."

The boy started to moan, and William could see the woman getting tired. Suddenly, the boy screamed and made the second mistake of the day, which was to be his last.

"You bitch, I'm going to come after you and shove this stick so far up your cunt . . ."

The boy started to choke, stopped stabbing his hand, and dropped the stick. William thought the woman had grown too tired to continue and instead wanted to choke him to death, but he was wrong.

William sat on the ground and watched the boy loosen his belt and pull down his pants with his undamaged hand. William knew the boy's fate, and he tried to get up and get away, but he couldn't move; his legs had no strength. He looked over at the woman who smiled at him.

"You're not going anywhere, you self-riotous prick; you are going to sit there, watch and pray to your maker, I let you go."

The boy now bent down, his mangled bleeding hand hanging by his side, and picked up the stick with his working hand. As William watched in horror, the boy began stabbing himself between his legs, and his once white underpants were now turning red with blood as he screamed louder than William had ever heard anyone scream before.

Even though the boy was foul-mouthed and maybe a thief, William wanted the torment to stop—the couple was wrong to hurt the boy. William got his wish as the boy stopped and then thrust the stick deep into his ear and collapsed to the ground with his body shaking in the last throws of life. When the boy's body remained still, the man turned to William, who the women now released.

"Get up and go before we change our minds!"

William stood and walked away as the couple watched. Ashamed for not having done anything to help and embarrassed, he walked away to try and put the horrible scene out of his mind.

He walked for a couple of hours before he reached the Brandywine Creek. He would picnic with his family along the creek when a young boy. The memory briefly made him smile until he remembered the encounter from a few hours ago. Although he did nothing wrong, he felt dirty, and he needed to get clean.

He saw about fifty yards up the way, a small waterfall behind some thick trees. It would be the perfect spot to clean the filth of humanity from his body. When he felt well-hidden behind the trees, he stripped off his clothes and stood under the waterfall. For William, it became a significant accomplishment to be able to stand in the open, exposed.

The cold water made him cringe and stiffened his muscles, but he was determined to suffer for his inaction earlier. He remained surprised he didn't feel afraid or ashamed to be standing there naked. Maybe his ordeal with Phillip and Robert hadn't scarred him as much as he first thought, or he felt more ashamed of not doing more to help the boy.

After a few minutes, he could no longer tolerate the cold water; he got out and waited for the breeze to dry his body, now covered with goosebumps. He remained so cold, that his undershirt rubbing against his ice-hard and scabbed nipples, caused him discomfort as he moved—

another reminder of how Robert would torment him as Philip watched.

Nightfall approached, and William needed somewhere to spend another evening alone. He walked away from the creek into the backyard of a darkened house and made his way to an unlocked garden shed that conveniently had some not-too-worn blankets lying next to an old lawnmower. When he picked up one of the blankets, a cloud of dust filled the shed, and he barely contained the urge to sneeze. Although the shed had dirt and dust everywhere, it also contained some food. The homeowners had used the shed to store onions and potatoes. It wasn't easy to consume the raw food, but it was at least something to eat. He had only two more energy bars left in his pack.

The following day, he headed farther down the creek until he reached an abandoned railroad bed. The rails were mostly overgrown and in places hard to pass, but the former rail line lay below the grade level, which he hoped would keep him hidden.

He walked along the old tracks and noticed the right of way had become well maintained, and he realized he walked along a restored tourist rail line. Again, he thought about his childhood, and he wondered if this was one of the lines he rode from time to time with his parents.

A few hours had gone by with mostly no sounds but the birds chirping in the trees and a few dogs barking. At one point, William heard a girl scream, but he kept walking. He had no power, no ability; he remained a useless man in this new world. He was helpless and unable to help others.

An hour after William heard the scream, he arrived at Kennett Square Station. He cautiously approached the little, old station house, and when it looked clear, he moved closer and peered in one of the windows. Someone had ransacked the place, but he could tell it used to contain railroad memorabilia as well as refreshments dispensed from an old-style, bright red, soda vending machine.

He walked on for another hour when he came to the first level crossing, he had encountered along the line—Penn Greens Road. According to a sign, a short distance down the road was the D&N Mushroom Farm located past RT 41. His first thought was of food. Mushrooms were not his favorite, but it would be better than the onions and potatoes he stuffed in his backpack earlier.

His second thought regarding the farm was caves—a place to hide. He knew some mushrooms in this area were still grown in caves. A cave would be a great place to hide from the world. He had only been free for about a week, but he wanted nothing to do with the new world. William wanted to hide, and a mushroom cave seemed like the perfect place.

He walked down the road with the breeze blowing through his hair and a newfound determination. His head and back were hot from the burning sun, seeming to say farewell as William sought out the safety of darkness. After a few minutes, he stood outside the main building of the D&N Mushroom Farm.

William stood quietly, listening for any sound to betray anyone else's existence in the area. Behind the main building rose a plume of what looked like white smoke. He was about to walk away when the stench of rotting vegetation and animal shit assaulted his senses. The smoke was most likely steam coming from mulching piles, but he decided to be cautious. He still heard nothing other than the birds singing goodbye to him from the trees, so he walked around the side of the rusty metal building. He stayed close to the structure and had to walk around piles of wood pallets and rotting mushrooms, which imparted its foul smell to the air.

He approached the back edge of the building, peered around the corner, and confirmed what he had expected. The smell and white smoke, actually steam, came from vast piles of the rotting matter converting into fertilizer. He could glimpse through the steam a conveyor belt, which led into a smaller building standing in front of a small line of hills.

William had never been in a mushroom farm cave before, so he wasn't sure what to expect. The building he now stood before measured only about twenty yards wide, with a small opening where the conveyer built entered the building. A row of windows ran across the building and a single door, which he found unlocked.

The first thing he noticed when he shut the door behind him was the God-awful smell. Worse than the mulch piles outside, and he felt certain it also contained the scent of a rotting corpse or two. He wished he had a mask to cover his face. He thought there had to be one somewhere around the farm.

In front of William stood another long wall with a larger double door and an opening on the left where the conveyer belt went further into the building or cave. To his right, he saw what looked like an office based on the small amount of light coming from a lone window facing out the direction he came.

The door to the office was also unlocked when he tried the handle, so he went in before going deeper into the farm. When he closed the door, he felt relieved when he noticed the smell wasn't as bad. He saw an almost exhausted room air freshener sitting on one of the desks, which someone had probably put there right before hell day. As he thought, the room was an office, but it also had a sofa with a pillow and cover still sitting at one end. The supervisors probably slept here at times, or the room is or had been used recently by someone else, maybe trying to hide.

If someone did stay there before, he felt sure they weren't there now. The place was unnervingly quiet; no sounds from birds, and of course, all the machinery sat idle. He tried a light switch on the wall behind him, but it didn't work, as expected. The electricity stopped at his former prison nightmare a few weeks ago. He expected there had to be a generator around somewhere, but did he want to start it and draw attention to himself? Probably not, but he couldn't live in the dark all the time.

He noticed another door on the far side of the room and was elated to find flashlights, many new and unopened, and an ample supply of batteries. He also discovered a camping lantern that worked on batteries and a good amount of that type.

Time to explore. To his left stood another door with a sign that read, 'D&H Mushroom Cave #2'. He grabbed the lantern, put in the batteries, and headed into the cave, where again, an intensified smell assaulted his senses. He had no choice but to put up with it for now as he explored the farm. In front of him, there were rows of stacked tables taller than his head, running farther back than his light could illuminate. To the side stood another double-doored, rusted storage cabinet. The squeak of the door was the only sound in the cave, and it reminded him of horror movies he watched as a child, which gave him a chill.

Knock it off, William, it's just your imagination; you need to be brave to survive.

"Yes!" he exclaimed as he saw by the light of his lantern a couple of face masks, more lanterns, and containers marked lamp oil. When he checked the lanterns, he found they were oil lamps. He pulled out the cleanest lamp, filled it with oil, and stopped when he realized he had no way to light the wick. On the top shelf, he found a small metal box. He had a feeling, and it paid off. The box contained matches, protected from the dampness.

A few minutes later, he had worked his way down the center aisle, following along the conveyor belt with his old-style lamp lighting a few yards in all directions. He had to push away spider webs and crunched on other critters as he walked. In the lessening darkness ahead, he could see what looked like a figure standing by the conveyor belt.

"Hello, is someone there?

"Hello, I mean you know harm, I'm just looking for a place to stay, a place to hide, same as you maybe?"

William didn't receive an answer, so he continued at a slower, cautious pace. When he reached the figure, he now understood where most of the smell had originated. A man's body hung from the belt, head on the floor in a puddle of dried blood, with one foot stuck under the belt and attached to what looked like a broken leg. William had no idea what the person was doing, and he didn't care. The middle-aged man must have slipped and fallen to probably a slow death.

An hour later, William found an old tarp by the cabinet and some gloves, which he put on to extricate the body, wrap it and drag it all the way back to the farthest reaches of the cave. Finally, before he went back to the office, he covered the tarp-wrapped body with dirt from one of the mushroom beds. He didn't care about the person; why should he? William cared only about lessening the smell of the body. He hoped it worked.

Now exhausted, William headed back to the office and collapsed on the sofa, where he slept better than he had for many weeks. In the morning, he awoke ravishingly hungry and ate the last of the remaining food, which consisted of one energy bar, an onion, and a bottle of water. He was never a big fan of mushrooms, but he needed food.

William spent the next hour with a lantern in hand, picking through the scraps and rotting mushrooms, looking for ones he could eat. He found enough to last him a couple of days, but he knew he needed more, and he remembered most of these farms had a country store, and he recalled passing one on the way into the farm.

He didn't want to go back outside; he remained afraid of being seen; he was fearful of being made to do horrible things again that made him sick to his stomach. William hated the world out there, but he knew he had no choice.

He could barely open his eyes when he walked back into the bright sunlight. He stood a moment leaning back against the door, waiting for his eyes to adjust. The breeze now blew away from the farm, so he couldn't smell any of the rotting mulch piles which lined his path back to the front parking lot.

He walked cautiously, staying as hidden as possible and often stopping to listen. Finally, he made it to the front, and bingo, there it was—the D&N Farm Country Store. Two large and broken windows lined the front, and the door stood open, swinging back and forth from the increasing breeze, which also blew his lengthening hair into his eyes. Dealing with his hair was a task for later; now, he needed to wait and watch, making sure no one remained, hiding in the store.

He waited for more than a half hour, afraid to move away from the building he hid against, crouched down like a frightened child. William calmed himself, stood, and began to run to the store, praying to the God he felt abandoned him, not to let anyone see him enter the building.

He reached the door and walked into a mess. Rotten mushrooms were lying on the floor mixed with broken glass from dried fruit preserves and jellies. Who would waste food needed for survival? Another reason to hate this new world in which he now existed. The soda machine also was smashed, but there were some intact cans scattered across the floor. William picked up two though it certainly wasn't what he wanted to drink. The sign on the machine indicated it once held juice and water, but he found none; however, scattered among the rotted and dried food littering the floor were a few unspoiled snacks and energy bars.

At least this trip wasn't a total waste.

He could see they had also sold hotdogs and Italian sausage, but they were also spoiled after weeks with no electricity. He walked behind the counter with the cash register and entered the closed-door marked private. Behind the door, he found an office with another door on the far side of the room.

There was nothing of interest he could see in the office, and he didn't expect to find any meaningful food stashed in a drawer or filing cabinet, so he proceeded across the room and opened the other door to find a gold mine of food. Whoever ransacked the store never bothered to go to the back.

Too bad for them and great news for me.

In front of him were shelves half-filled with a variety of snacks: peanuts, jerky, dried fruit, trail mix, power bars, and of course, junk snacks like potato chips and candy. Farther back in the room were shelves with water, juice, and soda. It was a paradise to a man who had mostly been eating mushrooms for the last couple of days.

William picked up a canvas bag lying on the floor and filled it with enough food, water, and juice to last him at least two weeks. Two weeks before, he would again have to venture out of his dark sanctuary, where he felt safe. Even now, as he filled the sack, he worried someone would find him and use him again like before. The grown man twitched and shook like a child; he had enough—time to leave.

William made his way back to his sanctuary without incident. The sweat that appeared on his brow as his fear took over was now drying and helping him cool off. The trip took all his energy, and he dropped his sack of goodies before laying on the sofa and sleeping for the next few hours.

The following two weeks were uneventful as William adjusted to his new life of seclusion. His food and water lasted longer than he anticipated, and he felt happy he wouldn't have to venture outside again for another week. But all wasn't well, and he started to have doubts about his current situation.

He remained safe and had been content, but his sleep had become restless over the last few nights as he dreamt of being trapped forever buried in the mushroom cave. In the dream, he aged quickly and died alone in the cave. At one point in the nightmare, he saw his own shriveled body decaying with mushrooms growing where his mouth had once been.

William started to wonder if maybe it was time to leave. Yes, he was used and abused by Philip and Robert, and he knew there were evil people out there, but he couldn't live in fear his entire life. It wasn't the man he was before, and it wasn't the man he wanted to be for the rest of his life, no matter what that life had in store. William decided on one more night, and then he would leave in the morning.

The New William

He slept well that night, which made him confident of his decision to leave. He gathered up the remaining food and water, walked out into a damp, miserable day with puddles filling the ground. He realized it was the first time it rained while traveling since he escaped. He had nothing to stay dry and didn't like the idea of walking around soaked all day. The rain became more challenging, and he knew this wouldn't be a quick passing storm.

He planned to stop at the store on his way out to get more supplies and figured he could find something there to wear to keep warm. He hurried to the store with a much quicker gait than the last time he cautiously, like a coward, made his way to the building. He recognized he no longer remained afraid; he felt excited to be on an adventure.

He gathered up as many supplies as he could carry and, on his way out, found a lightweight waterproof jacket. William put it on, surprised it fit well, and hurried quickly on his way. He reached the end of the property and stopped while the increasing wind pelted him with rain.

Where the fucking hell am I going?

He looked up and down the road, temporarily startled by a loud crack of thunder, when he noticed a sign to his left. The sign read, Downingtown, 17 miles. He had a friend that lived in Downingtown, and though he was sure his friend wouldn't be there, it remained as good a destination as any other.

William turned to his left and began walking down the middle of the road, not caring who saw him. It could take eight hours to walk to town, so he thought he might find shelter in a house along the way. He proceeded along Newark Road, following the signs meant for cars that might never be seen on these roads again. He turned right onto RT 842 and then left onto RT 162 and followed it into the town of Newlin, where he stopped in a partially dry bus shelter to have some food and drink.

He continued until the signs directed him to turn left onto RT322, also known as Downingtown pike. He walked for another half hour before deciding he had enough of the damn rain—again heavy with lightning flashes. To his right ahead stood a two-story renovated farmhouse that looked intact and empty. He wasn't foolish, so he walked around the grounds before trying the back door, which he found unlocked.

William walked into a kitchen, surprised to find it clean, when he noticed a candle's odor. He was beginning to think someone already lived—

No stop. You can't.

William had grown as a man during his time with the reverend, but there were some things from his journey he still couldn't deal with, and he refused to ever allow into his thoughts. The day had turned nasty as he stood looking over the fields of weed. He decided to go back to his room and meditate, but his mind couldn't easily banish all the painful memories.

His meditation had turned into a dream about her and their relationship. He woke at the point she discarded him like trash. He often dreamt of that time though he refused to let the memories affect him. The meditation had worked as intended, and he thought about his journey after her.

He considered trying to find his friend but figured it too late. He was probably dead, a slave, or a slave master. He felt warmth on his face and squinted as the sun moved from behind the church steeple across the street. He turned away from the sun hating it and the world until he remembered what the . . . boy . . . what he had told them.

"I'm only passing through on a mission to spread the word about Reverend Larson's place up in Limerick. He created a community where you aren't allowed to use powers, and you can be safe if you have no abilities. We need more people, so I volunteered to be one of those going out to spread the word."

A place in Limerick where powers were not allowed. Could it be true such a place existed? A sanctuary from this hell on Earth in which he now lived. He had been in Limerick before, and he had a good idea of how to get there. He remembered mention of a reverend; William had never been overly religious, but he knew he could pretend if it meant freedom from these bastards who only wanted to use him for their pleasure. Decision made, he stood tall and proud, feeling renewed as he started the next part of his journey. He was his own man now, and he would never be anyone's plaything again.

William now had a new destination for his journey and a new determination to live, as he walked head high through Downingtown. A few hours later, he stopped in a vacant house outside the town of Lionsville. He ate and tried to sleep but found it challenging. He couldn't get images of his recent life out of his mind as he listened to the far away screams moving through the night. He realized others were near, and he would have to be careful in the morning.

Morning came and started cloudy and damp as he cautiously stepped out the door. He couldn't hear any screams or other noises to indicate any others nearby. He walked mainly through fields and parks as he roughly followed the road, which would lead him to Phoenixville and eventually Limerick.

He reached a 'one mile to Phoenixville' sign late in the afternoon and headed across another field to go around the town when he heard laughter coming from a distance ahead. Even though he felt more confident and less afraid, he was no fool. He realized it still best to avoid contact with others, so he retreated the way he came and went around the other side of town. Darkness drew near, so he scouted out another vacant house for the night and settled down without hearing any laughter or screams until the morning.

He awoke startled by a loud series of screams, sounding like they were from out front of the house. He had slept longer than intended, and it was already mid-morning. He got up to peek out the window but quickly changed his mind when he heard a voice from outside.

"Grab her legs, and we can take her into the house."

"You shouldn't have struck her so hard; what if she dies?"

"What if she does? I never fucked a dead one before—could be fun."

Inside the house, William began to panic. He made sure he grabbed everything and headed upstairs when he remembered he had seen a half-opened door to a basement and decided to go there instead.

Cobwebs brushed his body as he hurried down the stairs and almost fell flat on his face when he missed the last step. He looked back and realized he didn't shut the door—too late now. He heard the front door open and listened as the floorboards creaked above his head.

The next two days were the worst of his life, second only to his captivity. He listened to what sounded like three boys repeatedly raping a woman who screamed and cried as they used her in various ways. After a day, the only sound above became the creak of the floorboards, as the boys discussed how many times, they could do her, while the boards groaned from the boys' vile movements.

William hoped the girl was dead and free from the repeated torment. He felt helpless and worthless for not helping, but what could he do, he had no powers, and from what he heard, he knew they had been well-gifted. He listened to them talk about all the mayhem they had caused since the event, and he hated them for being so much like his previous captors.

He awoke the third day of his self-imprisonment in the basement and heard nothing—no crying from the woman, no sound of the boys talking of their exploits, and no creaking floorboards. William waited a few more hours before cautiously making his way back up the stairs where he found the woman dead, with a pool of dried blood on the floor between her legs. He was sure the boys were gone, but he checked the entire house before taking a comforter off a bed and covering the woman's body.

William desired to leave immediately, but he needed to eat and drink. His stash remained still where he had left it in one of the kitchen cabinets. After eating, William decided to wash and look for some new clothes in the bedrooms upstairs. He prepared to wash up with a cloth and cold water until he noticed a propane tank in the yard. If he were lucky, it wouldn't be empty.

Minutes later, William stood under a heavy stream of hot shower water. He washed off the dirt and cobwebs from the basement and mentally washed away the guilt for not doing something to save the woman, now dead downstairs.

He finished the shower and found fresh clothes to fit well enough. He dumped all his old clothes and packed fresh ones from the large assortment. He wondered who the clothes belonged to before and where that person existed now, if at all, months after the event.

William was ready to go by mid-afternoon but decided it would be best to wait for the morning. As if to confirm his decision, he heard a couple of gunshots from a distance, followed a few minutes later by what sounded like a short, all-out war. He didn't want to stay downstairs with the body; it freaked him out the way she looked lying there, so he stayed in the master bedroom and went to sleep early, haunted by dreams of the dead woman below, screaming for help.

The following morning William walked out of the house with a bright, cheerful disposition matched only by the weather. He needed a light jacket to protect him from the temperatures while the sun rose to do its job warming the world.

He knew the way to go, having driven with his friend a few years ago, out of Phoenixville and past Limerick on their way to Schwenksville for a music festival, back before the world went crazy. William wanted to restore the world he knew by finding a way to eradicate the scourge the event had brought. He hoped Larson would agree with him and help him find a way to clean the world of all like his former neighbors and the bitch who tossed him aside.

William walked through Phoenixville instead of going around the town. He thought taking the risk would be worth getting sooner to Limerick. He needed to cross the river, but he wanted to be careful. A few hours later, he crossed the Schuylkill River along the RT 29 bridge and was greeted on the other side by a sign that read 'Welcome to Montgomery County,' and the sound of gunshots.

The sound wasn't near, but he intended to be careful. He was going to walk on or along Highway 422, but now he thought he should stick to side roads and fields as much as possible. He heard more shots and realized they were coming closer, so he ran to a warehouse across the street and hid behind the building listening.

William's good mood, which started the day, had now descended back into darkness and despair. He couldn't go on immediately; he had to go somewhere to hide. He cautiously got up and walked farther behind the building until he came to a backyard of a small home. He jumped the fence, smashed a back window to get in, and collapsed on the floor of a small bedroom. He didn't care if anyone was there, and he almost wished someone would be there to end his torment.

The following day, William awoke still on the floor and still alive, so he decided it was time to grow a pair and move his ass. He could do nothing about the evil spread across the world, but he could join others who, like him, despised the abilities and those who used them. He needed to get to Limerick by nightfall, find shelter, and then find Reverend Larson's group tomorrow.

He rummaged through the home before continuing his journey. He walked out into a dark rainy day, considered going back in to look for an umbrella, but decided it would be more of a hassle, and he was a man, not a child or a woman afraid of getting wet.

He walked up to RT 422 and decided to walk along the highway as much as possible. He walked around the dead vehicles and decayed bodies, only stopping when he heard or saw something from which he needed to hide. He stopped three times and hid inside one of the abandoned vehicles until the danger passed. He stopped one additional time for lunch, and by late afternoon he walked down the offramp to Limerick.

The sky had grown darker from the rain-filled clouds, and night approached, so he found an inviting house, intact but empty, to spend the night. The place William chose had three bedrooms, and after some checking, he found a room filled with clothes in his size he put aside to pack in the morning. He stripped off his wet clothes and slept comfortably naked on the still made bed.

After eating and drinking juice and dry cereal he found in the house, he packed some extra drinks for his journey and set out to find the reverend. He had no clue where to go or what to look for, so he decided to walk farther into town, and then if still no luck, maybe walk around the area. As he walked, he noticed he heard no gunshots and no screams from anyone in distress. There was a light breeze he enjoyed as it blew through his hair, now longer than he ever let it grow in the past. William had just about made it to the other side of town when he was startled by a loud voice.

"Drop your pack, put your hands up, and get down on your knees. We have you surrounded, and any attempt to use your abilities on anyone of us will result in your immediate death. No second chances."

William did as instructed before responding.

"I have no abilities, and I mean, you no harm. I'm looking for Reverend Larson's place. I heard it's a safe place for people like me who hate the cursed abilities."

"How did you hear about the reverend?"

William hated to think of the messenger, but he had no choice.

"A boy I met told me. He said Limerick would be safe."

"Stand up, grab your things, and follow me. Don't try anything stupid. My friends will be following close enough to kill you at the first sign of abilities."

"I understand."

William stood and slowly grabbed his backpack before following the man giving instructions, who had emerged from behind a building. The man who looked older than William stayed many yards in front and made sure William never got too close.

They walked out of town and down a side road until they came to Swamp Road, which ran past a community park. On one side of the road stood a small apartment building, and all around, he saw houses with signs of being inhabited. A bit farther up the road, he saw a church, the building to which they were heading.

They entered the church, and the man instructed William to stop halfway down the aisle. He was about to speak to the man who led him there when a robust authoritative voice boomed from the alter.

"Put down your weapons. I'm sure this man means us no harm. Welcome son. I am Reverend Thomas Larson."

"Check him for weapons, then escort him into my office, and post a guard."

The reverend walked away while the guards frisked William and rummaged through his backpack. Two guards led him into a room behind the altar, where they instructed him to stand and wait. One guard stood in the room by the door, while the other left the room with William's belongings.

A short time later, the reverend came in and instructed the guard to wait outside as he sat behind his desk. He didn't offer a seat to William, so he remained standing.

"What's your name, son?"

William did not like being called son but understood it to be what religious types always did when speaking to others. He believed it made them feel superior.

"My name is William, William Paterson."

"William, why have you come here? What do you want?"

"I want safety and security. I want to be where this curse is despised as much as I despise it, and I want to forget. I need to forget all the hell I've seen."

William could hold in his feelings no longer, and he broke down and cried. The reverend rose from behind his desk and led William to the chair in front. He poured a drink of water for William before sitting behind his desk.

"It's okay, son, let it out. You are welcome here as long as you want to stay. We will protect you, and maybe someday we can find a way to rid the world of this damn curse."

William spent the next hour relating most of his travels to Reverend Larson and asking for forgiveness for his sins and lack of courage. When finished, he felt like a new man. And he vowed to himself he would never again be a victim.

William smiled after recalling the first time he met Thomas. The wind picked up outside as he sat on his bed. A storm front was moving in across the land. William had decided the day he met the reverend, he wanted to be a storm front—a force to rid the world of the abilities. The time had come to discuss with Thomas how they would use the weed bombs to begin the task of ridding the world of the curse. A small smile appeared on his face. It wasn't the smile of a sane person.

Larson

Thomas finished his meditation and stood to look out his room's one lone window toward his church, with its high steeple reaching up to God. The room, an empty, white-walled space with nothing but an old yoga mat on the floor, was his private sanctuary outside the church grounds. His haven to strengthen his mind and plan the end of the curse.

Many years ago, the building was a convent for the Roman Catholic, Saint Joseph nuns, who used to teach at the school farther down the road. The building had only recently completed a conversion into apartments a few weeks before the event. Some of the higher-ranking members of his congregation had rooms below, but Thomas reserved the entire top floor as his domain.

His meditation this day had been extremely beneficial. Ideas of how to conquer the curse freely flowed when he meditated, and he had new ideas to discuss with his team. William worked with his group on ways to use the weed, and Thomas had a substantial feeling success approached his community.

He rarely acknowledged his slight ability to know little things before they happened. He thought his ability a gift from God to help him fight the curse—part of the test God put upon the Earth to separate the evil from the good.

No one knew of his ability other than Mary. He missed her so much and didn't understand why she felt she had to leave. He accepted her abilities and considered them a gift given by God to help him bring as many followers as possible through the test without faltering. He missed not only her skills but also her guidance and emotional support. Her leaving left him with a void no one else could fill. Even after almost three months, he still missed her presence.

Thomas had a prayer session in an hour, but first, he had Melissa waiting for him next door. He was amazed at how easy the girls in his flock fell for him and wanted to be with him in the most intimate way. He knew God graced him with good looks and charm and wondered why, in the past, so many missed the opportunities he had to offer.

Over the last few years, he had his choice of women who wanted to be with him, and he had fathered a few children to grow the flock. He ignored the sin of adultery because he knew he had God's blessing. Why else would so many women be attracted to him, if not God's will?

The truth, Thomas would never acknowledge. What he called the curse, gave him the ability of persuasion. It gave him the ability to convince others to follow him and give themselves to him willingly. The gift didn't work on everyone, especially not Mary or William, and Thomas was too conceded to ever fully recognize his abilities as anything other than natural charm. Thomas would also never come to realize his ability even gave him some power over Jonathan. His talent helped him convince Jonathan to leave them alone as long as they ran the power plant and supplied the Overlord's domain with constant electricity.

Thomas moved from the window, ready for his union with Melissa, when there came a knock on the door. Everyone knew he wasn't to be disturbed while meditating, yet he had a feeling this would be important. He opened the door to find William about to knock a second time.

Thomas and William

William knew the reverend's routine when it came to his sexual exploits. He didn't know if Thomas meditated to ask for God's forgiveness for the sins he committed, or if he did something else in his chambers. William did understand not to interrupt Thomas until he completed both parts of his routine, but this matter took precedence over Thomas's need for sexual gratification.

William decided to interrupt Thomas before he exited the mediation room. He nervously knocked once and waited.

If I didn't need this idiot and fake, I'd expose him and reach my goal in half the time.

Growing impatient, he prepared to knock again when the door flew open.

"William! What is so important you need to interrupt my meditation and administrations?"

"Thomas, they've done it. We have a way to use the weed, and we need to plan."

Thomas stood still a moment as William watched the anger drain from the reverend's face as William's words set in.

"That's wonderful news, tell me all about it. No, wait! I must administer to poor Melissa before we plan. Come to my office in one hour."

The door shut on William's face. If the reverend could see his assistant's face, he would catch the combination of surprise, disgust, and anger. William had no choice but to wait. He went to grab lunch; an hour later, he sat in Thomas's office waiting.

William let himself into the reverend's office and sat in the more comfortable of the two chairs facing Thomas's desk. The room's furnishings were basic and plain, part of the image Thomas portrayed to most of the congregation, but William knew the reverend's private chambers differed. Thomas liked nice things and excellent booze. He had a well-stocked liquor cabinet, and the bottles the scavenger teams brought back never lasted long.

William grew impatient. He put up with Larson only as a means to an end, and that end was to destroy the curse, and, if necessary, everyone who used it to take advantage of others. If he didn't need Larson and his resources, he would have left a long time ago. Not using powers wasn't enough and supplying the pervert in Philly with electricity for protection, sickened him.

William prepared to get up and leave when Thomas finally arrived.

"I am sorry I'm late; Melissa needed extra consoling today."

"I'm sure," was William's only response, which elicited a watch yourself look from Thomas.

"Now, William, tell me about the weed; how can we use it to rid the world of this scourge."

William gave the reverend all the details, stressing the need to take out Jonathan and free their community from his servitude. Thomas listened quietly while writing notes on a pad he always had on his desk. He asked no questions while William continued, but his expressions told William he wouldn't be happy with the reverend's response. He was correct.

"We have to be cautious, William; if Jonathan gets word of what we are doing and the weapon we have, he may get rid of all of us before we're ready to attack. We need to test further and build an arsenal to use farther west away from the Overlord. Then we will be prepared to go after him and free Philadelphia."

"We can't wait that long, Thomas; your plan could take years. Yes, we need to manufacture as many bombs as possible, but we can't waste them on countless tests. The team has tested the weed and the gas long enough."

"William, my boy, getting rid of his abilities is only half the battle. What about his soldiers? Do you really think they will quietly give up and lay down their weapons? He treats them well, and they share in his depravities. They may not desire freedom from the curse."

The universe works in mysterious ways, or maybe the reverend had more powers than he realized. Immediately upon finishing the discussion about soldiers, a loud, forceful knock startled both men. Thomas yelled; his displeasure evident.

"What do you want?"

The door thrust open, and one of Thomas's personal guards rushed in, out of breath with a fearful look on his face.

"Sir, Mary has returned; with soldiers."

CONVERGENCE

The Meeting at Creagerstown

A few days before Mary's return to Limerick she had pleaded her case to the Resistance.

"I have been waiting for hours! I would think you would be a little more appreciative of someone offering their help and an advanced warning of a danger heading your way."

"Not the start I was hoping for; how about we back up," Jim said as he sat nonchalantly across the table from Mary, not bothered by her frustration. He had been in this business long enough to know how to have the upper hand in any conversation or interrogation. Nicole and Susan followed into the room and took seats on the two sides of the conference table. Brian and one guard entered last and stood by the door. Brian smiled at Mary in a way that reinforced the fact he didn't trust her or want her around the Resistance.

"Hello, Mary, my name is Jim. I'm the head of the group here, which I'm sure you know is referred to as the Resistance, and I am also the leader of Sanctuary, a town we established to allow people with and without abilities to live and work together. To your right is Nicole, and to your left is Susan. Welcome to our town. Now tell me how we can help each other."

Mary spent the next few minutes talking about Reverend Larson, their group, and their relationship with Jonathan. Jim wasn't surprised Larson worked with Jonathan, as his spies had reported activity at the power plant. She briefly told them how she came to be with the Reverend Thomas and how she came to realize his cult was as dangerous as Jonathan, only in the opposite way.

"I don't know how we received these abilities, but I do know they can be used for good and can be used to rebuild our society in a new and better way. Unfortunately, much must be done first. I believe there is no place in a new society for people like Jonathan or Thomas."

Nicole listened intently and believed Mary to be sincere in her beliefs and desire to help rid the world of Jonathan and people like him. She had always been a good judge of character, even in her high school years. What Mary said next surprised everyone in the room.

"Thomas—calling him a reverend is close to sacrilegious—is working on a plan to defeat Jonathan as well as a desire to destroy what you have built. His ultimate goal is to rid the world of what he calls the curse. I know it sounds ridiculous, but recent developments have given him the means to accomplish his goals, at least on a local scale."

Jim interrupted before she could continue.

"I don't see how such a thing would be possible. We have been working on ways to resist and become immune to some abilities, but to do away with them seems unlikely, if not impossible."

"Have any of you ever heard of the purple weed, any of you?"

"I have," both Nicole and Brian said simultaneously. She gave Brian a nod to indicate he should speak. This facility was his house, and she didn't want to intrude.

"It has been called the poor man's high. It's horrible stuff to smoke or eat and doesn't do much but make you sick. It's invasive and was one of the most difficult weeds to control years ago when I worked on the family farm."

"That is correct, but for some reason, about two years ago, a fool in Thomas's cult—as I now know it to be—decided to drink old weed oil he found. After getting violently ill, he realized he felt different. I don't know the details, but somehow, he figured out the weed took away all his abilities. The effect was temporary, but it led to Thomas's exhaustive research to discover ways to use the weed to eliminate all abilities."

Nicole could tell by looking at Susan, she wasn't buying any of what Mary told them. Susan sat with a look of dismissal on her face, hands clasped in front of her, in a manner Nicole had come to realize meant, I'm not buying what you're selling. Nicole still believed Mary but wondered if she looked for a way to save Stephen, more than anything else. She missed him and was secretly afraid of letting her feelings get in the way of doing whatever they needed to do to defeat Jonathan.

"They have cultivated acres of the weed and have found various ways to use it as a weapon. I believe they have succeeded in finding a way to weaponize the weed and are getting ready to attack Jonathan in his fortress. They will lose, and they will die. I have foreseen it in my dreams."

"In your dreams!" Brian responded with impatience. "We are to listen to you when all you come here with is dreams and visions. We don't believe in this priestess crap."

Brian leaned against the wall; his arms crossed against his chest. He couldn't believe they were wasting time listening to this crap. He knew Jim for many years and respected him, but Jim never served his country and never fought against enemies who would use these kinds of tricks to gain access to vital information. Brian believed it all to be a ruse; he was determined to ensure this woman never left here without him at her side or in a body bag.

"It wasn't my choice to be called the 'Priestess,' that was Thomas's doing, but my abilities are real. Among other things, I can see glimpses of the future. If somehow Jonathan is not stopped, what I see is a terrible future, beyond your comprehension. Thomas can't do it alone, and neither can you. However, in my visions, I have seen success by the Resistance and the Abolitionists working together."

Mary paused and looked directly at Jim as if staring into his soul. It made him uncomfortable, a fact Brian noticed.

"I always had abilities to see little glimpses of the future, though not like a medium. I don't see spirits, and I can't tell an individual's prospects, but I would know when a visitor was coming to my door. I would realize to stay away from places and, I could see trouble or disasters if they involved me somehow.

"You understand this, Jim. I know you do."

Jim abruptly sat back in his chair, surprised, and not sure what to say. He never admitted it to anyone, but she wasn't wrong. Brian watched Jim even more intently as he began to understand why this woman had such an influence on his friend. Brian was only partially surprised by Jim's response.

"Yes, Mary, I do know. I have never admitted it before, but I guess the cat is out of the bag. It doesn't sound like my pre-event abilities were anywhere as strong as yours. However, I have seen things since the event. They haven't been clear visions, but I did see someone coming to us and helping. What exactly do you propose?"

"What I'm proposing is an alliance to defeat Jonathan and destroy his evil reign of terror. Time is running short; if you are willing, we must proceed with haste.

The Rage of the Overlord

The Overlord stood on his throne, his feet sinking into the soft cushioned fabric. He had displayed extreme emotion not witnessed before in the chamber, his anger evident on his bright red, distorted face. Across his brow, veins protruded, large and throbbing, ready to explode. Jonathan had tapped into a power he hadn't experienced before, a force so immense it would have killed any other person.

A fierce wind blew around the chamber as loose objects sailed across the room, some impaling those in attendance. Glass cracked in many of the massive windows lining the walls, while in other ornate windows, glass shattered, flying inside the chamber and out onto the street and courtyard below. Once priceless portraits and paintings of old Philadelphia ripped in their frames, as some flew off the walls and scattered across the chamber.

The guests in his throne room were terrified, beholding the display of power in front of their eyes. One visitor hid behind a chair, his face buried in his trembling hands, while a few others shook and cringed in puddles of their own making, for fear the Overlord would next use his power against them, like the woman lying dead on the floor.

One woman in attendance who had brought her children to meet the Overlord, he threw against a wall. The pressure against her body mounted as fiercely as the pain in her head, which caused her to scream. As her bones broke from the force, she screamed louder still; using the last breath she could gasp in her crushed and burning lungs before passing out and dying. Her children, who appeared to be immune to the Overlord's powers, watched in horror as blood continued to discharge out of their mother's lifeless body.

A few of his visitors tried to run for the doors before they slammed shut, and the Overlord directed his anger towards their fragile bodies. They were all now collapsed on the floor, their bodies writhing in pain, as Jonathan's power first seared their bodies from the inside and then drew out all the life they contained. He had used this ability on a lesser scale to power his capabilities to new heights when needed to accomplish a significant task, such as defeating a line of fools trying to attack him and when he destroyed the statue of William Penn. In those instances, he used their lives to give him enhanced power, but now he was in a fit of rage, ripping the force from their bodies and throwing it back at them with a vengeance he had never released before.

If Jonathan ever had an ounce of sanity, it became clear it was now gone. He let his power and rage destroy his mind, so only the insanity of an evil person existed. Stephen witnessed this display of anger from the back corner of the throne room, where Jonathan instructed him to stand after his performance. He too, lay on the floor as if in pain, but Stephen faked the intense pain others experienced till their death. Susan had taught him well how to harness his abilities to defend against the use of another's capabilities against him. It worked well, but it was difficult, and Stephen wasn't sure how much longer he could defend against Jonathan's power.

The day had started so well for Stephen, considering what his life had become. Hours ago, the latest guard of the last few weeks woke him. The newer guard, Mikal, who was more compassionate than Ander, had been visiting a friend of his from their time attending college in England. The friend moved to Philadelphia for his research, and Mikal became trapped in the States when the event happened.

Having grown up in Russia, Mikal knew the way to survive in a bad situation was to hide your true feelings and work for the power in charge. He confided in Stephen and Mark; he hated the Overlord and what he had done, but Mikal knew he had to be on the inside to survive. He never abused his position and always tried to be as respectful and kind as possible without being caught.

Mikal instructed Stephen to put on the new costume he brought him for Stephen's performance to entertain the Overlord's guests in a few hours. More flamboyant than usual, the costume contained pink and purple feathers creating wings to wear on his back. The pants were a shiny gold material, tight and barely large enough to be called briefs. There was no shirt, only the silver-studded harness for the wings.

Stephen had hoped Alfredo would personally bring the costume. He wanted to receive an update on how the plans were proceeding to destroy Jonathan. Alfredo was Stephen's contact with the Resistance and the outside world. He didn't know how the Resistance arranged the connection, but Stephen was glad he had a way to communicate with the world beyond the fortress. Mikal's respect for Mark and Stephen's privacy made it easy for him to swap vital information with Alfredo when he came in to measure or perform fittings of the latest costumes Jonathan forced them to wear for their torture and his pleasure.

Stephen wondered if the latest costume existed to degrade and embarrass him or if he was to be a gift to one of the guests to satisfy their sick sexual perversions. He hadn't been used in that way before, but Jonathan had threatened it for some time. Knowing the Overlord's depravity, Stephen wouldn't have been surprised if he had to sexually perform while the Overlord watched or be forced to strut in front of the entire audience in the throne room.

When they announced him to the Overlord a few hours later, Jonathan directed him to perform a dance where he acted out various sexual movements. When the dancing didn't please Jonathan, Stephen could feel his body taken over. He could have resisted, but he couldn't let his abilities show, so he acted out displays that embarrassed him as Jonathan compelled him to touch himself in many suggestive ways.

Things looked about to worsen when he felt his hands move toward the golden briefs he wore. Stephen almost had them pulled down when he saw Ander come rushing into the room, halting the performance. Jonathan had instructed Stephen to stand in the corner and wait to continue the performance later.

Aspen approached the dais slowly; Stephen could tell the man he knew as Ander was afraid, something Stephen had never detected in the man before this time. After a brief conversation, Stephen watched, as Jonathan, with a jerk of his hand, flung Ander across the room, his body many feet above the floor, as all hell began to break out. The Overlord had said little as his tirade began, but from what he had screamed at Ander, Stephen suspected someone had tried to harm Patricia.

Stephen could feel his body and willpower start to fade, and for the first time since becoming a prisoner, he feared for his life. He couldn't hold on much longer; soon, his body's fake writhing would become all too real. Stephen was within seconds of losing control when he felt the Overlord's hold on him quickly diminish. When he looked up, Stephen saw Jonathan step down from his throne, collapse in the chair, and fall to the floor. The Overlord appeared extremely weak and drained, his entire body shaking as if having a mild convulsion.

Stephen watched as Nathan rose from the floor, apparently unhurt, and helped his Overlord. Stephen sluggishly managed to get himself off the floor before being grabbed by another nearby guard who hadn't been a victim of the Overlord's rage. It appeared to Stephen, the display of power had exhausted Jonathan's body and mind. A brief moment passed while the Overlord regained composure and called for the guards to clear the room and dispose of the dead and injured bodies down the garbage hole. As the guard who grabbed him took Stephen out the door, he saw Ander's body pushed to the hole and watched it disappear.

Stephen had escaped possible death by mere seconds, but now he had the beginnings of a plan. It would be extreme and risky for those involved. Many might die, but if all went well, they could be free of the Overlord.

Stephen and Patricia

As the guard pulled him away, Stephen recalled the first time he met with Patricia in person, and he hoped no harm had come to her. He liked Patricia, and even before the first time they met, he could sense in her some abilities. He believed she kept them hidden from Jonathan, or maybe he knew and didn't care. She certainly hadn't abilities as strong as Jonathan's; no one could. Many times, Stephen watched her sitting next to Jonathan as he performed or waited in the wings. On more than one occasion, she begged Jonathan to show mercy to those brought before him. On most occurrences, he agreed, at least while she remained in attendance, but Stephen knew Jonathan made the pain of their death far grander after his betrothed was no longer in attendance.

Their first face-to-face meeting occurred when he had been summoned to Patricia's reading chamber a couple of weeks ago. Ander led him to her chamber, where Stephen first met and became the future charge of Mikal. Being his usual bastard self, Ander had not told him anything before they arrived at Patricia's reading room. As they walked, Stephen wondered if the ruse was up and if Ander led him to his death. It wouldn't be beyond Jonathan's or Ander's sick humor to force him to wear a ridiculous costume to his demise.

He hid his wonder when Ander handed him over to Mikal, who then led him into the chamber. Stephen was surprised and pleased when he saw Patricia sitting on a velvet couch waiting for him; it certainly wasn't what he expected. She apologized for what Jonathan made him do, and Stephen could tell her hatred for Jonathan remained strong. He felt sorry for the future she would be forced to endure if they couldn't eliminate Jonathan soon. He knew the wedding would be a perfect time, but he had no idea at that moment what they could do against his power.

Stephen thanked her for the apology before he began to dance for her in the heavy costume. Unlike the usually skimpy outfits he wore to the throne room, this costume wholly covered every inch of his body. The feathered and beaded regalia reminded him of one's worn by a Mummer on New Year's Day. It was hot, but it didn't bother him as his abilities did their magic. He only danced for a minute before Patricia stopped the performance and asked him to sit next to her, so they could talk. Mikal objected at first until Patricia threatened to tell the Overlord Mikal made inappropriate advances. Patricia instructed Mikal to wait outside the door, which he reluctantly did after a brief objection. Her gumption impressed Stephen.

"Again, I am sorry. I have seen you forced to perform in the throne room, but I don't believe I know your name."

"My name is Stephen, my lady."

"Oh, please drop the lady shit. That bastard forces people to use the title only because he knows I hate it so much. He may genuinely love me in his special sick way, but it doesn't stop him from getting pleasure by making my life miserable. He keeps me locked away most of the time, and I rarely ever get to have a normal conversation with anyone. I know you came to this insane asylum only a short while ago; tell me, what are things like out in the streets?"

Stephen hesitated, unsure how much truth to divulge, but he believed her hatred of Jonathan was genuine, and he decided to trust her.

"Things are bad out there in and around the city. Jonathan continues to expand his control, and he feeds on the weak by stealing their life to help power his objectives; however, all hope is not lost."

He paused in thought and made a decision he felt correct. Stephen explained to her his true identity and purpose but didn't divulge his abilities. He thought it best Patricia didn't know more than necessary to form an alliance he hoped would help defeat Jonathan. If things went wrong, he didn't want her to suffer for what she knew, and he didn't want to take a chance Jonathan, would notice a difference in her behavior.

He confided about Sanctuary and the Resistance without divulging his contact with the outside to protect her as much as possible. Patricia appeared surprised anyone around would willingly defy Jonathan. She had lost all hope of ever escaping his grasp.

"Stephen, for the first time since being brought here, I now have some hope. You have made me feel better, and for that, I am grateful. Wouldn't that jerk be surprised to know sending you here genuinely did make me feel happy."

She stood and walked over to the barred window, lost in her thoughts as Stephen waited. He knew she had more to say, and he could understand the emotional struggles she had to deal with every day. He wanted to join her at the window, put his arm around her to give her comfort, but he knew that would be a bad idea for many reasons.

Patricia hated to leave Stephen sitting there waiting while she tried to deal with her emotions. The brief glimmer of hope he had given put butterflies in her stomach and brought glints of moisture to her eyes. She didn't want to break down and cry in front of him, and she worked to control her emotions before asking the most important question on her mind.

"How is Mark? I miss him so much. Please let him know I still love him, and I don't want him to do anything to get himself killed. Does he know the truth about you, Stephen?"

"To answer your first question, he is fine. Jonathan prefers to torture me more than Mark. I'm his most favored play toy, which I believe is a good thing for Mark. I have told him my secret and given him some hope as well, and I assure you I will protect him as best I can. I will not involve him in any plan unless necessary, and of course, I will let him know how much you miss him."

They talked for another ten minutes, speculating on what happened to bring the abilities to the Earth. He told her more about the work at Sanctuary and how their goal was to build a new society to use the powers for good and more significant development of the human species. He began to ask Patricia about her abilities when Mikal interrupted, saying the Overlord waited to have lunch with his betrothed. Stephen could feel the disappointment and reluctance from Patricia as he said his goodbyes.

Stephen and Mikal

Stephen's recollections of his conversations with Patricia were interrupted by the sound of Mikal's voice as he took charge of Stephen and instructed the other guard to go back to the throne room and make sure it was secure.

"Stephen, are you okay? I heard about an incident in the throne room, and the Overlord killed many people."

"An incident is one way to describe what transpired; welcome to hell would be another. He didn't just kill people, Mikal; he ripped them apart from the inside and stole their life energy; it was horrifying. I heard stories of how he used people to power his abilities, but to see it happen, will cause me to have many nightmares."

Stephen laid it on thick. He needed Mikal on his side, and the best way to achieve the task would be to make Mikal realize how genuinely evil Jonathan had become with his total disregard, even for innocent women and children.

"Mikal, he didn't merely kill the visiting human slime like him, who came to buy his favor; he also killed innocent women, one while her children stood there and had no choice but to watch. Somehow, I was lucky. He forced me to stand aside in a corner while he spoke to Ander. I don't know what Ander told him, but Jonathan lost his mind and unleashed power I have never seen before. He directed his power more at others, and I only experienced intermittent pain as waves of his anger moved around the room. I'm sure though, had he not stopped when he did, I would be down the hole with the others, breathing my last, if I lasted that long."

"Breathing your last? Did he have people tossed down the hole who remained alive?"

Stephen could detect the surprise and revulsion in Mikal's tone. Evidently, he had never been present in the throne room when Jonathan dispatched those he found useless. Stephen stopped them in their tracks and stared directly into Mikal's eyes, while with a raised voice to indicate his anger, Stephen responded.

"You seem surprised, Mikal. It's not the first time, and I'm sure not the last . . ."

Stephen drew nearer and lowered his voice before continuing closer to Mikal's ear so no one else could overhear.

". . . if we can't do something to stop him."

Stephen put the thought out there, hoping Mikal's uneasiness of Jonathan's actions would be the motivation Mikal needed to switch sides, but it appeared he wasn't yet at the point where he would be willing to betray his master. Mikal was about to respond when Stephen cut him off, this time in a tone of friendship.

"What happened, Mikal? From what little Jonathan said before lashing out, it sounded like something transpired with Patricia."

"Yes, a recruit brought in by Ander to join the guards had approached Patricia, making sexual advances and asking her to satisfy his needs. When she refused, he tried to use his abilities on her, and when that didn't work, he used physical force to try and rape her; he almost succeeded. Luckily Ander was nearby and heard her screams for help."

They had arrived at Stephen's room; he dreaded telling Mark what had almost happened to Patricia. He knew Mark still loved her very much and hoped one day their nightmare would end and they would be together. Stephen liked Mark, and their love for each other increased his determination to bring Jonathan down, one way or another.

"I assume Ander is helping restore order to the throne room. I know he was dreading having to give the news to the Overlord."

Again, raising his voice to make his point, "Ander is dead, Mikal! Your Overlord tossed him aside like a piece of trash and had the body tossed down the hole. I'm not sure if he remained alive, and frankly, I don't care."

Mikal hesitated for a moment, lost in his thoughts. Stephen tried to continue the conversation, but Mikal unlocked the door and pushed Stephen in with more force than he had ever used against him before. As the door closed behind Stephen, he knew he now had a possible way to turn Mikal. He yelled as loud as he could before Mikal moved too far away to hear.

"Go, run back to your Overlord! Maybe you can take over for Ander and end up just like him someday!"

Unknown to Stephen, the words had the intended effect. Mikal stopped a little way down the hall and slumped against a wall. His hands were shaking, part in fear and part in rage. Unable to control his emotions, he put his hands over his face like he had not done since his early years in prayer. His throat burned, and his heart pounded faster as he began to cry.

Why did this happen? How did this happen? How did I allow myself to be dragged down so low, one wrong decision after another? I would be better off dead and free. If only I had let that bastard have his way with me and kill me, I would be in heaven and free. Dear God, forgive me for what I have done and for the lives I have taken.

Mikal pulled himself together, stood, and walked back to his quarters. He knew they probably needed him but didn't care. He was glad to find his roommates were elsewhere, so he could sit and think about what to do. Could he help Stephen? He could end up dead and in hell a lot sooner, unless maybe, giving his life to defeat the Overlord would absolve him of his sins.

He lay down on his cot and thought back on one of the mortal sins he had committed.

Two years ago, the incident happened while he walked to a shelter someone set up in Bensalem, a couple of miles north of Philadelphia. He tried to avoid people, but unknown to him, someone followed close behind. Without any warning, a man grabbed him from behind and dragged him around an old railroad switch house along the former northeast corridor mainline. The man appeared older than Mikal. Well-built and tall, the man was dirty and wore ragged, torn clothes under a heavy coat the man now removed and dropped to the ground.

The assailant had long stringy hair, which added to the look of someone who had lost his mind and had no regard for himself or others. He tied Mikal to a horizontal pole that had once been part of a fence and began to rip and cut Mikal's clothes from his body with a knife the man brandished in Mikal's face.

"I'm going to slowly cut you with this knife and watch the blood run down your body and onto your dirty cock before I violate you with this knife the way you did to me. Then I'm going to slice that pretty cock of yours little by little. If you try to use your tricks on me again, remember you will still be tied to the pole with no one to help you this time."

Mikal had no idea what the man was talking about; he never met him before. He evidently had Mikal confused with someone else who hurt him tremendously. Someone who used their abilities to abuse the man sexually, and now he wanted revenge. Mikal tried to explain to the man he never hurt him and had no special powers, but the man wouldn't listen.

The crazed man took the knife and cut a line across Mikal's chest. The pain caused him to scream, which only made the man laugh and cut again, this time down across Mikal's stomach, which made him cry out in pain louder than the first time.

"Go ahead, scream, and scream some more. I like it!"

The man stopped for a moment as if listening to something, probably in his mind. He then moved closer to Mikal, got up close into Mikal's face, the breath and the odor coming from his body causing Mikal to wince.

"Change of plans. Before I have my fun violating you, I think I'll start by slicing away your manhood, piece by dirty, filthy piece."

Mikal's heart raced, the veins in his neck throbbing; his entire exposed body exuded sweat mixing with his already spilled blood even though the temperature was almost below freezing. He couldn't take any more pain; he had to make the man stop.

"Let's begin."

The man put a ragged old glove on his left hand and grabbed Mikal's penis, but before the knife in his right hand could touch him again, Mikal screamed and cursed at the man while something inside him he had never experienced before, erupted with tremendous force. He effortlessly managed to break the bonds, which held him, and without touching his adversary, he flung him yards across the air and onto the long empty tracks.

Mikal could have run, but instead, what he did next haunted him ever since. He grabbed the knife the man had dropped, and ignoring the man's pleas for mercy, he stuck the blade deep into the man's heart, killing him instantly.

The memories caused Mikal to cry as he lay on his cot while his hands absentmindedly ran along the scars across his body. He needed God's forgiveness to avoid going from one hell to another. He knew what he had to do. Even if it weren't enough to buy his way into heaven, he would help Stephen in any way he could to defeat the Overlord, even if it meant he had to kill again.

Jim and Brian

Jim waited in the rear vehicle down the street from the reverend's office. Accompanied by six of his finest soldiers, Mary walked to Thomas's office to prepare him for the meeting about to occur, if he allowed. Jim thought it best she go first and make Reverend Thomas understand; they were not there to take over or harm them in any way. The purpose of the meeting was to plan a possible alliance and attack against a monster. If Thomas chose not to help, they would leave, but not without ensuring no one could depart the area to warn Jonathan of their plans.

They had to strike soon, and if Thomas didn't agree to participate, they would have to attack even earlier, possibly before they were fully prepared and before they could get word inside to Stephen. The future of everyone who remained within one hundred miles of Philadelphia was at stake. Jim thought it a risk worth taking, even though not everyone agreed.

Jim waited with six additional soldiers and Nicole in a convoy of one heavily armored military Jeep and two trucks equipped with machine guns he hoped not to need. Brian, of course, wanted to attend, but considering his extreme vocal objections to this alliance, Jim ordered him to stay behind and continue to prepare. Jim and Brian were great longtime friends and worked well together, but they didn't always agree. Brian didn't trust Mary and did not want an alliance with her cult. As Jim waited for word to move forward, he thought back on the heated discussion.

"Jim, have you become a crazy idiot? Have you lost your fucking mind? You can't trust this woman. You—"

"Stop right there, Brian. We are friends who go back a long way. As much as I want and respect your opinion, I will not stand here and be insulted.

Immediately after Mary concluded her argument, Brian motioned for Jim to follow him outside. When Jim walked out the door, Brian was pacing back and forth across the grass, like a caged bull.

Jim's comment about being insulted caused Brian to slow down and stand directly in front of his friend. Brian's face became red, and Jim could see veins popping out of Brian's forehead, which he knew from experience to be a sign of the man's anger.

"I'm sorry, Jim, but I don't like this. Maybe it's my military training and distrust of everyone, but I have a bad feeling about this whole endeavor. You could be walking into a trap. If you meet this man, this supposed reverend, I'm going with you to make sure you don't do anything . . . stupid or get yourself hurt.

Before the last comment, Brian backed away and diverted his eyes. Jim knew Brian cared about him as more than just a casual friend. Brian remarked many times how Jim reminded him of his brother.

"I'm sorry, Brian, but I'm going to meet Reverend Thomas, and you are not going with me."

Brian turned back to face his friend, about to raise his voice again when Jim put up his hand and gave his friend the look he knew too well.

"I understand your concern. Yes, this could be a trap, which is why you will stay here, just in case. If we don't make it back, you will need to take over. You will need to be a leader of the fighters and the civilians. I know you can do it; I know inside you is the man with the compassion to do what is needed. Your willingness to put our friendship second to what you believe is right proves your strength and resilience."

Jim, hesitated, finding it hard to control his emotions, which he found disturbing. He usually didn't become emotional, and he turned away from his friend briefly before moving closer to Brian and laying a hand on his shoulder.

"I trust you, I trust your instincts, but she is probably correct. We can't defeat Jonathan alone. We must take this chance. I will leave it up to you to plan the number of vehicles and fighters to accompany Mary, Nicole, and me."

"I will reluctantly agree, Jim. But I . . ."

Brian hesitated a moment, a strange look on his face.

"I have a bad feeling about all of this, Jim. It's not an ability I have perceived to have picked up, but nowadays, a bad feeling may be more than just a feeling. Let's get back in before they start asking questions we don't want to answer."

The remainder of the meeting turned to plan when and how they would travel to meet Thomas. Brian did his best not to let his feelings show, but they were uncharacteristically evident.

Jim knew Brian would have liked to send more soldiers, but he knew Jim would object to overdoing with too much show of force. Jim was also sure there were support soldiers and armaments close behind and out of sight.

It had been over half an hour since Mary and the advance team headed to meet Thomas, and he started to worry. What if Thomas had more support than Mary led them to believe? What if this all were a trap? Jim could tell without any abilities, Nicole also worried. He reached out and took hold of her hand to comfort his friend and even himself. He sensed something more bothered her, but he didn't want to pry.

"Don't worry, Nicole; I'm sure everything is okay. We would have heard some gunshots if it were a trap—unless they use powers they purportedly hate."

"Are you trying to comfort yourself or me, Jim?"

"Both. If things go well, this could all be over in a month or so, one way or another. Hopefully, it will end well for us, and you can reunite with Stephen. I don't need powers to know you are thinking of him often."

Before Nicole could respond, Cody, one of the soldiers who accompanied Mary, came back and confirmed Thomas was willing to meet. Nicole didn't get to tell her friend the news she confirmed.

"We have been granted permission to move the convoy up to his office, if you wish. Our men checked out the area and have seen no apparent danger."

"Yes, we will, so we are not walking as much out in the open. Cody, instruct the lead driver to move out and be on guard."

"Yes, sir!"

As they began to move, Jim's heart raced faster. One way or another, this was it, the beginning of the battle soon to start; the campaign for Philadelphia. Over two hundred and fifty years later, it was time to fight against another tyrant, only this time, he wasn't an ocean away.

Meeting the Reverend Thomas

Thomas, Mary, and his two guards moved to the conference room to receive the delegation from Sanctuary. He said little to Mary, and when they entered the room, he began to pace. Mary could tell Thomas was deep in thought. He stopped by the window and stared out at the hills in the distance.

How could she do this to me? She ruined our chance to take out these imbeciles and then get rid of that bombastic fool in Philly. He is the biggest menace, a fact I understand, but we don't need help to destroy the Overlord and his grip on the city with the weed at our disposal.

Thomas was angry, but more so hurt, that Mary would betray him in such a manner. Their relationship had always been considered complicated, but now he didn't know what to do, how to proceed. He had feelings for her, he could never let show, but most likely, she already knew.

She is, after all, the Priestess. Maybe she is correct; perhaps she saw the future and knows for certain we need them, but then what. If we successfully destroy the Overlord and all he assembled, will she be willing to turn against Sanctuary? Would she next turn on him and everything he built?

He was awakened from his musings by the sound of Mary's voice.

"I'm sorry, Thomas. I didn't do this to hurt you or to be in any way vindictive. We need the resources of Sanctuary and their Resistance arm to defeat the Overlord. We can't do it without them. I have seen it, and you know my visions are to be trusted."

Thomas turned from the window with a sigh. He looked at Mary without immediately speaking, turned away, walked to the head of the table, pulled out his chair, and sat. Most people would consider his behavior rude, but Mary knew he processed her words in his way.

"Mary, I missed you. You hurt me, but the hardest part was not knowing why or if you would ever come back. I hope we can start anew, and I sincerely hope you come back to me when this is over. I need you, and more importantly, the community needs you."

"I know, Thomas and I will—"

Mary was cut off by the knock on the door. A second later, the door opened, and another of Thomas's guards led in the delegation from Sanctuary.

Damn, she was about to let me know her intentions, and now I will have to wait and hope we can talk later.

Thomas stood and politely held out his hand. He hated acting differently from how he felt, but Thomas knew he had to put on a good show.

"I am Reverend Thomas Larson; welcome to my version of Sanctuary, a place where people can be free of the curse."

"Hello Reverend Larson, I'm Jim Oswald, and this is my assistant, Nicole. We don't consider the abilities to be a curse. They are a gift if used properly. We use the gift to help people, to cure them of illness, and to learn. If used properly, the gift can help us build a new and better world. It's not the abilities that hurt people; it is the abuse of those abilities, which is why we are here.

"We need to do whatever it takes to stop Jonathan. We know it; I'm sure you do as well. I don't know what deal you have with him, but when the Overlord no longer needs you, he will wipe your community off the map. We have our differences, but we must work together, or we all will probably die."

"I think you are overly melodramatic, but please sit so we can have a civil discussion.

"Jordan, bring some food and drink. The rest of you wait outside."

The guards left as Jim and Nicole sat on opposite sides of the table with Thomas and Mary at the ends. A moment later, Jordan returned with a tray of juices, water, and another plate of pastries.

"One of our members was a pastry chef in Reading before the . . . gift, as you say, arrived and destroyed her life. The curse has in one way or another hurt everyone here—"

"I'm sure they have been hurt, Thomas, but not by the gift. Evil people who were waiting for a chance to abuse and deceive others hurt them, just as—"

"Enough!" Mary shouted, startling Thomas and Jim. I didn't risk my life to come here and then leave to find Sanctuary just so the two of you can argue your different philosophies of life after the event. We have a common enemy; it is time to work together."

Jim put up his hands as if in surrender. He felt embarrassed for letting his emotions get away from him. He vowed he wouldn't allow it to happen and hoped the rest of the meeting went better.

"I'm sorry, Mary, I shouldn't allow my emotions to get the better of me. Please let me show my sincerity by first putting all my cards on the table."

Jim faced Thomas before continuing.

"We currently have two operatives within Bartram Fortress. The first one, Stephen, is being held captive, and they routinely force him to entertain Jonathan and his guests. He has access to Jonathan and his intended wife, Patricia. His roommate was Patricia's love interest before Jonathan hunted them down, so he is more than willing to participate in any action against Jonathan.

"Our second operative is a costume maker who gets to have direct contact with Stephen and is free to come and go out of the fortress. He passes his information on to our operatives in the city. Our network of operatives and contacts is quite large. Finding recruits to work against

Jonathan is rather easy."

Thomas put his hand up and asked him to stop. All the while, Jim spoke; the reverend had a look of dismissive disbelieve on his face.

"I find this all hard to believe. How does your operative inside manage to get so close to the Overlord without him detecting his subterfuge?"

"Stephen has many abilities which allow him to withstand almost any torture. He allowed Jonathan's men to capture him for spying, but when Jonathan was unable to break him, he decided to use Stephen for entertainment. Our belief is Jonathan still suspects him of being a spy, and using him in this way keeps him close, easier to watch."

"Nicole, I noticed you squirm a bit when Jim mentioned torture, and I sense Stephen is special to you?"

"Yes, Mary, he is my husband."

The room remained quiet for a moment before Thomas continued after giving a strange look toward Nicole.

"So, you have one useful operative; what is that going to accomplish."

"It gets us the information we need, Thomas. It enables us to plan. Without getting into too much detail at the moment, we hope to strike during the upcoming wedding. Jonathan scheduled the ceremony to happen in less than a month. We have teams already in position hiding in plain sight all around the city, with more training. However, brute force will not defeat a man like Jonathan, which is where you come in. Your turn, Reverend Thomas."

Mary could hear the disdain in Jim's voice, the almost dismissive way he said, Reverend Thomas. She hoped the meeting would not again disintegrate into name-calling and arguments of philosophy. This alliance needed to work, or they would all end up dead. She had seen it in a dream the prior evening, but she kept it to herself for now.

"There isn't much to tell," Thomas began. "We are a small community, and we have managed to stay below the Overlord's notice. We have nothing to offer you."

Again, allowing his anger to get the better of him, Jim shouted.

"Cut the crap, Larson, we know damn well you have contact and a long-standing agreement with that bastard to work the power plant to keep power supplied to Philadelphia. Your control of the facility alone, is in itself, a strategic advantage. And then there is the weed."

"What weed? What the hell are you talking about? I know nothing of—"

Mary stood up, knocking her chair to the floor. She smacked her hands on the table, causing water to spill from her glass, as she continued in a loud voice.

"Enough? Thomas, you will tell them everything or I—"

"What do you know? You haven't even been here for months."

"I know everything—I have seen it."

Thomas looked a bit panicked, and at the same time, lost, as he sat thinking of what he should do. He took a long drink of water, giving himself a few seconds to think, stall, and come to grips with how so many things had suddenly and without warning changed.

"Alright, I will tell you everything. Yes, we do have an agreement with the Overlord. He leaves us alone, as long as we supply him power. He knows we are no threat to him since we refuse to use any abilities in the community. In fact, most of the people here have no abilities at all."

Thomas's heart raced, his distress evident on his face; he didn't want to do this, and he inwardly cursed the bitch, Mary, for forcing him to divulge all their secrets. Ultimately, he had no choice but to work with Sanctuary—for now.

"The weed has grown wild in this area for as long as anyone can remember. Some time ago—"

The door flew open, interrupting Thomas, as William barged in and stood before the group, glaring at his leader.

"Are you crazy? Are you going to give away all our secrets to these people? You want them all gone as much as I do."

Jim was about to rise and speak. He became angry to know the Abolitionists secretly listened to and plotted against them when Nicole reached over and touched his hand while shaking her head, no.

"William, please sit down. I feel Mary has put us into a predicament we can't escape."

"I swear to your damn God, if you continue, I will get word to the Overlord, and he will end this treason."

Jim stood and approached William.

"Such a move would be the last mistake you ever make."

A few seconds after Jim's statement, the group heard a loud but distant explosion. Thomas's face went white. He feared he was about to lose everything. He put his hands over his face in prayer, asking for guidance, while William became even more enraged.

"What the hell did you just do, and how?"

Jim moved closer to William, sensing the man to be a problem now and in the future.

"Regardless of the outcome today, William, we will be watching you closely and making sure you have no way of contacting Jonathan until our plans are complete one way or another. Now I suggest you sit down as asked.

"To answer your question. I prepared a demonstration of our resolve and capabilities in case needed. I promise, we mean you no harm and don't want to interfere with what you have built here, but we will never let you betray us to your Overlord."

Nicole had no idea Jim had prepared what he had called the demonstration. She was ready to use her abilities to get them out of there when she first heard the explosion. She gave Jim a look of annoyance as he returned to his chair, for not including her in his plans as her heart rate returned to normal, and she let her body relax. From the corner of her eye, she watched Mary move over so William could sit next to her.

"Please, William, sit with me."

He reluctantly pulled over a chair and sat.

"This is a mistake."

"I guarantee you, William, it is not." Mary took his hand to offer him comfort. "Please continue, Thomas, tell them everything."

Reverend Larson removed his hands from his face, revealing bloodshot eyes. Mary noticed for the first time since returning how much older and tired Thomas looked. She felt sorry for him and sorry for the way the situation developed.

She also noticed how strong and confident William had become. He clearly had been building his mind as well as his body. She feared that no matter the outcome of this meeting, Thomas's days in control of all he created were in jeopardy. Her dreams were beginning to make sense, and it saddened her deeply.

Thomas continued.

"I do want to apologize for the interruption. As I was about to say, we discovered a few years ago, the weed could temporarily suppress all abilities. It grows wild in this area, and some people have, in the past, used it for a cheap high. One of our residents found an old vial of the oil and decided to drink the liquid. He realized what minor abilities he had, which he was working to suppress, were suddenly gone. The effect lasted only a short while, but some here realized its enormous potential.

"The problem is, you must eat it or drink the oil. It is bitter with no way to hide the taste in food. The intended target would immediately stop eating before consuming enough to be effective."

Thomas hesitated, not wanting to reveal their latest accomplishment, but he realized they had no choice.

"A recent discovery by one of our members has changed the circumstances, and we believe the weed can now be properly weaponized on a large enough scale to use against the Overlord. We were working on plans to use the weed to attack him, and we were confident of our success."

"You are wrong, Thomas. I have seen it in my visions. You cannot defeat him alone."

William shook his head no as he spoke.

"So, you say, Mary."

"William, you have known me long enough to know my ability is real."

William nodded and dropped his gaze down to the table, feeling defeated for the moment.

"Please continue, Thomas. I know of the weed but never thought anything could suppress abilities. I'm quite interested."

"Yes, Jim, I'm sure.

"We have been cultivating the weed for a couple of years and have many acres growing around the area. A few months ago, some of our people started working on ways to make it more useful. I had just received an update from William when you arrived.

"William, I think you should continue."

William raised his head and gave Thomas a look of contempt. He would play along for now, but his day would come, and he would eliminate all who stood in his way.

"To keep this short, we found a way to create a super-concentrated fine powder version of the weed flowers. The powder, when inhaled, works in seconds to suppress all abilities. One exposure to the substance lasts anywhere from thirty to forty minutes, depending on the individual. Jonathan appears to have extraordinarily strong powers, so there is no way to know precisely how long it will work on him, if at all.

"We have developed explosive devices, which will allow us to disperse the powder quickly. We have five devices ready to go, and we can have another twenty ready to go in a week. They can be large enough to spread across a city block or small enough to be smuggled into a building."

"This is unexpected and fantastic news."

The look on Jim's face, couldn't hide his excitement as he continued.

"Do you have gas masks? Will they work against the powder?"

"Of course not, Mr. Sanctuary; why would we need them? I have no idea if they will work."

William's angry response flowed through the room, and Mary had a sudden vision building upon her dream that disturbed her a great deal, but she didn't let it show. She didn't usually have these images while awake; this was a new development for her.

"Don't worry, Jim, we have more than enough for all our soldiers. If we can get one of these devices, I can arrange a test with Brian and some volunteers."

"Sounds like a plan, Nicole."

"Now let's talk schedules, we have less than a month, and we will need time to get some of the devices to our contacts."

Madness and Perversions
of the Overlord

The Overlord entered his private chambers flanked by two nervous guards, earlier stationed outside the throne room when all hell broke loose. They didn't see what had happened, but they could hear the commotion and screams. They entered the throne room as ordered by Nathan and the Overlord just in time to see Ander's body slide over the edge of the hole, down into the pit.

"My God, what has he done."

"Just shut up and move your ass before we end up like Ander."

As Nathan instructed, they escorted the Overlord back to his chambers, where they now stood at the doors of his bedroom awaiting orders. The two nervously watched the Overlord pace back and forth like a caged animal looking for a way to escape. Neither one wanted to say a word for fear of feeling his wrath. Jonathan stopped in his tracks and turned to the guards, causing their hearts to race faster in their chests.

"What the fuck are you two assholes doing standing there? Get out!" he screamed. "Get out now and stand watch outside the main chamber door."

The guards inwardly sighed in relief as they started walking out the door.

"Wait! Bring that red-haired whore from the chamber down the hall. Now! If she is not here in less than five minutes, I will skin you both while alive."

After the outer doors closed, he screamed, and in his continuing rage, he used his power to rip his clothing from his body before continuing to pace across the floor.

"Idiots, how could they be so careless?"

You should flay them all, Jonnyboy.

"Grandmum, is that you? I miss you, I miss your touch, but I can't; I need them, don't you see?"

Why? You are all-powerful. You are like God—no, you are God.

Silently, he let her words sink into his mind and came to a new realization.

I am. I am God; I'm better than God. My fool parents should see me now. I should pull their bodies from the ground and hang them on the wall to watch me take my pleasures with these fools.

Yes, do it; make your dad pay for calling you a worthless piece of shit.

Maybe I'll hang one in the throne room to watch me rule over these stupid bitches and bastards. They will all pay; they will all pay for what they have done to me. How dare they deny me what I wanted? How dare they not give themselves to me freely? They had their opportunity in the past before I received my gift. The gift the universe granted me, the abilities, the powers to make them pay. I have made them pay for their mistakes, and I'm not done.

Yes, make them pay. Make them pay, Jonnyboy.

I miss you; I miss your touch. Touch me, grandmum, like you used to.

You don't need me to touch you anymore. You're a big boy now; touch yourself as I taught you—yes, just like that.

Had anyone been witness to the events playing out in the Overlords chambers, they would have seen him stop his pacing and stand still, swaying back and forth. They would have witnessed the Overlord fondling himself like an unsure teen, just discovering the pleasure of self-gratification. If they stood before him, they would have seen the empty yet disturbed eyes of the Overlord and observed bloody drool slowly fall out of his mouth.

With a knock on the door, he awoke from his trance.

"What is it?"

"We have the woman you ask for, my Lord."

The Overlord went to his bed and lay down on the covering, which used to be the oversized flag of the city of Philadelphia.

"Send her in and stand guard at the outer chamber."

"Yes, my Lord."

"Lord is no longer acceptable. You will call me Lord God. Spread the word! Anyone who does not address me adequately will be tossed into the pit, alive.

"Yes, Lord God."

When he heard the outer door close, he called the woman to his bedroom and told her to stand in front of his bed.

She did as told, trying to hold back tears. She stood at the bottom of the bed, eyes down, but she knew the Overlord was naked on the bed, waiting for her. The last time he took her, she needed to stay in the medical ward for days to recover. She gave herself willingly, afraid of the consequences if she didn't. After all, he wasn't the first.

This time the choice wasn't hers to make.

The Overlord gazed intently at the young redhead. When he first brought her to the fortress, she was barely what in the past had been considered legal age; however, that was before all laws ceased to matter. She now stood before him wearing the standard white linen robe all his whores wore when not entertaining him.

"This will not do."

He raised his hand, and immediately the robe ripped in half and fell from her body. He then used his powers to direct her hands across her breast and down to her crotch. He made her explore herself with her fingers as he watched and became aroused.

The girl trembled with fear. She had no control of her hands. It brought back terrible memories of other hands moving and forcing her hands to do much the same, many years ago. She began to cry.

"How dare you cry. Your trembling should be from the reverence of my powers, but I sense your trembling is fear. Let me give you something of which to be afraid."

Without another word, he took complete control of her body and forced her to lay below his crotch and take his now immense, erect manhood. After a minute, he released her, and she knew better than to stop.

Minutes passed, and Jonathan had not achieved the release he so desperately wanted, so he retook control of the redheaded girl, and he moved her head up and down faster and forced her mouth tighter. The pleasure changed to pain, but he didn't care as he moved her head faster and faster.

He moved the woman so quickly it caused her to have a concussion. After another minute, he manipulated her so impossibly fast, she died and became nothing but another lifeless body used up for the Overlord's sick desires.

Eventually, he reached his goal, a mirror on the wall shattered, and he screamed with pleasure as he tossed the now lifeless body aside to reveal his bloodied manhood. He enjoyed the pain as he fell asleep and dreamed of again being a child with his grandmum in bed beside him.

The Overlord of Bartram Fortress fell deeper into madness.

He slept for well over eight hours, and when he awoke and looked down at the dried blood on his abundant manhood, he cried. He went to his shower and gently washed. He could control the pain, but he couldn't fix his mangled cock. Nature would have to take its course.

He had wanted to move up his wedding after what happened

yesterday, but now he could not. He needed to be whole on his wedding night when Patricia willingly gave herself to him. The Overlord began to feel something he had not felt since obtaining his powers—remorse. He wanted Patricia to be with him and love him for who he was, without fear.

He dried himself and went back out to the bedroom to find the lifeless body lying on the other side of his bed. He looked down at the young redhead's still beautiful body and began to cry.

"Why do they not love me for who I am?"

Love? What do you care about, love? You are the Overlord.

I want to be loved.

No, you want to take love and toss it down the pit. You are the Overlord; you are God; you take what you want. Take Patricia, mangled manhood or not. If your sight repulses her, kill her!

I mustn't; I love her.

No, there is no love, only power, and the power is yours.

Power.

Yes!

"I will take want I want!"

Yes!

"Guards, come here now."

Two different guards, not the two from the prior evening, came into his bedroom to find the Overlord standing still naked, looking out his window and down on his conquest.

"Take the whore and toss her out in the street for all to see."

"Yes, Lord."

"What?"

Without turning around, the Overlord mentally grabbed the guard and broke his neck.

"You will now dispose of both bodies on the street."

"Yes, Lord God."

The Overlord smiled. He was God, and they better not forget.

"Bring Patricia to me immediately when done disposing of this trash."

"Lord God, I believe she is busy with your jester, Stephen, at the moment."

"Busy? Where?"

"I believe they are in the library."

Patricia Seeks Comfort

Patricia sat on the grand appointed chair in her room, which faced the also beautifully appointed vanity. Jonathan's troops took both pieces from bedrooms of the once rich and powerful of Philadelphia. He had raided the former houses of the Philadelphia elite to furnish most of the rooms in his fortress. He also took all the gold and other precious metals and jewels merely because he could. If anyone happened to be in the houses when he raided them, the individuals soon would be wishing there were dead. Jonathan didn't wait long to grant their silent wish.

Patricia dressed in a soft robe, having just come out of the shower. Even though the assault had happened many hours before, she still needed to clean her body. The sick individual who tried to rape her managed to get his fingers into her womanhood before Ander stopped him. After everything she had been through with Jonathan, the man's touch and violation of her body sickened and disturbed her more than any of the times she had been with Jonathan. At least the times she remembered. Patricia knew he had taken her by force when first captured, but he somehow manipulated her mind so she still couldn't remember.

Jonathan hadn't been with her in that way for months—not since before she agreed to marry him, to again spare Mark's life and force Jonathan to stop tutoring the true love of her now miserable life. It surprised Patricia when Jonathan had said he didn't want to force or coerce her again to be with him. The next time they were intimately together, he wanted it to be as a happily married husband and wife. If she had to, she could fake the happiness if it meant Mark would be left alone and maybe even someday freed.

The future wife of the Overlord was amazed, in a way, how she did still pity Jonathan. Yes, he always appeared a bit odd, observing and leering at her years ago back in the office, but she imagined some trauma, some event, or series of events from his childhood caused him to be as he became. She felt confident he was merely a victim, who now possessed the power to take his revenge on the world; and that he did with a vengeance.

Patricia noticed, as she combed her hair, her hands continued to shake. She needed comfort, but not from Jonathan, and Mark was out of the question, as Jonathan would never allow him to visit, especially now. She needed someone to talk to, and she realized who. Patricia knew he had more to tell her, but it was much too late in the day. She decided to have him brought to her in the morning. She would say she needed the distraction of watching him perform to give her comfort.

She awoke the next morning feeling better than she had in years, and she wasn't sure of the reason. Patricia knew she had dreamt of a man rescuing her from danger, but she couldn't now awake, remember what the threat had been.

No matter, today is another day, and I still want to talk to Stephen, now more than ever, but why?

She pushed the thoughts out of her mind and called for her attendants. She instructed them to tell the guards she needed entertainment, and she wanted the Overlords favorite jester brought to her in the most outlandish costume he possessed. She needed a good laugh after the events of the previous day.

Patricia felt terrible to have Stephen brought to her dressed as a fool, but she had to make it look good. She didn't need him for amusement;

she needed him to talk to as a confidant. She also realized something special about him, something different beyond the fact he indeed spied for a Resistance.

Stephen wasn't too surprised when Mikal unlocked their door and entered to inform him Patricia wanted to see him immediately. He somehow expected the summons.

"She wants you in your funniest costume. Put on the fancy joker one and be ready in five minutes. I think she will like that one."

"Why does she want to see me?"

"I don't know, just do as I tell you."

Stephen could sense by Mikal's tone that he wrestled with his conscience due to their conversation the previous day. Mikal was uncharacteristically gruff, maybe to hide his decision to help or perhaps his anger at having to choose.

"Mikal, I can't go perform smelling like this. I haven't had a shower in days, and I also need to shave again."

Mikal's expression changed to one of annoyance, his face a shade redder than a moment ago.

"Fine, then strip here and follow me to the showers."

Stephen now understood what decision Mikal had made. He had decided to help them and now overcompensated, treating Stephen less like a friend and more like a prisoner. No matter, as long as he helped them when needed.

Mark said nothing as he listened to the exchange and hoped only to give Stephen a message for Patricia before he left to meet her. He felt jealous, she asked for Stephen, but he knew Jonathan would never let her meet with Mark unless promising him something in return. Whatever reason she had for requesting Stephen, Mark suspected it was a good sign of hope for the future.

Stephen had helped Mark to develop some ability of his own. Thanks to Stephen, he could now resist some of Jonathan's lesser commands. A fact Mark knew had to remain a secret, but he did hope Stephen could do the same for Patricia no matter what their future held.

Patricia decided she would meet Stephen in the library, as it was a perfect place to talk and be left alone by the guards. She knew they would be reluctant to leave the room, but she also knew they didn't want her to tell their Overlord of her displeasure.

She asked one of the servants to bring tea and some pastries. They only brought enough for her, but no matter, the intention was for Stephen to have them anyway; she already had breakfast.

"Please also bring me a tomato juice, sorry, I forgot previously."

That will give Stephen a bit more nourishment since they didn't send many of the pastries.

Patricia sat by one of the windows to wait while looking at the collection of books still lining the walls. They mainly were law and history books about the founding of Philadelphia. Many people had fought and died to create the best country this world had ever known, and now it meant nothing.

The servant arriving with the requested refreshment woke her from her thoughts.

"Madam Patricia, the tea has been prepared as per your usual request. Is there anything else I can get you?"

"No, thank you, and please make sure no one disturbs me here. The guards will let you know when I'm back in my chambers."

"Yes, mam. The Overlord's fool is waiting for you."

"Do not call him that! His name is Stephen. Have him brought in."

"Yes, Mam, sorry."

As the servant left the room, Patricia scolded herself for raising her voice and not knowing the servant girl's name. She wanted to treat them with the respect she knew Jonathan would never show to those he called his minions.

"My Lady. The Overlord's jester, as you requested."

"Thank You, Mikal; you may wait outside, all the way outside."

"But my Lady, I must stay at least in the other room—"

"You will do as I say or—"

"But my Lady, after what happened yesterday."

"Mikal, you know she is safe with me. I trust you Mikal, do you trust me?"

"Yes, Stephen. Yes."

Mikal turned and walked out, closing the main library door behind, and moved to keep watch in the hall after closing the reception area door.

Patricia sat in the chair, a bit stunned and confused. She wasn't sure what exactly happened, but she felt sure there was more to the exchange than the words they spoke.

"Do you always talk to your guards in such a manor, Stephen, and please take off that stupid hat, sit here and have some pastries."

"Thank you, Patricia. Mark sends his love and hopes to see you soon."

"You haven't answered my question. I know your secret, don't be coy with me."

"I believe Mikal is a tortured man, torn between his survival instinct, his sins of the past, and his desire to atone for them, if possible. I think Mikal will be an asset to the cause."

"And what cause would that be, Stephen?"

"Killing Jonathan."

Patricia wasn't surprised by Stephen's response, though she didn't understand why.

"You make it sound so easy. Only someone with abilities stronger than those Jonathan possesses would be able to defeat him."

"Maybe. You weren't there when he heard the news of your attack. Jonathan freaked out, for lack of a better term, and went crazy. He used a power I don't think he knew he possessed. He threw most everyone against the walls with such pressure that bones broke and heads crushed. Some who tried to escape appeared to burn from the inside, fire erupting from their eyes and mouths as they screamed their last breath. I even witnessed him rip—"

"Is there a point to this, Stephen, other than making me sick? You appear to be just proving my point; no one can stop Jonathan."

"The point is this—what happened afterward. Jonathan became weakened, unable to stand, his body shaking. When his guards picked him up off the floor, they had to walk him out of the room. Whatever he did, whatever he tapped into, was more than his body could handle without repercussions. If someone were to attack him at that weakened state, the attack could be successful."

"If the person didn't die first trying."

"They would need help; help from outside. I'm in contact with my people outside; I won't tell you how, so as not to put you in even more danger. All I can tell you now is we plan on making our attack on the day of the wedding."

"It's insanity; he will kill you and anyone else trying to kill him."

"Not if he is weakened."

"How can you get him back into such a weakened state without causing others to die."

"I know, many people will die, some deservedly so; however, I'm sure his feelings for you will keep you safe. It's his feelings for you we can use for his downfall.

"As I said, I don't want you to know too much, but I plan to pretend to attack you on the day of the wedding. My hope is he will lose control again, and that's when my friends can strike."

"I say again; it's insanity; you will get yourself killed."

Her words hung there as he decided to come totally clean with Patricia.

"I am not without the ability to defend myself to some degree."

Stephen thought the shock on her face was the revelation of his abilities, but that wasn't the case.

"He's coming."

"How do you—"

Stephen stopped as he understood immediately; Patricia had some abilities of her own. He quickly ran out to the reception area, opened the door, and pulled Mikal into the room. He was relieved to see no one else in the hall, but he could hear the approach of Jonathan with his guards.

"Shut up and listen, Mikal, he's coming. Leave the doors open and stand guard as if you have been watching us and protecting her the entire time."

Stephen went back into the library before Mikal could say a word, but he did as Stephen instructed, his heart pounding as he took up his position at the doors, looking into the library. He watched Stephen stand in front of Patricia, hat back on in full costume, head bowed as if he had just finished a performance.

From behind Mikal, Stephen heard the doors open hard and slam against the walls. Mikal turned around in a defensive position as if he didn't know who had entered the room. He then began to stand at attention and address the Overlord, as he was silently and without physical touch, pushed out of the way.

"What is going on here!"

Stephen backed away from Jonathan's path, head down and silent. He knew he wasn't to speak; Jonathan had directed the question to Patricia, his voice filled with rage. Stephen noticed Jonathan acted differently—he was enraged more than usual, his voice almost imperceptibly quivering—all signs Jonathan's control and sanity were slipping.

Patricia almost gasped when she saw Jonathan. The look in his eyes that wasn't there before was, for some reason, she could not define—frightening. She composed herself as best she could before speaking.

"Good morning, Jonathan, I—"

"You will call me Lord, or I will make you regret your existence! Be thankful I do not make you call me by my proper name—Lord God."

"I am sorry . . . Lord, it will not happen again."

"Good, now tell me why you are here with this dirty spy."

"Spy? I did not realize—"

"He won't admit it, and I can't prove it, but I know it. I keep him around only for my amusement since you will not let me use the bas—, Mark, in such a manner. He is also useful for keeping an eye on Mark. After all, I have to make sure he stays healthy so as not to offend my Lady."

Patricia was surprised when Jonathan appeared to calm down when he thought of her and their arrangement. Stephen noticed it as well and felt sure he could use it to their advantage.

After a brief pause, Patricia continued.

"If I may continue, Lord?"

"You may."

"I felt despondent after what happened yesterday, and I needed some cheering up. I didn't think you would mind me using your jester. I am sorry, Lord, if I was mistaken."

Jonathan said nothing, so she continued.

"He just finished a wonderful dance, which made me laugh. It felt good to laugh. There is so much misery all around, and I . . ."

Patricia hesitated but wanted to test how receptive Jonathan would be to her request.

". . . May I make a request Lord?"

"More requests? Don't push me."

"I only ask that you don't in any way punish our jester or Mikal. He did want to ask your permission first, but I made some regrettable threats against him to do as I commanded. You and your, our, guards need to trust me if I'm to be your Lady, and this is to be a marriage in more than appearance. Our servants need to realize they should obey and service me appropriately. I must admit I enjoy these silly performances of our jester, but there is no need to be overly cruel and distrustful."

"You are correct. As my Lady, you should have the freedom to command my—our servants and use them as you see fit, with obvious exceptions. I tell you now; I will kill you if you ever fuck anyone but me, your Lord!"

"I would never. I know my place and what you expect of me."

"Good. Now, are you done with this pathet—forgive me, person?"

"I would love to see some of his tricks, if I may."

"Fine, carry on."

Jonathan turned away to leave but stopped and turned back to Patricia. He gently put his hand below her chin to raise her head, bent down, and gave her a gentle kiss.

"Mikal, watch them; they are not to be alone."

"Yes, my Lord God."

Minutes later, after Jonathan left, Patricia again ordered Mikal out of the room. This time, she allowed him to stand guard in the outer chamber, still with the door closed. She motioned for Stephen to sit back down so they could finish their conversation.

"I figured Mikal wouldn't now accept standing in the hall. I hope having him stand in the other room will suffice."

"I don't believe, Patricia, we have anything to fear from Mikal. I'm confident he will be on our side when the need arises."

"Which I want to hear more about now while we are free to talk. And don't think I forgot about your comment of being able to protect yourself."

"Okay, one thing at a time. I told you of my plan to weaken Jonathan at the wedding. The ceremony is to start at noon that day. At a time we choose, probably close to ten minutes past the hour, I will attack you in some manner yet to be determined. Five minutes later is when the full attack would commence."

"What kind of attack, how do they expect to defeat him?"

Stephen stood. He was restless and couldn't sit any longer. He began to pace, leaving Patricia waiting for an answer.

"I don't yet know. My contact will hopefully have more information when I see him tomorrow. We have less than three weeks to the wedding. I hope we can all be ready."

Stephen paused, and Patricia jumped in immediately.

"Continue, Stephen; you're not finished yet."

He was mindlessly looking at the titles of the books on one of the shelves.

"You are relentless!"

He turned, approached her, and sat back down close so even Mikal could not overhear.

Patricia said nothing but smiled as she waited.

"I discovered, Patricia, a few weeks after the event, I had some abilities. As the months went on, I worked on my body, mind, and abilities. Four years later, I have progressed more than even I expected. I can use my abilities to shut down my body and protect it from extremes without needing food or water. I also can resist attacks from others using their abilities. I'm not the only one."

He stood again and walked to one of the windows.

"I have told you more than I believe to be prudent."

He turned back to Patricia with a coy smile on his face.

"Now, let's talk about your abilities, Patricia."

It wasn't a word Stephen found much use for, but the look on Patricia's face he found to be precious.

The Plan Develops

"We have slightly over two weeks, Jim, before the wedding, and much to accomplish, but I think the plan is coming along."

Brian sat across from Jim, looking tired with bags beneath his eyes, which was unusual for him, and he wasn't sitting as straight and tall as he usually would. The United States Marine showed his age and frustration as he updated his friend on the plans for the attack on Jonathan's fortress.

On Jim's desk, between them sat diagrams of the Philadelphia City Hall building, known now as Bartram Fortress. Brian had been working long hours with his teams and the fools in the cult, as he called them, finalizing plans for the attack.

"We have thirty-two bombs ready, and we should have over forty fully operational bombs of a few different sizes before the attack. We worked with the abolitionist's team to alter the original design to allow my men to fire them from bazookas and rocket launchers. I will also have the teams equipped with a substantial supply of hand grenade-sized devices."

"So, the test went well?"

"Yes, Jim. It went extremely well!"

Brian perked up as he discussed the test. The gas worked far better than expected. He reached for his coffee but didn't take another drink before continuing, his excitement evident.

"We had twenty volunteers, all with more substantial than average abilities, and we spread them out around the test area, the size of a city block. The gas's effect started twenty seconds after the explosion and spread to the farthest subject within thirty seconds. The gas suppressed most of the subject's abilities for well over two hours—far more time than we should need to secure the facility and his soldiers.

"It's a damn good thing that witch woman told us about these freaks before they had a chance to use the gas bombs against us and destroy all you have built here."

"We, have built Brian, and her name is Mary. It's not helpful for you to be so negative against her. With all that has happened, all we have seen over the last four years, I would expect you to be a bit more open-minded."

"Oh, I know Jim, you are right, but she was a part of that cult; they were her life and her friends for a couple of years. It makes it hard for me to have full trust in her."

"I understand."

After a short pause, Jim continued.

"Did you also have control subjects with gas masks to test their effectiveness?"

"Absolutely, and the masks worked as designed, with no leakage. We have more than enough, and we will have extra with us for Stephen and anyone else he has convinced to help; however, we believe Alfredo should be able to smuggle in some small masks, which will last a couple of minutes."

Jim pushed his chair back from his desk and stood to fill his coffee cup. He was tired of sitting and anxious. He worried things wouldn't go as planned. The Sanctuary and the Resistance leader stood in front of his Philadelphia map, sounding like his mind was somewhere different from his words.

"Alfredo is due to meet with Stephen for his wedding costume fitting in two days. He will give Stephen the full details. Stephen knows nothing of the gas; he knows only the day and time of the attack."

Jim turned from the map; the far-away sound of his voice no longer evident.

"How do you plan to approach and enter the city?"

Brian pulled a folded piece of paper from a file he had placed on the desk.

"Here is a map showing my plan. We are pre-staging in Chester Heights. As you know, I've had teams there for a couple of years to coordinate our Philly activities. We have secured a larger area, and we have most of our equipment, resources, and fighters hidden there already.

"The night before the attack, we will move up to Drexel Hill, where we also have been securing the area with additional equipment. An advantage for us, Jonathan has concentrated most of his resources north and south. He hasn't moved much farther west than Upper Darby."

Jim nodded his approval, making mental notes of his questions.

"The morning of the attack, we will use the Grays Ferry Bridge to get into the city since it has the least number of patrols. We will use the weed gas bombs and mustard gas to incapacitate the guards and then move across the bridge. We have an abundant supply of weed powder which we will shoot out of air cannons as we move through the city.

"The group will split after we cross the bridge. One group, I will lead and go farther along Grays Ferry up to 23rd Street. We will then move up 23rd and work our way to 17th and Chestnut, where we will ditch the Jeeps and trucks. The other group will head over Washington Ave. a few blocks and then zig-zag their way up to 13th and Walnut, where they will ditch their Jeeps.

"I'm sure we won't be able to prevent Jonathan from being alerted, but he won't be expecting anything this large, and I hope he will be too preoccupied to care. I'm confident he will expect his forces to be able to defend the city.

"If all goes well, we will be outside Bartram Fortress on schedule."

"We? Are you going to be in one of the final attack groups?"

"Yes, I will be with the main attack force, group one. Don't try to persuade me otherwise; I need to be there, it's what I did in many other wars, and it's what I need to do in this one."

"I knew you would, and I know better than to tell you no. Not that you would listen to me anyway. So, what about your contingencies?"

"You know me all too well. I will have operatives in place around the fortress a couple of days in advance, and a smaller second group is coming in the long way from the north via Kelly Drive and the old Reading Subway. We will equip all forces with bombs and gas masks, but only the larger group will have vehicles all the way into the city. Our north group will ditch their transports before reaching the Strawberry Mansion. Bridge."

"What about communications?"

"We will establish relays; however, teams will go silent except for a few coded messages."

As expected, Jim had more questions, but he appeared increasingly restless. He stood again and gazed out the window.

"And the reverend's men, do they have a part in the attack?"

"The Abolitionists are part of the main attack group. We have been watching them closely and listening in on them whenever possible. Let me tell you, they are not all that religious. We have heard some things—"

"Stop, Brian! I don't care."

"Sorry.

"I don't have any of his men in the other group, and they don't know of the north group's existence. Not many others do, just as a precaution."

Jim continued looking out the window, feeling uneasy. He knew this was what they had to do, even though he worried about the possible failure and assured loss of life. Many people in the city were victims of Jonathan—forced to do countless things against their will and out of fear. He hoped many didn't have to die.

"The plans sound good. In a couple of days, we will know if Stephen has any updates. Will you be able to get some devices to Stephen?"

"I have put together two small devices. I think it's the best we can do. With your approval, I will give one to Alfredo to sneak in, and then he can take the second and maybe a third when he goes to drop off the final costume for Stephen."

"You have my approval. Now I need a real drink,"

Jim moved back to his desk and pulled a bottle of Johnnie from the desk drawer.

Patricia Confesses

"My abilities, Stephen? What makes you think I have any abilities?"

"You knew Jonathan was coming. I would call that an ability."

Patricia walked to the door and slightly opened it to make sure Mikal wasn't standing directly outside the door. She saw him standing near the outer doors to the hallway with his back turned away. Satisfied, she returned to her seat and poured herself more tea.

"Yes, I do know when Jonathan is near or when he will soon show up. It's something that slowly developed the more he spent time with me. He spends some nights here and forces me to lie next to him. He doesn't force me to have sex with him. According to Jonathan, he wants me to be with him willingly and is content to wait for our wedding night. It's the one tiny bit of decency, I believe he possesses.

"The three of us used to work together in the same office, a few blocks up Market Street. I always thought him odd but sweet. I was always nice to him and he to me, but Mark always hated him and called him a sick pervert. He said he caught Jonathan staring at me a couple of times in the office."

Patricia started to cry. Something she hadn't done for a while.

"I didn't need you to go into so much detail. I'm not trying to pry, I just—"

"I know, Stephen; it's not your fault. You are the only person I have had to talk to, so now it's all flowing out of me. I don't trust the attendants he has taking care of me, though I do think some do truly care about me out of more than just fear of their Overlord."

She turned away before continuing, and Stephen could sense her embarrassment.

"I believe some of the servants pity me. I wish I could control them and make them stop, the same way I—"

She stopped, stood, and walked away.

"I believe you started to say more than you intended. You have some power over your

attendants as well, I presume."

He waited.

"You can trust me, Patricia. I'm here to help."

"It's hard to trust anyone, but you are correct; I can persuade them with the proper tone of my voice to tell me many things they shouldn't and normally would not."

"That's good; it may be helpful.

"I promise. I will try to get you and Mark out of here."

"That would be wonderful. We had started to have a decent life in Pennsauken before Jonathan found us. We were officially engaged two days before the event. Mark took me to dinner at the Crystal Tea Room, and before dessert, he got down one knee while the waiter brought my cake, with the ring sitting on top.

"After things went to hell, we tried to quickly get married at one of the churches in the city, but we couldn't find any priest still alive. Mark owned property in Pennsauken, so we grabbed his car and had just enough gas to get to one of his properties. With all the people, some dead and some crazy along the roads, I didn't think we would make it, but, eventually, we made it to the house, which sat far back from one of the less-traveled roads in the town.

"We managed to hide out there and have a life together of sorts. There was already a garden area on the property, so we could grow food, and we had managed to grab a large variety of canned goods and meat products from a local grocery store. The property had a propane generator and a large storage tank so we could freeze the meat and have some light at night."

Patricia's eyes went moist and had a faraway look as she continued.

"We loved each other tremendously, so one evening Mark and I stood looking up at the stars and pledged our love directly to God. It was the only wedding we could ever expect to have."

Patricia laughed and stood before continuing as she paced the room, nervously wringing her hands together and unconsciously looking for the ring, no longer on her finger.

"I know, hokey as shit, but we were in love, and we considered ourselves as safe as possible, given the circumstances. We had food, shelter, and each other until he came. We had some good years before Jonathan turned our lives into a nightmare far worse than the one in which we already lived."

She had to wipe away tears before continuing.

"Neither one of us had any abilities of which we were aware. It wasn't until Jonathan brought us here that I realized I had some small ability to manipulate people. I feel like a jerk when I do it, but we do what we have to for survival. Mark and I had to do far worse while in Pennsauken a couple of times.

"Stephen, I hope you can help us, but I think I need to be alone now. Thank you for listening."

"Patricia, don't be too hard on yourself, we didn't ask for this, but we have a right to survive. I will see myself out."

William Confronts Thomas

Reverend Thomas stepped out of his shower, wrapped a towel around his waist, and headed to his bedroom to continue his morning routine. He was startled to find William waiting for him instead of Josette, his latest partner.

"What the hell are you doing here, William? Where is Josette?"

"I sent your latest bitch back to her room, where she belongs. You know you could at least act like the man of the cloth you claim to be; this behavior of yours is disgusting."

"William, I will forgive your outburst and judgment of my life only because I know your past and how many times others hurt you, but my patience only will go so far. I know my past behavior has been less than chaste; however, Josette and I have a special relationship, and I'm planning to ask her to be my wife. I assure you if she says yes, I will be wholeheartedly faithful to her and my vows. Now, again, why are you here?"

Thomas began to get dressed and had only his underwear on when William grabbed his arm and spun the reverend around to face him.

"I'm here to talk some damn sense into you before it's too late! We need to stop this madness before we all end up dead. I have a team set up to attack the Sanctuary fools in our community, and I have additional weed gas bombs ready to go beyond our borders. Let me kill these invaders and warn the Overlord before it's too late."

"You are a fool!" Thomas yelled before regaining his composure. "If you touch me again, I will have you locked in the church basement for forty days, where you can go without food and water like our true Lord."

William released the reverend's arm and paced the room while talking, almost as if he was talking to himself. While William continued to pace, Thomas tried to finish getting dressed but to no avail as William approached him again, standing directly in front of him.

"You are under their spell; they use their abilities to control people, and they are using them to control you. We had so much here; we had peace; we had the freedom not to be controlled; you will lose it all— everything you built."

William moved away and again began to walk back and forth across the floor like a caged animal.

"I will kill the ones here, and then I will march into Sanctuary and kill every last one of those mental freaks."

"Are you mad, William? You will stand down, or I will kill you myself!"

"You're the one, Thomas, who is mad. You are mad for the witch. She has you under her spell. How many times have you fucked her, Reverend? How many times have you let her use her abilities to bewitch others to you and your bed? You talk about not using abilities, but you let her use hers and bewitch people. You, Reverend Larson, are a—"

Thomas's face turned red; his hands quaked with anger as he made a fist and slammed it on his desk.

"Enough!

"Mary has bewitched no one, and we are not lovers; never have been and never will be. I consider her my sister—like the sister I never had."

Thomas appeared lost in his thoughts. He took a deep breath, and now calmer, continued.

"She could see the future and see danger long before this curse arrived on our doorstep. It only made her ability stronger, more accurate. She cannot control anyone and wouldn't use the ability if she could."

Unwavering, William continued his tirade against Thomas.

"I swear to your damn God, Thomas, if you continue, I will get word to the Overlord, and he will end this treason."

"William, such a move would be the last mistake you ever make."

Thomas, still half-dressed, walked over to William and put his hand on his shoulder. It was time, he thought, to use some of his hidden abilities.

"William, I think of you as my brother. You came here late, same as Mary, but together we have built much, and we have a better chance of keeping what we built here, with the help of Sanctuary. Please, William, my brother, don't destroy what we have built—together."

"Please, William, my brother, don't destroy what we have built—together."

"Please, William, my brother, don't destroy what we have built—together—together."

Thomas's words echoed in his mind: brother, built, together. William began to feel light-headed, went to the bed and sat, as the words continued to echo in his head.

"I'm sorry, Thomas, I love you, and I admire you, but I think you are wrong. However, I will not interfere, and I will cooperate fully with our Sanctuary allies."

"Thank You, William; I love you too. Now, can you let me finish getting dressed for the morning service?"

"Yes, sorry to make you late. Anyway, I think I need to get something to eat; my head is feeling funny."

William left the room, and Thomas felt a pronounced concern for his friend. He did consider William to be a brother, and he feared William had become insane and likely a future problem.

William walked out of the building and sat on a bench underneath one of the sprawling oak trees surrounding the old church building. He still felt a bit dazed and confused by what had happened. He knew he was right, but why did he give in so suddenly.

His mind cleared, and the answer, as well as extreme anger, came to him immediately. He clenched his first by his side and would have screamed if he wasn't out in the open. He had let Thomas violate him, almost as bad as what happened to him before coming to Thomas's Abolitionists.

The bastard had used some ability on him. Thomas forced William to calm down and see what the reverend considered reason. It explained much that happened since he had arrived to join the group. Thomas was gangly and not at all good-looking. William now understood how Thomas had so many women in his bed, night after night, why he had at present six children with more on the way.

The man, a so-called reverend who preached rightfully of the evils of the cursed abilities, used them on his flock. He betrayed everything his believers had come to his ministry to experience as well as to forget.

William clenched his fist so tightly; small drops of blood were in his palms when he opened his hands and buried his head between them.

"How could I have been such a fool?"

William vowed there and then to himself, to the world, and the reverend's God. I will make Thomas sorry for his deceptions and stupidity. One way or another, I will stop this lunacy, and I will punish Thomas for all the wrong he has done, and then I can be the leader.

"I will earn it.

"I deserve it."

Stephen and Alfredo

Alfredo was an older gentleman of Italian descent who came to the United States at the age of thirty-three. He brought with him his clothing design skills and soon found a lucrative job in New York City, designing clothes for some of the biggest Broadway hits.

He found himself now a senior citizen in a world gone to hell. He had left Broadway over six years ago to start a small shop in downtown Philadelphia where he made custom-tailored suites for the city's wealthiest inhabitants and still dabbled in costume work for the local theaters.

Today, he was a member of the Resistance working to bring down the *bastardo,* who considered himself the Overlord of the city. Alfredo wished him nothing but *la dannazioe,* for all eternity.

Mikal escorted Alfredo on this day to do the final fitting of the costume the *bastardo* wanted Stephen to wear to entertain at the wedding. He had never met this guard until today, and Alfredo sensed goodness in the man, the other guards didn't possess. While there, he received instructions to fit Stephen's roommate Mark for a fancy, old-style tuxedo. Mark would be escorting Patricia down the aisle to give her away to the *bastardo.* Alfredo didn't understand why, nor did he care.

Stephen and Mark were, of course, waiting for him in their room.

"I will wait outside so you can have some privacy and more room to work. Knock on the door when you are finished."

"Thank you, Mikal."

"You were awful chummy with the guard, Stephen, and I'm surprised he left us alone."

"His name is Mikal; he has become a friend and possible collaborator. Not everyone here is evil, Alfredo. Good to see you again, by the way."

"Good to see you as well, Stephen. Nicole, of course, sends her love, and yes, I did sense certain goodness in the man just by the fact he introduced himself to me when we met."

Stephen smiled as he thought of his wife and how much he missed her and her touch. Mark awoke Stephen from his reminiscing as he stood to shake Alfredo's hand.

"I'm not sure why I had to be here, not that I have anywhere to go."

"I assume you are Mark."

"Yes, why?"

"I am to measure you for a tux for the wedding."

"Why, Alfredo, would I be wearing a tux at the wedding? I figured Jonathan would have me dressed in one of our standard but less outlandish costumes."

"It is my understanding, Mark, you are to be giving away the bride."

"What!" that fucker is determined to rub it in and humiliate me as much as possible. I won't do it; I can't do it."

"Calm down, Mark. We have no intention of letting this thing happen. Remember the training we have been doing; it will help you to remain calm and focused."

"Now, Alfredo, fill me in while you measure Mark."

"Do you think the guard is listening?"

"I expect he is pretending to be listening should his superior walk by, but even if he hears the plans, he won't report anything he hears. Of that, I'm sure."

Feeling assured by Stephen, Alfredo passed on all the attack plans as he measured Mark. Stephen and Mark were surprised to learn about the powder and how they turned it into a semi-gas weapon.

"This should make it much easier to be successful. Yet, I worry the gas will stop me from my plans."

"What was your plan before now, Stephen?"

"The wedding is to start at noon. Shortly after, I plan to threaten Patricia, hopefully causing Jonathan to lose control as he did a few days ago. It made him obviously weak—"

"And also killed many people, Stephen. I worry his anger will hurt Patricia."

"I don't think you need to worry about Patricia getting hurt, Mark. He is sure to direct all his anger at me, the threat to his bride.

"So here is the new plan. I will first off need a weapon."

"I think I can take care of supplying a weapon," Alfredo answered. "Go on."

"Mark will escort Patricia in at noon. I expect Jonathan to speak for about five minutes showing off for the crowd in attendance. Five minutes or so later, at 12:10, I will attack Patricia. I will goad him on, and after a few more minutes, I expect the storm to start. The troops should launch their attack at 12:15. By that time, I expect Jonathan will be out of control and possibly weakened."

Alfredo finished with Mark, so he had Stephen put on his costume.

"Now, let me show you what I have done."

Alfredo reached into the second layer of the costume and produced a small gas mask.

"This, I am told, will last for two minutes, hopefully, enough time to get a complete mask inside for you. You can keep this one for Mark, and I will sew a hidden pocket into the left breast of the tux. You can put it there, Mark, before the ceremony.

"I will put another mask in here for you, Stephen. And I will also sew in a ceramic knife you can use as a weapon."

They talked a few more minutes about additional plan details before Alfredo knocked on the door for his escort out of the fortress. There remained nothing left for the conspirators to do but wait. In three days, one way or another, it would be over. They all hoped to survive.

Wedding Eve

Nathan arrived at the Overlord's chambers almost immediately upon being summoned. It annoyed the guard when the Overlord called for him. He was enjoying a bit of torture testing on a not-too-willing recruit. The former guard hadn't followed orders, so he volunteered to be a practice dummy.

Oh, well, he isn't going anywhere without his legs. Nathan smiled as he thought of the young man hobbling around.

He arrived at the Overlord's door, knocked lightly, approached his master, and waited for an acknowledgment. The Overlord sat on the side of his bed, obviously lost in his thoughts as if talking to another person.

"Nathan, report now!"

"Yes, Lord God. All preparations for the wedding are complete, and I—"

"No! You idiot. Tell me about the spy and the bastard. What have you learned?"

"Lord God, if Stephen is a spy, he hasn't indicated it in any way. He hasn't had any conversations with the bastard indicating any thoughts of a plot. He has no communication with anyone outside the Fortress."

Nathan wasn't entirely truthful, and he began to worry, thinking as his Overlord spoke.

I need to talk to that idiot, Mikal. He is late with a recent report. Stephen's only contact with anyone other than the bastard and Patricia was the old fool costume designer. I wonder if—

319

His thoughts were interrupted.

"It is time we use other methods. The bastard's usefulness is near over. After the wedding, you are to take them both and torture them until either we learn the truth or they are both dead.

Nathan stood before the Overlord smiling at the thought of the pleasure he would receive from their pain.

"Leave me and go tell my bride-to-be to expect me in five minutes. I want to speak with her before I retire."

"Yes, Lord God."

Go, Jonnyboy, take her and show her what it means to be your bride.

Yes, I should—No! Grandmum, I want her to love me. I want my love with her to be different, not like those whores who fear me.

You are Lord God, the Overlord of all you see—to hell with love. Love is useless; show her your power, make her bleed with your passion.

"No, Grandmum. Shut up, shut up now!"

Patricia sat in her elegant chair, stolen from somewhere in the city, looking into her mirror, wondering what Jonathan wanted. Would he go back on his word and rape her tonight, or would he save his further sexual torment for after the wedding?

Whether forced or consensual, before or after, to Patricia, it would always be unpleasant and only to keep her true love alive.

While she waited for Jonathan, she thought about Mark. She loved him so much and missed him. Their life together in Pennsauken was the best it could be in this new world of pain and misery. Their little house behind the trees, secluded from the terrible world beyond, with its gardens of vegetables and flowers, she missed tremendously.

A soft knock at the door awoke Patricia from her musings.

"Come."

Patricia was surprised to see Jonathan enter the room with a pleasant smile on his face, not the usual smile of subterfuge and deception. In his hand, he held a single, tiny, red flower.

"My love, I wanted to wish you a good night's sleep, and I hope you are happy with the arrangements for tomorrow."

Take her now, throw her on the bed, and take what is yours!

She watched as Jonathan twitched a bit as if experiencing pain.

"Thank you . . . Lord God."

"Please, Patricia, call me Jonathan. I know what I said before, but I want your true respect as your mate and friend."

You little pussy boy. Tear off her clothes and ram that cock of yours deep inside her. Make her feel pain, the way I made you feel pain in your backside when you were a bad boy.

Patricia watched in astonishment as a small tear appeared in Jonathan's eye. She stood, approached him, wiped the tear from his eye, and kissed him in a moment of weakness.

"I love you, Patricia; however, I must go before I lose control and ruin this moment.

"Good night. Till tomorrow, my love."

WEDDING DAY

6:00 AM

Patricia awakened to the sun shining along the edges of the ornate curtains, covering her room's windows. The night had brought her a happy dream of her time before the event, back when she and Mark had started dating and made love for the first time.

Her happiness quickly faded as she became fully awake and remembered where she lived and what fate waited for her on this day. She looked to her right and saw the dress brought to her the prior evening, and she began to cry.

She hated Jonathan, and last night's kiss was a moment of weakness brought on by the surprise of his words and tear. True, she felt sorry for him at one time, but now only the hatred and contempt remained. She had no choice that she knew, but she also doubted he would ever keep his word regarding Mark. Patricia's biggest fear continued to be Jonathan wouldn't keep his promise, and Mark would soon be dead. If her fear became a reality, not even Jonathan's powers would prevent her from ending her life.

Stephen ended his deep meditation sleep to find Mark sitting on the side of his cot, a look of fear and misery on his face.

"You're up early, Mark. Did you sleep at all last night?"

"No, not much, and when I did, I had only nightmares haunting me, nightmares of seeing Patricia standing next to that fucking bastard as his wife. I can't do it; I can't walk her across the floor and give her to him. I would rather be dead."

"Mark, look at me. I promise you, one way or another, this will end today. Either we will both be dead, or we all will be free. I have full confidence in our plan, and I will do everything in my power to keep you and Patricia safe. To do that, I need you at your best and most capable. I need you to be ready to act and move Patricia out of harm's way. Can you do that? Can you be there for Patricia and me?"

"Yes! Yes, I can."

The Overlord of Bartram Fortress had risen early that morning to find the naked, bloodied body on the floor of the girl he forced to his bed the night before. Many thoughts entered his mind as he looked down on the cold corpse.

I promised Patricia I would be with no one but her. I have broken my promise the night before our wedding, and it wasn't the first time.

Before a smile broke on his face, Jonathan felt remorse for barely a second, thinking about the joy he would have with Patricia and any other whore he chooses to invite to his bed.

Yes, Jonnyboy, you are the master; you control all.

Yes, Grandmum, I will take her and use her any way I want. We will be married; she will be mine to do with as I please, and when I'm married, the bastard will die.

The bitch at his feet disturbed him for some reason, so he called his guard to have her taken away. He didn't remember this one's name. Nathan had assigned the man to guard duty, while his presence was needed elsewhere.

"Guard, Come in here now!"

The man quickly entered the chamber and found last night's whore dead on the floor as expected. The Overlord's encounters recently ended no other way.

"Yes, Lord God, how may I be of service?"

"Take this thing out of here, have it dumped in the pit, and tell Nathan to make sure everything for today is prepared and ready to go as planned."

"Yes, Lord God."

"And remind him, if anything goes wrong, he will regret his life."

The guard tried not to let his anxiety show as he called for a second sentry to help, and they carried the body out of the chamber.

Now, Jonnyboy, let's talk about the death of the bastard. Why not kill him now, or kill him at the ceremony?

Yes, Grandmum, yes. The bastard will die at the ceremony. After I kiss my new wife, she will watch her former lover walk to his death in the pit. He should rejoice, I don't torture him first.

Mikal stepped out of the communal shower, disgusted by what he heard while drying off. Many of the other guards enjoyed talking about how they used their status and non-event powers to force men, women, and even children to participate in vile sex acts and fights to the death, arranged merely for their amusement. The few guards who had abilities they weren't afraid to show and use around the Overlord, also told of exploits worse than the horror and slasher movies he watched as a youth.

He quickly dressed and went to the mess for breakfast. It was a big day, a day he now hoped would see the end of the Overlord and the restoration of some civility to the once-great city. The city he had expected to one day call his home.

In Mikal's youth, the instructors taught him Americans were evil and exploited the less fortunate for the gain of the powerful. While recent events would prove that to be true, he did learn a different truth from visiting the city's historic sites before the event. Yes, evil was abundant in the United States, the same as in Russia. Still, the U.S. had a system designed to protect the individual and provided a constitution developed to help ensure freedom. He never could understand how the American people could let the framework be so diluted over the years, but he hoped the vision he learned about could return to his new home.

Mikal had decided days ago, he would do everything in his power to help Stephen and his friends destroy the Overlord and hopefully restore the freedom to Philadelphia countless individuals had died to achieve in the past. He had many sins for which to seek atonement; today would be the day.

"Is everything ready Alfredo, have you secured the items in the costume for Stephen?"

"Yes, Patrick, I have. Any luck in reaching Stephen?"

"Yes, we exchanged messages; all is ready. There isn't much more we can do but wait and pray."

"Pray to whom? I no longer believe in a God. No God would allow this to befall the world. I think back to my Catholic upbringing in Italy as a child and everything the nuns and priests taught. I realize now; it was all a lie, all a waste."

"No, it wasn't, or so I believe. I was born, raised, and educated as a Catholic all my life, and I haven't lost my faith. I believe this world is merely a test to prove our worthiness for heaven. I pray to God every night, not to help us, but to help me be worthy of Him."

Alfredo stood, about to leave, but paused, looking at the little cross Patrick had hung on the wall. He sighed, remembering so much from his youth and life.

"Patrick, if he does exist, I'm sure he has lost faith in me."

Alfredo paused again while Patrick watched him and understood; the older man wrestled with beliefs long forgotten. He turned to Patrick with an expression of sorrow and frailty.

"If you would permit me, Patrick, I would like to take a moment to pray with you before we start this day."

"I would be honored, Alfredo."

Nicole sat at the table, alone with her thoughts and coffee. Jim stood at the door and watched a moment before taking a drink of his own and deciding to join his friend.

"Good morning, Nicole, may I join you?"

"Yes, of course, Jim. I expected you would also be up early and hoped you would find me here."

"Hoped, or nudged?"

They both laughed. In a world of abilities, sometimes, you never knew when the simple, innocent wishes and desires of others were encouraging your actions.

"Maybe both, Jim."

Nicol took a sip of her coffee before continuing.

"I can't reach Stephen, but I do sense him. I feel determination and hope coming from him, and it makes me feel better. I wish I were there; I wish I were part of the team."

"You know I do as well. And you know Brian would never allow it to happen, especially in your current condition. If this mission is not successful, we are necessary for the survival of what we have built here in Sanctuary."

"I know, Jim, but I feel useless."

"I understand. On a good note, I received ready signals from all teams this morning. Everything is proceeding as scheduled, and the weather is cooperating. Light winds will help keep the powder where the assault teams need it to be, to make the mission a success."

8:00 AM

William peered out the back door of the compound's main utility garage to see if anyone stood nearby. He wasn't going to let Thomas decide his fate; he wasn't going to let those with abilities rule him ever again. He had one of the Jeeps gassed and ready to go; he just needed to make sure he could get out without being seen.

His fellow Abolitionists were only half the problem. He still needed to be wary of the guards posted by the fools from the so-called Sanctuary. *Those bastards will stop me if they can; I need to make sure they can't.*

He had a few low-powered weapons already stowed in the vehicle, a last resort if needed. The coast looked clear.

Time to open the garage door and get a move on—running out of time.

The wedding was to take place in four hours; he needed to reach Philly to warn the Overlord in three. Possible, but not easy, he knew; the roads were close to useless in some areas—still littered with wrecks and even traps. William pushed the button, and as the door slowly opened, he became startled at first and then angered by what greeted him.

"Hello, William, where the hell do you think you're going?"

"You know where I'm going, and so help me, I will not hesitate to run you down if I have to—I need to warn the Overlord before it's too late."

"Are you even listening to yourself? Do you want to give complete control of your life to a madman who is no better than the men who sexually abused you?"

William's demeanor changed; the resolve fell from his face as he began to pace in front of the Jeep. The look in his eyes when he dared to look at Thomas, frightened the reverend.

"Shut up! Don't you ever talk about . . . about that to me. You don't know what it was like—the way they tormented me day after day."

Thomas knew he had struck a nerve; he hoped this to be the correct path to get William to stop.

"No, I don't; however, I do know what it's like to have another person control your life, and that is what Jonathan is doing, and he is doing it for his personal sick pleasure."

"Sanctuary will lose this war, Thomas, and we will suffer the consequences. If I warn the Overlord, we will be in his favor and debt."

Thomas laughed, which caused William to get angry, and he began to feel something in himself he had never felt before. He stopped his pacing and looked up at Thomas to see a gun in the reverend's hand.

"You would pull a gun on me, Thomas. Are you really willing to shoot me?"

"William, I consider you a friend, but I have to stop you. Look, if Sanctuary wins, the Overlord is gone, and we will be completely free to live as we want. If Sanctuary loses, our hands are clean, Jonathan will never know we were involved, and things will be as they were."

William thought for a moment.

"No, if Sanctuary wins, they will be our new masters, they will force us to use these accursed abilities, or they will use them against us, making everyone their slaves. I'm leaving; get out of my way, Thomas."

William moved to get into the Jeep and heard a shot ring out from the gun—the bullet missed him and ricocheted off the vehicle's hood. He now experienced a new power in his body, and his face contorted in a mixture of rage and confusion. He focused on the gun, and it went flying out of his former friend's hand and landed under a tool cabinet.

"So, William, you are now one of them."

William barely heard the words Thomas spoke as the rage continued to build. Almost unconsciously, he grabbed Thomas from across the garage and threw him upside-down against the wall. His body slammed against the side of the building and stuck there via the force of William's mind.

William had now lost all control and had become another madman like the Overlord. He remembered a story his former friend had confided to him, and he knew the perfect punishment for Reverend Thomas Larson.

Across the room lay a pile of metal rods used for reinforcement in one of the group's construction projects. Slowly at first: the rods began to shake. Against the wall, Thomas could feel his feet pulled together as his shoes burst from his body.

Tears fell from Thomas's eyes as he knew what was to come. His heart pounded, and he prayed to the God he had used and, at times, abandoned.

One rod flew across the room from the pile and penetrated Thomas's feet and the wall behind. The invisible force of William's mind then pulled Thomas's hands away from the floor and stretched them across the wall. Silently, two more rods flew across the garage, spread out and impaled each hand as the reverend screamed in further agony; he hoped someone would hear.

"Now, Thomas, you can't stop me, and after I warn the Overlord, I will take over the flock and guide them to a new beginning."

"You are mad!" Thomas cried out while William prepared to leave. He believed they were far enough away; no one would have heard the gunshot or Thomas's screams, but he wasn't positive, so he wanted to check outside again.

William tried to move and found he couldn't. He couldn't walk, he couldn't raise a hand, and pain shot through his head. He looked at Thomas, crucified upside-down on the wall, and noticed a smile on the reverend's face.

Marine First Lieutenant Aaron Diemon felt proud of his association with the United States Marine Corp and displayed his insignia proudly on his non-marine fatigues. The U.S. and the Marines may be gone, but Aaron still held the values they instilled.

He served under Marine Captain Brian Crawston in the Middle East, and they had for each other, a mutual respect. They were now great friends, but to this day, Aaron called him Captain Crawston around others.

Aaron understood the honor to be chosen by Brian to lead the northern assault team. He recognized the faith Brian had in his ability to lead. He knew they were a backup, a decoy, or maybe the last resort if the main attack failed. Aaron relished his job, and he was determined not to fail.

His team completed preparations an hour ago; they were packed, armed, and resolute. Aaron's well-chosen seven men and three women stood before him, awaiting the order.

"Time to move out. I will be in the lead vehicle—we stop for nothing until we reach the park.

"Give the signal."

Brian received the signal from the northern team as he stood before his group of fighters, ready to give the order. He had faith in Aaron, but he worried. They were a small group, well-trained but heading into a dangerous situation.

"No different than any other mission, Captain Crawston; we are marines; it's what we do," Aaron had responded to him when they discussed the details of the mission. He expected no less of a response from his friend.

Brian faced his team, two teams in reality. They were ready to fight— ready to win. He completed his pre-mission briefing, and prepared the group of seventy-six fighters to go. He could have pulled a few more soldiers off other patrols, but he liked the number; he felt it fitting.

"Everyone, proceed to your transports: next stop, the Grays Ferry Bridge. We stop for nothing in between.

"Mr. Granderson, give the signal."

Jim paced his office. He tried to read reports about supplies and the advance team's findings, but he couldn't stay focused. He wasn't a fighter; he felt useless. His friend would tell him he had other essential leadership qualities, but Jim's friend wasn't working by his side. Brian was preparing for one of the most important missions of his life.

Jim stopped pacing and headed for the door to visit the radio room. Before he reached it, someone knocked.

"Come in!"

He smiled as Debra entered.

"Susan would like to see you."

"Please send her in."

"Yes, and Jim; they just received the go signal."

9:00 AM

Thomas had been crucified to the wall, bleeding slowly to death for almost an hour. William, angry and determined, still tried to fight against the reverend's power, but to no avail. He remained stuck, unable to escape.

William had spent most of the hour cursing and screaming at Thomas to no avail. The reverend ignored him. William wasn't sure if it was punishment or concentration.

The bastard can't hold on much longer, but I'm running out of time. The man who preached against the curse has his own skills, and he is now using them against me. God-dammed hypocrite and fool.

William had tried to use his abilities to move more poles, with the idea to put one through the reverend's eye, but he appeared to have lost all abilities. No matter how hard he tried or how much anger he tried to raise in himself, he could do nothing.

Ten more minutes passed, and finally, Thomas spoke.

"William, at one time, you were my friend—no longer. You are an instrument of the devil himself. With my last breath, I curse you and pray to God, you rot in the real Hell, far worse than the time you spent as the play toy."

As William watched, Thomas raised his head from the wall and looked up.

"Father, into your . . ."

Thomas's voice faded as he died, and William found he could move. He wasted no time making sure he had all the supplies he gathered, jumped in the Jeep, and sped out of the garage, almost running down two guards from the accursed Sanctuary.

Mikal and another guard escorted Stephen and Mark to the showers to prepare for the big event. Jonathan wanted them to look and smell good for the ceremony—part of the show.

Stephen couldn't talk to Mikal due to the presence of the other guard Stephen didn't recognize. Mikal called him Paul; he looked surprisingly young, still in his teens. He seemed reluctant to order them around like most of the other guards. He appeared timid and acted pleasantly. Maybe he would help, but Stephen couldn't take the chance; it could all be an act.

On the way back to their room, Mikal gave Stephen a look and a nod to let the younger man know he remained on his side. Stephen couldn't give him details, but Mikal was smart; he would know what to do when the time came to act.

When they arrived at their room, Alfredo waited with their clothes in hand. Mikal opened the door and instructed Paul to stand guard across the hall. They entered the room, and Mikal closed the door. Mark and Alfredo had a look of concern on their faces, which Mikal noticed.

"I am with you. What do I need to know and do?"

"Thank you, Mikal; I knew I could count on you to do the right thing.

"Alfredo, what do you have for us today."

Alfredo placed the clothes on the appropriate cots.

"Stephen, when you wear the costume, you will find a few surprises. The implement you asked for is in a pocket on your left side undergarment. It will be easy to reach when needed. This seam here under the belt has a left pocket hiding your temporary mask, and as an added bonus, on the right are two very small um . . ."

Alfredo glanced at Mikal, unsure what he should say.

"It's okay, Al; you can speak in front of Mikal."

"Okay. There are two, small, weed gas balls. Suitable for use in a small room. You may not need them, but space was there.

"As I mentioned, your mask is meant to be temporary. It's small and only good for a few minutes. Team members will have additional full-sized gas masks."

"Excellent, now what do you have for Mark."

Alfredo stepped over to the other cot and reached for the top hat.

"There is a compartment under the top of the hat which holds one of our gifts. I had to design this suit to look good, so it doesn't have room for any other secret areas."

"Yes, unlike my outlandish costume. This thing reminds me of another old-style mummers' outfit."

"Then, I have done my job well, Stephen. The Overlord wanted outlandish, and you needed space for gifts. Job done!"

"Job well done, my friend," Stephen said with a warm smile.

"I will have Paul show you out, Alfredo."

After Mikal gave Paul his orders, he again stepped into the room and closed the door.

"Stephen, I will be of the best help if I know what is to transpire."

With a smile on his face, Stephen answered.

"Hopefully, the end of the Overlord."

Aaron's team arrived in Fairmount Park shortly after 9:00. The group broke into two as pre-arranged and prepared to abandon the vehicles. The two Jeeps, including the one in which Aaron rode, drove to the Chamounix Equestrian Center, and the former army truck proceeded to the Ford Road playing fields. If all remained clear, they were then to rendezvous Greenland Drive and Ford Road, at precisely 9:20.

As expected, both teams arrived without incident, and Aaron sent a two-member advance team to within eyesight of the bridge. Five minutes later, they advised all clear. It was time to move.

At 9:30, the team began to cross the bridge preparing for the altercation they knew awaited on the other side. If Aaron's team was nervous or worried, it didn't show, and he sensed no feelings of fear from anyone.

Brian's team arrived at State RT 13 and 52nd Street by 9:15—fifteen minutes ahead of schedule. They had little trouble working through the main roads, and streets still littered with rusting vehicles. They didn't want to cross the bridge into South Philly until 10:30. It would allow plenty of time to make it up to the fortress before 11:45 if everything went well.

Brian gave final instructions to the advance team. They were to drive to 47th and Woodland Avenue and ditch their Jeep. They were then to proceed as close to the bridge as possible to scout the situation. What time the remainder of the team advanced to the rendezvous would depend on their report. If all looked good, he would depart with the team at 10:00.

10:00 AM

"Lord God, may I approach."

"What do you want Nathan, I'm busy contemplating my conquest of Patricia and the death of the bastard."

Why do you tolerate such fools, Jonnyboy?

"Sorry, Lord God, but I need to report the illness of seer Randy. He has contracted some virus and wasn't able to report for duty this morning."

"Where was he to report, and why am I just receiving word now? I believe his duty was to start at 6:00 this morning; it is now past 10:00!"

Jonathan used his seers to keep an eye on all major approaches to the city and spy on his subjects and guards. He had fifteen in all and cultivating them took much effort and time on his part. He had to wipe away almost their entire mind and create essentially a new individual by altering select areas to give them the ability to report back to him everything they saw, from as far as four miles away. Some couldn't transmit that far, but Randy was one of his best.

The connection wasn't constant—even he, with all his glorious power, could not manage such a task; however, he had them trained to send him whatever discrepancies they found. He instructed them well on what they needed to report.

"I'm sorry Lord, Lord God, my—"

"You had best be careful; I have killed for less. No one, not even you, are indispensable, as Ander learned.

"Now continue!"

"Randy's station was up by the Strawberry Mansion Bridge. The overseer failed to notify my staff until only a half-hour ago. His excuse, preparations for the wedding—"

"Does he still live?"

"Yes, I didn't think—"

"Think? You don't think; you do as I say!"

"You are to kill him, slowly for his failure, and dispose of Randy too before he spreads his disease."

"But Lord God, he is your best seer."

It would be best, Jonnyboy, if you killed this fool. First, he interrupts, now he questions your orders. He is a waste of your greatness.

"You are treading on thin ice."

"Yes, Lord God, I shall do as you command, but what should I do to man his position? All the other seers are already out in position due to the importance of the day."

No matter, Jonnyboy. No one would dare to attack the Lord God of Bartram Fortress on his wedding day!

"Dispatch an extra couple of guards up to his position, and don't bother me about this matter again."

Nathan excused himself and headed back to his office. He had no one left to disperse up to Strawberry Mansion; all guards were assigned and deployed. He realized his only option was to pull two guards from the throne room honor detail. The pompous ass would never notice.

Patricia stood up from the little table, which held her mostly untouched breakfast. The meal was a lavish spread of pastries, meats, sunny-side-up eggs, juice, and coffee.

"The last meal of the damned," she said to the empty room.

She often talked to herself since there was no one else other than the servants and him. She longed to speak with Mark or Stephen. She wondered what they were doing and hoped all proceeded as planned.

The Overlord's fiancée stood looking out one of her windows at what would be a beautiful day if not for the coming events. She decided then and there if things didn't go well today, and she ended up married to that monster Jonathan, she would take her life. She didn't know how she would do it, but she would find a way, he would not win.

A lone tear fell from her eye, the bright sun glistening in it as the tear fell to its death.

"Concentrate Mark, feel the pressure of my command and push back with your mind. You can do it."

"I'm trying, but it's difficult."

"Think of Patricia, think what he will do to her tonight if we—"

Stephen stepped back from the force of Mark's defense.

"We certainly know what motivates you. I should have tried that trigger before, but I didn't want to put those types of thoughts in your mind."

"Don't worry about it, Stephen; the thoughts are always there."

"Yes, but your anger is not. Passion can be a powerful weapon when used correctly. We have done all we can; I guess we need to get ready. Mikal will be here for us soon.

"Remember, put on the gas mask quick, and use your anger as a defense for as long as you can. The little mask Alfredo provided will not last long, and the weed bombs will not be the only gas they will deploy."

Aaron led the team across the bridge, but not on the road deck.

Thanks to extensive plans available of the historic bridge, they knew of the maintenance walkways underneath. The advanced team saw only six soldiers stationed on and near the bridge; he suspected there would be more around, so everyone had silencers on their sniper rifles. No machine guns unless necessary.

His team lowered themselves from below the bridge and took up positions enabling them to take out the soldiers quickly without raising any alarms. They were not all within sight of Aaron, so he had to use radio signals to count down.

Three, two, one, silently ten bullets flew, taking out the six guards, who collapsed dead on the bridge and grass. Aaron radioed his praise of a job well done, and the team met below the historic structure. It was only 10:05, and they were on their way to the fortress via the once picturesque East River Drive.

The advance team reported to Brian on schedule. They witnessed over a dozen soldiers stationed on both sides of the bridge; only three were on the west side. Other than the guns they carried; the team saw no other weapons. One odd thing they did report; a man was sitting under a canopy who appeared to be meditating.

The report gave Brian an odd feeling, and he knew, maybe instinctively or through an ability, they would need to launch a first strike with weed and mustard gas bombs. He instructed the advance team to wait for his signal, then fire gas bombs at both sides of the bridge. The advance team carried short and long-range launchers, so hitting the targets would not be a problem. They would then use silenced guns to shoot as many soldiers as possible on the western side of the river, as the main caravan would storm the bridge shooting all the way.

The bridge was south of center city and beyond a sharp curve of the Schuylkill River, which would prevent posts up north from seeing their attack, but the noise would be another issue. His team wouldn't use machine guns, which didn't have silencers unless the Overlord's men used them first. Hopefully, if the soldiers had radios, his team could take them out before they could send any messages.

Brian knew when they made their way to Grays Ferry and 34th Street, they would need to be prepared to eliminate any opposition moving off the 34th Street bridge to investigate.

"Time to move up and into position to start the attack. Everyone to their positions. We will hold at 47th and Woodland, pick up the advance team's Jeep, and I will then give the signal."

Brian looked over his soldiers and silently wished them all luck. An hour from now, they would be dead, wounded, or hopefully making their way north to confront Jonathan.

Before taking his position, Brian said a silent prayer.

At 10:25, he gave the signal, and bombs flew.

11:00 AM

Brian stood in the middle of the Grays Ferry and Washington Avenues intersection, looking north at the Liberty Towers, thinking about the past. He knew Jonathan had shut them down and blocked all entrances. He hoped someday to see them reopened and filled with workers and residents.

Brian wasn't aware, but the so-called Overlord would love to have had them and the other buildings taller than his fortress destroyed, but it would require the life force and sacrifice of two many of his subjects to make it possible.

Brian turned to his second in command and asked for a report.

"All teams are ready to proceed. The medics have dressed the wounds, and the teams have been re-briefed."

"Thank you, Scott."

Scott was young and not formerly military trained, but he caught on quick and earned his position. Brian checked his own wound's dressing and found it adequate; he had worse. The first part of the mission stood completed as a success, but everything didn't go as planned.

With his signal given, bombs flew and exploded on both sides of the bridge. The blasts incapacitated, killed, or knocked unconscious most of the soldiers. The team quickly took out the remainder of the Overlord's soldiers on the west side of the bridge, and the convoy proceeded across the structure, well above the previously posted speed limit.

His men fired at will, killing most of the soldiers on the east side of the bridge, but unknown to his scouts, a surprise awaited. Hidden to the side remained a gunner equipped with a machine gun and rocket launcher. As the lead Jeep, Brian's transport, approached the end of the bridge, a blast destroyed the road in front of the vehicle. The Jeep went onto the sidewalk; Brian was thrown out of the vehicle and luckily into a garden full of cushioning bushes. On the way through the air, one of the bullets gave him a nasty flesh wound on his left shoulder and, unfortunately, killed two of his men.

His remaining team made quick work of the Overlord's soldiers still alive, and the full squad met up at 34th Street. As Brian had expected, the battle's noise attracted soldiers from the 34th Street bridge, and they were speeding down the road. Brian's team was prepared and took out the truck and all occupants with a traditional shoulder-launched rocket.

Brian knew there was no way the battle wasn't heard by other of the Overlord's fighters. He didn't realize, however, and would never know; the weed gas prevented the man meditating under the canopy from reporting directly to his Overlord—the first of many lucky breaks.

The seer stationed on the 34th Street bridge sat back on the west side of the river. The soldiers with him were fighting one another over a prank gone wrong, and the seer remained hungover from the previous night's carousing, when he should have been meditating and reporting. It would be sometime before they realized the east sides' team was missing. The Overlord, for now, would remain mostly unaware of the attack.

Brian didn't know how lucky they were. However, if he did know, being a religious man, he would have said God was on their side.

At 11:05, Brian gave final orders, the team split into two, and the final battle was closer to reality.

Patricia stood before her full-length mirror, her gown showing behind her, draped across the chair. She sighed as a tear appeared in her eye.

One hour. One more hour before my life becomes more of a hell than it already has become. What does it matter? It will be a sham marriage, and there is no law of the land to consider whether it is illegal. God, if you're out there, please spare me. Don't let this fake wedding happen.

All these thoughts ran through Patricia's head as she stood looking at the gown she had to wear for the wedding. She desperately wanted to take a knife to it or set it on fire. She thought back to when she was a child imagining this day in her play wedding dress. She thought of her mother and father, who thankfully died before the world became Hell.

Her eyes shed additional tears, and she collapsed to her knees.

Aaron led his team down East River Drive, passing numerous statues—dirty but mostly undamaged—occupying overgrown sculpture gardens that once were the pride of the city and exercise stations, now overgrown with weeds.

Shortly below Fountain Green Drive, the old Reading Railroad line came within thirty yards of the river drive. They moved off the road to follow the old rail line the rest of the way into Broad Street. A few minutes after they started walking along the rail bed, they heard a truck's approach. They took cover behind a few large bushes and waited while the vehicle came into view carrying three soldiers. Aaron quickly fired a standard shoulder-launched rocket at the vehicle, killing or severely wounding its occupants. Had the soldiers made it up to the bridge, they would have found the guards dead, and Jonathan would have been alerted to his team's presence.

"That was a close call. Luckily, we were still close enough to the road. Let's move; I want to be at the tunnel entrance by 11:15."

The team continued south toward the city, walking along the tracks.

To their right, as they proceeded, they passed the grandstands for watching the many regattas once held on the river. A few minutes later, they could see the boathouses along the river, now falling apart from neglect, with rotting sculls and oars hanging on vine-covered walls.

At 11:10, five minutes ahead of schedule, they entered the tunnel, which, before the event, took freight trains under Eakins Oval and eventually along the river's waterfront. The tunnel was cold and dark. Water dripped from the walls, and the ceiling glistened in their lights, painting an eerie scene. Their flashlights only lit a small way ahead, but it would be enough.

Aaron motioned the team to stop. He listened for a few seconds but heard no evidence of anyone else nearby or in the darkness ahead. The only sound was the relentless dripping from above.

They proceeded to where the old and abandoned for over forty years Reading Subway—as the locals called it—branched off to the left. This tunnel would take them the rest of the way to Broad Street. The walls in the old tunnel were lined with stone, and in the ceiling were numerous skylights, which made their lights unnecessary. Again, Aaron motioned to stop before proceeding and then motioned to tighten up, and he softly spoke.

"We will move on in silence, no talk, no radios, only hand signals. Send the update signal to Sanctuary."

The advanced scouts in position throughout the city had informed Sanctuary of steps leading from the subway tunnel to the street level; at 11:40, they arrived at Broad Street, next to the abandoned Philadelphia Inquirer building.

Jim paced the small communications room, constructed a few doors down from his office. So far, all signals had been good to go. The final coded messages were to be received before 11:30 if all continued well, and then there would be radio silence except for go orders between the teams in the field.

Jim last saw Nicole a few hours earlier. Her worry about Stephen and her pregnancy took their toll, and he knew she went back to her room to meditate in hopes she could at the very least sense Stephen to confirm if he remained alive and unharmed. He believed she felt as he did.

I wish it were tomorrow. One way or another, the mission would be finished.

Of course, the thought wasn't accurate, for if they did win, a considerable amount of rebuilding and maybe even fighting would remain.

Jim's thoughts were interrupted when Susan came in, bringing a refill for his coffee. He took the coffee and kissed her on the cheek. He didn't care what the radio technician saw or thought. One way or another, the time had come to make their relationship known to all the community.

"Any word Jim, from the teams?"

"We are awaiting the final mission proceeding signal from team two. Team one gave the final signal shortly after 11:00. We should receive all go signals no later than 11:30, as of yet we haven't—"

"Sir, team two just sent the signal. All is go!"

"Mark, are you ready? Can you hold up through the next hour?"

"What choice do I have, Stephen? I will admit I'm nervous and don't feel I will be alive on the other end of this, but I will at least get to see and touch Patricia one last time."

"Remember your training, and try to get away if you can, at least to a far corner of the room."

Mark reached out his hand. Stephen met his hand, shook it, then pulled Mark in for a quick hug.

"I will, Stephen, and thank you for everything."

Before entering, Mikal knocked on the door, something he had never done before, even when alone. Stephen was surprised to see Jordan follow Mikal into the room—the young guard they placed in the isolation chamber next to him as punishment. Stephen hadn't seen him for a few weeks and knew his presence here at this time was a good sign. They had two allies in the fight.

"Good morning, Mikal!"

"Good morning, gentleman. Are you ready? Mark, you look great, Stephen; forgive me if I laugh."

"You are forgiven—for everything."

Mikal looked away, not sure how to respond. He only wished Stephen had the power to forgive him all his sins.

"It is time to go."

"Wait, Mikal, Jordan, I have something for you. Alfredo made them as a good luck charm. He gave us a couple extras. I don't believe in such things, but he does. Alfredo told me you should wear them over your heart."

"Thank you, Stephen."

Mikal took the two small, flower-like charms and gave one to Jordan. They had pins on the back he used to attach his charm to his uniform.

"Do you think we should, sir?"

"Yes, Jordan, it will be okay."

They exchanged a look. Mikal knew how Jordan felt about his forced service to Jonathan and knew as Stephen did; this was the right thing to do.

Mark glanced at Stephen with renewed worry showing on his face. Stephen also worried about them and the lives of the two guards now escorting them to the throne room.

I hope the charms work for their sake.

William stood on the top of his Jeep, looking southeast toward center city Philadelphia. The time now 11:45, and he had to accept there was no way to make it on time to warn the Overlord—he failed. He had come down RT 422 to the Schuylkill Expressway because he knew the Overlord's men had mostly cleared those roads, but he encountered nothing but problems on the way into the city. A trip that would have taken no more than an hour before the curse now took him more than two.

First, William developed a flat tire three miles out from the expressway and then detoured around the King of Prussia area since someone had blocked all the ramps onto the expressway. Finally, he made it onto the expressway but didn't get too far before encountering another disruption.

As he approached Conshohocken, William felt a pull on his mind. His hands started to turn the wheel of the Jeep toward the exit ramp ahead. He resisted, which caused pain to build along the back of his neck and into his head. He sped up to try and outrun the power of whoever wanted to control him, but they only increased their hold. He continued to fight, but in the end, he blacked out—for how long, he wasn't sure. William found he had crashed the vehicle into the guardrails a few miles farther down the road when he awoke. He was bruised but not injured in any significant way. No one came for him, but he thought they might be on the way. He was relieved to discover the Jeep still drivable. However, the best speed he could maintain was only forty miles an hour. He knew he would never make it on time, so he pulled off at the Girard Avenue exit where he currently stood on the bridge.

Now, what do I do?

William thought for a few minutes before deciding he didn't want to be a servant to the Overlord if he did win, and the Resistance would probably kill him if they won. He had to go out on his own with the treasures he had brought—bags of seeds and weed sprouts—the new beginning of his abolition of the curse. His day would come; William felt sure, and he would not fail like the pathetic reverend he left crucified for his sins against humanity.

William pulled an old map from the Jeep and planned a way back out of the area. He wanted to avoid Conshohocken, so he decided to follow Girard out to RT 30 and take it out to RT 29, where he would get on the turnpike at Malvern. From there, his eyes scanned the map and found a little place called Nantmeal Village. He was sure to find lots of farmland to rebuild and replant. This new world had not heard the last from William Paterson.

Jonathan looked at himself in the mirror and saw only a God. A God dressed to perfection, ready to take the one last thing he had denied for himself.

I should have taken her many, many months before and ravished her to my heart's content.

He was God, and she, his subject.

Yes, Jonnyboy, don't make the same mistakes again. Get this over with and have Patricia again and again. Do it there in your throne room in front of your guests. Let them marvel at the manhood of their God.

Yes, I shall—no! I love her; I want her to be mine by choice. I want her to love me; I need to be loved, not just feared, I need—

No, Jonnyboy, you need no one; you need nothing, give nothing, and take everything. Let me comfort you, Jonnyboy, like I did when you were a child.

The Overlord stood in his fortress before a mirror now displaying the outlines of his erect manhood.

"It is time."

12:00 Noon

The Overlord of Bartram Fortress stood waiting at his private entrance to his throne room, ready to start the ritual to make Patricia his wife and conquest. He was two minutes behind schedule, starting his ceremony, and he wasn't happy. A minute before giving the signal to announce his entrance, Nathan came to him with what his advisor considered troubling news.

"Lord God, I'm sorry to disturb you, but I have received word of a possible attack beginning in the city's southern region. There are reports of—"

"And you are disturbing me now. Why? Do I not pay you and reward you for leading my army and protecting my domain? Are your fighters not able to do the job, or are you the problem, Nathan?

"I have received no warnings from my seers, and I'm sure this is nothing more than a few misguided idiots trying to ruin my day."

He is a fool, Jonnyboy, kill him for his ineptitude, make him pay.

I mustn't, Grandmum, I need him—for now.

"Go, Nathan, lead your fighters out into the city and destroy anyone causing a disturbance. Show no mercy, or I will show you no mercy when I punish you for your failures."

The time was 12:02 when the Overlord gave the signal and triumphantly walked to stand upon his dais and await his bride.

Two minutes behind schedule. Hopefully, this isn't a sign of trouble to come.

Stephen's thoughts turned from his worries to his prior conversations with Patricia and Mark.

Mikal brought Mark and him to the throne room five minutes before noon, where Patricia already waited.

When Mark saw his wife, he wanted to run to her and hold her tight, but she warned him against showing any affection with Jonathan so near.

"I have missed you so much, Patricia; no matter what happens today, remember you have always been the only love of my life."

Mark's eye's glistened, and Patricia wiped away his tears before wiping her own.

"Remember, to stay calm and act surprised at whatever happens."

They both acknowledged Stephen's instructions as Mikal came up to them with two brightly colored flower bouquets. He handed one to Patricia and then the other to Stephen.

"They told me to give this to you, Stephen. You are to walk the carpet first and stand to the right after you bow before the Overlo—Jonathan."

Mikal smiled before continuing.

"I guess you are the flower girl," Mikal said, enjoying the moment to tease his new friend.

Before walking away to stand guard at the door, Mikal looked at Stephen, stepped close to him, and whispered, "I'm with you friend, good luck."

Two minutes past noon, the music started, and Jonathan stepped out to his dais, and Stephen silently sent Patrick an update as he walked toward the Overlord, flowers in hand.

Three short signals beeped in Aaron's ear as he took up his position on Filbert Street, a few yards off North Juniper. The messages received were from the other members of his team, confirming their positions and readiness. Stationed with Aaron were two others from his team and three fighters who joined them from the leading attack group. They reported to Aaron and were now under his command. The time—12:05.

Aaron's team reached Broad and Arch without incident, staying along back alleyways most of the way down. The few people they did encounter were uninterested. To be safe, they deployed a few weed bombs to stop anyone from wordlessly communicating with the fortress. Sanctuary was well aware Jonathan had spies everywhere in the city. They could do nothing about the old-fashioned communication methods, and their orders were explicit. If trouble broke out and they lost the element of surprise, attack in any manner possible, at will. There would be no turning back.

Aaron didn't worry about the smoke from the bombs attracting too much attention since numerous fires were being used for cooking by Jonathan's homeless, lower-level minions. If he had treated his people better, they would most likely have been more concerned about his team's presence in the city. Many probably assumed they were security details put in place for the wedding.

Their updated orders were to deploy both mustard and weed gas around the fortress when the main attack started and watch for fighters coming up from behind. Aaron and his team were ready, just a few more minutes to wait.

Brian stood in the middle of South Broad Street, ready to give the order. Getting there wasn't as easy as they hoped, and he was certain Jonathan's forces knew they were coming, but no soldiers were visible.

Brian knew there were old subway entrances behind them, but he made sure they were well guarded. Jonathan's soldiers couldn't sneak up on them from below, so he looked forward, waiting for the appropriate time, as he replayed in his mind the trip up from South Philly.

His team split into two attack groups as planned, and the first group made it up to 13th and Walnut Streets without any significant incidents. They used a few mustard gas and weed bombs as a precaution but encountered no visible soldiers. All the updates he received were sent via pre-arranged codes, just in case anyone monitored radio channels.

Brian's team moved up Grays Ferry to 23rd Street as planned; however, when they reached Pine Street, they were ambushed by a group of soldiers hiding in Fitler Square Park. His men were well-trained and quickly dispatched all eight of Jonathan's soldiers, losing only one from their group. His name was Shane, he just turned twenty-three, and his wife expected to deliver their baby in a couple of days. Brian vowed Shane's sacrifice would not be in vain.

The remainder of the journey up to 17th and Chestnut was uneventful. They dispersed weed powder as they went to eliminate the abilities of anyone trying to follow or engage the group as they traveled.

All was ready; both teams had abandoned their vehicles and moved into final positions roughly one city block around the former City Hall building. Patrick contacted the teams and informed them he received a message from Stephen stating everything remained ready and on schedule. Brian had only to give the signal, and his teams would advance quickly and attack, showing no mercy to anyone who tried to stop them. The battle for Philadelphia was soon to begin.

The time—12:05.

As Stephen led the little procession up the makeshift aisle lined with flowers, soldiers, and onlookers, he observed many things, some of which would be useful in the moments to follow. Many extra guards and soldiers were in attendance. However, Jonathan dressed them in fancy uniforms, some even looking like pictures he remembered of the Swiss Guard that used to secure the Vatican in Rome. Only a few soldiers were armed, and they stood back along the walls and behind the dais.

He noticed many men and women guests he had seen in the audience with Jonathan in the past. He imagined many weren't comfortable attending the ceremony based on the last time they were in the room with their Overlord. Stephen also noticed two operatives from the Resistance in attendance. He wasn't sure how they managed to be on the guest list but seeing them in the crowd was comforting.

Along the sides of the dais stood several slave girls, scantily dressed and holding flowers similar to those he carried—three on the left and two on the right. As instructed, when Stephen reached a few feet in front of the dais, he bowed to Jonathan and then felt his body pushed to the side and silently forced into place next to the two slave girls on the right.

Stephen watched as Patricia walked toward the dais, arm, and arm with Mark, who looked defeated and ready to accept his fate, whatever it should be. Stephen had no doubt Jonathan planned to kill Mark and him, possibly as soon as the ceremony ended. Jonathan liked to create a spectacle for his worshipers.

Patricia and Mark reached the dais, and immediately Mark was pushed aside by the invisible force of Jonathan's mind. Mark almost stumbled before he took his place behind Stephen. The veil Patricia wore raised from her face and moved back over her head as if by a soft breeze. Jonathan approached the front of the dais and, as expected, addressed those in attendance. Stephen estimated the time to be 12:05.

Welcome friends . . . *worthless subjects* . . . and worshipers of the Lord God of Bartram Fortress, and welcome to my wedding. Today you are privileged to witness my . . . *latest conquest* . . . marriage to the radiant Lady Patricia. This day has been many years in coming, and I am truly blessed . . . *much entitled* . . . to accept Lady Patricia . . . *the bitch* . . . as my wife.

End this charade, Jonnyboy, kill the bastard and the spy now. Take your bitch on the dais for all your worshipers to witness!

Jonathan stepped down from the dais and took Patricia's hand to escort her to the platform's top level. He motioned with his hand, and a man Stephen didn't know, dressed in robes he had seen worn by the priest at Sunday mass, stepped before the betrothed to begin the ceremony.

Stephen had noticed Jonathan's slight stumble over his words and didn't know what to make of it but thought it didn't matter. He estimated the time to be 12:09, and he prepared to act, but he didn't expect Patricia to be so far away. He had an idea, but it would be risky.

"Lord God, if I may approach. Lady Patricia was to pass her flowers to me, so her hands were free for the ceremony. May I step forward to receive them from her?"

Stephen waited as Jonathan thought for a few seconds before answering. He hoped Jonathan wouldn't just use his abilities to rip the bouquet from her hands. Stephen prepared to take a riskier maneuver when Jonathan agreed.

"Lady Patricia, let me take those flowers from you."

Stephen walked up the steps to Patricia, grabbed her arm, and pulled her down the stairs, using his abilities as best he could to keep her from stumbling and bringing them both to the ground. Once at the bottom of the stairs, he reached into the secret pocket and pulled out the knife Alfredo had placed in the costume. He held the knife at her throat and pressed as far as possible to make it believable without drawing blood.

"Don't even try it, Jonathan, or I will slit her throat!"

"Jonathan, Lord God, please save me from this madman!"

Stephen inwardly smiled to hear Patricia playing the part of the maiden in distress, almost like the old Robin Hood movies he watched years ago. He was about to start taunting Jonathan when Mark, unplanned, started to play the role of the concerned former lover.

"Stephen, please don't hurt her, don't take your anger at the Lord God out on Lady Patricia."

As Mark spoke, he moved from his position to stand closer to Patricia and Stephen. Before this drama started, he felt unsure what to do, but now he wanted to be close to his wife no matter what.

Stephen could sense the soldiers in the audience move closer behind the three as they stood before the Overlord of Bartram Fortress, waiting for him to make his move. Stephen didn't have long to wait.

"Guards, hold your ground. I can deal with this pathetic piece of waste without endangering my fiancé."

Use your significant power to rip off his head where he stands. Make it a show for all to see, Jonnyboy!

Stephen watched as again the strange look appeared on Jonathan's face, swiftly followed by a look of frustration. It was time to taunt.

"What's the matter, Jonny, can't get your power up to defeat this piece of human waste as you called me?"

Stephen quickly whispered to Patricia.

"Act like I'm hurting you."

"Ouch, Jonathan, he is hurting me; make him stop. Why aren't you saving me?"

Perfect, Stephen thought. She is taunting him too. Suddenly, Stephen felt a pain in his head and a heaviness in his arm. Jonathan began to exert more force, and it started to be more than Stephen could withstand.

"I feel you, Jonny. Stop now, or I will run this knife into the luscious neck of Lady Patricia, and you can watch your whore die, right here."

Stephen leaned closer to Patricia and licked her neck. Before pulling away, he whispered in her ear.

"Sorry. Taunt him some more."

"Jonathan, please. Are you going to allow him to defile me in front of all our guests?"

As Stephen watched, the odd look appeared once more on Jonathan's face.

Jonnyboy, kill this bastard, kill him now! Take power from these bitches in front of you, use them like you used the slaves to enable you to get rid of that horrid statue. Do it. DO IT NOOOOWWWWW!

Jonathan screamed, and every one of the slave girls standing along the dais fell to the ground and became motionless. A wind came from nowhere blowing around the room, and Stephen felt an increased pressure in his head and pushing now on his entire body. This time, Jonathan had unleashed a massive amount of power by stealing the lives of his slave girls. Stephen felt his arm being pushed away from Patricia; he knew the attack from outside would start within seconds, but could he hold on long enough?

Mark could tell from where he stood, Stephen was weakening, so he took off his hat, grabbed the little weed gas bomb, pulled the trigger, and threw it towards Jonathan. When Stephen saw what Mark was doing, he dropped the knife, pulled out his grenade, and did the same. Both men simultaneously pulled out their tiny gas masks as Stephen felt Jonathan's force weaken right before all hell broke loose in the Overlord's throne room.

The time—12:10. Brian gave the order, and his teams advanced on Bartram Fortress. The Resistance fighters didn't slowly move in or with stealth; they progressed with haste; silently with purpose. They were not to stop. The orders were to advance to City Hall, shoot any of the Overlord's soldiers they could see or anyone else trying to stop them while firing weed powder bombs and mustard gas as needed.

Their goal, the former City Council Chamber, now the throne room, was on the north side of the building on the fourth floor. The second attack group would proceed up 13th Street to Commerce Street, and from there, they would start firing weed and mustard bombs into the fourth-floor windows making their way around the north side of the building. The objective assigned to one section of the fighters was to secure the north portal; the entire second group would then enter the north portal to access the stairs and make their way up to the fourth floor.

Brian secured his gas mask and led his group up Broad Street, heading for the south portal entrance. Two minutes after he gave the order to attack, he heard the sound of bombs and knew it was the north support group beginning their assault. One minute later, Brian crouched across the Street from the south portal entrance when about ten of Jonathan's soldiers appeared heading towards them through the ornate archway.

Brian noticed the surprised look on the lead soldier's face a split second before he fired a shot hitting the soldier in the head. The man fell to the ground, dead. The other soldiers fired their guns at Brian's team as they moved to take cover behind the columns and within the alcoves, which lined the entrance.

One of Brian's men took a shot to the shoulder; another looked dead. Brian advanced, firing on fully automatic as he crossed the Street, and his men fired a volley of weed and mustard gas into the portal area. Jonathan's soldiers were blinded and choking as Brian's team advanced and killed them all without any additional loss of life on his team.

Brian led half his team up the east stairway while the rest went up the west stairway. At 12:17, both groups made their way along the fourth-floor corridor heading for the throne room, with little opposition.

Stephen pulled Patricia away from the dais and handed her off to Mark.

"Go as far away from Jonathan as you can. If possible, leave the room and look for our fighters to give Patricia a mask."

The words no sooner left Stephen's mouth when one of the Resistance members he saw in attendance when he entered now handed Patricia and Mark proper masks and led them away. Stephen could no longer let himself be concerned with their safety; he had other work to do.

Gas and mustard bombs had now smashed through all windows of the throne room, but their effectiveness didn't last long. Again, a huge wind came from nowhere and everywhere, clearing the gas from the area. It did nothing to help Jonathan's guests or his soldiers since they had already inhaled too much gas, but Stephen knew they were not all incapacitated and certainly wouldn't be for more than a few minutes. As if to confirm his thoughts, a bullet struck him, which went through his right arm, causing him to fall from the unexpected pain. The soldier who fired the bullet tried to get off another shot; however, the gas in his lungs overpowered him as he fell to his knees, choking.

Immediately after stumbling from the pain and falling, Stephen felt his body lifted in the air. He raised more than five feet above the floor when gravity, suddenly allowed to take hold, pushed him back to the hard surface. He quickly stood of his own accord and looked up to see Jonathan on his knees. Apparently, the gas had weakened him, but he still had powers. Stephen turned away from Jonathan when he heard his name called, and the other Resistance member guest in attendance tossed him a full-size mask, which he quickly pulled on in place of the small one about to give out. He used his abilities to control the pain in his arm and stop the blood loss as another volley of bombs came through the window, and the Resistance assault teams entered the throne room.

Aaron, his original team, and the additional backups from the leading assault group now assigned to him, launched their bombs on schedule and watched as the first assault team entered the north portal. He ordered two of his squad to the far end of Filbert Street to watch the team's back. One member stood watch from the team's original position as Aaron and two others moved forward to sweep the area around the north and east sides of City Hall. Aaron didn't get far when he was alerted to trouble back on Filbert. The time for signals was over, as in his ear he heard trouble.

"We have a line of Jonathan's soldiers heading toward us from 12th Street. We are going to fall back to Juniper and take up positions. They won't have much room to move if we can trap them on Filbert."

Aaron agreed and sent one of the squads back to Juniper while he and Warren, an experienced former U.S. Army sniper, headed to Commerce Street. He planned to go down Commerce, and when Jonathan's men entered the thirteen hundred block of Filbert, he and Warren would pick them off from behind while the others picked them off from the front.

Two minutes later, Aaron and Warren had taken out six of the Overlord's fighters while the rest of the squad killed the remainder; however, not without a cost. Warren had been hit in the neck and was gone.

Aaron's remaining squad had just about rejoined when they received word from Brian inside the building.

"Send in whatever you have left; we need more gas in the throne room."

Brian witnessed the wind clear away the gas, and saw Stephen get shot before moving back into the hallway. Immediately he called for his fighters to fire more bombs into the throne room as two of Jonathan's soldiers approached him, wearing the flower pins, which identified them as being on the side of the Resistance.

"I believe your name is Brian, I'm Mikal, and this is Jordan. How can we help?"

"Go back in and act like you are loyal to Jonathan. Maybe point your weapons at Stephen and be ready to move against Jonathan when the time comes."

Brian watched them go back into the room as more bombs came through the windows. He wished he could have given Mikal and Jordan gas masks, but how would they explain that to Jonathan? Before the bombs stopped exploding, he ordered a full assault on the throne room and advised the team not to shoot the two identified individuals aiming their guns at Stephen.

Immediately upon entering the room, Brian's team killed or wounded all of Jonathan's soldiers they could see. Brian was sure there were more hiding up in the observation balconies. He had sent fighters up there, and he now saw them in position with guns pointing at Jonathan. Brian hoped they hadn't lost too many of their fighters, but he did see a few of his team dead or wounded on the floor.

Only a few seconds had passed as Brian made all his observations, and he became dismayed to see again the wind caused by Jonathan, clear away most of the gas. They had additional smaller bombs with them, but they would be useless unless they could weaken Jonathan first. Stephen stood back on his feet and faced the man that considered himself an Overlord.

On the dais, Jonathan screamed, raised his hands, and pushed back against the Resistance fighters who dared to attack him, but his power wasn't as great as he hoped. A few soldiers fell back to the ground; however, the ones pointing their weapons at him from the balcony barely staggered at all. Brian felt reassured, seeing the weed powder did weaken Jonathan to some extent.

They did something to me, something in the gas.

You know what to do, Jonnyboy. Why do you hesitate?

"Yes, I know what to do. I will take their lives and use their life force to destroy the rest, along with this spy and the bastard hiding in the hallway with my beloved Patricia."

Stephen watched as the strange look appeared on Jonathan's face while he could hear some of what Jonathan said. Stephen realized Jonathan talked either to himself or to voices in his head. He sensed Jonathan was about to do something drastic. He looked to the side and saw Mikal and Jordan pointing their weapons at him while resistance soldiers pointed weapons at them. Good, Jonathan will think they are still loyal to him. Before Stephen could taunt Jonathan again, he heard Brian from behind him.

"Give it up, Jonathan! We have more than enough guns pointing at you and your soldiers. Surrender, and no one else needs to die."

Standing tall on the dais, Jonathan laughed and yelled.

"Sorry, sir, but more will die, many more, I assure you!"

When the ceremony began to go wrong, most of the Overlord's guests ran away, but some could only take cover around the room as they choked on the gas. Jonathan could feel them; he reached out with the power he had and ripped the energy out of their bodies as he did with the slave girls, but it still wasn't enough; Jonathan needed more.

He reached out again with more strength and attempted to take the lives and power of those threatening him, but he became angered to find he could only take the lives of a small number of the fighters attacking his fortress. Somehow, they were able to resist.

It will be enough, it has to be, or Grandmum will be mad at me.

"Now, you will witness my full power to destroy my enemies, but first, my love should be at my side.

"Patricia, come to me!"

Out in the hall, with Mark, Patricia couldn't resist, and Mark couldn't hold her back. She slowly walked back into the chamber and toward the Overlord, fear, and pain evident on her face as she began to walk up the steps to Jonathan.

To the left side of Stephen, Jordan watched and knew he had to do something. He liked Patricia and hated the Overlord. He swiftly turned his gun toward the Overlord and fired multiple rounds, but Jonathan's power remained too strong, and he was quick to respond. Jonathan repelled the bullets back toward Jordan, and all three projectiles Jordan fired now hit him. One struck in his head, and he went down.

Mikal recognized an opportunity while Jonathan was distracted, and he began to fire his weapon at Jonathan, but to no avail. Jonathan caused the bullets this time to go around his body while he raised his hand and threw Mikal across the room, where he hit the wall hard and fell to the floor.

Brian watched and thought now or never and gave the order to fire. Hundreds of bullets flew as Stephen grabbed Patricia and pulled her close to him as they both ducked down. Jonathan's power over her momentarily weakened as he defended against the bullets, some of which did make it through and struck his arms and stomach.

Stephen gazed up and saw a look in Jonathan's eyes, unlike anything he had ever seen before. He was beyond mad, and Stephen thought there probably wasn't much remaining of who Jonathan had been before the event.

"So, Patricia, you choose this spy and that bastard Mark over me? Are you going to fuck them both? Oh wait, Mark can't fuck you; he cut off his cock."

Kill them, Jonnyboy, kill them all.

"Yes—no, I can't kill her. I love her, Grandmum. I will kill the rest."

Patricia pushed Stephen aside and stood. She wanted no one else to die in her defense, while she coward like a child.

"Jonathan, please, I beg you to stop. Too many have died; too many have suffered. Give up and let them help you. Let me help you."

"You would help me, Patricia; why?"

It's a trick; the bitch is trying to confuse you.

"Jonathan. Look, you are bleeding. Let me clean that for you."

Mark had moved into the throne room and stood only a few feet away from Patricia, and he watched in horror as she ripped a piece of cloth from her gown and walked up the stairs to wipe the blood from Jonathan's arm where a bullet passed through.

"I love you, Patricia," Jonathan said as she began to tend to his wound.

No, Jonnyboy, she is a whore like the slave girls you devour for power. Take her power, rape it from her as you would rape her with your cock.

"No, Grandmum, no, I love her."

You don't need love. She is using you. She wants to fuck the young spy boy. You caught them together, remember; think about it.

Brian watched, unsure what to do. He didn't want to hurt Patricia, but he now understood, Jonathan was losing control of his mind. He walked over to Stephen.

"What do we do? We can't shoot him with her up there."

"I know Brian, but I believe she is distracting him or maybe trying to talk him down, I don't know for sure, but I can almost sense the conversation he is having in his mind. I think I can use it to drive him over the edge."

Above them, on the dais, Jonathan screamed and pushed Patricia away from him and down the stairs as he thought about what his Grandmum said.

"What did you do with the spy boy, Patricia? Did you fuck him? Grandmum says you did."

Jonathan began to walk down the steps to where Patricia had fallen.

Kill her, Jonnyboy; she is making you look the fool.

Stephen heard a word in his head. A name he knew he could use. This approach would be risky, but he needed to drive Jonathan over the edge.

"Maybe you should listen to your Grandmum, Jonnyboy. Maybe—"

"Don't call me that name! Only she can call me that name."

Kill him!

"Do you want to know the truth, Jonnyboy? I fucked Patricia in the room where you found us. Right after you left, but it wasn't voluntary. I attacked her, raped her, violated her, and you were not there to protect her. You are nothing. you have no power!"

Kill him. Kill him now!

Jonathan raised his hands, and Stephen felt a force push him backward, but only a few feet and only onto his ass. Without getting up, Stephen continued to taunt Jonathan.

"You're weak, Jonnyboy, and you have run out of people to steal from except for maybe, Patricia."

Yes, Jonnyboy, kill her, take her power.

"No, Grandmum, I can't kill her; I love her."

You are weak! Take her life and use it to kill them all.

"All I wanted was to be loved. I wanted to be loved and to love the way Grandmum loved me. Touch me, Grandmum; touch me, Lady Patricia; I want to be touched again."

NO. KILL HER!

Jonathan put his hands to his head. Immense pressure and pain filled his skull.

Kill her, Jonnyboy, and then I will make the pain stop.

No, Grandmum, please stop hurting me.

KILL HER!

"Okay, yes, I will kill her, just please make the pain stop."

Kill her first!

Jonathan moved toward Patricia, and both Stephen and Mark charged him, only to be tossed back by Jonathan's power.

"Jonathan, no, stop. How can you hurt me if you truly love me?"

"Grandmum says, I must. She will stop hurting me if I kill you."

Tears fell from Jonathan's eyes as he appeared to Patricia to be like a child.

Jonathan reached toward Patricia but then quickly pulled away.

"I can't, Grandmum, I can't," he cried.

THEN YOU WILL SUFFER!

"NO," Jonathan yelled as he grabbed his head again. He staggered around the dais, and then he realized what he had to do. He started walking toward the pit. We walked a few steps and then felt as if a force pushed him back.

No, Jonnyboy, you can't; I forbid it. You must kill Patricia; you must kill them all.

"No, shut up, Grandmum! You no longer can tell me what to do."

Jonathan screamed again and ran toward the hole in the corner of the floor.

Brian thought Jonathan was trying to escape and ordered everyone to fire. Bullets flew through the air, most hitting Jonathan as he continued to move toward his goal. Stephen yelled for them to stop.

The room became quiet as Jonathan turned around to face Patricia. "I'm sorry!"

It was his last words before he threw his bloodied body into the pit.

The room's atmosphere immediately changed as if a force no one had noticed beforehand lifted. Jonathan's power, now extinguished, would never torment anyone again.

The battle for Philadelphia was over, and the Resistance had won.

AFTERMATH

The Way Forward

Jim stood at the lone window of the conference room, looking out at the rolling hills covered with pine and oak trees. His thoughts wandered, but mostly he thought about all that had happened since their victory in Philadelphia. Things were progressing well with restoring liberty and order to the city and the surrounding areas. There was talk of elections and requests for him to run for mayor, something for which he had no desire.

He watched as Nicole and Stephen arrived for the meeting, walking from their car, hand in hand, with her baby bump starting to show. He knew better than to mention it to her or suffer the consequences. They had decided to relocate to Philadelphia and now lived in one of the historic houses near Rittenhouse Square. Jim felt Stephen would be a good mayor or a fine member of the new regional council, but he also expressed no interest in politics.

A minute later, he welcomed them when they entered the conference room. Jim expected the rest of the attendees to arrive in a few minutes, which would give them a short amount of time to converse.

"Jim, great to see you again."

Stephen extended his hand, which Jim shook, and then grabbed his friend to hug him.

"I hope I'm getting a big hug as well, Jim!"

"I would never miss an opportunity to hug you, Nicole. You look well."

"I don't feel well. My abilities haven't been able to diminish my morning sickness."

"How are the second wedding plans coming along."

Stephen jumped in to answer since he had a question to ask Jim.

"Extremely well. Several priests have returned to the city and our ministering out of The Cathedral Basilica of Saints Peter and Paul. Surprisingly the building remained largely unscathed by everything that happened in the city. One of them, Father Brennen, has consented to make our marriage official in the eyes of God. We will be setting a date soon. You will, of course, be my best man, again?"

"Stephen, I would be honored. Now, please sit and have some breakfast. Brian should be here, momentarily. He is bringing Debra and Susan. Debra has been out at Creagerstown, helping set up a new computer system for the town, and Susan was cleaning out the last of her things she had left at the school.

"How are Mark and Patricia? Have you heard from them?

"Yes, Jim. We visited them in Pennsauken just last week. They finally managed to get the house cleaned up, and they have established a community center for the area. At some point, we may be able to re-establish a bus service between Pennsauken and Philly to tie together our two communities."

They spent the next few minutes in idle chit chat waiting for the others to arrive. Nicole looked at her husband and friend while realizing how happy and content she felt even though there remained much to accomplish. She smiled as she sensed the rest of the group approaching in the hallway. After a round of kisses, hugs, and numerous updates, they sat down to discuss the progress of various projects. Brian spoke first.

"We have continued to look for William, but with no success. Based on reports from our team at the Abolitionist camp—sorry, I need to remember to stop using that term. Based on the reports from Limerick, it had to be William that killed Thomas. We have access to an old but working crop-dusting plane, which we will use in the coming months to look around the area for signs of weed cultivation. We are sure he took seeds and maybe some small plants."

"Have you gotten rid of the fields out at Limerick?"

"Yes, Jim. Mary reported they burned and plowed over the fields. We can't do much about the wild growth, but I don't consider them a problem. Mary says hello to everyone, by the way."

"How is she doing with rebuilding the community?"

"It sounds like she is progressing well, Nicole. They buried Thomas a few weeks ago and are constructing a memorial. She works with the people who remained in the community to help them cope with the new order of things. She has explained they will still be a community for those who want to be away from or learn how to suppress their abilities, but they won't base it on any religion. She will not let it become a cult.

"Creagerstown will continue to function as our training ground for our fighters. Our numbers are back above seventy-five, and we have several new recruits. There have been many reports of people using their abilities to hurt and control others around the region, especially near Conshohocken, so the need for our fighters remains.

"That's all I have to report, so I can now stop talking and have some of these delicious-looking pastries."

The meeting continued as they discussed the progress of restoring the Philadelphia City Hall building. There had been some concern as to confirmation of Jonathan's death, but when they saw the razor-sharp blades Jonathan had installed sticking out from the edges of his pit, they knew there was no way he could have survived the fall as well as all the bullet holes in his body.

They buried the remains from the pit in a mass grave outside of the city, and there were plans to install a memorial plaque. Workers removed the shaft, and the repairs are well underway. Former guards of Jonathan's, not in confinement, worked to clear out the former prison areas. The

Broad Street underground walkway had been re-opened, and Jim talked about the possibility of soon restoring limited subway train service.

Before the meeting ended, Jim had one last bit of news. He stood with Susan, and they announced their intention to get married in the coming December. Susan always loved Christmas and looked forward to celebrating the season again and their union.

A New Beginning

Mark sat on his porch, looking out at the garden behind the house. Thanks to the limited phone service now available, he just heard from the doctor confirming he should have no problem harvesting Mark's sperm to inseminate Patricia artificially.

Mark cried when he heard the news. They would always have a reminder of what Jonathan did to them, but at least they had each other and the possibility of children.

Patricia attended a meeting at the new community center and wouldn't be home for a few more hours, but he was content to wait with butterflies in his stomach and a massive smile on his still-damp face.

Mikal looked out the window of his little house on Front Street, overlooking the Delaware River. The United States no longer existed and may never again, but his new friends officially welcomed him as a citizen of Philadelphia, and whatever form of the country may eventually emerge.

He felt fortunate to be living in Philly and not back in Russia. He spent two weeks in the hospital after Jonathan had thrown him against the wall during the fight. The doctors told him they didn't think he would make it, but he always was and continued to be a fighter. Mikal felt blessed to be alive.

When released, the first thing he did after visiting his new friends,

Stephen, and Nicole, was to look at the Liberty Bell. A group of historians who survived the initial event had managed to move the bell into a hiding place to keep it away from anyone trying to destroy the treasure. It was no small feat, but now it stood back in its original, historic location.

During Jonathan's terroristic reign over the city, his minions had severely damaged Independence Hall, but work had already begun to make the extensive repairs needed. Mikal had his time to heal; the city of Philadelphia, and the surrounding areas, now worked towards its healing, including working to put the William Penn statue back in its rightful place.

Nicole and Stephen had returned from the hospital, where the ultrasound technician confirmed they would have a girl. They were elated over the news, especially Stephen. He wanted to name his daughter Cynthia in remembrance of his sister. Nicole thought it was an excellent idea.

Later that evening, they sat in Rittenhouse Square Park, enjoying the light summer breeze.

"Stephen, do you think our baby or future children will have abilities?"

"Future children? Just how many were you planning?"

"Well, it is a big house."

They laughed together. It was good to laugh, Stephen thought, as he also considered how to answer Nicole's question.

"Well, no one knows how we managed to get the abilities, so I doubt anyone knows for sure. Mary said some children were born in their community, but all are still under one year old and exhibiting no strange behavior. I guess we will have to wait and see what the future brings next."

William's Vision

William Paterson, the new and improved Abolitionists Commune leader, stood alone on the roof of the barn he had picked to be his home and office. The light hurt his eyes as he looked to the west and rejoiced to see the first of the purple weed fields starting to bloom. His group remained small, but all righteous movements began with a few individuals willing to fight for justice. He had confidence he would achieve his goals.

The world had not heard the last from William Paterson. He had become a new man, no longer afraid, no longer going to take orders from anyone. He was strong in mind and body, determined to succeed where the fool reverend had failed.

He watched a wind from the west move across the distant field of purple. It reached where he stood and blew his long, newly blond hair into his face. William turned away from the wind to face the direction of his enemies. He pushed the hair out of his face to reveal his eyes, haunting and full of hate with a touch of madness.

www.ingramcontent.com/pod-product-compliance
Lightning Source LLC
Chambersburg PA
CBHW070807030726
47504CB00003B/731

* 9 7 8 1 9 5 4 3 9 6 2 2 7 *